THE BOOK OF YOU

Clarissa is becoming more and more frightened of her colleague, Rafe. He won't leave her alone, and he refuses to take no for an answer. He is always there.

Being selected for jury service is a relief. The courtroom is a safe haven, a place where Rafe can't be. But as a violent tale of kidnap and abuse unfolds, Clarissa begins to see parallels between her own situation and that of the young woman on the witness stand.

Realizing that she bears the burden of proof, Clarissa unravels the twisted, macabre fairytale that Rafe has spun around them — and discovers that the ending he envisions is more terrifying than she could have imagined . . .

THE BOOK
OF YOU

CLAIRE KENDAL

LARGE
PRINT

First published in Great Britain 2014
by
HarperCollins*Publishers*

First Isis Edition
published 2015
by arrangement with
HarperCollins*Publishers*

A catalogue record for this book is available
from the British Library.

ISBN 978–1–78541–046–8 (hb)
ISBN 978–1–78541–047–5 (pb)

This book is printed on acid-free paper

For my father, who gave me
my first book of fairy tales.
And for my mother, who
taught me to read.

As for this little key, it is that of the closet at the end of the long gallery, on the ground floor. Open everything, and go everywhere except that little closet, which I forbid you to enter, and I forbid you so strictly, that if you should venture to open the door, there is nothing that you may not have to dread from my anger.

"Blue Beard", Charles Perrault

Contents

Contents

Week 1

The
Spinning
Girl

Monday

Monday, 2 February, 7.45 a.m.

It is you. Of course it is you. Always it is you. Someone is catching up to me and I turn and see you. I'd known it would be you, but still I lose my footing on the frozen snow. I stagger up. There are patches of wet on the knees of my stockings. My mittens are soaked through.

Any sensible person would be at home on such an icy morning if he had a choice in the matter, but not you. You are out, taking a little stroll. You are reaching to steady me, asking if I'm okay, but I step away, managing not to unbalance myself again.

I know you must have been watching me since I left my house. I can't stop myself from asking you what you're doing here, though I know your answer won't be the true one.

Your eyelids are doing that flickering thing again. It happens when you're nervous. "I was just walking, Clarissa." Never mind that you live in a village five miles away. Your lips blanch. You bite them, as if you guess they've lost what little colour they normally have and you're trying to force blood back into them. "You behaved strangely at work on Friday, Clarissa, walking out of that talk. Everyone said so."

3

It makes me want to scream, the way you say my name all the time. Yours has become ugly to me. I try to keep it out of my head, as if to do so will somehow keep you out of my life. But still it creeps in. Barges in. Just like you. Again and again.

Second person present. That's what you are. In every way.

My silence doesn't deter you. "You haven't answered your phone all weekend. You only replied to one of my texts and it wasn't friendly. Why are you out on a morning like this, Clarissa?"

The short term is all I can see. I have to get rid of you. I have to stop you trailing me to the station and figuring out where I'm going. Ignoring you won't get me the outcome I need now; the advice in the leaflets doesn't work in real life. I doubt anything will work with you.

"I'm ill." This is a lie. "That's why I left on Friday. I've got to be at the doctor's by eight."

"You're the only woman I've ever seen who looks beautiful even when she's ill."

I really am beginning to feel sick. "I have a fever. I was vomiting all night."

You lift a hand towards my cheek, as if to check my temperature, and I flinch away.

"I'll come with you." Your hand is still in the air, an awkward reminder of your wrong move. "You shouldn't be alone." You punctuate this by letting your hand drop heavily to your side.

"I don't want to give it to you." Despite my words, I don't think I sound concerned.

"Let me take care of you, Clarissa. It's below zero — you shouldn't be out in this and your hair's wet — that can't be good for you." You're taking out your phone. "I'm calling us a taxi."

Again, you've cornered me. The black iron railings are behind me so I can't back away from you any farther; I don't want to slip and fall through the gap — there's a three-foot drop to the road below. I step sideways, repositioning myself, but this doesn't stop you towering over me. You look so huge in your puffy grey jacket.

The hem of your jeans is sopping, from dragging in the snow — you aren't caring for yourself, either. Your ears and nose are red and raw from the bitter cold. Mine must be too. Your brown hair is lank, though it's probably freshly washed. Your closed, frowning mouth never relaxes.

Pity for you steals upon me, however much I guard against it and recoil from you. You must be losing sleep, too. To speak meanly, even to you, goes against the kindness my parents taught me. Rudeness won't make you vanish now, anyway. I know all too well you'll only follow me, pretending not to hear, and that's the last thing I want.

You're punching numbers into your mobile.

"Don't. Don't call." Your fingers pause at the sharpness in my voice. I push the point further. "The doctor's not far from here." I make myself more explicit. "I won't get in a taxi with you."

You press the red button and pocket your phone. "Write down your landline for me, Clarissa. I seem to have lost it."

We both know I've never given it to you. "I had it disconnected. I just use my mobile now." More lies. I give a silent prayer of thanks that you didn't somehow find the number and note it down when you were in my flat. I'm

5

amazed you overlooked such a chance. You're probably kicking yourself for that. But you were busy, then.

I point up the hill. "You should try along the top edge for your walk." I play on your desire to please me, a callous move, but I'm desperate. "It's one of my favourites, Rafe." There's too long a pause before I manage to get out your name, but I do use it and that's all you notice; it doesn't occur to you that I've only thrown you this treat in the hope that it will lure you into going away.

"I'd like that, if it's special to you, Clarissa. All I want is to make you happy, you know. If you'd just let me." You attempt a smile.

"Goodbye, Rafe." I force myself to use your name again, and when your smile becomes deeper and more real I'm amazed and a little guilty that such a crude trick can work.

Hardly daring to believe I've got away, I step carefully down the hill, checking periodically that the distance between us is increasing. Each time, you are looking back and raising your hand, so I have to make myself wave half-heartedly in response.

From now on, I'll take taxis to the station in the mornings and check through the windows to make sure you aren't following. Next time I'm faced with you, I'll consider the long term and obey the leaflets. I'll refuse to speak or I'll tell you for the zillionth time — in no uncertain terms — to leave me alone. Even my mother would think such circumstances warranted bad manners. Not that I would dream of worrying my parents by telling them about you.

My teeth chatter as I stand on the platform, anxious that you will materialise while I listen to the apologetic announcements about cancellations and delays due to the extreme weather.

I lean against the wall and scribble as quickly as I can in my new notebook. It's my first entry. The notebook is tiny, so that I can always carry it with me, as the leaflets advise. The pages are lined and wire-bound. The cover is matt black. The people on the helplines say I need a complete record. They say I mustn't miss out anything and I should try to write as soon as I can after each incident, no matter how small. But your incidents are never small.

I am shivering so violently I regret not drying my hair. I rushed out the door to avoid being late after over-sleeping because of bad dreams — about you, always about you. There would have been time to dry it, though I couldn't have predicted that as perfectly as I can predict you. My hair feels like a wand of ice, channelling the cold through my skin and into my veins, a spell freezing flesh into stone.

There had to be a world where he wasn't, and she thought perhaps she'd entered it at last. Portraits of stern-looking judges hung on the wall opposite the marble staircase. Climbing to the first floor, Clarissa felt as if they were watching her; but she couldn't give up the hope that this could be a place where she wasn't spied on, a place she could keep him from.

She let the jury officer inspect her passport and pink summons, then sat down on one of the padded blue chairs. The room was wonderfully warm. Her toes thawed. Her hair dried. It seemed a magic place, away from his eyes. Only jurors were allowed in, and they needed to tap a code into a keypad before they could even get through the door.

She jumped at the crackle of the jury officer's microphone. "Will the following people please come and stand by the desk, for a two-week trial that is about to begin in Court 6?"

Two whole weeks in the safe haven of a courtroom. Two whole weeks away from work and away from him. Her heart was beating fast in the hope that she'd hear her name. She sank back in her chair in disappointment when it never came.

At lunchtime, she made herself leave the sanctuary of the court building; she knew she needed fresh air. She hesitated just outside the revolving doors, scanning up and down the street. She worried he might be hiding between two custodial services vans, parked a few metres up the road. She plunged past them quickly, holding her breath. When she saw that he wasn't crouched by one of the bumpers she exhaled in relief.

She wandered through the outside market, watching local workers buying quick wholefood or ethnic lunches from stalls, glimpsing barristers sitting around a large table in an expensive Italian restaurant.

Checking over her shoulder, she disappeared into the familiar comfort of a sewing shop. As always, she was drawn to the children's fabrics. Mermaids floated absently as little girls swam after them, under enchantment; she imagined a toddler's peasant dress, its tiers alternating between plum and fuchsia seas.

Henry would have hated it. Twee, he would have said. Sentimental, he would have said. Too pretty, he would have said. Unoriginal, he would have said. Plain colours are best, he would have said. Perhaps it was just as well that the failure to make a baby had driven them apart.

She aimed herself firmly at the thread display, then searched her bag for the scrap of mossy green quilter's cotton traced with crimson blossoms. She found it, chose the best match for the background colour, and headed for the till with two spools.

"What will you be sewing?" the girl asked.

Clarissa saw eyelids vibrating beneath pale brown lashes, a gaze she couldn't escape, lips dripping cuckoo spit: flashes of Rafe's one night in her bed.

She would exorcise him. "New bedding," she said.

It would feel lovely against her skin. And she was surprised by a funny spark of curiosity about who might someday sleep beneath the tiny crimson blossoms with her.

Monday, 2 February, 2.15 p.m.

I am trying to piece it all together. I am trying to fill in the gaps. I am trying to recollect the things you did before this morning, when I started to record it all. I don't want to miss out a single bit of evidence — I can't afford to. But doing this forces me to relive it. Doing this keeps you with me, which is exactly where I don't want you to be.

Monday, 10 November, 8.00p.m.
(Three Months Ago)

It is the night that I make the very big mistake of sleeping with you and I am in the bookshop. The shop is open just to your invited guests, to celebrate the publication of your new book about fairy tales. Only a couple of your English Department colleagues have turned up. Encouraged by my presence, they are whispering venomously about Henry. I am pretending not to notice by picking up books and acting as though I'm intensely interested in them, though the words are jumbled and about as comprehensible to me as Greek.

I'm still not sure why I've come, or what possesses me to mix the red and white wines you press upon me. Probably loneliness and loss: Henry has just moved from Bath to take up the professorship at Cambridge he's been plotting all his life to get. Compassion also plays a part; you sent me three invitations.

I can't leave until after your reading. At last, I am seated in the back row, listening to you recite from your chapter on "The Test of the True Bride". You finish and your handful of colleagues asks polite questions. I am not an academic; I say nothing. As soon as the smattering of applause dies out I weave my way towards the door to escape, only to be stopped by your plea that I not leave yet. I sneak up to the art section and sit on the grubby beige carpet with a book about Munch. I turn to *The Kiss*, the early version where the lovers are naked.

I visibly startle when your shadow falls on the page and your voice cuts through the first floor's deserted silence. "If I hadn't found you you might have been locked in all night."

You are standing above me, peering down from what seems to be a very great height and smiling.

I quickly close the Munch and set it aside. "I'm not sure that would have been such a terrible fate, sleeping with the artists." I wave your heavy book like an actress overdoing her use of props. It makes my wrist ache. "This is wonderful. It was so kind of you to give me a copy. And you read brilliantly. I loved the passage you chose."

"I loved the painting you chose, Clarissa." You set down the overstuffed briefcase you're carrying in one hand and the two glasses of wine you're balancing in the other.

I laugh. "Have you got a body in that briefcase?"

Your eyes flick to the briefcase's lockable catch, as if to check it's properly closed, and it occurs to me that you have secrets you don't want exposed. But you laugh too. "Just books and papers." You stretch out an arm. "Come out of hiding. Let me walk you home. It's a dark night for you to be out on your own."

I reach up, letting you help me to my feet. You don't release my hand. Gently, I pull it away. "I'll be fine. Don't you have a dinner to go to, Professor?"

"I'm not a professor." There is a quiver in your eyelid. It vibrates several times, quickly, in succession, as if a tiny insect is hiding inside. "Henry got it, the year I applied. Not much chance against a prize-winning poet. Being Head of Department didn't hurt him, either."

Henry had more than deserved the professorship, but of course I don't say this. What I say is, "I'm sorry." After a few embarrassing seconds of silence, I say, "I need to get home." You look so crushed I want to comfort you. "It's a really

11

interesting book, Rafe." I try to soften my impending exit. "You should be proud."

You retrieve the wine and offer me a glass. "A toast, Clarissa. Before you go."

"To your beautiful book." I clink my white to your red and take a sip. You look so pleased by this small thing; it touches and saddens me. I will replay this moment too many times over the next few months, much as I would like to shut it out.

"Drink up." You gulp down your own, as if to demonstrate.

And I follow your example, though it tastes like salty sweet medicine. But I don't want to dim your already lacklustre celebration.

"Let me walk with you, Clarissa. I'd rather walk with you than go to some stuffy dinner."

A minute later we are out in the chill late-autumn air. Even in my wine-fuelled light-headedness I hesitate before what I say next. "Do you ever think about Bluebeard's first wife? She isn't specifically mentioned, but she must be one of the dead women hanging in the forbidden chamber."

You smile tolerantly, as if I am one of your students. You are dressed like a preppy American professor — not your usual look. Tweedy blazer, soft brown corduroy trousers, a finely striped blue-and-white shirt, a sleeveless navy sweater. "Explain." You shoot out the word peremptorily, the way you must do it in English Literature seminars.

"Well, if there was a secret room right at the beginning, and he commanded the very first Mrs Bluebeard not to enter it, there wouldn't have been any murdered wives in there yet. There wouldn't have been the stream of blood for her to drop the key into, and no stain on it to give her away. So what reason did he think he had for killing the first time? That's always puzzled me."

"Maybe he didn't invent the room until wife number two. Maybe wife number one did something even more unforgivable than going into the room. The worst form of disobedience: maybe she was unfaithful, like the first wife in the *Arabian Nights*, and that's why he killed her. Then he needed to test each of the others, after, to see if she was worthy. Except not a single one was." You say all of this lightly, jokingly.

I should have seen, then, that you don't joke. You are never light. If I hadn't accepted the third glass of wine I might have seen that and averted everything that followed.

"You sound like you think she deserved it."

"Of course I don't." You speak too quickly, too insistently, a sign that you're lying. "Of course I don't think that."

"But you used the word disobedience." Am I only imagining that I'm beginning to wobble? "That's a horrifying word. And it was never a fair promise. You can't ask somebody never to enter a room that's part of her own house."

"Men need secret places, Clarissa."

"Do they?" We've reached Bath Abbey. The building's west front is illuminated, but I can't seem to focus on my favourite fallen angels, sculpted upside down on Jacob's Ladder. The vertigo I'm beginning to feel must be like theirs, with the world up-ended.

You take my arm. "Clarissa?" You wave a hand in front of my eyes, smiling. "Wake up, sleepyhead."

That helps me to remember the point I'm trying to make, though I have to concentrate extra hard to form sentences.

"There must have been some truly dreadful secrets in that room. It was a place for his fantasies, where he made them real."

We're passing the Roman Baths. I imagine the statues of the emperors and governors and military leaders frowning down at me from their high terrace, willing me to drown in the great green pool below them. My mouth tastes of sulphur, like the spa water from the Pump Room's fountain.

"You're better on 'Blue Beard' than any critic, Clarissa. You should be the professor. You should have finished that PhD."

I shake my head to deny this. Even after my head stops moving, the world continues to waver from side to side. I hardly ever tell anyone about the abandoned PhD. I wonder vaguely how you know, but halt abruptly, distracted by a ring in a shop window. It is a twist of platinum twinkling with diamonds. It is the ring I dreamed Henry would one day surprise me with, but he never did. Moving lights glitter and flash inside the gems like bright sun on blue sea. White and gold fairy bulbs rim the window, dazzling me.

You pull me away from the glass and I blink as if you've woken me. By the time we've passed the closed shops in their deep gold Georgian buildings, my steps are no longer straight. Your arm is around my waist, aiming me in the right direction.

I hardly remember going through the subway, but already we are climbing the steep hill and I am breathless. You are holding me close, pushing or pulling me, half-carrying me. Flashes from the diamonds and fairy lights come back, tiny dots before my eyes. How is it that we are already at the door of the old house whose upper floor is mine?

I sway gently, like a funny rag doll. Blood rushes into my head. You help me find my keys, help me up the stairs to the second floor, help me to put two more keys into the locks of my own front door. I stand there, dizzily, not knowing what to do next.

"Aren't you going to invite me in for a coffee?"

It can't fail to work, your manipulative little call to my politeness. I think of idiot-eyed Snow White opening the door to the wicked queen and practically grabbing the poisoned apple out of her hands. I think of Jonathan Harker crossing Dracula's threshold freely and of his own will. I think again of Bluebeard and his bloody chamber. Did he carry each new bride over the threshold and into his castle after she'd leapt happily into his arms? After that came the room of torture she never imagined.

I try to smile but my face seems not to move as it should. "Of course. Of course I am. You must come in for a coffee and warm up while I call you a taxi. It was so sweet of you to walk me home on your special night." I'm jabbering. I know I'm jabbering.

I stand in front of the sink, letting water run into the kettle. "I'm sorry." My words sound smudgy, as if spoken in a language I barely know. "My head is feeling funny."

It is such an effort to stand up. I feel like a spinning top. Or is it the room that is revolving? My body seems to be made of liquid. I float down, my legs folding with such pleasing neatness, until I find myself sitting on the slate tiles of my galley kitchen. The kettle is still in my hands, sloshing water from its spout. "I'm very thirsty." Though the water is splashing onto my dress, I can't imagine how to get any of it into my mouth.

You find a glass and fill it. You kneel beside me, feeding the water to me as if I'm a child drinking from a sippy cup. You wipe a drop from my chin with your index finger and then put it to your lips. My own hands still clutch the kettle.

You rise again to set the glass down and turn off the tap. You lean over to take the kettle from me. "It hurts me to think you don't trust me." I can feel your breath in my hair as you speak.

You pull me to my feet, supporting my weight. My legs are barely working as you move me towards the bedroom. You sit me at the edge of the bed and crouch in front of me, leaning me into you to stop me from falling over. I can't keep my back straight. I am weeping.

"Don't," you whisper, smoothing my hair, murmuring that it is so soft, kissing away the tears streaming down my face. "Let me put you to bed. I know just what to do with you."

"Henry . . ." I try to say. Speaking seems too difficult, as if I have forgotten how.

"Don't think about him." You sound angry. You look deeply into my eyes, so that I must close my own. "The Munch painting, I know you were thinking of us, imagining our being together. We both were."

I am completely floppy. I feel as though I am made of waves. I am slipping backwards. All I want is to lie down. There is a rushing in my head, like the sea. There is a pounding in my ears like a drum beat, my own heart, growing louder.

Your hands are on my waist, on my stomach, on my hips, on the small of my back, moving over me as you unfasten my wrap dress.

I only ever meant for Henry to touch this dress. I made it for the birthday dinner I had with him seven months ago. Even though we both knew it was all but over, he didn't want me to turn thirty-eight alone. Our last night together. A goodbye dinner, with goodbye sex. This dress was never meant for you.

I am trying to push you away but I might as well be a child. You are pulling the dress the rest of the way open and sliding it off my shoulders. And then the room tips, and everything that follows is shadowy. Broken images from a nightmare I don't want to remember.

She was so immersed in writing that the rasp of the jury officer's microphone startled the pen from her fingers, making it shoot across the quiet area where she was sitting. "Will the following people please come and stand by the desk for the trial that is about to begin in Court 12?" Her name was the first to be called, giving her an electric shock. She shoved the notebook into her bag as if it were a piece of incriminating evidence she didn't want to be seen with.

Two minutes later she was hurrying after the usher with the others. A heavy door sprang open and they were in the hidden depths of the building, winding their way up several flights of draughty concrete stairs, padding across the linoleum of a small, overly bright waiting room, then stumbling through another door. She blinked several times as she realised that they were in the courtroom. Her name was called again and she filed into the back row.

Henry would have refused the Bible but Clarissa took it from the usher without wavering. She meant every word of the oath, though her voice was faint.

Sitting next to her was a prettily plump, dark-haired woman whose necklace spelled her name in letters of white gold: *Annie*. As if through a haze, Clarissa glanced farther to the right, where five defendants sat only a few feet away, flanked by police guards. Annie was studying the men with undisguised interest, as if daring them to notice.

The judge addressed the jurors. "This trial will last for seven weeks."

Seven weeks. She'd never dreamed she'd be that lucky.

"If there are compelling reasons as to why you cannot serve on this jury, please pass a note to the usher before leaving. Tomorrow the Crown will make his opening remarks."

She groped for her bag, tugged down her skirt as she stood to make sure it hadn't ridden up, and lurched after the others. As she passed the dock she saw that if she and the nearest defendant were each to stretch out an arm, they would almost be able to touch.

She squirmed off her mittens as she boarded the train, found the last empty seat, and took out her mobile. A sick wave went through her. Four texts. One from her mother. The others from Rafe. It was actually restrained for him, stopping at three.

She didn't smile, as she normally would, when she read her mother's — *Coffee is not a breakfast food.* Nothing could inure her to his little series, however harmless they might seem to somebody else.

Hope you're sleeping. Hope you're dreaming of me.

Keep getting your voicemail. Will phone later.

You'll need juice and fruit and things with vitamins. I'll come to your flat.

She wanted a friend to turn to, to show the texts to; she wanted a friend to tell her what to do. She used to have friends before Henry and fertility treatments took over her life; before she let a married man leave his wife for her; before other women stopped trusting her; before she found it too hard to look at their disapproving faces and see her own bewilderment at what she'd done mirrored in them.

Henry and her friends wouldn't mix, but she still should have found a way to obey that cardinal rule, the one that says you should never let a relationship interfere with your friends. Now Henry was gone, and Clarissa was too abashed to try to get her friends back. She wasn't even sure she deserved them, or that they'd ever forgive her.

She thought of her oldest friend, Rowena, whom she hadn't seen for two years. Their mothers had met in the maternity ward, cradling their new babies as they gazed at the sea from the hospital's top-floor windows. There'd been play dates in infancy and toddlerhood. They'd gone all through school together. But Rowena was another friend who didn't get along with Henry. She and Rowena had grown so different, though; perhaps Henry only hastened a breach that would have happened anyway.

She tried to shake away the self-pity. She would need to try harder to make new friends. And if she didn't have friends to consult at the moment, at least she had the helplines; their information leaflets had arrived in the post on Saturday, just one day after she first spoke to them.

She texted him back. *Don't come. Don't want to see you. Very contagious.*

As soon as she pressed send she regretted it, remembering the advice every one of those leaflets repeated in countless ways. *Wherever possible, do not talk to him. Do not engage in any kind of conversation.* She knew her lost friends would have said that too.

She wished she hadn't given him her mobile number. Nothing else had worked to get rid of him the morning after his book launch party. Not being audibly sick in the bathroom. Not swallowing three painkillers right before his eyes for her throbbing head. Not even her visible trembling made him see she was so unwell he needed to go. The number had been a last-resort payoff to get him to leave — if only she'd had the foresight to make up a fake number instead of using her real one to fob him off. But she'd been too ill to think clearly.

She dialled Gary. Compelling reasons, the judge had said. What might these be? Pregnancy, perhaps. Or breastfeeding. She had no compelling reasons. A line manager who would be mildly inconvenienced by her absence was not a compelling reason.

Clarissa tried to sound sorrowful and as if something shocking had been done to her. "I thought it would only be nine days. Two weeks at most. That's what all the stuff they sent us says, but I somehow got picked for a seven-week trial. I'm so sorry."

"Didn't they give you a chance to say you couldn't? You're vital to this university."

She couldn't help but laugh. "I'm not. Not like doctors or teachers. Even they don't get out of it. Even judges don't. The secretary to the Head of the Graduate School is hardly a key worker — though of course I'm touched by your unique sense of my importance."

"But you didn't answer my question." On rare occasions Gary could muster a serious boss tone with her. "Didn't they give you a chance to get out of it?"

She felt no qualms about the lie. "No," she said. She was home; the train was pulling into Bath. Her skin prickled, usually an unfailing warning that she was being watched, but she knew Rafe wasn't in the carriage. She couldn't see him on the platform either. "No, they didn't."

Tuesday

The traffic fumes were making her eyes burn. She was walking from Bristol Temple Meads station to the court and the roads were so wide and alike she wondered if she was lost.

She was trying to concentrate on the route, the barely known landmarks — she was sure she remembered that purple wall to her right from yesterday — but Rafe was crowding out everything else, as usual.

Friday, 30 January, 10.00 a.m. (Four Days Ago)

It is my last day at work before jury service; my last day of having to avert you. On Monday I will disappear into the court building and you will not know where I am.

I place my documents and reports on one of the fixed wooden chairs in the large lecture theatre and my bag on another. I take the seat between them, hoping these small battlements will deter you from sitting beside me. Such a visual signal of my wish for space would work with anyone else. But not with you. Of course not with you. Nothing works with you.

22

You are standing over me and saying "Hello, Clarissa" as you move my papers onto the floor and sit down. I'm unfairly, irrationally furious with Gary, for insisting that I attend this meeting in his place. You are in the aisle seat, making escape more difficult — I'd been foolish not to see that coming.

You lock your eyes on me, your eyeballs quivering. There is nowhere to hide from your eyes. I want to put my face in my hands, to cover myself. Your cheeks flash crimson, then white, then crimson again with the sharpness of a car's indicators. I hate to see such clear evidence of my effect on your body.

And your effect on mine. I am growing hot and my chest hurts so much I fear I will stop breathing. I might faint in front of everybody, or be sick. It must be a panic attack.

The ceiling is high. The fluorescent lights are speckled with desiccated fly corpses. Though the bulbs are far above my head, they burn into the top of my skull. Even in winter the flies survive in the building's warm roof space. I can hear one hissing and frying, unable to escape the trap of the lamp in which it has found itself. I fear it will fall on me. But better a fly than you.

You touch my arm and I shrink away with as little violence as I can manage. You whisper, "You know I love your hair that way, off your neck. Your neck is so lovely, Clarissa. You did it for me, didn't you? And the dress too. You know how I love you in black."

And I just can't bear it any more. As if the top has blown off a pressure cooker I jump up, abandoning my papers, tripping over your feet and legs. You take advantage — of course you do, you always do — and put your hands on my waist in a pretence of helping to balance me. I slap your fingers away, beyond caring whether I affront the Vice Chancellor, who pauses in his opening remarks as all the heads in the room turn to watch me rush out. It makes me want to cry, knowing that it appears as if I'm the one out of control, rather than you.

Somehow I flee the campus and get myself into the centre of Bath and stumble along my near-automatic walk to the Assembly Rooms. I don't follow my usual descent into the dimly lit basement, my favourite place, where they display gowns from hundreds of years ago; they are spun of silver and gold, brocaded in shimmering silks, embellished with jewels. Instead, I walk straight through the sage-green entrance hall, between marbled columns the colour of pale honey, and stop just outside the Great Octagon.

The room is closed. A sign explains that a private function will be taking place in it later today. But I slip between the double doors as if I have a right to, and close them behind me. It is hushed and peaceful in here, surrounded by these eight stone walls; soft light falls on me through the paned windows. I take out my phone, inhale deeply, and dial 999.

"Police emergency." The operator's greeting is sing-song and chirpy, as if she's working in a dress shop and I'm a potential customer.

I don't know what to say. I manage "Hello," though I'm breathing heavily. I must sound like a nuisance caller.

"What is your emergency, please?"

Queen Charlotte aims her gentle gaze at me from her high portrait, as if to offer encouragement. "At work this morning . . . A colleague . . ."

"Has there been an incident in your place of work?"

I try to explain. *He sat next to me in a meeting when I didn't want him to. He whispered suggestively. He invaded my body space. He made me feel upset.*

"Right. Is this man with you now?"

Queen Charlotte's eyes follow me in concern as I circle the room. "No. But he's stalking me all the time. I can't get rid of him."

"Did he physically injure you?"

The Drake Family are too happy in their ornamental golden frame, posed in their manicured eighteenth-century landscape with their perfectly behaved children. "No."

"Has he ever physically abused you?"

The sweet Drake baby, sitting on its mother's lap, should not be hearing this. "No," I say again, after a long pause.

"Has he ever directly threatened you?"

Once more I hesitate. "Not directly, no. But he makes me feel threatened."

"Are you in any danger at this moment?"

I look up, up, up, above the elegant frieze of curling tendrils, craning my neck. Captain William Wade poses in his red Master of Ceremonies coat and stares disapprovingly at me. "No."

"I can see you're very upset, and that's understandable. But this isn't a life-threatening matter. 999 is really meant for life-or-death emergencies."

The room seems smaller, as if the tastefully muted yellow walls are drawing closer together. "I'm sorry." The high ceiling doesn't seem so high any more. There isn't enough oxygen in here.

"You don't need to be. But I think you'd be able to help yourself better if you calmed down." She clearly thinks I'm hysterical.

There are four pairs of brown double doors in the Great Octagon. One pair bursts open. A middle-aged tourist blunders in, takes one look at me, and quickly backs out, shutting the doors behind him.

"I am calm." The words come out as a squeaky croak.

"I can see you made this call in good faith." She clearly thinks I'm a crazy time-waster.

My face is red and hot. "I didn't know who else to turn to. I thought that was what you were there for."

"You're obviously distressed. Have you thought of going to see your GP?" She clearly thinks I'm just plain mad.

I press my temple against the jutting plasterwork of one of the chimney-pieces. "My GP isn't going to make him leave me alone."

Her voice is kind, even apologetic. "The police cannot act unless there is evidence that a crime has been committed. From what you are telling me, there hasn't been a crime. I'm not saying I don't believe you, but you have no evidence. And as much as I'd like to help, you are not in mortal danger, so I can't send anyone out to you in these circumstances."

George III looks off to the side. "Are you saying he has to hurt me before you'll help?"

"I'm saying that nothing can be done at this stage. There are specialist organisations and helplines that can advise you on how to document persistent harassment from a stalker. You're going to need to be proactive about gathering evidence, if you want to put a stop to what he's doing. Get in touch with them. That's the best course of action you can take right now."

I press end on the call and sit for a few minutes in the middle of the scuffed wood floor. Above me is the huge crystal chandelier. I think it might just fall on my head. I get to my feet, my knees stiff and sore, and hurry from the Great Octagon, casting one last look at Queen Charlotte before they find me and throw me out.

She was relieved to be torn from these recollections by the sight of the court building. Somehow she'd made it, despite being so distracted by bad memories she'd missed the left turning and walked on for twenty minutes before seeing she'd have to backtrack. It was only day two, but she worried that the judge might be so strict about lateness that he'd kick her off before the trial had even begun. Again she practically stumbled into the jury box.

A ring binder lay on the desk she shared with Annie. Together, they opened it and read the charge sheets. *Kidnapping. False imprisonment. Rape. Conspiracy to supply Class A drugs.* Shocking, dramatic words. Words that made her wonder how she'd ended up in such a place.

The prosecuting barrister couldn't have been more than fifty. The lines beneath his eyes had the slant of a good-humoured man, but Mr Morden looked deadly serious as he turned to the jury box. "I'm going to tell you a story," he began. "A true story. And not a pretty one. It's the story of Carlotta Lockyer, and what happened to her was no fairy tale."

Four of the five defendants were studiously looking down, as if trying, politely, not to eavesdrop on a conversation that had nothing to do with them.

27

"A year and a half ago, on the last Saturday of July, Samuel Doleman took a ride with some friends."

Doleman's grey eyes were military-straight before him, though his face turned pale. His red hair was cut so close Clarissa could see his scalp. It made him look vulnerable. So did his freckles.

"He drove them from London to Bath in a van. They were on a hunt. Their prey was Carlotta Lockyer."

Clarissa remembered exactly what she was doing then. She wondered if anybody else in the courtroom, other than the defendants, could. She had just finished her fourth attempt at IVF. Twenty-eighth July was the date of the last pregnancy test she'd failed. She replayed the tense drive to London early on the Saturday morning to get to the lab for her blood draw. Perhaps she and Henry had even followed the van along the motorway as they returned to Bath that afternoon, Clarissa sobbing wretchedly after the clinic's call to her mobile, Henry brooding and silent.

"If you turn to the screens, you will see CCTV images of the defendants taken outside the entrance to Miss Lockyer's flat."

Clarissa tried to shake herself back into concentration, willing her heart to slow down. She knew that flat. The building was a ten-minute walk from her own. If Rafe had caught her a few minutes later the previous morning they'd have been standing in front of it.

Despite the jerky, grainy footage, she could see the men moving about, fidgety and circling, peering through the glass door, banging on it with their fists, shaking the handle.

28

She imagined Rafe doing that to her door. Miss Norton would have something to say about it if he dared. Miss Norton was the little old lady who lived in the ground-floor flat. Only Clarissa and Miss Norton occupied the building: the first-floor flat was always empty, an investment property owned by a rich Australian who seldom used it.

"Miss Lockyer, evidently, is not at home. Sadly for her, Mr Doleman and his friends don't give up easily."

The same could be said of Rafe. She tasted her morning coffee, soured.

"They searched for her. They found her. They stalked her. They pounced. They dragged her onto a terrifying journey from Bath to London, into the darkness of their sadistic world."

Yet again, she imagined going to the police to complain about him. Yet again, she saw all too clearly what would happen if she did: they'd end up thinking she'd brought it on herself.

He'd say she liked attention. He'd say she went to his party and wanted to sleep with him. He'd say she invited him home. There was probably CCTV footage of the two of them walking up the hill that night, with his arm around her.

She thought again of the leaflets' warnings. *If there is any doubt that you are being truthful, it may harm your case and credibility.* But when it came to the truth, it was her word against his.

She was remembering something she usually kept buried. Walking home from school with Rowena when she was fifteen. That strange girl on the seafront who'd punched her in the stomach, grabbed her bag and knocked her to the ground before running off. It had all seemed to happen at once. The only thing Clarissa could do was gasp for breath as Rowena crouched beside her, her arms around her.

Her parents took her to the police station and made her report the incident, but the sour-faced police-woman clearly thought it was a schoolgirl argument that wasn't worth her time and kept asking what Clarissa might have done to provoke it. Had she been showing off? Flashing valuables at a girl who was less fortunate? Arguing over a boy? Clarissa left the station with her cheeks bright red and her face burning hot, feeling like a criminal.

A random act of violence. That was what Rowena had called it, holding her hand afterwards. But Clarissa wasn't sure. There must have been something about her to draw that girl's attention. And something about her to draw Rafe's too. There was certainly nothing random about him.

Her eyes ached; briefly, she squeezed them shut. Her shoulders were stiff. The man sitting in front of her was annoyingly tall, well over six feet; she'd had to crane her neck to see over his close-cropped brown head and keep Mr Morden's face in view; it had been like that yesterday, too. After seven weeks of this she'd need a chiropractor.

The man rose and gave her a small nod, waiting for her to precede him out of the courtroom. It was his stance that she noticed: standing solidly, feet a foot and a half apart and exactly parallel, weight back on his heels, arms crossed over his chest. She'd never seen anybody look so straight but so relaxed at once.

Any expression of thanks could only be muted in the theatre of Court 12, but it seemed important to cling to small habits of courtesy in such company. She stepped ahead of him with a slight nod and almost-smile, answering his public display of good manners with her own.

Tuesday, 3 February, 6.00 p.m.

It doesn't last. Of course it doesn't last. It is amazing enough that the lie about being sick bought me even one day of not being under your eye. It's only been thirty-four hours, but it's still the longest break from you I've had in weeks.

You would say it's a love letter. I call it hate mail. Whatever its name, it is propped on the shelf in an innocuous brown envelope, neatly arranged by the ever alert Miss Norton.

No other man can do to you what I can. No other man will love you like I do.

For once, I want your predictions to come true.

Wednesday

Wednesday, 4 February, 8.00 a.m.

When I open my front door you are standing so close I breathe in the scent of your soap and shampoo. You smell fresh and clean. You smell of apples and lavender and bergamot — smells I would like if they weren't your smells.

"Are you better, Clarissa?"

Fairness is not something you understand. It is not something you deserve. But I will be fair by talking to you one final time before refusing ever to talk to you again. This morning will be very different from Monday.

I speak calmly to you, in a polite voice. It is far from the first time I say it. "I don't want you near me. I don't want to see you. I don't want anything to do with you. No form of contact. No letters. No gifts. No calls. No visits. Don't come to my house again."

My speech is perfect. Just as I rehearsed. I move away quickly, not looking at you, though you are clear enough in my head to provide an exact witness description.

You are six feet tall and large boned. Your belly used to be flat, but you must be drinking more because it isn't now. Your hips have widened, too, over the last month. Your nose is ordinary in the blur of your puffy round face, which has lost its definition.

More than anything else, you are pale. Pale in mind. Pale in soul. Pale in body. Your skin is so pale you flush easily, going from white to ruddy in a flash. Your pale brown hair is straight and short, not at all thinning. It is unusually soft and silky for a man's. Your brows are pale brown. Your eyes are pale, watery blue. They are small. Your lips are thin. They are pale too.

You touch my arm and I shake you off, walking down the path to the waiting taxi.

"I was coming to check on you," you say, as if I haven't spoken at all. "Your phone's still not on," you say. "I worry when I can't get hold of you," you say.

With you beside me it seems a long walk through the path of Miss Norton's wintering rose bushes, but I am at the taxi and must have reached it quickly.

I open the rear door and get in, trying to pull it closed behind me, but you catch it before I can.

"Move over, Clarissa. I'll come with you." You are bending over. Your head and torso are inside. I can smell your toothpaste. The mint is strong. You've probably used mouthwash too.

The composure I have practised so carefully dissolves. "This man isn't with me," I say to the driver, the same one who picked me up yesterday morning. "I don't want him getting in."

"Stop bothering her. Get the fuck out of my car or I'm calling the police," the driver says.

My mother has told me all of my adult life that taxi drivers see it as part of their job to be protective; they know that's why women pay for taxis. My mother is often right, and I am

33

lucky with this driver. In my mother's visions of taxi drivers as heroic saviours, they are always big and burly men.

This one is a woman, middle-aged and short, but stout and tough and fearless seeming, with beautiful cropped spiky grey hair that I am certain she would never dream of dyeing. She wears jeans and a fuzzy orange wool sweater. She does not show you the warmth and joviality that filled her car during yesterday's brief journey. She is opening her own door, showing you she's prepared to enforce her words.

You withdraw your head and torso and stand just inches from the door as I slam it closed and the driver slams hers.

You bang a fist on the roof. "How can you treat me like this, Clarissa?"

The driver presses the button to lower the front passenger window, shouts threateningly at you, and moves off.

"Clarissa? Clarissa! I don't deserve this, Clarissa."

I still refuse to look at you. I'm trying so hard to stick to the advice, to do this right. I can see in my peripheral vision that you are running beside the taxi to the end of the street, slapping the trees and lamp posts as you pass them. I can hear you calling my name. The driver is muttering under her breath about what a fucking crazy idiot you are. She is apologising for her language and I am apologising for being so troublesome. We each tell the other that no apology is needed, though I know she is just being nice and mine is. I thank her for being so kind.

Before I get out of the taxi I take her card: she is a potential witness against you.

Despite the film of sweat on my back and brow even in the cold of the morning, it has been a fairly successful start to the day in terms of managing you.

As I move in a daze through the station my new phone bleeps, announcing that I have an email. I look at the screen like a little girl daring herself to stare into a mirror in the dark, frightened that the face of a monster will appear. To my astonishment, the email is from the long-silent Rowena. She's visiting Bath tonight, and she's commanding my presence at a French restaurant I've never been to but Henry once said was gruesome. I email back, *I'll be there*, and two kisses. Then I switch off my phone and step onto the train to Bristol.

Clearly, the witness box was placed so its occupant would directly face the jury. But still the woman seemed so far away. In front of the jurors was an orchestra pit of twelve barristers in their wigs and black robes. Clarissa had to look over them all to get the witness in view.

She was extremely thin, almost worryingly frail. High cheekbones. Small straight nose. Rosebud lips. Delicate chin. Softly arched brows. Tiny seashell ears that belonged on a fairy. Her dark blonde hair was in a short ponytail.

But the closer Clarissa looked, the more she saw that the woman's ethereal beauty was damaged. Her skin was too thin, too transparent. The firm set to her mouth and the lines etched around her huge green eyes were at odds with Clarissa's guess that she was in her late twenties. Something had taken an unnatural toll on her.

"She looks like you," Annie whispered. "She just needs to grow her hair longer and you'd pass for twins. But she's the mean version. She's hard."

35

And probably ten years younger than I am, Clarissa thought.

The woman sipped from the glass of water that the usher poured for her, giving him a weak nod of thanks. Her skin was so drained of blood it was hardly darker than the white gauze of the top she was wearing. The top wasn't warm enough; she probably had goose bumps. Her hands were shaking as she held the Bible. Her voice was trembling as she took the oath.

The judge spoke. "You are not to infer anything about the defendants from the presence of the blue screen blocking Miss Lockyer from their view. That is a very usual sight in court, simply to make witnesses feel more comfortable. That is all it means."

Clarissa nodded agreement up at his high bench. She could see that the others had turned their heads to the left to do the same. She wasn't sure she believed him, though.

"This witness will need a break every forty-five minutes," the judge said.

The woman nodded gratefully at him and then it really began. Carlotta Lockyer seemed to be the only person in the room. And though Mr Morden was speaking too, and asking questions, he, and everyone else, seemed to disappear. There was only Miss Lockyer's voice.

I started dealing for Isaac Sparkle the summer before last, to fund my habit. Within a week I'd smoked it all myself and was money down. I thought if I ignored it, tried to avoid him, it would disappear.

On Saturday, July twenty-eighth, I was walking home. I'd gone out to shoplift, but hadn't managed to get anything. There was a white van on my street, partly on the pavement. When I was level with it one of Sparkle's couriers, Antony Tomlinson, got out the front. Sparkle got out the back with one of his dealers, Thomas Godfrey.

Sparkle said, "Get her in the fucking van." They picked me up and forced me in.

Sally was in the back seat. She's a working girl, another user. The van stopped after about five minutes. Godfrey said to Sally, "Get the fuck out." There weren't no door handles in back. Sally had to climb between the front seats, over Tomlinson, then out the front passenger door. I was screaming, begging them to let me out too, but they drove up to the motorway.

Godfrey told me to shut up. He smacked the side of my head. Then he took out one of those green disposable lighters. The flame was on high. He put it to my right earring. I could feel the hoop getting hot, really burning. I was crying. I was pleading with him to leave off.

We stopped on the way to pick up another man. He got in the van and said, "You got her. Good." The van driver, Doleman, said, "Someone should fuck her up the ass. Teach her a lesson."

They took me to a flat in a poor part of London. No electricity. So cold. The only light was from a street lamp outside the lounge window. The boy they'd picked up played music from his phone. They were yelling, "Strip off and dance." I begged them not to make me.

Godfrey punched me in the stomach. "Do it." I was crying but not proper crying — he'd knocked the wind from me.

I took my clothes off, and I danced. I can't describe how humiliated I felt. Like I was an animal performing for them. "She ain't doin' nothin' for me," Godfrey said.

"We're gonna teach you some discipline, like my father taught me," Sparkle said.

I had to stand on one leg with my arms out. I was still naked. They was cheering like they was at a football match. Look at her tits wobble. Look at her hairy cunt. I wanted to cover myself, to lean over, but if my arms drooped or I put my leg down I'd be whacked with a broom.

I wanted my clothes so bad. To stop them looking at me. And also 'cause I'd gone longer than usual without any heroin or crack cocaine, and withdrawing makes you get even colder.

They said I had to earn the clothes back by doing naked press-ups. For every ten press-ups I'd get one thing, but only ten seconds to put it on. They were counting together, shouting numbers. I had to start more press-ups as soon as they got to ten. I got my bra and my knickers, my top and my jeans. I didn't have time to put any of them on properly.

Tomlinson and Doleman went off clubbing. I was sat in a chair. Godfrey and the boy they'd picked up went to sleep on the couch, Sparkle on the other chair. The door was locked. I didn't dare move.

It was about three in the morning when Tomlinson and Doleman came back. Tomlinson grabbed me under the arms and Doleman took my legs and they carried me into the bedroom. They threw me onto the mattress and Tomlinson held my chest and arms down while Doleman pulled my jeans and knickers off. I kept saying no and begging them to stop. But they didn't stop. They raped me.

Doleman in my vagina and Tomlinson in my mouth. Then they switched places. Doleman said he'd use a knife on my face if I bit him; he made me swallow it when he came. All the time they were forcing me, holding me down.

When they were done I said I needed the toilet and Tomlinson said fine, go. Tomlinson had come in my face. I wiped it on my jeans and on my T-shirt — they hadn't taken the shirt off me. It burned when I peed. There weren't any hot water or soap or towel. I washed my vagina in cold water and dried it on my jeans.

My knickers got sticky and wet as soon as I put them on. It was too dark to see but I was scared it was blood and if they made me strip again and saw it they'd take the piss out of me. There was a freestanding cupboard, so I hid my knickers behind it. I put on my jeans and hoped there'd be no more blood for them to see.

Miss Lockyer covered her face with her hands. Her shoulders were shaking. Not a sound came out of her.

The judge sent them home for the rest of the day. "Please remove the defendants from the dock so this witness can leave," he said.

Clarissa's heart was beating very fast, as if she'd just watched an unbearably tense scene in a horror film. She knew her face must be red. Tears had been welling in her eyes but she'd resisted wiping them, not wanting anyone to notice.

She went straight to the cloakroom to blow her nose, grabbed her coat from the locker, and hurried down the stairs and out of the revolving doors, holding her face up to the blast of freezing air. She'd only walked a few feet before a car slowly drove out from beneath the court building. It paused, blocking the pavement as the driver waited until it was clear to turn left into the street.

Something made Clarissa peer inside. Slumped against the window in the rear passenger seat was Carlotta Lockyer, weeping. She met Clarissa's eyes with her own, seemed, briefly, to register a kind of puzzled recognition, and the car smoothly moved on.

Wednesday, 4 February, 8.00 p.m.

When I hug Rowena just inside the restaurant's entrance her breasts bounce against me without squishing at all. They are improbably high and seem to have grown two cup sizes.

Her first words to me are an answer to my unvoiced question. "Yes. I had a boob job." Her chest is shimmering, dusted with sparkling powder. "You wear your body every day. You've got to be happy in it."

Rowena runs her own one-woman company. She is a Discourse Analyst. She looks at every mission statement, advertisement, and logo a business produces. Then she tells them what messages they're really giving out. Maybe Rowena worked for a plastic surgeon and got seduced by the brochures she was supposed to critique.

"Just because we *are* thirty-eight doesn't mean we have to *look* thirty-eight." She is examining her face in her compact mirror, looking so worried it makes me think of the queen in "Snow White" with her terrible looking glass. Rowena's forehead is shiny smooth. It is out of synch with her jaw and cheeks.

I want Rowena to look less sad and strained, so I ask how she gets that dewy fresh glow; a little teasingly, but affectionately too.

"I have a strong will not to raise my eyebrows at all, and to limit my expressions. Movement gives you lines."

She's not intelligent, Henry said.

There are different kinds of intelligence, I said.

Henry haunts me too, but not as much as you. You're fast overtaking him.

Despite the freezing night and slippery pavements, Rowena is wearing a plunging sleeveless dress of deep purple velvet, and high heels. I think it's a little odd, because it's not like Rowena to make so much effort just for me. I tell her that her dress is beautiful.

"So many women get stuck in their look," she says, and I'm pretty sure she means me.

Is this the Rowena who used to sneak her favourite clothes to me whenever I wanted to wear something my mother hadn't sewn?

I glimpse my reflection in the window. My hair is piled on top of my head and held with silvery geometric clasps, though a few blonde wisps have escaped around my face and neck. The bodice and sleeves of my charcoal dress are tightly fitted, the skirt like the upside-down bowl of a wine glass, the hemline just above my knees.

Rowena looks down at her chest. "It's not just to attract men." The emotion behind the last sentence is too strong; her mouth trembles as she struggles not to frown. "It's for me. I owe it to myself. And these new boobs don't move at all. They're so pert and perky I don't even need a bra."

I think of the defendants jeering at Miss Lockyer. *Look at her tits wobble*.

Pert and perky are not Rowena words. When did they become so?

Rowena goes on, seeming to need to convince herself more than me. "The women at my gym are always asking, 'Who did your face? Who did your boobs?'" She speaks as if her body parts can be purchased by anyone, like a new gown or bag.

The defendants say tits. Rowena says boobs. I say breasts. I don't know what you say. I don't want to know. What I do know is that these differences matter.

"It's a huge compliment. You should try Botox, Clarissa. At the very least. If you don't do something soon you'll wake up one morning looking like a deflated balloon."

She's not even nice to you, Henry said.

She's comfortable being honest with me, I said.

You have nothing in common, he said.

I blink hard several times, as if this will clear my vision so that the Rowena I thought I knew will come back to me. This version of her would probably advise Henry to get a hair transplant. I can picture his response if she dared: the scornful, incredulous eyebrow he'd raise, wordlessly. I think

Henry is beautiful as he is, even if he's no longer mine to think this about.

"I'll give it some thought. Are you well, though? Recovered from the operations?"

"The only downside is that I can't feel my nipples any more." Rowena says this mockingly, like a dieter who has given up chocolate but never liked it much anyway. I work hard to disguise my sadness for her, and my horror that she has mutilated herself and her own pleasure in this way. "The scarring's rather shocking. But the surgeon's hopeful it will improve."

Is this the Rowena who used to float in the sea with her eyes closed, humming to herself and pretending to be a mermaid as she let the currents rock her?

I picture Rowena's areolas sewn on like buttons, a dark ring circling each one. For a few seconds my own nipples seem to burn and tingle. "I'm sure it will. I'd imagine it just takes time."

She studies my face. "You've got circles under your eyes. You should cover them up. You should consider an eyelid lift. It's very rejuvenating. You'd feel so much better about yourself. If the people you work with see you looking tired, they'll believe you *are* tired. They'll believe you're not effective at your job, that you're unprofessional."

Many women are disinclined to tell others about what is happening to them.

I bite my lip. "I'm not sleeping very well lately, Rowena. It's this man."

She misunderstands. "I want to hear all about him. But can it wait?"

Is this the Rowena who rushed from Edinburgh to London so I could sob in her arms when my boyfriend broke up with me in my second year at university?

"Of course," I say.

She only ever talks about herself. She's not interested in you, Henry said.

But I've withheld the most important things, I said, *to try to hold on to her. How can she be interested in me when I've kept the essential parts of my life hidden?*

Both of Rowena's husbands said they didn't want children, then left her to have them with other women. She'd never have forgiven my taking Henry from his wife. Sometimes I even wondered if it was my guilt about what I'd done that somehow stopped me from getting pregnant. The attempted baby-making would certainly have infuriated Rowena further. Henry knew this, and helped me with the cover-up, though he mumbled about how one-sided a friendship it was.

She checks herself severely in the compact mirror again, and I realise that her failed marriages are probably what made her so susceptible to this cult of plastic. "Did I do the right thing with my face?" She brushes powder above her eyebrows, which seem higher than I remember.

"You did absolutely the right thing. You look like an American soap opera star." This brings a near smile to her lips, which I have just noticed are plumper. "If it makes you happy, more confident, then that's what matters. That's what shows."

She nods in enthusiastic agreement. "It's a firmer, more youthful and sculpted look." Henry would pull a face at this, but I do not.

The waiter leads us to a table in the corner. Hanging on the restaurant's walls are pseudo Art Deco paintings of nude women, easily overlooked in the dimly lit room. I get sidetracked by one of them, of a dancer. It makes me think again of the men in the dock and how they forced Miss Lockyer to strip and perform for them. "What made you choose this place?"

"I didn't."

"Then who did?"

She ignores my question. "Do you think it looks natural?" There's a tremor in her voice that makes my heart hurt for her.

The flickering candlelight gives Rowena's frozen face an illusion of expressiveness, though I'm alarmed by how pronounced her cheeks have become, and scared that whatever the beauty technicians shot into them might harm her. "I do. Like you've been to a really great spa."

Is this the Rowena who used to play with my hair and tickle my arms when we had sleepovers, then swap places so I could do the same to her?

"I believe that each of us has a responsibility to look our best at every age."

Who are you, and what have you done with Rowena? I silently ask her.

I take her jewelled hand to get her attention. "I need to talk to you. It's something very bad."

She looks towards the restaurant's entrance and it's as if somebody's flipped a switch: her dazzling white, cameras-are-on-me smile appears in a flash. She makes no attempt to restrain it.

I follow her gaze and nearly choke on the sip of water I've just taken. The warbling French jazz seems to grow louder

45

and the room plunges from dim to almost dark. Have they done something to make the lighting even worse? Because I cannot process what I'm seeing.

What I'm seeing is you. Striding towards me like it is the most normal thing in the world.

There was no sign of you when I left my flat. No sign of you when the taxi dropped me off. No sign of you at all until now. How did you work out I was here? Only Rowena knew.

You are beaming. You look radiantly happy, so happy that I'm astonished by a small stab of sadness that I am the one who must wreck this crazy joy of yours. Something you make me do over and over. Don't you know how exhausting it is? Doesn't it make you tired, too?

You are moving your mouth, saying words I don't understand. You are standing beside Rowena. You are bending to kiss her on each cheek.

"D-d-don't touch her." I've never had a stutter, but for a few seconds I do. "G-go away."

Rowena pulls out the chair beside her in welcome. "Rafe's joining us."

How can she know your name? None of this is making sense. "He can't."

"I invited him." Rowena puts her hand on yours. You are first to break the contact but she seems not to notice. "Sit down, Rafe."

My flight response nearly hauls me out of my chair, but I don't want to leave Rowena alone with you and she doesn't look like she's going to follow me out anytime soon.

"If you're sure." You drape your coat over the back of the chair, declining the waitress's offer to hang it up for you. I'm certain there's something in the pockets that you don't want

46

to risk having discovered. I'm certain also that you want to keep your things near so you can grab them quickly to chase after me when I run away.

I look only at Rowena, as if she is a lifeline I must grab. "I don't understand."

"We wanted to surprise you." Rowena adjusts her carefully highlighted brown hair.

I force myself to use my brain and use it quickly. I puzzle out how you linked Rowena to me. It must have been that awards ceremony for business women eight years ago. Rowena was between husbands, then, so I went with her. When they called her name I clapped so hard my palms smarted; I smiled so much my jaw hurt. There'd been a photo of me and Rowena, with both of us named in the caption. It's the only thing that comes up on me in an Internet search.

"We thought you'd be excited that we know each other." Rowena sounds hurt, but my horror of you is even stronger than my usual inclination to comfort and reassure her.

"How?" My vision is blurring in this stupidly dark room. "How do you?"

"We met face to face for the first time at lunch today. But we've been emailing the last two months. It's amazing how close you can get to a person when you write to each other." She waves away the approaching waitress. "Rafe follows my business blog. He gets his students to read it to enhance their employability. But he noticed a reference to my creative ambitions in my profile so he got in touch. He's advising me on that memoir I've always wanted to write."

The blood is pulsing behind my eyes. "He cyber-stalked you."

"That's melodramatic. And paranoid." She apologises to you. "Clarissa didn't mean it."

"Yes I did." Everything is in shadows. I shake my head several times to try to clear it and then I make myself focus on you, the very thing I hate to do. "You don't know anything about writing a memoir. You're just a literary critic." I say the last two words like they're the worst insult I can think of.

"I have a number of talents and interests you haven't yet discovered, Clarissa."

There you go again. Punctuating every sentence with my name in your freakish way. Why doesn't Rowena see how weird it is? A sob comes out of my throat before I can stop it. "You don't need him, Rowena. You can join a writing group. He's using you to get at me."

"Not everything is about you. That's so unbelievably arrogant. Not to mention ridiculous. Rafe and I only just discovered a few weeks ago that we have you in common."

I squeeze my eyes shut, then open them again, not caring how peculiar I must look. "What a coincidence."

"Isn't it, Clarissa," you say.

"We both care about you," Rowena says.

"Very much," you say.

"Did he tell you about this morning? When he was waiting outside my house? When the taxi driver had to threaten him with the police? When he knew I didn't want him to be there?"

You are shaking your head in a pantomime of how wounded and misunderstood you are. Your performance is clear even through the murky vapour of this awful room. "Clarissa," you say. "Oh, Clarissa. How could you think this way?"

I can barely stop myself from dashing your face with iced water from the nearby jug.

Rowena touches your arm. "Rafe's concerned about you. That's why I came down."

The irony isn't lost on me that it's only because of you that she got in touch after two years of silence.

She is regarding me with disappointment. "He told me you haven't been yourself lately. That you've been acting strange at work. I asked him to keep an eye on you until I could get here. I never dreamed you'd be so unkind to him."

A vein throbs in my forehead as I fully grasp how much trouble you took to set this up, how much time you spent plotting and manipulating, how much advance planning you did, how much patience and discipline you exerted over yourself in waiting for tonight. Rowena was the ideal target for you. She is visibly injured, her vulnerability and desperation carved into her new breasts and face. You groomed her. You totally manoeuvred her. You actually charmed her.

If you have friends in common he may turn them against
you by dismissing your worries or claiming you behaved
unreasonably to him.

It's as if you've read the anti-stalker leaflets too, and you're using all of their advice against me. We have no friends in common so you went and made Rowena into one.

My throat is tight but my vision is clearing. "That's not how it was."

You're smirking now, enjoying yourself: two women fighting about you. You've put me in a position where I have to talk to you and look at you and pay attention to you.

49

Already you've forced me to break the resolution of silence that I made only this morning.

"You can't not believe me, Rowena." If my own friend trusts your story over mine, if she actually thinks you're plausible, then there's no hope that the police will ever take me seriously. There's no hope for Miss Lockyer either.

You are sucking on an olive, watching me. You take the stone out of your mouth slowly, sensuously. There's a sheen of oil on your lips. It makes me shudder and I tear my eyes away, wishing my vision hadn't snapped into this new hyper-acuteness.

Rowena pats my hand lightly. "Let's change the subject, Clarissa, and put the evening back on track. You've always encouraged me to be creative, and Rafe's got me started on writing about my childhood. I thought you'd be pleased. I told him the things we used to get up to when we were teenagers. I've been writing about when that girl beat you up on the sea-front. Remember how horrible that policewoman was to you, afterwards?"

There's a hot radiator on the wall behind me but I'm shivering in my wool dress. Goose bumps are springing up on my arms. The person I least want to be exposed to now knows every detail of the story I least want to tell. I open my mouth to speak but nothing comes out.

Rowena's too excited to notice. "It's all in the explicitness — that's what Rafe's getting out of me. Remember how I got you home and cleaned you up?"

"I do," I say quietly. "Nobody could have helped me like you did."

"It's a great story. Clarissa will be proud of you when she reads it."

I'd kick you under the table but I don't want to touch you even with my boot and I'm not about to let you prove to Rowena that I'm unbalanced. To my amazement, you stand up. For a second of reckless hope I actually think you're going to leave. But of course you're not. You're just going to the bar.

I'm on my feet, ready to walk out, but almost immediately I sit down again. I couldn't abandon my worst enemy to you, let alone my oldest friend, though right now Rowena is acting more like the first than the second. Whatever Rowena may be, I am my parents' daughter; they taught me too well the importance of loyalty to friends and family, even when — especially when — that loyalty is tested. The Rowena I loved must still be in there, though right now she's buried so deep I'm not sure I'll ever be able to find her again, or if I even want to try.

It's as if she gave you a tour of my underwear drawer. But I know I need to sound calm if I'm to have any chance of getting through to her. "I don't want you talking about me to him. Please don't."

"It's my story. You just happen to be in it. You have no right to dictate to me."

"You may want him here, but I don't. I've made that clear. Any normal man would respect my wishes. Don't you see that?"

She doesn't answer. For an instant I think she does see it. Rowena's ears always redden when she's upset and that's what they're doing now. Their heightened colour makes me notice the scars just in front of them, and I look away so she doesn't see me seeing.

"He tricked me into coming here. He knew I never would if you told me he was joining us. Don't you think it's odd that he asked you to keep it a secret?"

She hesitates, considering, but she wrestles with whatever doubts she may be starting to have about you and spits out the word "No".

I don't want to say what comes out of my mouth next, but I know I must. "He's not interested in you at all."

Rowena's lips curl into disbelieving rage. "Not every man on the planet's in love with you. You can't take them all." Perhaps she has guessed the truth about Henry. Maybe you actually told her. You probably just let it slip out casually while talking about something else. That's exactly the sort of thing you'd do.

"What he does isn't love. It's the opposite of love." I'm speaking gently, softly, as tenderly as I can. "It's as if he's trying to steal me. And now he's stealing you from me."

"I'm not yours to steal. You haven't been real with me in years. You're so full of secrets I hardly know you any more. Don't you realise how much that hurt me?" Her voice cracks at the last sentence.

I put my hand over hers, moved by this glimpse of the old Rowena's need for me. "I know. And I regret that. But right now I'm trying to stop you getting hurt. That's the only reason I'm sitting here when all I want is to run out that door. He knows that. That's why he set this up."

She rips her hand away. "How very generous and selfless of you." Her voice is cold, clipped. "You don't want him. So leave him to me."

"He's dangerous. He's making my life hell. That's what I wanted to talk to you about. It's a hard thing for me to trust anyone with. I'd call the police on him this minute but you wouldn't back me up if I did, would you?"

"You're being hysterical. He's an invited guest. I actually think you're sick. I've got to know him well."

"You've no idea what he's like. He's just using you to spy on me."

"You're the most egotistical woman I've ever known."

Already you're back and so is your smirk. "Peach Bellinis," you announce proudly. "Tonight's special. The bartender here is great. That's why I suggested this place."

Rowena lights up again. "I adore Bellinis." She truly does like you.

I try to see you as Rowena does. Henry thought you were a buffoon, but he admitted that students sometimes got crushes on you. Tonight you're wearing black jeans and a deep blue shirt, untucked. It's my favourite shade of blue. Midnight blue. I actually like what you're wearing. It occurs to me that Henry sometimes dressed like this, and you're deliberately copying him.

You set the Bellinis on the table, and a bottle of French beer for yourself. "Let's all have fun now." But you already are: the most fun you've had since November. "I hope you like Bellinis too, Clarissa." You look at me, then at the naked woman on the wall above the table.

She is sitting on a stool, her legs together at the knees to stop it being too graphic. She is wearing a suspender belt, stockings, high heels and nothing else. There's a riding crop across her lap. You gesture towards the painting and arrange your face in a grimace of fake embarrassment. "Sorry. I'd forgotten about the decor here." But you and I both know you're getting off on this public porn: on seeing me surrounded by these pictures. That's why you chose this place.

"I think it's beautiful. Tasteful." Rowena reaches for her glass.

I wonder again about the wine you fed me in November. "Don't drink that." I grab her hand but she snatches it away. I try again and she actually smacks my wrist — hard — and picks up the glass. After an absurd struggle I spill her peach Bellini all over the basket of dried-out baguette slices.

"You're being insane, Clarissa," she says. "I can't believe you did that."

"I think Clarissa isn't well." You manage to appear sorrowful. "She needs our understanding and support."

"She needs professional help," Rowena says.

I pick up the other peach Bellini. I don't want to leave it on the table now that I've made Rowena so determined to drink it. I grab my bag and coat from the back of my chair. Like you — because of you — I have a habit of keeping my things close, so I can make a quick getaway. I consider rushing out of the restaurant, but I know you'll only come after me and I'll end up alone on the dark street with you. There's only one place I can think of where I can call a taxi and hide until it's here. And I have a plan, formed crudely only in the last few seconds. It means facing you once more, on my own, but it's fairly safe and because of Rowena I can't see an alternative.

You start to rise and my hand flies up in warning, like a traffic policeman's. "Don't you dare follow me." I can count on you to ignore my wishes. You always do. I'm so loud the people at the tables around us stare. I choke out a goodbye to Rowena but she doesn't answer. I speed towards the metal stairs that spiral down to the basement, where the cloakroom is.

54

There's another piece of fake Art Deco porn down here, just outside the cloakroom. This one is of a man and woman together, to show that the cloakroom is unisex. In keeping with the rest of the art, they're both naked. He's standing, looking down at her. She's on her knees before him. The view of her is from behind; her head blocks the centre of his body.

The cloakrooms are so trendily dim I feel blind again. I head towards a stall, hurling the peach Bellini into the chrome sink as I move. The stall has the kind of door with no gaps at its top and bottom, so there's no chance of you crawling under or peering over. I phone for a taxi. The dispatcher tells me a driver will be along in ten minutes. I plan to stay behind this locked door for the first nine of them.

When I emerge you're in the room, just as I expected. You're barring the exit. The cloying smoke of the incense they're burning down here makes it hard to breathe, and you're blocking what light there is. My head is pounding, maybe from eye strain, or maybe because I'm being choked by a poisonous fog of synthetic jasmine. I remind myself that the taxi driver will come into the restaurant any second to ask for me. I calculated before I came down here that someone was bound to walk in, so I don't think you'll risk doing anything too uncontrolled. Still, I don't want to be trapped here long enough to find out; I've staged this collision with you as exactly as I could, leaving the smallest amount of time possible to say what I need to without Rowena hearing.

I get straight to it. "I'm not going anywhere near Rowena again. Hang around her all you want. I don't care. It's not going to help you get near me." I know you. I know Rowena won't be in any real danger from you. Rowena is throwing herself at you. You're not interested in women who actually want you. Only the ones who clearly don't.

"I care about what you care about, Clarissa. I want your friends to be my friends. I want to help Rowena. For you, Clarissa. I'm only interested in her because you are. Don't be jealous."

"I'm not —" Your last point is so outrageous I begin to deny it, but I manage somehow to bite back the end of the sentence. I start again, trying to sound indifferent and cold. "Rowena and I have grown apart. It's been too long. She doesn't interest me any more. I don't even like her any more."

As soon as the forced betrayals are out of my mouth I want to disavow them. But I can't, despite my spasm of grief for Rowena. It's impossible for me to try to help her as a friend should. Or her me. Not now that you've hijacked her. Saying these things is all I can do for her: I need to make sure she's of no use to you. But she won't thank me for it.

I take a small step towards the door. "Get out of my way."

You don't move.

"If you don't get out of my way I'll make you." It sounds ridiculous as I say it. We both know I can't make you do anything.

You smile, indulgently. "You're charming when you're angry, Clarissa."

My hand is curling around the frosted glass soap dispenser. It's heavy. It's as ludicrous as everything else in this supposedly atmospheric, irritatingly trendy unisex cloakroom.

"It pleases me that you're jealous, Clarissa. I want to pull those clips out of your hair and run my fingers through it and kiss you. I want to see what you're wearing beneath that dress."

56

I raise the soap dispenser as if it were a weapon.

You actually laugh out loud. "You'd never be able to hurt me, Clarissa. I know you."

My hand stops doing what hands are supposed to do. The soap dispenser slips from my fingers, shattering like a bomb on the monochrome-tiled floor just as the main cloakroom door slams into you, propelled by Rowena. You stumble and then skid on the mess of liquid and glass, only just catching yourself by grabbing the sink. The whole evening has been a surreal nightmare, but the unintended choreography caused by Rowena's entrance is straight out of a slapstick comedy.

"I have to go, Rowena."

She seems not to know what to do. For an instant, her face softens, and her eyes fill with tears that she manages to keep in. Then she says, "Nobody's stopping you."

I stagger up the twirly stairs and out of the restaurant and into the waiting taxi. My lips taste of salt because I'm crying; I realise I must have been biting them, because the tears are stinging. Rowena is lost to me. Lost to herself. I saw that in my first few minutes with her. Even before you walked in and did what you did.

Thursday

Thursday, 5 February, 8.02 a.m.

There is another envelope from you this morning, waiting for me on the mat inside the front door. You must have pushed it through the slot very early for it to have escaped Miss Norton's notice. I hurry along the path to the taxi, relieved that at least you aren't actually here.

As the taxi zooms down the winding hill I dial Rowena's hotel. She's going back to London today. Out of your reach, I hope. But also out of mine.

She answers with a slurred, "What?"

"It's me."

"He's not here, if that's why you're calling. He only stayed in the restaurant long enough to tell me he can't help me with my writing any more, or have anything to do with me. He says he won't come between two lifelong friends."

But you already have: Rowena slams the receiver down with a clang and the line goes dead.

At least I know she's safe. At least you've pulled back from her as I predicted. You've got what you wanted. You've got as much of me as she can give you.

58

I tear open your envelope. In it is a ticket to the ballet. Tonight's performance. And a letter.

You must be stressed, Clarissa. I know you don't mean to treat me unkindly. You can't have meant the cruel things you said. I only want to make you happy. I wanted last night to be special for you, reuniting you with your friend, but I can see I misjudged it. I promise never to see Rowena again. Please let me make it up to you by taking you out. On your own. Just the two of us. I'm all yours. No gooseberry. I know you'll love the Prokofiev Cinderella. We share so much, Clarissa. Meet me in the foyer at 7. Don't forget your ticket! We'll have a drink first. And a late dinner after.

Love, Rafe.

I hardly know where to begin to rip apart the madness of your letter. Do you not hear the things I say to you — no, no, and no — again and again? I think you must not take it in; you're in the grip of a crazed kind of shifting reasoning, even a terrifying sincerity.

Did you rifle through my CDs and DVDs when you were in my flat? Because you are right, guessing how I adore that ballet. But you can't imagine how I'd hate it with you. From a different man the gesture might have been sweet. It might have been romantic. But not from you. The man who exploited my oldest friend and turned her against me. From you this ticket is an assault, not a gift. Surely you must know, deep down, that you won't be sitting next to me in the theatre tonight?

But I can't shake my dread of what you will do when the curtain rises and I'm not there. I can't help picturing you standing on the tiled floor, watching yourself in the elaborate gilt mirror, waiting, angry and upset when I don't turn up, the man behind the ticket collection counter noticing you, guessing you've been stood up.

You were a baby once. What could have happened to you, to make you like this?

"Are you able to continue this morning, Miss Lockyer?" Mr Morden looked sad and concerned. His voice was soft and gentlemanly.

The defendants all gazed ahead, their faces blank, sitting very still in their shiny wooden box, on chairs that were covered in the same royal blue woven upholstery as the jurors' and barristers'. It was all very blue, but for the judge's deep brown leather.

"I'm okay. Thank you." She spoke as if the conversation were just between the two of them. Clarissa saw then that her voice could be pretty, in different circumstances.

"I know yesterday was very difficult for you."

Miss Lockyer's hair was in two low ponytails, like a little girl's. She tugged at one of them.

"Can you please tell the jury what happened next?"

Her voice was decided and unashamed. "I went back into the bedroom. I know it might seem strange that I got back into bed with the two men who'd just raped me, but I thought if I didn't they'd come and look for me and that would be worse. I huddled in the corner of the bed, in a kind of ball, hugging myself. You just can't imagine how cold that flat was. Their weight was on the duvet, so I could only pull a bit of it over me. I was

60

scared if I tugged at it too much they'd wake. I dozed, I was that tired, but I kept jerking out of sleep. Then it was morning and Sparkle came and stood in the doorway and signalled for me to follow him into the lounge."

Tuesday, 11 November, 9.00 a.m. (Three Months Ago)

It is the morning after your book launch party. I fight my way out of a nightmare, thrashing to get free of a very dark place. I am in my own bed, lying on my side, my back to you. You are pressing the front of your body into me, spooning me, and I can feel your erection. Your hand is over my breast, stuck to it like a suction cup. You are kissing the nape of my neck and whispering that you've been watching me dream. You are holding me so tight I have to struggle hard to wriggle out of your arms and snatch my dress from the floor to cover myself as I rush into the bathroom to be sick. When I'm finished, grabbing the sink to balance, I look down at my body. Spots of blood have dried on the insides of my thighs, where there are red marks that I don't want to think about. They will turn into bruises the next day. My lips and wrists and ankles are chafed. My hair is matted and tangled. My eyes hurt too much. I turn the lights off. I stand beneath the hot shower in the dark, shampooing my hair and soaping every inch of my skin. It stings, when I wash between my legs. I brush and floss my teeth. My jaw aches. The last thing I can recall is your taking my dress off. After that, there is only blackness. The bathroom door is locked behind me. I ignore your repeated knocks and concerned questions from outside. Late that afternoon I need an emergency appointment at the doctor's to get antibiotics for a bladder infection. I am ill for three days, after: I have a pounding headache that just won't go; I vomit and vomit until there is nothing left but bile; I sleep and sleep. No matter how much I sleep, I cannot wake up.

Miss Lockyer began to pant. Abruptly, dramatically, her skin paled. It was easy to see this in the clear light pouring through Court 12's domed glass ceiling and the row of windows on the wall behind Clarissa — the only windows in the room and far too high to look out of. It could have been a ballroom. Maybe it was, long ago.

"I need a break. I'm sorry. I need a break." Miss Lockyer covered her face.

They were sitting in the small, windowless waiting room just outside Court 12.

"She's not coming back," Annie said.

Clarissa said softly, "I'm sure she'll be back."

Annie rolled her deceptively gentle brown eyes and swung her shiny black hair and puffed her apple blossom cheeks. Beneath the artificial lights, her creamy skin was faintly yellow.

"You're probably right," Clarissa said quickly. "You watch all the time. I write too much. I take too many notes. I'm probably missing something by not looking."

Annie's face was cherubic and heart-shaped. Her angelic features seemed to relax a bit. She tapped her sweet little chin several times with her index finger.

62

"What did she think was going to happen, stealing those drugs from them?"

Clarissa pulled out a Japanese pattern book. There was a nightdress with a crossover bodice she loved the look of — she had some silk the colour of a bruise that she'd use. She'd make two, and send one of them to Rowena once she'd managed to get Rafe safely out of her life.

"My wife used to sew."

The owner of that voice must have noticed what she was looking at. Her face reddened as she hurriedly shut the book. In the chair opposite was the tall man who sat in front of her in the jury box. She liked his dark brown hair, so short it made her wonder if he was in the military; she'd spent a lot of time over the last two days with that hair in her view; she thought it would feel bristly.

"Does she not any more?" she said.

His jaw — strong and square and so unlike Henry's — stiffened almost imperceptibly. She had the impression that he was considering what to tell her, though his pause probably seemed longer than it actually was. "She died. Two years ago."

"Oh — I'm so sorry."

His name was Robert. She told him her own name as the door into Court 12 opened and the usher invited them back in. She stood and lined up with the others, but Robert's voice soon made her turn around.

"You left this on your chair." He was holding out the Japanese pattern book. The nightdress she'd been studying — very pretty, but a little revealing — was featured on the cover, hanging against a wooden wardrobe. The picture was covered by his large hand.

She bit her lip slightly and shook her head in ironic embarrassment, surprised at the same time to find herself noticing how symmetrical his lips were, and that they were perfect — not too big and not too small, not too red and not too bloodless, but just right. His eyes were the brightest sapphire blue she'd ever seen in human eyes. She thought she might be blinded if she looked too long at them.

Despite its remarkable features, his face was neutral, perhaps even expressionless. "I think you're right," he said. "I think she'll be back."

And she was, though her eyes were rimmed in red and she had to swallow hard several times as she spoke.

"They made me lie down on the floor. They threw a quilt over me. They started . . . kicking me, hitting me. I was in a ball, trying to shield my breasts, my head. I thought they were actually going to kill me, and they'd covered my face so they wouldn't have to see me while they did it. I started screaming that I'd call my grandfather, that he'd give me the money.

"Sparkle took the quilt away, handed me my phone. 'Dial,' he said. I told my grandfather I was desperate, that I needed fifteen hundred pounds, but he said no. I thought they'd start beating on me again then but Sparkle said I could pay him back by dealing for him. He gave me three hundred pounds' worth, so I could get started. Then he drove me to the train station and let me go."

Thursday, 5 February, 8.30 p.m.

At eight thirty the doorbell rings. And rings and rings and rings. I've known since this morning that you'd come after me for jilting you at the ballet. I don't answer, of course. But I do experiment: I take the intercom phone off its cradle but this fails to disable the buzzer; worse yet, your voice is now incessant. Without a word I put the intercom back in its place and refuse to pick it up again.

I go into my bedroom and grab the handset for my landline. I press the 9 once. I press it twice. Remembering my call to the emergency operator last Friday, I pause before pressing it a third time.

I am fifteen again, reporting the bag theft. The policewoman is firing her questions at me and I'm wishing that my parents were beside me instead of in the waiting area with Rowena and the shouting relatives of criminals. Had my bag really been stolen? Perhaps I'd simply lost it and feared telling my parents the truth? Surely they'd be upset by the expense and inconvenience such carelessness would cause: getting the locks changed, replacing my school books, giving me another week's worth of lunch money? I said that my parents would never mind about such things. I said I could never fear them. I said they cared only about my safety. The policewoman's incredulity seemed to deepen with every word I spoke. I managed to persuade her to let me drag Rowena in, but the policewoman regarded her as an unreliable witness, a loyal friend to me whose confirmation of my story couldn't be trusted.

They didn't find the girl who assaulted me. Of course they didn't. I doubt they even looked for her.

The police cannot act unless there is evidence that a crime has been committed.

I press the red button instead of the third 9 and toss the handset on my bed, knowing I can't go to the police yet. I still don't have enough evidence. And by the time they got here you'd be gone — then they wouldn't take me seriously. You're not stupid enough to let them catch you at my front door. Maybe they'd even charge me with wasting police time for making another inappropriate 999 call only six days after the last one. They'd think you're a phantom just like that girl who punched me on the seafront.

By nine o'clock the endless scream of the bell is more than I can stand. I pick up the intercom phone but I say nothing. Knowing it won't be long, I wait for your voice.

"Clarissa?" you say. "Clarissa? I waited for you, Clarissa. Is something wrong, Clarissa? How could you be so horrible to me, Clarissa? I thought you'd be sorry after how you treated me last night, but now this."

Until you, I loved my name. I don't want you to take that away from me too. I can't let you do that, though I cringe each time you repeat it.

The way you veer between solicitousness and anger, conciliating and scolding, makes me so fearful I hug myself and rock back and forth.

I go into the bathroom and shut the door, though it hardly does anything to block out the noise. I turn on the tap at full force and that helps, but doesn't completely drown you out. I shake lavender bath salts over the tub: Gary's Christmas present, which is the same every year, making us both laugh as he hands it over. I do not feel like laughing right now. I drop my clothes on the floor and as soon as the bath's full enough for the water to cover my ears I get in with a clumsy splash.

That does the trick entirely. I can't hear you at all now. But the bath salts do nothing to relax me and after only a few minutes I'm weak and faint from the heat, and the steam is making it impossible to breathe. Not being able to hear anything at all is frightening in a different way. I have a tiny kernel of hope that when I break the water's surface and re-emerge there will be silence, but you are still there, of course, making your noise. I get out too quickly and feel dizzy.

The nice word for you is methodical. Obsessive compulsive is the meaner phrase, and one you've truly earned. Nobody lives up to that one better than you. You press the buzzer for a shrill sixty seconds exactly, then allow me precisely two minutes of precious quiet before repeating the cycle. You probably keep a stopwatch in your bag of tools. It's a good thing Miss Norton is near deaf and goes to bed early, taking her hearing aids out before sleep. I am grateful that I'm not in a public place where you can ambush me like you did with Rowena.

I swaddle myself in towels and go into my bedroom. Again I shut the door and again it does almost nothing to muzzle the screech of the bell. I turn on the radio. They're playing a Chopin Prelude. I turn up the volume and you're seriously muffled but for the pauses between the piano's notes. It's only when I crawl under the bedclothes and pull them over my head that you entirely disappear.

Soon though, my ears are hurting in a different way. This music was not meant to be blasted. You have ruined the Chopin for me for ever. To have it at such a high decibel level, competing absurdly with your finger on the buzzer, makes it ugly and uncivilised — it was never meant to be used as a weapon. I'm suffocating again, unable to get enough air into my lungs with the comforter over my nose, and I must quickly abandon this homemade sensory deprivation unit too. Once more, there is the stab of you in my eardrums.

By ten I cannot endure another minute. I grab the intercom phone. You win again. It is impossible to stay silent.

"I will never let you in. I don't want to go out with you; I never asked for that ticket; I'd never have shown up at that restaurant last night if I'd known you'd be there."

You say, "I don't want to upset you, Clarissa." You say, "I'm just trying to make you happy, Clarissa." You say, "That's all I want. But you've hurt me, Clarissa." You say, "I know you're lonely, Clarissa. I'm lonely too." You say, "I'm just trying to help us both, Clarissa." You say, "I know your heart's been broken, Clarissa. Mine's been broken too. Again and again by you." You say, "I'm going now, Clarissa."

I jerk the handset onto its cradle in such distress it falls off and dangles and I have to put it back. The new noiselessness is so quiet it makes a low hum in my ears. But I can't get rid of my anxiety that you are still standing there.

Friday

It was difficult to focus on Azarola's barrister after barely sleeping the night before.

"Please confirm your description of the man you said they picked up en route to London." Mr Williams made Clarissa think of an actor in a legal drama who'd mastered his lines and moves. "You said 'About five foot nine, mixed race, slight build, with long plaits".'

Azarola leaned forward. He was well over six feet. His skin was golden, his eyes were hazel, and his hair was straight and short and thick and medium brown. His shoulders and chest were broad, like Robert's, beneath his fitted black sweater, which she thought looked expensive and fine, and was probably cashmere. He made her think of a Spanish pop star.

"Yes. That was my description," Miss Lockyer said.

There was no way that description matched. Could Clarissa herself make such a mistake, if she were in too much fear to look? Or had the police got the wrong man?

Tomlinson's barrister looked like a seasoned Shakespearean actor. "Mr Tomlinson had consensual sex with you. It

69

was not the violent encounter you portrayed. It was a cold-blooded commercial transaction for drugs. You are a professional, Miss Lockyer. You even gave Mr Tomlinson a condom."

Clarissa shuddered. She hadn't been able to remember enough of that November night to know if Rafe had worn a condom. Knowing him, he probably hadn't. She'd been inexpressibly relieved when her period had started a week later, as expected: a novel experience for her to wish not to be pregnant. What would Mr Belford make of her, if she were sitting in that witness chair?

Clarissa spoke quietly to Annie as they got their coats and slowly made their way out of the building. "That's what happens when you press charges, when you complain. They just rape you up there all over again and say you're a prostitute."

"But she was a prostitute, Clarissa," Annie said. "Nobody could possibly believe her when she says she wasn't."

Clarissa stuffed her tattered copy of Keats's *Collected Poems* into her bag. The book was a relic of her abandoned PhD, and something she always reached for when the world around her seemed especially dark and uncivilised. She glanced out the train window. Robert strode assuredly along the platform and disappeared down the stairs. She hadn't realised he'd been on the train; it hadn't occurred to her that he might live in Bath too. Somehow he'd climbed off and got himself almost out of the station before the other passengers had even begun to alight.

She surveyed the platform for Rafe, peering into the crowd that was pressing her towards the stairs. Her body was aching from sitting all day. She wanted fresh air. She wanted to move. She'd already had to give up her morning walks. She didn't want to lose the walk home, too. The fact that the taxi-queue was so impossibly long helped her to make up her mind, but she was glad there were so many people about.

Still, she was nervous when she stepped into the railway arch behind the station. She paused to look inside the tunnel: no Rafe. And on the bridge, before she stepped onto it to cross the river: again he wasn't there.

But there was someone, in the middle of the bridge, crumpled inside a heap of shabby blankets and encircled by empty beer cans, clutching a bottle of cheap spirits. There were several plastic bags around her, with her meagre belongings.

Normally, Clarissa would keep as much distance between them as she could. This time, she approached the woman, though she fought a stab of the same mixture of fear and pity that Miss Lockyer made her feel. She gripped her bag more tightly.

The woman's hair was so greasy and matted Clarissa couldn't tell what colour it was. Her flimsy shell jacket was torn and filthy on her skeleton frame. Her wrinkled skin was so rough and red and flaky it must have hurt; she appeared at first glance to be an old woman, but probably wasn't more than forty. Would this be Miss

Lockyer, some day? There was a stench of sour flesh — an unmistakable mix of unwashed genitals and anus and armpit sweat — that made Clarissa gag and try to breathe through her mouth, hoping the woman didn't notice.

"Money for the shelter?" The woman held out a hand that was almost blue with cold. Clarissa took off a mitten and drew out a twenty-pound note, knowing it would probably be used to purchase a wrap of crack cocaine and a wrap of heroin. "Bless you," the woman said.

Clarissa peeled off her other mitten and offered the pair, uncertain if her mother's knitting would be wanted. The woman hesitated, then took them and put them on, slowly and clumsily. "Bless you," she said again, not meeting Clarissa's eye, and Clarissa moved forward, pressing her now frozen fists deeply into the pockets of the warm coat she'd cut out when Henry had still been there.

Henry, smiling faintly then, a glass of wine and the paper in his hands as she kneeled on the living-room floor, bending over the indigo wool she'd quilted into diamonds, immersed in her plans for it. Henry, crackling with energy even when he was still. Henry, shaving the few hairs he had left in the shower each morning, so he was entirely bald — a style choice rather than unwanted fate, and yet more evidence of his infallible aesthetic judgement. Henry, in Cambridge now, a world away from this woman and from Clarissa.

Clarissa hurried on, wanting to get home as fast as she could. She reached the old churchyard within

72

minutes. Miss Lockyer must have passed it countless times, including the day they took her. Had she ever noticed the only tomb that hadn't been torn out? Green with mildew, the grey stone box marking the location of the bodies was the size of a large trunk. Many centuries ago the graveyard had been a wood. It was another of Clarissa's special places. She liked to think it was a source of magic for her, and that someday that magic would take effect, though it hadn't happened yet.

A woman had been buried there with her two babies in the middle of the nineteenth century. Three deaths in two years. Clarissa couldn't see the inscriptions in the dark and the engraved letters were losing their definition, but she knew them by heart.

Matilda Bourn, Died 21st August 1850, Aged 4 Months
Louisa Bourn, Died 16th September 1851, Aged 6 Weeks
Jane Bourn, Mother of the Above Children
Died 22nd December 1852, Aged 43 Years & 6 Months

Clarissa always imagined the two babies cradled in their mother's arms, beneath that damp earth, and the mother happy at last to be able to hold them to her. Had they been her only babies? Probably there'd been many others; that was more likely. Probably her health had been ruined by too many pregnancies too close together — that might have been what killed her. Clarissa could have researched it, but she didn't really want to know. She preferred the story she told herself, in which the woman waited and yearned, childless, for a long time. Then, miraculously, she had her babies after she turned forty, the age Clarissa would be in a year and a half. Only to lose them.

No husband was mentioned. No father. As if the only relationship that mattered was the one between the dead mother and her dead babies. But somebody had valued them enough to put up that stone.

Clarissa's surname was a variant of theirs, but she knew that that wasn't why she felt such a powerful connection to the dead mother and her dead babies. She had an almost superstitious ritual of praying for them — and to them — whenever she passed the grave. Sometimes she climbed over the iron gate at the far end to clear away crumpled cans or greasy fast-food wrappings.

Tonight, it was pitch-black there. The people who'd seemed to share her walk home from the train station had somehow melted away without her noticing; she'd loitered too long with the woman on the bridge. Regretting her decision to give up on the taxi-queue, she considered doubling back. But she quickly calculated that wouldn't help matters — she'd be as alone and isolated retracing her steps as she'd be pressing on.

She tried to reason with herself that Rafe knew nothing about her daily trips to Bristol; he had no reason to suspect she'd be walking home from the station in the evenings. Nonetheless, she couldn't help but imagine shadows moving along the walls, where they'd leaned all the old gravestones; those who'd wept over them were long dead; they'd probably never imagined that the carefully wrought markers would be ripped from their places.

She plunged ahead, only just holding herself back from running in case she slipped on the icy footpath. She was certain he would suddenly step into her line of sight, materialising out of the starless night.

She only began to breathe freely when she reached her street. She wouldn't walk any more on her own after daylight. Not anywhere. No matter how long she had to wait for a taxi. And when she did walk, she would only go to places that were dependably teeming with people.

Friday, 6 February, 6.15 p.m.

A small padded envelope waits for me on the shelf in the communal entrance hall. In it is a tiny box. You've wrapped it in gold embossed paper and decorated it carefully with curled silver ribbons. You've enclosed a heavy, cream-coloured card, imprinted with a rose. *I notice what you love. Wear this for me.*

My hands tremble as I climb the stairs to my flat, tearing open the box as I move, tripping on the landing at the sight of the ring I was caught by that night back in November, as if under a spell. You would never have bought it if you'd known I was thinking of Henry while I looked at it. I wasn't thinking of you. Not you. Never you. My visions of you are only dark.

Madly, I think that the tips of my fingers will bleed as they brush over the small circle of cold platinum and the tiny diamonds that encrust it. The ring has flown to me like an evil boomerang.

As soon as I'm in my flat, I shove it all back into the padded envelope, including the card, slapping on parcel tape and fresh stamps, scribbling your name and the university address on it, crossing out my own. Above all else, I can't let you think I've accepted something so costly from you. I'll post it back to you first thing tomorrow morning.

But as soon as I begin to stuff the parcel into my bag in readiness, one of the leaflet's commands freezes my hand.

Retain all letters, packages and items, even if they are alarming or distressing.

I have to hold onto the ring, however much money you spent on it. The ring is a gift, after all. Just not in the way you intended. I will add it to my growing collection of evidence. A grim assortment, but not yet irrefutable as proof.

Week 2

The
Fire Dance

Monday

Clarissa was watching Robert. He was leafing through the jury file. He stopped at a photo of the van's interior, studied it, and scribbled a note for the usher to take to the judge.

Mr Belford was peering dubiously at Miss Lockyer. "A story," he was saying, "of systematic beatings and torture, and violent acts of rape and forcible restraint. But hardly a mark on the victim."

The judge interrupted with his usual formal courtesy, asking them to look at Robert's photo. Behind the driver's seat, nestled on top of a greasy and crumpled fast-food wrapping, was a green disposable lighter.

Mr Morden was beaming at Robert. Nobody had noticed that lighter before. It exactly fit with Miss Lockyer's account of Godfrey burning her earring in the van.

It was another of the many breaks occasioned by Mr Morden and Mr Belford's whispered arguments. Clarissa sat in her usual chair. Robert had taken to sitting opposite her, in the corner of the unnaturally bright, glaringly white little annex.

"Poor girl," Robert said, not in the least afraid to state his sympathy directly.

Clarissa wondered how many men would speak up like that, in front of the others. "Yes," she said, nodding a little, her expression slightly sad. "Poor thing." And then, "I can't believe you found that lighter. Are you a detective in your day job?"

"I'm a fireman." He shrugged it off, modestly. "Most people don't look around for potential causes of fires. It's what I've been doing since I was twenty. Half my life."

The usher was back already, calling them to return.

Clarissa picked up her bag and cardigan. She'd never met a fireman before. She'd surrounded herself with academics, though she'd decided not to be one herself. But it wasn't lost on her that she'd run straight into the arms of one, in Henry, even if he was mostly a poet. She thought what Robert did was interesting and important.

"It's just a job," he said, as if he'd read her mind and was putting her straight. He spoke matter-of-factly, but in his friendly, even way. "We all do our part."

"You are yourself capable of violence, aren't you, Miss Lockyer?"

Miss Lockyer shook her head at Mr Belford's question as if it wasn't worthy of an answer, Mr Morden jumped to his feet to object in absolute fury, and the jury found themselves walking out once more.

Again Clarissa was seated opposite Annie and Robert in the little annex.

She was remembering Wednesday night. The soap dispenser slipping from her fingers and shattering against the cloakroom tiles instead of Rafe's skull.

You'd never be able to hurt me, Clarissa. I know you.

"I'm not sure I'd be able to damage another person," she said, "but I'm beginning to wish I could."

"You don't look like you could damage a moth," Annie said.

Robert was looking hard at Clarissa. "Hurting someone isn't about physical strength. You've never been in a situation where you've had to. Anyone could do violence, Clarissa. I promise you could too, if you needed to."

"Have you, Robert?" Annie asked.

His face was expressionless. He didn't answer.

"I didn't really need to ask," Annie said. "Of course you have."

Mr Belford gave the impression that he hadn't taken his eyes off Miss Lockyer during the jury's absence; a kestrel hovering above a field mouse, waiting for his chance.

"Is it correct that your ex-partner has a new girlfriend?"

Clarissa looked in concern at Annie, whose husband had just left her for another woman. She thought of Rowena, too. And of Henry's wife.

Miss Lockyer gazed at her hands.

Clarissa wondered what she would feel when Henry found someone else. She knew she'd feel a stab if he went through successful fertility treatment with a new girlfriend, and she should be bigger than that. Not that he'd be quick to put himself through such a thing again. Henry wanted people to think testosterone oozed from his every pore. He'd made her vow never to tell anyone that his small population of misshapen sperm all possessed five heads and ten tails and swam in demented circles, bumping into each other.

Mr Belford prompted the still silent Miss Lockyer. "Did you threaten to kill her?"

"Of course not."

He shook his head, making it clear that her responses were so absurd it was not worth speaking further to her.

She'd been so focused on Miss Lockyer and Mr Belford and her note-taking she hadn't looked at the public gallery. A movement in the back row caught her attention.

A pale man leaned forward from where he'd been resting his pale head against the pale wall, looking only at Clarissa, forcing her to see him looking.

As Robert paused to let her exit the jury box before him, she stumbled, her cheeks growing warm, her breath speeding up, her heart pumping so fast she thought it must be visible, pounding beneath her dress.

Monday, 9 February, 5.55 p.m.

I sit in the jurors' room pretending to be so lost in my book I don't notice that everyone has gone. The jury officer is looking at me, loudly packing up her things. Finally, she tells me that the room needs to be vacated for the night and I see I cannot put you off any more.

Just as I expect, you are waiting for me right outside the court building. I march past you to the end of the road and turn left, acting as if you aren't here.

"Clarissa." You've caught up to me. "It's ridiculous of you not to speak to me, Clarissa."

I halt in front of the coffee stall, closed for the day now like everything else. I have never seen it so quiet, but there are a few people around. It still gives me the safety of public space.

"Darling, please talk to me."

I can't help myself. The leaflets' commands of silence are impossible. "I'm not your darling." You step closer. "Don't come near me." My voice is shrill. I try to lower it. "Don't you *ever* come here again. You had no right."

"It's a public gallery."

Unless I stop you from ever coming again, I won't be able to enter that jury box and continue with the trial. Court 12 will become a trap, a place where I'm pinned down and on display for you. I realise how powerfully I care about the trial, how much it matters, that I'm actually immensely proud to be serving on a jury — it's something I'd always hoped to do. Corny thoughts about public duty and citizenship are banging around in my head even in your presence.

"If you come again I'll tell them I know you. They may call off the whole trial. They don't want jurors disturbed by people they know. I need to concentrate."

"The testimony upset you, Clarissa — I saw that it did."

You are right. I hate your being right about me. I hate that I wasn't even aware of you, watching. I hate that I don't quite know what I would have done if I'd noticed you there while

Court 12 was still in the throes of its ugly business instead of its last seconds.

"There's no law against the friends of jurors sitting in the public gallery."

"You aren't my friend."

"You're right." You correct yourself. "Lover."

"You're not —" I bite my lip. You look so sad anyone else would pity you.

"I thought you'd be happy to see me."

"I'm not." It isn't so difficult to be mean. I'm almost shaking with anger. My mother never could have imagined a man like you.

"I'm not seeing Rowena any more."

"I don't care who you see or don't see."

"You're cruel, Clarissa. I was worried. You were ill."

"I lied to you. I wasn't ill. I didn't want you to follow me that morning. I didn't want you to find me. I didn't want you to know I was here. I have a right for you not to know where I am. I don't like being followed." This is better: firm and honest.

"That was an evil thing to do. I thought better of you."

"I don't care what you think of me. I don't want you to think of me at all."

"Your mobile still isn't on."

"I changed the number. You're the reason I changed it. I want nothing to do with you. I've told you this a million times."

"I went into every courtroom in the building until I found you."

I move my head slowly from side to side. "Don't you see that that's not normal?"

"No. No, I don't. It shows how much you mean to me."

You hold your arms out, as if expecting for me to fall into them, and I step back. How can you imagine that I'd want that? "Did you like the ring, Clarissa?"

"No."

"You've kept it, though. So you must like it."

"Don't send me any more things. I want you to stay away from me." As I start to walk away you grab my arm. I jerk it free. "Don't touch me. You make me sick. The things you do make me sick."

"You can't just sleep with me and then change your mind. You can't make me feel what you have and then ignore me."

A phrase from one of the leaflets stabs at me.

One third of all stalkers have been intimate with their victim.

"It was only one night. It meant nothing to me. It was the biggest mistake I've ever made and I wouldn't have made it if I hadn't been drunk. Or worse. Was there something worse?" For once you don't have anything to say. "Why can't I remember any of it?" And still nothing. "Why were there marks on me?" For once I have more to say than you do. "Why was I so sick, afterwards?"

At last you speak, though I wish for your silence again as soon as the words are out of your mouth. "You were crazy with passion for me, Clarissa. You were out of control, the way you responded, the things you begged me to do to you."

"I was unconscious." I clutch my bag, trying to stop my hands from trembling. The coffee I drank during lunch is halfway up my throat. I swallow it back down. "Did you put something in my wine?"

"Now you're sounding mad. You wanted me, Clarissa. You wanted me as much as I wanted you. Why are you trying to deny it? You were lying back and enjoying it."

"I didn't want you. Not then and certainly not now."

Your mouth twists. Your hands are in fists, releasing, clenching, releasing again. "Bitch." Your face is scrunched in hatred, but you struggle to smooth it away. "I didn't mean that, Clarissa. I'm sorry. You've upset me too much. Say you forgive me. I didn't know what I was saying."

The leaflets stab at me again.

Eight women die every month in England as a result of domestic abuse.

I wish those leaflets didn't keep ambushing me. I don't want to think about them. I don't want to imagine they can be right. The leaflets are like friends whispering uncomfortable truths that I don't want to hear. I want to think that those numbers are just made up. *Eight women die every month.*

"I'm going now. If you follow me I'll walk straight back into the court building and tell the security guards. They haven't left yet."

"Say you forgive me and I'll go."

"I'll never forgive you. If I ever see you in that courtroom again I'll report you to the judge."

"I didn't mean it, Clarissa, calling you that."

"And I'll tell them at work too that you did it, that you followed me here, that you upset me so much I couldn't go through with something so important." I am merciless. I am no longer quaking and the nausea has gone. I know what I need to say to keep you out of Court 12. "I'll make a formal complaint to Personnel. They take seriously their responsibilities to employees who are on jury service." This is perfectly true. "I can see that you don't want work to know what you're doing." And this is true too. Your eyes light up, confirming I'm right — you never send me emails on the university system.

"You *are* a bitch. You're not the woman I thought you were."

"You're right. I'm not. You don't know me at all. Just leave me alone. That's all I want from you."

I walk away, and this time you don't follow.

They say you shouldn't equivocate. They say you should be direct and firm. They say you should never try to soften the blow. They say that "No!" is a one-word sentence. They say to use it with force. They say you should never elaborate on No.

Tuesday

Clarissa was waiting for the train to start its journey from Bath when Robert stepped on, only just making it before the doors locked; but he didn't look as if he'd rushed. She was in the aisle seat, and watched him walk towards her, thinking how rare it was for someone to move so sure-footedly in a lurching carriage.

The seat across the aisle from her was empty. He took it and smiled good morning over the narrow passage. "Fancy seeing you here," he said. "Going anywhere interesting?"

She affected a mysterious appearance. "Maybe."

"On your way to work, perhaps?"

"I thought I'd skip work today. Just a whim. In fact, I've decided to skip it for the next six weeks."

"So have I," he said.

"What a coincidence," she said.

"But seriously." He stretched his long legs into the aisle, relaxed but alert; she knew he'd move them out of the way if anyone needed to pass, before they needed to ask. "You know I'm a fireman. Am I right in thinking you're an academic? I heard you telling Annie you worked at the university."

She shook her head, as if shocked and horrified by the idea. "I nearly was, but no. I'm an administrator." She paused. "My father — he wanted me to be an academic. He was a school teacher. He taught English before he retired." She laughed at herself. "It's too early in the morning for true confessions."

"Never too early for that. But I'm interested in why you changed your chosen path so dramatically." He appeared to be mulling it over. "Every time I see you you're reading. Or writing."

She nodded. "Academics never escape work. Nights . . . weekends . . . There are always essays to mark, or articles to write, or research papers to read, or forms to fill in, or students to email. Not to mention the teaching and meetings. It's unremitting. Some people love that life, but the idea of it made me feel trapped. I wanted to leave work behind at the end of the day when I went home. And I wanted my imaginative life to be my own — I didn't want to have to account for it to other people." She bit her lip, surprised to find herself telling him this. "So I abandoned my PhD."

"What was it about?"

"How Pre-Raphaelite painters responded to Romantic poetry. Henry — my ex-partner — thought the Pre-Raphaelites were absurd. He was probably right, but I can't help but love them."

"Did you and Henry like any of the same poets?"

"Yes," she said quietly. "Henry made me fall in love with Yeats." She didn't say that Henry used to whisper whole verses of Yeats to her in bed.

"You don't strike me as someone who gives up on things."

She didn't want to bore him with the story of her father's heart bypass in her second year of the PhD, and how the research seemed meaningless after she helped her mother to nurse him. But she knew her father's close brush with death only hastened an inevitable admission that she wasn't cut out for a life of abstraction and sterility, of thinking endlessly about other people's ideas and words in an alien language; academic conferences and journals just made her head hurt. She'd rather look at the paintings and read the poems than theorise about them. And she needed to use her hands; to make things herself.

"Those Pre-Raphaelites did paint some beautiful dresses," she said, "and fabrics. I like to sew, you see. So I was spending all my time recreating those dresses instead of writing my PhD thesis."

"I can see the temptation," he said, making her laugh. "You should have done a PhD in textiles instead. Is there such a thing?"

"Probably. I think you can get one in pretty much anything these days."

"The history of the fire engine?"

"Almost certainly," she said. "But that's not good as a facetious example — that's actually something important."

The train had arrived in Bristol. His dark blue backpack was on the floor in front of him. It appeared huge and heavy, but he lifted it with one hand as if it

90

contained nothing more than feathers, and the two of them made their way out.

Just past the ticket gates was a man dressed as a chicken. Thinking of the addict on the bridge, Clarissa dropped a worn and slightly torn five-pound note into his cup. It was all the cash she had. But Robert added five more.

Mr Tourville was red faced and portly. His wig was crooked and seemed about to slide off as he wiped his brow. Doleman's pale eyes were glued to the back of his would-be saviour, who was passing round a newspaper cutting.

Carlotta Lockyer was sitting on dandelion-covered grass that matched her eyes. She was wearing faded bell-bottom jeans, trainers and a floaty purple blouse. Her blonde hair was loose, skimming her shoulders, pushed behind her ears. Her pretty chin was tucked towards her chest as she looked up at the camera. Squinting in the soft spring sunshine and frowning slightly, she was sad and brave at once, as if newly serious after a sobering close call; not the image Clarissa would have thought Mr Tourville wanted to publicise.

She took in the headline — *Young Woman's Escape from Evil Sex Murderer.*

She scanned for the date — nearly three years ago, in late April.

She read the caption beneath the photo — *Carlotta Lockyer, above, was nearly Randolph Mowbray's victim.*

Then she began the article itself.

91

Party girl Carlotta Lockyer only narrowly avoided the fate of Rachel Hervey, 19, who was murdered last August by deranged sex beast Randolph Mowbray, 26. Pretty Carlotta, 25, met the sadistic rapist and killer at a London nightclub. She admits that she found the calculating, vain and devious Mowbray charming. "It embarrasses and terrifies me when I think how easily I agreed to visit him, but I got ill at the last minute and couldn't go. I learned afterwards that that was the weekend he killed that girl. It could have been me."

Mowbray, who was writing a PhD thesis about serial killers in literature, had been obsessed with Rachel for several months before he raped, tortured and strangled her. He then hid her body under the floorboards of his house, where it lay undiscovered for ten days. The English undergraduate's disappearance sparked a national search and a televised reconstruction of her last known movements. During the five-week trial, the family's harrowing ordeal was made worse by Mowbray's wholly false allegation that Rachel had sought him out for a consensual kinky sex game that he claimed had then gone wrong and led to her accidental death.

Detective Superintendent Ian Mathieson described the case as "one of the most horrific and tragic things I've ever had to deal with in a 35-year career. The life of a talented and beautiful young woman was viciously stolen by Mowbray's particularly brutal and distressing crime. Rachel's last moments were of darkness and terror and pain."

"Miss Lockyer's a trouble magnet," Annie whispered.

Clarissa nodded, though she hardly heard Annie. She remembered reading about the case at the time. There'd been something in Mowbray's trial about how Rachel had complained to the police about him a few weeks before she went missing, but she didn't have enough evidence for them to do anything.

Darkness and terror and pain.

She wanted to cry. She was picturing Rachel's bruised and bloodied body beneath floorboards, her parents frantic, praying against hope for her safe return.

Mr Tourville glared at Miss Lockyer. "You sold your story and your picture to a national newspaper."

"They didn't pay me a penny. I came *that close*" — she pinched her thumb and index finger together to demonstrate — "to that boy murdering me."

"You exploited the tragic rape and murder of Rachel Hervey in order to feed your love of attention."

"I never wanted that sort of attention. I hated the way they wrote about me. It wasn't fair. They twisted everything."

"You say you'd been raped. The other men were in the next room while this was supposedly happening. Why didn't you scream for help? Fight back?"

"They were holding me down. Doleman threatened me with a knife. And the other men were hardly likely to come to my rescue, were they?"

93

"Please. You know there was no knife. You asked for it. You were lying back and enjoying it." His delivery was so crude and venomous Clarissa couldn't quite believe what she'd heard.

"No." It was sob more than language.

Mr Tourville returned Miss Lockyer's outraged stare without flinching, puffing up his chest and setting his weight more squarely on his feet, as if he had just said something very brave when nobody else had dared.

She could hear Rafe's voice, playing over and over again in her head, as she sat in the waiting room. *You were crazy with passion for me, Clarissa. You were out of control, the way you responded, the things you begged me to do to you. You wanted me. You were lying back and enjoying it.*

"Clarissa?" She felt a light touch on her shoulder and looked up at Annie. "Time to go home." The others were rising to follow the usher downstairs. It was only two thirty, but they were being let out early so the judge could conduct court business.

Robert peered at her. "You don't look well. Are you well?"

"Fine." She tried to smile. "Just sleepy."

"Take a long walk this afternoon," he said. "Get some fresh air. We don't get many chances for that these days."

"Yes," she said. "I think I will."

Tuesday, 10 February, 4.30 p.m.

I dump my things in my flat as soon as I'm back. Quickly, I pull on two pairs of wool socks and my wellies. I walk straight out the door again, still bundled in my coat and hat and mittens.

I can't help but check up and down my street. There is no sign of you anywhere, which is just as it should be. I happen to know you're trapped in London at a postgraduate English conference — it's one of the perks of my job that Gary had me book you into it.

I need to be in a place I can think, one of the places I love best. I need to pretend that killers only torture women and hide their bodies beneath floorboards in the newspapers. Not in real life. I need to pretend that it is normal to go for a walk in the late afternoon, even if the sky is already starting to darken. If I pretend all of this hard enough it might become true.

I walk as briskly as I dare on the icy pavements until I reach the park.

The park is round. I think of it as a giant watch face. The black iron gates marking the main entrance are in the six o'clock position. I go through them and move clockwise, in the direction of nine o'clock, keeping to the road that rims the park's circumference. I always imagine the clock's twelve numbers spaced along this road, and measure my location against them at any given point. The road encircles the huge island of grass at the park's centre. The grass is covered thickly in snow, too difficult to trudge through.

I have reached eight o'clock. To my left is the path along the cliff. Below it is a steeply sloping forest and my favourite view of Bath. The Abbey will soon be bathed in blue light.

They have gritted the road, so I can move quickly, enjoying my blood pumping and the quiet wind in my face. It is peaceful here, unearthly in the twilight. A child would think the mound of snow-coated grass was an enchanted realm. All I can hear is the crunch crunch crunch of my boots on dry sticks. The park seems to be my private garden; the cold is keeping everyone else indoors.

I am at twelve o'clock, halfway around, as far away from the park entrance as I can be. In the empty children's playground, a swing creaks gently, as if pushed by a ghost.

That is when you appear.

"Hello, Clarissa."

I am completely frozen.

"I wasn't feeling well. I had to give the conference a miss."

For several seconds I forget to breathe.

"I said I wasn't feeling well, Clarissa. Don't you care? Aren't you concerned?"

I put my hands on my ears and press hard to make myself think.

"You disappoint me." You shake your head sadly. "I stopped by your house. But I saw you walking towards the park."

You must be so skilled at following, close enough to keep me in sight without my guessing you are there. I had no idea. I didn't see. I didn't hear.

"I thought I'd lost you for a minute. You disappeared, but I found you."

You always find me. Always. When do you ever not find me? And this time it's my fault. All mine. All because I gave into that stupid impulse not to let my fear of you imprison me.

Reclaim the night. That idea was so important to me and Rowena when we were at university. We went on marches, thinking of the women who did that in the 1970s. We were wrong. They were wrong. It's not even night yet, but it soon will be and I shouldn't have come here. I shouldn't have tried to disregard that fear of dark places. I must never let myself disregard that fear again.

I consider leaving the road to cut in a straight line across the disc of grass, the most direct way out, but it's a ridiculous idea. The snow drifts are too high — it will take for ever — and there are too many trees and bushes, casting their shadows. I will not let myself be lured from the path like Little Red Riding Hood. I understand all too well the lessons those stories teach.

"My car's parked over there." Out of the corner of my eye I see you gesture towards three o'clock. "I can give you a lift."

The proposal is so absurd I ought to laugh, except that I'm growing way too dizzy to find it funny.

"I'm trying to be nice after yesterday, Clarissa. After all the days. After all of your insults and slights. But you don't make it easy."

Just leave me alone. That's all I want from you.

Did you not hear me say that?

"I need you to tell me that you forgive me for what I said yesterday, Clarissa. You know I didn't mean it, calling you that. I was angry. And you were very provoking."

I will never forgive you.

What about that? Clearly that didn't go in either. Which is why the leaflets are right, and speaking to you — even a tiny bit — is absolutely the wrong thing to do.

97

I'm looking ahead and moving counter-clockwise as fast as I can. I'm wondering if I am going to get out of this at all, but I can't afford to think like that; I try to tell myself I'm overreacting. I'm only at eleven thirty, still five minutes' walk from the black iron gates at six o'clock, but I retrace my steps along the loop the way I came. I'm not letting you get me anywhere near your car.

"You had your period last week, didn't you?"

I can't stop myself glancing up at you, briefly. You're smiling like a smug detective with a valuable secret source. I don't say, *How can you know that?* But I'm thinking it.

"I know you, Clarissa. I know you better than anyone knows you. That's why you were in such a bad mood, isn't it? That's why you lied to me that you were sick. That's why you ruined our evening at the restaurant. That's why you stood me up at the theatre. It was your hormones. I'm trying to forgive you for how you've been treating me. I'm trying to understand."

Despite the salt on the road, I nearly lose my footing and when you move towards me I lurch out of your reach.

"I only wanted to help. You could have fallen and hurt yourself."

And whose fault would that have been?

"You don't need those leaflets from the stalker organisations, Clarissa. You know that's not what this is."

How can you possibly know about the leaflets? But again I manage to keep the words in. I see too how hopeless it would be to argue with you. You've actually said the name of the thing you are and you don't even recognise yourself.

Three-quarters of female victims know their stalker. The leaflets say that too. I wish I didn't know you.

I continue to move along the road. I haven't got far. Only back to eleven o'clock. I scan hopelessly for CCTV cameras but there doesn't seem to be a single one.

"You wanted me to find you here, didn't you? You wanted me to follow you."

I consider screaming, but there's nobody around to hear and I'm not sure my voice will work.

"I like your new perfume, Clarissa."

Surely it's faded to nothing since I sprayed it this morning. I only used a little. Behind my ears. The nape of my neck. Just as my mother taught me. *Never overdo it*, she always says.

"Gardenia. You're wearing it now, aren't you?"

Since when are you so expert that you can identify perfumes?

"Come to my car and talk to me where it's warm."

Walk fast Walk fast Walk fast.

"I'll put the heating on."

Faster Faster Faster. Don't slip Don't slip Don't slip.

"We're going the wrong way."

And with that you grab my hand. I feel it before I see it, since I'm refusing to look at you as I continue towards the black iron gates.

"I tried to make you see sense, Clarissa, but you won't."

I try to snatch my hand away but you grasp it more tightly and that's when I notice that you are wearing fitted leather gloves.

"We do it my way, now."

Somehow I register that I've never seen you in gloves before, and my stomach does a full tumble. I look around wildly but the park is still deserted. I tell you to let go of me,

99

you have no right, to let go of me at once, but nothing I say or do makes you release me.

"Please walk with me, Clarissa. We can talk. We need to talk."

You've managed to pull me a few feet. The way I don't want to go.

"How are your parents?"

You speak as if you'd met them, as if we were taking a happy stroll and chatting like close friends, as if you weren't dragging me by force, as if you think you can make this normal by talking about normal things. If it weren't so awful it would be comical.

"I didn't realise they had a sea view."

That's when it hits me. That's when I see how you have learned these things.

You must have crept up to my house early on Friday morning and stolen the black bag full of my rubbish, including my used sanitary towels.

Freaky creep.

You must have taken the contents of my recycling box too — the return envelope with the stalker organisation's logo, the brown parcel paper with my parents' return address and Brighton postcode, the receipt for the perfume.

The most ordinary things that people do all the time. Meeting a friend for dinner is no longer possible for me. Putting the rubbish out is something I can no longer take for granted. Do you want me to know it? Or are you so out of control you don't see that you are showing your hand, alerting me to your covert intelligence tactics?

You've got me back to twelve o'clock.

"I just want to take you home, Clarissa," you say.

"With me," you say.

"Back to my place," you say.

"Just to spend time with you," you say.

"That's the only thing I want," you say, "the only thing I ever want."

"I'll cook you dinner," you say.

"I know you're not sleeping lately. You'll sleep beautifully if you're with me all night," you say, and I realise you must have found the discarded container for the sleeping pills in my rubbish too.

"The sun's nearly gone. You're not safe on your own in the park after dark," you say, and I can't help but be amazed that there isn't even a hint of irony in your voice.

You're towing me faster, clutching my hand and wrist in both of your hands, and you've got me to one o'clock.

Why didn't you scream for help? Fight back?

My heart is thump thump thumping so furiously I don't know how it manages to keep going, and my nose is running, and my scalp is tingling as if tiny electric shocks are falling on it from the sky. But I can't let you get me into your car. At any cost I must stop that happening.

I make another violent effort to break free.

"You asked for it." You yank my arm so hard I cry out.

You asked for it.

You smash me against you, knocking the wind out of me. You pin my arms behind my back with one of yours, hooking one of your legs behind me too, to stop me struggling or moving. From afar, we must look like lovers.

"I like having you in my arms this way, Clarissa."

I am entirely alone here. The leaflets are more useless than ever.

"This is all your fault, Clarissa."

Your breath is in my face. It doesn't smell like toothpaste this time. It's the sour bacteria breath a person gets before a sore throat comes on and I start to gag. I try to turn my head but you squeeze your other hand around the back of my neck so I can't.

"You left me no choice, Clarissa."

My hat has fallen off. Your lips are against my ear. You're biting the lobe.

I consider letting myself go limp, thinking that then maybe you won't be able to hold me up. Dragging a limp weight isn't easy. Robert told me that this morning during one of the breaks. But I realise that even if Robert's right, I don't want to be on the ground. I don't want to think about what you might do if I were on the ground. Staying on my feet is crucial.

"If you keep running away, if you keep avoiding me, what do you expect?" You pause for a few seconds before saying my name again, and this time it comes out like a groan.

Anyone could do violence, Clarissa. I promise you could too, if you needed to.

I know that Robert is right, and I would do great violence to you if I could. But a physical fight is not going to get me out of this one. I can't beat you that way. I can't damage you. I can't run faster than you. Right now you're making sure that I can't even move at all.

My only chance is with words. And tricks. And luck. I think I can pull off the first two, but the third is not in my control.

I say, "I'll go with you."

Your lips are on my forehead. They are wet.

102

I say, "I'll come with you to your car, but please let go of me."

You lips are against mine. "Really?"

"Yes," I say. "But you're hurting me."

"But you like that. I know your darkest secrets, Clarissa. I know your hidden talents."

"I don't like being hurt. I really don't. Please stop."

You run your tongue over my lips.

"You're holding my neck too tight. It's making it hard for me to breathe. It's hard for me to talk."

"Good." But you loosen your grip. "Talking isn't what I want any more, Clarissa."

Your tongue is in my mouth. My breath is coming in uneven rasps, very loud and fast. Too loud and fast.

Your hips are against mine and you grind into me harder. My knees want to fold, but you're clutching me with such force I cannot fall. "See what you do to me?" Your hand is on my breast. "We need to get you out of all these layers." You say this as if we are lovers sharing a joke. "They're in my way."

"You don't want to do this out here, do you?" My voice comes out in a tremble and you must think that this is because of passion instead of fear and repulsion.

Your hand is in my hair now, pulling so that my eyes fill with tears as you tip my head and make me look up at you. "Can I trust you?"

"Yes." You look uncertain, but I think you're wavering. "We're not going to get to your house any time soon if we stay like this." I try to make my voice sound teasing, and I think I fail, but it doesn't matter because I've said what you want to hear.

103

"I have plans for us tonight." You pull my hair harder. "More of what I know you want."

You're still pinning my arms behind my back with one of yours. You slide your gloved hand beneath my coat and dress and press it between my legs. "This is what you want." I sway, but do not try to stop you. You press harder. "Isn't it?"

"Yes."

"Good. Tell me again."

"Yes. It's what I want." And though my words come out like a sob you finally take away your hand and release my arms. I force myself to let them hang calmly at my sides, though what I want to do is brush them off, brush away your touch, and shove you as hard as I can.

"Good." Good is clearly one of your favourite words. You put your hand on the small of my back. "You haven't been making sense lately, Clarissa. Don't you see?"

"Yes."

"Take my hand."

I take your hand.

"You need to let me think for both of us."

"Yes." I step back, so our bodies are no longer in contact.

"You need to do what I tell you." You tow me a few more feet.

"Yes." And I see that yes is a magic word for you too.

You're moving me faster. "That's the best thing."

"Yes." And as the word comes out, a man and his big black dog step into the park at eleven o'clock, from the path that leads down to the allotments.

I have been watching for this since you found me. I haven't stopped looking even for an instant. It always seemed likely

104

someone would come; I hadn't stopped telling myself that the whole time; I couldn't let myself stop believing that.

You follow my eyes to the pair and you falter. My boot might be soft rubber, but I balance myself and then aim it as hard as I can at your shin.

You cry out at what you see as a betrayal as much as pain. "Bitch." That word again. What you really think. "You lied to me." You truly do look astonished.

I scream and shout but "Help me" comes out as a feeble croak, as if I'm in one of those nightmares where my voice won't work right.

"You were only pretending you wanted me."

"Yes." And I can't help but feel pleasure in this yes even though you manage to haul me a few more feet and I'm screaming at you to let go of me, shouting that you're hurting me. I'm trying to dig the heels of my boots into the tarmac to slow us.

"I'll never trust you again."

I don't know if the noises I'm making are loud enough, or if the man sees the struggle, or if he can somehow just tell that something's not right, but the man and his dog are speeding up as they approach us and you release me so abruptly I seem to fly for a few feet before slamming onto the road.

"You've pushed me too far this time."

I scramble up.

"That was your last chance."

The man and his dog are closer still.

"I'll punish you for this."

I shout again at the man and my voice works perfectly this time, cutting through the cold clear air with cold clear clarity. "Please come. Please help me."

You walk away, towards your car at three o'clock, towards the school just beyond the park.

When the man and his dog reach me you turn and take a few steps towards us again, so that the dog starts to bark at you and you freeze. You have to shout over the dog to make your voice carry the ten feet between us.

You say to the man, "She's my girlfriend. It's just a lovers' quarrel and she's acting crazy and refusing to come to dinner like we arranged. You should mind your own business. Everybody has domestics."

You say to me, "I'll see you later, Clarissa. When you've calmed down."

You say to the man, "Shut your fucking dog up."

As you move away, the dog allows short gaps between his barks. When he seems certain you aren't coming back, he is quiet.

"He's not my boyfriend," I say to the man, wiping my mouth with my coat sleeve. And then, beyond caring that I am asking a perfect stranger for a big favour, I say, "Can you please walk me home? It's only ten minutes from here. I'm scared he'll be waiting for me."

The man picks up my mitten, which has fallen off. I hadn't noticed. I run it over my forehead and lips and ear and neck, then shove it in my pocket. The man finds my hat too, and I wipe more at all the parts of my skin that you have touched. I am weeping, and trying hard not to let myself dissolve into outright sobs.

The dog licks my hand, as if he wants to comfort me. I realise there is grit in my palm. The man says, "This is Bruce. He likes you," and he rummages in his coat for a tissue and wordlessly hands it to me and I dry the tears that seem to be

106

freezing onto my cheeks and the snot that's beginning to make my lips and skin crack.

The man and Bruce walk me home. The man is tall. Taller than you. He is thin. Thinner than you. Even beneath his layers of outdoor clothes I can see this. He is nice. A million times nicer than you. And normal, I think. A zillion times more normal than you. He is a nerdy, clever computer geek. A trillion times more interesting than you. His name is Ted, a name I like infinitely more than I like yours.

I grow calmer as we walk. We don't talk about what happened in the park, as if something so ugly and embarrassing is best forgotten now that we are back in civilisation. We hardly talk at all, beyond the minimal and polite things strangers disclose. Our breaths puff out in frozen clouds. So does Bruce's.

But then he politely suggests that maybe it's time for me to look for a new boyfriend, and when I tell him once more that you are not my boyfriend I can barely stop myself from crying again.

The man saw you. He saw the tail end of what you did to me in that park. And even he isn't sure of what he saw. He is nice, but even he thinks that perhaps it really was just a lovers' quarrel. Even he considers the possibility that your account is the true one.

When we reach my house I rub the top of Bruce's silky black head to say goodbye. "Thank you, Bruce. You're very kind and good." The man smiles. I tickle the soft folds of fur beneath Bruce's snout.

The man stands at the bottom of my path and watches as I walk to the door and open it. Then he rushes home to his

107

wife and baby. And I rush straight into the hottest shower I can bear, where I scour off every trace of you.

Afterwards, what I want most is to swallow some sleeping tablets and crawl under my covers. But I don't. As usual I force myself to pick up the black notebook. I make myself put down every detail of what you did to me tonight, though it is the last thing I feel like doing. I have no concrete proof of what happened in that park. But I write it all down as if it were a story. Perhaps the leaflets are not completely useless after all. They have taught me that a time will come when the story matters a lot. And I already know that every story has a true name. I wish this story's name could be different, but nothing will change it. This story is *The Book of You*.

Wednesday

Clarissa was in the jurors' cloakroom. The smell of her shampoo was especially strong; she'd lathered and rinsed and repeated three times. She studied herself in the looking glass, surprised her face could be so pale despite her having scrubbed it so hard the night before. She half-expected to see his fingerprints on her throat, but there was nothing; she'd even checked the back of her neck at home with a hand mirror. It occurred to her that he had exercised quite deliberate control over the amount of pressure he applied.

Her phone signalled an email, startling her — she'd meant to switch it off. It was from Hannah. They'd been taking the same evening Pilates class for the past year. Hannah wondered where Clarissa had been the last few weeks, and whether she'd like to go for a drink after Thursday's class.

I want your friends to be my friends.

Rafe had targeted Rowena. Maybe he'd hurt Hannah. Maybe he'd already got to her and would be waiting in the pub with her if Clarissa turned up.

She emailed back that she wouldn't be able to make it to the class any more, and was busy tomorrow night.

109

Then she switched off the phone, knowing he'd isolated her even more. He'd done what he set out to do. It was all in the leaflets.

She was washing her hands again when Wendy came in. Wendy was twenty-three and had shown Clarissa pictures of her boyfriend. She met him for lunch each day and proudly took his shirts to the dry-cleaner's, enjoying the new game of playing house. Clarissa had silently shaken herself for the shot of jealousy that went through her heart.

"Look." Wendy was clutching the centre of her skirt. Her white-blonde, straight-as-straw hair fell over her pretty pink face. The navy polyester was sliced to the top of her thighs. "It's one of my office skirts. I need to run into work after court today."

Clarissa knew that Wendy was a secretary for a software company.

"I'm thinking that slash wasn't originally part of the design," Clarissa said, glad to be reminded that catastrophes could sometimes be of a relatively mild and easily reparable order.

"I caught it getting off the bus." Wendy tried to smile. "The defendants will love it. I don't think they get too many treats."

Clarissa moved away from the one hand-drier that actually worked, though she wanted to put her whole, freezing body beneath the stream of hot air. She rummaged for her hand-sewing kit, assembled by her mother in a bag made from scraps of poppy-and-daisy patterned fabric. Wendy peered at the contents as if they were instruments for performing brain surgery. "I can mend it for you," Clarissa said. There was self-interest as well as kindness in the offer; needlework always calmed her, and she liked Wendy.

Five minutes later they were in the quiet area. Wendy was in a chair. Clarissa kneeled on the blue carpet before her, stitching from the top of the gash towards the hem.

She was trying to ignore the fact that her fingers were stiff and her arms were aching from the way he'd gripped them. The skin on her wrist was patchy and red and tender, as if he'd given her an Indian burn with his leather gloves. She'd deliberately chosen a top with long, fitted sleeves to hide the marks, though she'd made herself take a photograph of them early that morning. It had seemed a futile thing to do, but she'd reasoned with herself that even if the image proved nothing on its own, it might help later, as part of a larger picture.

Robert walked in, raising a mildly quizzical brow.

"It's not what it looks like," Wendy said, laughing.

He sat down and opened a book, his eyes studiously glued to the pages.

Clarissa tried to concentrate on the skirt and not look too much at Robert. She reached for the scissors.

"Any other hidden talents?" Robert asked. "Aside from being a couture seamstress?"

She couldn't stop herself from replaying Rafe's voice. *I know your hidden talents.*

"Just the one." She snipped the thread. "But I'll be showing at London Fashion Week. Under a top-secret

111

label." She smoothed Wendy's skirt and stood up. "Done. Fifteen-minute repair."

She couldn't stop asking herself why he was wearing the gloves. She couldn't stop herself imagining the most frightening reasons.

"I want to know the label," Wendy said. "I'll auction my skirt as a Clarissa original."

She couldn't stop wondering, over and over again, what she might have escaped.

"My secrets die with me," she said.

The usher appeared, to check if they'd finished, and Wendy hurried over to talk to him.

She couldn't stop reminding herself that he'd only touched the surface of her. She couldn't stop trying to convince herself that she had washed him all away.

She knew Robert had deliberately hung back so he could walk with her up the stairs to Court 12. "How can I find out your secrets?" he said with a quiet smile.

She couldn't stop letting him poison everything else; she had to stop that.

"I'd probably hand them all over, for you," she said lightly. "But you mustn't ever say I didn't warn you. Some of my secrets aren't very pretty."

"I might have a few skeletons in my own cupboard," he said.

Sparkle's barrister was covered in acne and made Clarissa think of a bullying schoolboy. "The very day of your police medical exam you went and met Mr Sparkle. Why would you leave a place of safety, the police station, to meet this supposedly violent and terrifying kidnapper you'd just escaped?"

"Patronising git," Annie muttered, quite discernibly.

Why did you go and meet Mr Solmes in the park?

That's what Clarissa would be asked if she went to the police and complained.

You wouldn't have gone alone to that park unless you wanted to see him. He came to the public gallery the day before to visit you and you spent time with him afterwards. You had dinner with him and your best friend the previous week. Clearly you are very well acquainted.

That's what they would say.

You were never in any danger and you know it. You were even seen holding hands. You know very well that Mr Solmes never threatened you. You were a willing participant in that conversation. You said yes multiple times to Mr Solmes's requests, then you changed your mind without bothering to communicate this to him. Now you're out for revenge. You have since refused all of Mr Solmes's reasonable attempts to reach an amicable understanding.

She'd already spent enough time in Court 12 to know how it worked.

Mr Solmes tells us that you have recently started to take sleeping pills. Clearly you are not stable.

They'd say that too, with no mention of how Mr Solmes came by the information, or what was driving her to take them.

113

You were unsteady on your feet. When you slipped, Mr Solmes intervened to prevent you from falling and injuring yourself. For that — and the barely detectable mark on your wrist which resulted from his catching you — you rewarded him with false allegations of assault and attempted kidnapping. No good deed goes unpunished.

That's how they would conclude.

Miss Lockyer shook her head in weary disagreement. "The police wanted me to go. They said to act normal, not to let Sparkle suspect I was helping them. And I needed drugs."

Sparkle looked like he was trying to suppress his laughter in church.

"It's certainly true that you had the police eating out of your hand."

"They were kind to me, yes." She swallowed hard. "Go ahead and make something dirty out of that too. You lot are good at that. It's not hard for you to do with me, is it?"

It's not hard for them to do with anybody, Clarissa thought.

Wednesday, 11 February, 12.50 p.m.

Annie and I are wandering through the outside market during lunch. I am sipping coffee. Annie is eating a hummus sandwich from the deli stall. I have bought a bottle of organic grape juice. Annie has bought a pot of clotted cream, an apple cake, and a huge trout.

114

"Get some steak," Annie says. "You look like you could use some iron."

"The locker room's going to smell just lovely, Annie. I won't tell anyone who's to blame."

"Oily fish is good for kids."

I can't help wrinkling my nose. "If you can make them eat it. Those googly eyes will freak them out. I hope you'll decapitate it first."

Instead of the exasperated nudge I expect in response, Annie leans towards me. She speaks in a low voice. "That man keeps staring at you. The one by the butcher's stall."

I know it is you before I turn to look. My eyes are on you for only a few seconds. I tear them away as if frightened that they will meet yours and I will be turned to stone. But I take in your navy UCLA sweatshirt, your jeans, your dark trainers. I take in the fact that you are not wearing the leather gloves.

"Do you know him? Do you want me to leave you to talk to him?"

"No. God no. Please don't leave. I don't want to talk to him." I don't realise that I am clutching Annie's arm until she loosens my fingers, though she places her hand over them, gently, for a few seconds.

"He looks mean, Clarissa. He looks angry. He's glaring at you. He looks — I don't know — as if he's trying on purpose to look intimidating. Kind of like the defendant who smacked and punched Miss Lockyer and burnt her earring. What's his name again?"

"Godfrey," I say.

"That's the one. Except that your man's much better at being menacing."

115

"He's *not* my man, Annie. Please don't ever say that." I glance at my watch, a mere ritual, as if ordinary gestures have power, but I don't take in what it says. "We'd better get back."

"He's following us. Who is he?"

"Someone I used to know. Don't look at him. Ignore him." *Telling others can strengthen evidence and provide corroboration, thereby increasing the likelihood of a prosecution.*

My voice is very quiet. "I might — at some stage — I might need you to say you saw him here. Would that be okay?"

"Of course." Despite my command, Annie keeps checking behind her. "And if you ever need to talk . . ."

"Thanks."

But I can't drag Annie into this. Annie has enough problems of her own. Battling with her estranged husband over arrangements for their little girl, who is only six. Struggling not to let herself become obsessively jealous of the younger woman he left her for.

When Annie tells me these things, I think of Henry's wife and feel sick. Partly from remorse. And partly from dread that Annie would see me as the enemy if she knew and slam the door on our embryonic friendship.

Annie is nothing like Henry's wife, but she shares her talent for giving dirty looks. She's aiming one at you one right now, and that pleases me. Annie is doing more than she can imagine for me, just with that look.

I think of Rowena and how you fooled her, how you got her on your side. But Rowena was at a disadvantage. You infiltrated her. You were wearing your mask all the time with

116

Rowena. You got under her skin and set her up before she could see what you really are. Annie's first glimpse of you is in your monstrous form, your real self. To my great relief, she clearly doesn't like you one bit.

Furious, jumpy Godfrey made Clarissa think of Rumpelstiltskin. His barrister, Mr Harker, had a faint Irish accent. Mr Harker's thin face was kind, perhaps even sympathetic.

"I do not dispute any of your evidence, Miss Lockyer," he said.

Miss Lockyer was startled; she bowed her head slightly and seemed about to cry. Was she really not going to be attacked again? Could this man really be saying he believed her?

"Pathetic." Annie began her loud whisper as Mr Harker sat down. "Was that mind-numbing lecture on the unreliability of memory supposed to pass for Godfrey's defence?"

Clarissa could only answer with a baffled half-smile. She hadn't taken in a word of it. She'd been too busy replaying the lunchtime encounter with Rafe. It was his display of the UCLA sweatshirt that was niggling her. Despite the biting cold, he hadn't worn a coat. She was certain it was because he'd wanted her to notice the sweatshirt. It must be some kind of trophy, full of special meaning for him.

She couldn't recall any mention of his having been a student at the University of California, or of his teaching there, or even of his ever visiting Los Angeles. In truth, though, he could have done any of those things. She knew so little about him, really: a circumstance she was glad of — she hated having to force herself to learn more. There was a message in that sweatshirt — she was sure of it — but one she couldn't yet read. In the meantime, he was enjoying the power of whatever the secret was.

She could hear the phone ringing as she fumbled with her keys. She tracked the sound to her sewing room, peeking behind the door and peering into the corners before entering. There it was, on her cutting table. The battery was low, she saw, as she answered the call from her mother.

She was walking through the kitchen, filling the kettle and putting it on the oven, her head bent towards her shoulder to hold the phone.

"You sound distracted, Clarissa."

She was in the living room, picking up the stacks of sewing magazines and art books she'd left on the wooden floor her father had sanded and restored for her. She was placing them on the shelves he'd built for her, alongside the volumes of complete fairy tales by the Grimms, Perrault and Andersen that he'd read to her when she was a little girl. She had read them again and again since, endlessly fascinated, and thought that they were not at all for children.

"Can you stay still for a minute and listen to me, please?"

Her mother had covered the sofa for her. Crimson roses the size of Clarissa's fists weighed heavily upon their curling burgundy stems. They were scattered over

118

a background the colour of dried blood. Clarissa fell onto it.

"Are you looking after yourself properly?"

The subtext of this question was her grief about Henry. "Yes. Of course. You taught me well."

"I was worrying when you took so long to answer."

Clarissa was her parents' own fairy-tale child, born when her mother was forty-three, after sixteen long years with no baby. Her father liked to tease her that he'd had all the spindles in the kingdom burnt, to keep her safe. She always teased back about how great that plan had worked out.

"I promise I'm fine." She unzipped one boot and stripped it off, then the other, as her mother passed the phone to her father.

Clarissa was up again. In the kitchen, turning off the screaming kettle, lulled as usual by her father's voice. "Do you think it's silly," she asked, unable to resist confiding in him, "if I take taxis home from the station?" As she spoke, she felt walls closing in on her and the world growing smaller, but she knew it was the only thing she could do; she had to face that fully now.

"No. But why the change, Clary? You love walking."

She was angry at herself for saying so much and worrying him. "It's a long day, this jury service thing."

"Good idea, then," her father said.

She was in her bedroom, checking that nobody was hiding in the wardrobe, then lying on the bed, peeling off her stockings and letting them fall onto the deep gold rug she'd made from a heavy vintage fabric

119

covered in huge lilies. She bent her knees to her chest and wiggled her freezing toes.

Clarissa's mother had spent five and a half decades intervening in her father's conversations. Her voice was too clear. "Please tell your daughter that mango on its own is not lunch. And weak black tea is not a dinner food." As if the phone itself knew that her mother had finished and Clarissa was not to have a comeback, it bleeped three times and died.

Thursday

Thursday, 22 January, 2.30p.m. (Three Weeks Ago)

It is just over a week until I will leave work for jury service. I am on my way to deliver some papers to the new Head of the English Department and I must pass by your blue office door. It is propped open, despite the plaque warning that it's a fire door and must remain closed. The room is empty. But I spot something that halts me, my breath coming quicker, nervous that any second you will appear in the corridor. Still, I must look.

Only I would recognise the collection of items on top of your filing cabinet as a mini-shrine. Do you plan to use it all for some weird voodoo ritual? An envelope addressed to you in my handwriting, which must have contained some boring piece of post-graduate administration. A yellow coffee mug covered in orange and green daisies; I'd used it every morning until it disappeared a month ago; you haven't washed it. A plastic container of the strawberry yogurt I sometimes bring into work with me, streaked with the now-browning vestiges of what I failed to scrape from the pot. I can't begin to imagine how you got that. An empty tube of the hand cream I always keep on my desk. Leaflets and magazines about amateur photography. Some discarded papers from a meeting, covered in the tulips I always doodle.

110. They say that it takes an average of 110 stalking-related incidents before a woman goes to the police. I tell myself I can't have got anywhere near 110, though I wonder if that depends on how they count.

Does each thing on your filing cabinet count as one incident? Actually, they probably don't count as anything at all. I'd look like an idiot if I brought it up, and you'd be able to explain it all away, making me look paranoid and stupid. I can practically hear you, laughing conspiratorially at the utter nonsense of such an accusation.

Is every man who forgets to wash a coffee mug to be brought before the university harassment committee?

Am I the only one who's ever mistakenly walked away with someone else's teacup? Guilty as charged. But if she wanted it back she could have asked for it. I had no idea it was hers.

I will write Domestic Services a formal letter of apology for my negligence in dealing responsibly with food waste.

I admit that I'm blushing about the hand lotion, but it's winter — men get dry skin too.

I acknowledge that I ought to develop a better system for recycling envelopes and papers. Take me before a competency tribunal. Punish me with some staff development.

I'd get nowhere, complaining. I can't prove anything with any of this.

I look again at my tulips. Seeing them in your office puts me back in that meeting. You stop to write something, then look intently at me and nod to yourself in a satisfied way, as if you have confirmed some fact about me that you can now note. It makes me feel stolen. There is nowhere to hide from your eyes, whatever way I try to pull my chair back or sink down low or position myself to be blocked by Gary. I look down at the table. I squirm, self-conscious and embarrassed.

"Interesting," you say in a knowing tone, when I mumble something that is the very opposite of interesting in response to one of Gary's requests for dull information. To the others you sound engaged and attentive; you're on top of your job. The worst they'd think of you is that you're sucking up to Gary. None of them would dream that you're pestering me.

I shake away the meeting and remember where I am. There's the tread of an ogre on the stairs, so that the building seems to wobble. It must be you. Your steps are always noisy and hurried, as if you want everyone to think that you know where you're going; you're purposeful; you have a lot of extremely important things to do and you mean business. What a model employee you are.

I knock quickly on the new Head of Department's door, relieved when she answers immediately. I slip inside, the sound of your hello close behind me, and I pretend not to hear it.

I am so intent on plotting how I can get past you on my way back that I don't even think about the fact that I am standing in Henry's old office; I don't even take in how much the new Head of Department has changed it and erased him; I don't even replay the time he and I had sex on the mess of a desk that is now littered with her spreadsheets and files but was always carefully ordered and clear when it belonged to him. I invite her to come with me straight away to see a new computer suite for postgraduates. I want to hug her when she says yes, though I manage to restrain myself.

123

Escorted and busy in my improvised new role as tour guide, I see you watch in frustration as I pass your illicitly open door. The Head of Department pauses to scold you for defying fire regulations and disregarding health and safety training. There is no irony in her voice as she kicks away your improvised door-stop of a plastic folder.

I know you are glaring at her, though I don't look. You applied for her job and didn't get it. Now she has added this to the list of insults and grievances you must be collecting, and I feel a pang of concern for her, though I still want to cheer her as the heavy wood slowly swings, then clicks shut, with you on the other side of it.

The entire world seemed to be closed on Thursday morning. Clarissa knew from email that the university was shut because of blizzard snow. But there were enough trains and buses into Bristol for the court to go on.

She sat companionably with Robert, waiting for the others to struggle in.

Robert retrieved a clear plastic bag from his backpack and took out a chocolate croissant. He broke it into two pieces and wordlessly offered one of them to her.

She was about to say she never ate breakfast, but she stopped herself and accepted it. "Thank you," she said, taking a bite, waking up a bit more as the taste of butter and strong chocolate did its lovely work. "This is so good."

"The café just outside the court." He chewed thoughtfully. "Let's hope Lottie has an easier day today."

Lottie. It was affectionate, even intimate and loving. Along the lines of how Clarissa's father always called her Clary. Yet it was an endearment for a woman she and Robert would never actually talk to or know; a woman they ought to remain entirely detached about.

Clarissa had started it. Once, just once, she'd slipped and used the name aloud to Robert. Instantly, he caught it from her. That had only been on Tuesday but already the two of them were in the habit of using it with each other. Never in front of the other jurors, though. That was an unspoken, instinctive rule. It was their private, secret thing.

"Yes," she said. "Let's hope."

His phone buzzed. He stuffed the rest of the croissant into his mouth and scanned a text. "Drinks with the guys tonight after work. Want to text Jack back for me that I'll be there?" He passed her his phone.

"Are you sure you trust me?"

"Entirely."

She knew exactly what to say. Robert would know the message was for him rather than Jack, but there was just enough teasing uncertainty about this for her to dare.

I'm longing to be with you. xx.

Blushing a little, she flashed the screen at him for inspection. "Shall I press send?"

"Go ahead." He was entirely deadpan.

She went ahead.

"Clarissa!" He sounded completely shocked. "I didn't think you'd actually do it. I was only joking."

125

She gasped and began to apologise, but he only interrupted. "Got you!" A text came back almost straight away. He read it, grinning. "Not fit for your eyes."

"Are you going to tell him it was me?"

"Nah. Why spoil his happiness? So proud he even read it to the others. But I can see I'll need to watch out with you. You're a tricky one."

Court 12 began only an hour and a half late.

Miss Lockyer sipped some water, visibly relieved to be back in Mr Morden's hands.

"Can you describe your condition in the days following your abduction and rape?"

"I was withdrawing. I was extremely distressed. I couldn't stop vomiting. They had to give me pills to stop the anxiety and help me sleep, and I'm the last person doctors want to give drugs to."

Mr Morden never took his sorrowful, pitying, gentlemanly eyes, full of admiration, from his star witness. "Thank you, Miss Lockyer. You've been very brave."

Clarissa wanted one last look at her face, but Miss Lockyer had collapsed like a rag doll, her head dangling from her flower-stalk neck, hiding as well as she could in that very public courtroom, retreating back into her own world, now that she was allowed to.

The snow was whirling thickly outside the windows as they swept through the jurors' waiting area. All of the other courts had finished early that day, because of

126

the weather. The large room was uncannily empty and quiet. The jury officer's desk was deserted.

Of the twelve jurors, Clarissa and Robert were the only ones from Bath. "We might get stuck here," Clarissa said to him as they fought their way through the blizzard. "The trains may not be running."

"If that happens I'll phone the station. One of the guys will come and pick us up."

"They'd come all the way to Bristol to get us?"

"Yes," he said, with that simple, calm matter-of-factness he always used.

"Will it be a fire engine?"

He smiled at her as if she were a child, but his "No" was uttered with the same kind firmness. "It'll be a jeep."

"I'm disappointed," Clarissa said, as they squeezed onto the five o'clock train, miraculously running. "I wanted to ride in a fire engine."

"It wouldn't be —" He bit back the end of the sentence and smiled.

The previous three trains had been cancelled, so this one was packed. Clarissa couldn't move in much beyond the door. She leaned against the partition and Robert stepped in after her, standing only inches away. When the train moved off he swayed towards her for a few seconds and she found herself wondering what it would be like to kiss him. There was a drop of melted snow on his cheek, and she had to resist the impulse to reach up and wipe it away.

"Do you feel," Clarissa wondered, carefully, "that with each new question the ground shifts again, and then everything you thought just a minute earlier, you're no longer sure of it?" The judge couldn't object to that question, despite his continuous solemn warnings not to discuss the case.

"I do. Exactly like that." His breath was like toothpaste. She thought he must have slipped a mint into his mouth when she wasn't looking. She was pleased by the idea that he'd made that secret effort at the possibility of being in close proximity to her.

The train was approaching the platform. The door was opening. She was sorry it was already over. She was pulling on yet another hat and pair of mittens her mother had knitted her. Knowing Robert was behind her, she stumbled off with the same self-consciousness she felt whenever she entered or exited the courtroom.

They paused for a minute in front of the station. The night sky seemed to be under a spell; it was a backdrop of softly glowing light and whiteness from the snow instead of the usual dark. Robert's black fleece hat quickly looked as if it had been dusted in pale blossom.

"I live near Lottie's old flat." She blurted this out, wanting to delay their parting by finding something to say.

"Small world. Have you told the others?"

"No. I pass it sometimes, going to the station. But I've been getting taxis in the mornings — running late," she added quickly. "Anyway, I don't think I'll go that way any more after dark. I've started taking taxis home too."

She glanced across the street. Rafe ducked into a doorway.

128

"Is something wrong?"

She faltered. "The stuff we hear in court may be scaring me."

Robert was studying her carefully. "That's understandable. There's not much of you, and that hill's shadowy at night." After a few shy seconds, he said, "I'm on the other side of town. Not far from the scented garden for the blind."

She knew his street. A row of beautiful Georgian houses, slightly smaller scale than the grandest of Bath's listed buildings, but still pretty huge and rather special. "It can't be an attic flat," she said, thinking of a top floor's low ceilings, impossible with his height.

"It's not a flat," he said.

"Oh." She tried to conceal her wonder that he could afford a whole Georgian house.

"You're shivering," he said. "You better get home. Goodnight, Clarissa Jane Bourne."

There was no doubting whose fault it was that her mind jumped the way it did. She tilted her head, looking at him quizzically, trying to keep her voice casual. "What superpowers do you have to know my middle name?"

"No laser beam eyes or magical brain scanning or secret agent snooping involved. It's full names on the jury list. I see yours each morning when I cross my own off. Yours is at the top."

She bit her lip in mock embarrassment. "And how did I not notice that?" she said, laughing a bit, dismissing herself. "Silly."

"No," he said. "That's not a word I'd use about you."

And in truth she didn't feel silly. He wasn't a man who made her feel silly at all. Even when she had to face her own default paranoia, even when she lost control and couldn't help but let him glimpse it, he seemed to respond only with gentle good humour and kindness. And she truly did think that he saw so much. Names. Lighters. She wondered what else he saw.

"Say hello to Jack for me," she said.

"I'll do that."

She didn't want to look back, after they parted, to see if Robert was watching her, just as she never looked to see where the barristers' and defendants' eyes were as she went in and out of the jury box. But she did turn. She couldn't help it. Robert walked on, straight and purposeful and evenly paced, and never looked back himself.

She hurried into a waiting taxi, grateful there was no queue, refusing to search again for Rafe's horrible shadow. She knew it was there. She didn't need to see it to know that.

Friday

A short, plump, pasty-looking man was sitting in the witness box. The ex-boyfriend who'd broken Lottie's heart.

"How did Miss Lockyer seem to you when she returned from London on Sunday, July twenty-ninth?"

"She were in a state. She were a right mess. She were dirty looking. There were a bruise around one of her eyes. She were shaking and crying. She wouldn't let me touch her. She smelled bad. She weren't wearing any knickers. That upset me, worried me. I kept asking about that, but she wouldn't say. There was dried blood between her legs. Her breathing were rough, like it were hurting her in her chest."

Clarissa and Annie were wandering through the outside market at the end of the day. It had been Annie's idea to spend a little time together, shopping, before Clarissa caught her train back to Bath and Annie got her bus to the outskirts of Bristol.

"Our judge always lets us out too late," Annie said. "All the other juries are gone before us. There's never anything good left by the time we get out."

"We could go again together, during lunch. Like we did on Wednesday."

"You look as if all that passes your lips is mineral water from enchanted springs and purified air. The rest of us need to eat during lunch." Annie frowned as the owners of the craft stalls began to pack away the vestiges of their painted pots and handcrafted jewellery and artisan cards and tie-dyed dresses, seeming to snatch things from display tables faster than she could grab them. "At least your creepy friend isn't following us. He'd better hope for his sake that I don't see him again."

Clarissa reasoned with herself that Annie would be safe from Rafe. She was sure Annie would notice if she were being watched by him — Annie was way too observant and careful for him to get away with that. Plus, there was something about Annie that made Clarissa certain that Rafe wouldn't dare mess with her.

"I'm not inclined to hope anything that's for his sake." Clarissa blew her nose and tossed the crumpled tissue into a bin.

"What do you think of this?" Annie was studying a handmade wooden box decorated with Disney princesses. Clarissa thought it was hideous. She pointedly remained silent and Annie put down the box, deciding against it.

"This is pretty." Clarissa held up a child's dress. It was cornflower blue and embroidered with roses. She wondered if Annie's little girl might like it, but frowned as she inspected the hem. "It's unravelling."

Annie rolled her eyes. "You *are* a mistress of stitches, Clarissa. I'll give you that." Annie paused, as if unsure whether she should continue, but then she did. "Think about something this weekend. Consider whether that cliché's wrong about women lying down for artists. Ask yourself whether they lie down for firemen, and whether firemen know it. One of the perks of the job." Annie squeezed her arm. "You hardly know anything about him, Clarissa," she said, looking hard at her. "There's something about him I don't . . ." Annie stopped herself. "It doesn't take a mind reader to see how much you like him. Be careful."

Saturday

When I get to the bottom of the stairs I find Miss Norton in the hall. I'm on my way out to run errands and meet Gary for coffee, but Miss Norton is already returning from a busy morning of excursions. She is saying goodbye to the taxi driver who insisted on carrying in her tartan shopping bag on wheels, scolding him that she could have done it herself.

Miss Norton is ninety-two and likes her routines. Every day, as soon as she wakes up, Miss Norton walks twenty times around her flat, as fast as she can, for exercise. The pavements outside are too uneven and dangerous for old ladies to speed-walk, Miss Norton says.

I want a fairy godmother. She will look like Miss Norton and laugh Miss Norton's tinkling laugh. She will grant three wishes and I will choose wisely. One. I wish for a baby. Two. I wish for Robert. Three. I wish you would go to some place far far away for ever. The wand will wave and wave and wave once more. It will be so simple.

Miss Norton gives me a knowing look. "These came for you, dear. Chocolates. I only just put them on the shelf with

134

your other post. Such a lovely box, too. Someone left it in front of our door."

I walk to the door. I hesitate, but make myself pull it open.

You are standing opposite the house, on the other side of the road, leaning against a lamp post. Black jeans again. A black, long-sleeved shirt, not tucked in. You aren't wearing a coat or a hat, and your shoulders are hunched against the cold. You actually look vulnerable.

For an instant, I falter in my hatred of you. I see you as if you were a stranger. I see the trouble in your face, and I think what a lost soul you are. I think of when Henry first left and how it felt to be so hopelessly disappointed in love. Isn't that what you are, only to a pathological degree? But then you lift a hand in greeting, slowly, and start towards my house. You're moving closer to me, where I absolutely don't want you to be. And the stab of compassion that took me by surprise is gone as quickly as it came.

Your voice is too loud on my peaceful street. "Hello, beautiful."

Hello, beautiful.

Henry said that to me the day we met.

It happened five years ago, soon after I started working at the university.

The first time I ever saw him is still vivid. His sharp suit. His tie with quotations from T.S. Eliot zigzagging over it. The way his eyes shone as Gary introduced us at the start of the committee meeting that had brought us together that day. The electric shock he gave me when we shook hands. The fact that from the beginning it was impossible for me to look anywhere else in a room if Henry was in it.

135

During the meeting Henry actually winked at me, so I had to stop myself from laughing. When I got back to my office the two words were waiting for me in an email. *Hello, beautiful*. They seemed to blaze out of my screen.

I could have ignored him or rejected him or even made a complaint of sexual harassment. But I didn't do any of those things.

Hello, I wrote back, aware of how hard my heart was beating.

Have dinner with me tonight. His message appeared within seconds of my reply. It wasn't a question, but I could have said no and he would have respected that word.

Another big difference between you.

So is the fact that I can't even remember the first time I ever saw you. Until your book-launch party, I'd never had anything to do with you outside of work or taken much notice of you; you were just one of the many barely distinguishable academics I had to chase to fill in paperwork on behalf of their PhD students. That's all you were.

After the restaurant, Henry and I walked along the river, breathing in the wood-smoke from the barges' chimneys. The river was so swollen it covered the black iron barriers that were supposed to stop people from falling in. Henry recited Yeats's "The Mermaid" from memory and made me promise not to drown him. Despite being slowed by all the wine we'd drunk, we somehow solved the paving-stone maze, holding hands in the near-darkness until we reached its mosaic centre.

At the end of the evening, we stood by the weir, watching it foam just below the upside-down reflection of Pulteney Bridge, illuminated gold on the water's glassy mirror. "Perfect date," Henry said. He coloured the words with his usual ironic edge and his poet's awareness of the statement's retro feel. "Perfect date" wasn't naturally part of Henry's vocabulary. But I had to agree that that was what the evening had been, as he pulled me close.

It was a month later that I found out he was married, though he swore the relationship was over in all but name. I refused to see him for three weeks after he told me, ignoring his phone calls and messages and emails, not answering the doorbell, furious beyond expression that he had kept it from me. But I'd already fallen for him too hard, and it wasn't long until I broke my vow to renounce him. Two months after that, Henry left the house he'd been sharing with his wife and showed up at my flat, bearing wine and flowers and a suitcase.

I could have turned him away, as I've turned you away so many times.

Instead, I kissed him and pulled him in.

You've finished crossing the road. "Clarissa. I wanted to say —"

I slam the door before you finish.

Miss Norton raises a white eyebrow. "I've seen him several times before."

"Don't ever let him in, please, Miss Norton."

"As if I'd ever let a strange man in, Clarissa."

"Sorry. I know you wouldn't. I know I didn't need to say. Will you tell me if you see him here again?"

"Of course."

"Could you describe him if you were asked to? Or identify him?"

"Of course," she says again, looking hard at me.

137

"Good. That's good." But I'm worrying that I've asked even this much of her. It's not the job of a ninety-two-year-old to protect me. It's mine to protect her. Delicately, I touch the heart-shaped box, displayed so carefully by Miss Norton on the shelf. It is deep red. I pull my fingers away quickly, as if it burns me.

"You do get so many gifts, Clarissa." Miss Norton shakes her silky white hair in impressed amazement.

"I'll never eat these." I push the chocolates farther from me; they are weighty. "I wish I could throw them out." But I know I must keep them, locked away with your other things.

Miss Norton squints. Perhaps she is genuinely shocked at the thought of such waste.

"I'm sorry," I say quickly. Miss Norton must be wondering why I don't give the chocolates to her if I'm not going to eat them myself. "I know you're of the generation who experienced rationing. My grandmother did. She never got over it."

"You're of the generation who thinks everything will go on for ever, dear."

"You're right." I nod, abashed. "I know how careful you are." I decide to buy Miss Norton some chocolates of her own while I'm out and surprise her with them when I return.

"Can you speak up? My hearing aid needs a new battery." Patiently, I repeat myself.

"Yes." Miss Norton appears thoughtful. "I *am* on a pension." She has long been retired from her job as headmistress of a private girls' school. "Don't forget the card," she says. Her hand is papery white and traced with blue veins. It curls around the edge of the crimson container. She slides the envelope from beneath the curling pink ribbons.

The envelope is the colour of candyfloss. It is heart-shaped too. If it were from Robert I would smile in secret pleasure at the words. *For the Princess in the Attic*.

But you are not Robert. You are like a living version of the troll's mirror in *The Snow Queen*. From you, even the most beautiful things become ugly and distorted.

I want to hide from Miss Norton's X-ray eyes.

"It can only be for you. You do look like a princess, you know. And I'm too old to live in an attic." She reaches out a finely boned hand and lightly, briefly, touches my forehead. The hand is soft and dry. Surprisingly, it smells of eucalyptus. "You don't look well."

I try to smile. "I'm fine. You're so kind, Miss Norton."

The hall falls into near-darkness and the card slips from my fingers.

"Oh dear," says Miss Norton.

I fumble for the light switch's timer and the chandelier's silvery crystal droplets are illuminated for another ten minutes. I retrieve the card from the dark gold matting and slide it out of the envelope. *Be my Valentine*.

Your handwriting is more familiar to me than anyone else's. *I will never give up*.

"You're trembling. Come into my flat. Let me make you a cup of tea."

Despite my powerful instinct to shelter and spare lovely Miss Norton, the words spill out. "I know I must seem ungrateful to you, and spoiled. But I don't want it." I shove the card back into the envelope, not wanting to touch it or look at it as I do. "I told him I didn't want it. I want nothing from him." I wipe away a tear. "I won't have any tea now, but thank you."

Chocolates and diamonds and leather gloves. You assault me in the park. You put your hands on my body when I don't want them there. And then you give me a Valentine's card. Are all of these things of the same order for you? You're practically schizophrenic.

I will still go out. I will march right past you. It is daylight. My neighbours will hear me if I call for help. You cannot do anything to me on a morning like this. If you follow me I will lead you straight to the police station, and I'm pretty sure you wouldn't like that at all.

But I am still shuddering in the aftermath of my walk in the park. I plan to drop my coat off at the dry-cleaner's while I'm out, so they can wash your touch from it. I plan to buy a shredder, too; you can search my recycling bin as much as you please, but you will never again find anything interesting there.

You will not see the receipt for the book about sex that I chose during the lunch break yesterday, thinking perhaps I should consider my skills, just in case. You will not see the receipt for the book about natural fertility that I bought at the same time, also just in case. I will be donating the barely used bottle of Gardenia to a charity shop. The receipt for my new perfume will be turned to confetti. You will never know what it's called.

Suspiciously little is known about you. Maybe there is a missing key; one that can help me. I remember Gary mentioning that he knows someone who worked with you years ago. Maybe Gary can tell me something useful, despite my wish not to have to think about you.

But it isn't all about you. Not everything is about you. I mustn't let myself forget that.

140

I want to see Gary. I want to hear about the people at work and the things that are going on in my absence. You're no danger to Gary. You can't hurt him like you could hurt Rowena or Hannah. You can't use him to get to me like you would use them; he'd see right through you if you even tried.

And Gary is a man. A big man. A man from work. A man from work whose position is higher and more powerful than yours. You don't pick on people your own size.

I brace myself as I open the door. "I'm meeting a friend, Miss Norton. And there are a few things I must do. I have to go." Without actually stepping out of the house I look as far as I can, both ways, along the wide, gracious street. No ugly, cowardly shadow. Unless you are hiding in one of the beautiful front gardens, all different, like the Georgian buildings themselves in their various heights and shapes and pastel shades and window styles.

I wonder vaguely if the seasickness I'm feeling is akin to pregnancy nausea.

"Can I get you anything while I'm out, Miss Norton?"

She scolds me for missing an obvious fact, though fondly. "I've just been to the shops, dear," the ever-sharp Miss Norton says.

Week 3

The
Steadfast Lover

Monday

Monday, 16 February, 8.12 a.m.

I see you as soon as the taxi turns into the road in front of the building. You're leaning against the wall by the station entrance. As soon as I get out you intercept me, like a hack journalist dogging a celebrity. You stick close as I head towards the ticket gates.

God, you're annoying. The most annoying person in the world. When I'm not in a state of complete terror I can see that at your best you are just plain irritating. But you're long past your best. You're getting closer each day to your worst, and I don't want to let myself imagine what the final stage of this trajectory might be.

"Did you enjoy the market with your juror friend on Wednesday, Clarissa?"

My mouth goes dry at the thought that Annie has come to your notice. But I tell myself you can't imagine there'd be anything to gain from a woman I've only known for two weeks, purely because our names were both pulled from a hat. I swallow hard and clear my throat. I tell myself again that Annie can't be in any danger from you; she'd give you nothing of me: Annie is no Rowena. But I know also that I

145

have to keep away from Annie outside of court from now on — I need to make sure you never look at her again.

"Why aren't you wearing your ring, Clarissa?"

My eyes are on the electronic departure board. I don't pause in my step as I search for the train to Bristol. To my great relief, the 8.22 is running on time.

"If you'd read your fairy tales properly you'd know that there's always a terrible punishment for failing to appreciate a gift."

I bump into the last person in the queue for the turnstile and mumble an apology.

"I didn't know you were such good friends with Gary, Clarissa."

I'd felt you on Saturday morning, following, spying, despite my not seeing you after I parted from Miss Norton. I noticed Gary looking over his shoulder as we walked into the café, as if he felt something too.

"Did you like the chocolates, Clarissa?"

I've never known the procession through the ticket gates to move so slowly.

"It's rude for you not to say thank you."

You're no longer held in check by the hope that you can win me over. Even you must see that you never will.

"It wasn't polite of you not to invite me in, Clarissa."

I remind myself that all you want is to get me to react. I won't. No matter what you say or do I won't.

"I'm going to need to teach you some manners, Clarissa."

I remind myself that I'm in a crowded place in broad daylight.

"I don't appreciate having the door slammed in my face."

I remind myself that you cannot touch me here.

"I don't appreciate it at all."

At last I am at the barrier, praying you won't follow me. I know from the university timetable that you have a lecture at nine, so there's a good chance you won't. I feed my ticket in and push through the turnstile. But I can hear you, calling out from behind me.

"I don't like that fireman, Clarissa. I saw you talking to him here last week. Stay away from that fireman."

My breath catches. Already, you know who Robert is. You know what he does. It wouldn't have been difficult to learn these things if you followed him home on Thursday night. You could have peeked through the letter-box slot and seen his name on a piece of post, then searched for him on the Internet.

I've searched for him myself and found several news stories. Laying a Remembrance Day wreath in memory of serving firefighters who'd perished, with a photo of him looking so handsome and serious in his full dress uniform, medals and ribbons pinned over his heart. Part of a team that put out a fire in a tower block where six people died, and attending a memorial for them, after. Rescuing a child from a burning house — to do such a thing must be sheer elation for a fireman. Ten years ago he'd been pulled from the rubble of a collapsed building and spent a week in hospital afterwards; a fireman on his watch had died beside him.

Of course you don't like Robert; you can't fail to see that you're no match for him.

I don't falter in my step, walking away from you. I don't look back. The leaflet people should video me. A short film: *How to Deal with Your Stalker When Severely Provoked*. I am exemplary. You don't exist. You can say the most awful things but you are a mere ghost talking to air. For now, the lecture keeps me safe. You do not follow.

She sat on the train, examining the special bag she'd made that weekend. She'd researched and planned and pattern drafted and sewed until very late each night. She thought of it as her anti-stalker bag, and was struck by how odd it was that something could look so beautiful yet have such an ugly function. As she inspected each of the inner pockets, and tested the security and accessibility of the things she'd slotted into them, she replayed what Gary had told her.

Rafe had lived with a woman ten years ago, in London. Gary's source for this information was a friend who'd lectured in the same English Department as Rafe, then, at a different university. The woman had worked there too, as a secretary, which is how she and Rafe met. As soon as Rafe got his lectureship in Bath she left him and quit her job. Nobody knew what happened to her after they split up; she had vanished with absolute completeness.

But Clarissa had a name: Laura Betterton. She'd done some Internet searches, over the weekend, and found nothing. Somehow, she'd been expecting news stories about a missing person or even reports of an unsolved murder. But Betterton wasn't that common a name. Even if she couldn't find Laura, the online phonebook offered her an address and number for a James Betterton, in London. Not expecting anything, Clarissa dialled. A man answered and she asked for Laura.

"Who is this?"

"You don't know me, but —"

"Then why are you calling?"

"I'm trying to find her — I mean Laura."

He grunted; almost a choked-back, bitter laugh. "And you can't even tell me your name?" He put down the phone.

Lots of people were abrupt and irritable when interrupted by a wrong number. But she thought there was something else in the man's voice. He'd sounded startled. Angry, too.

For now, though, she didn't want to pester him with more phone calls — she knew all too well how upsetting that was. She realised also that the power of her desire to find someone who knew more of Laura's story could make her imagine she was hearing something unsaid, when there was nothing out of the ordinary there at all.

Sally Martin fiddled with her Pre-Raphaelite red hair as Mr Morden took her through the Saturday when she witnessed Lottie's kidnapping. The defendants had made her direct them through Bath as they drove around searching for Lottie.

"They didn't want anybody to see what they were going to do. They tracked her to her street. We'd only been there a minute when Tomlinson said, 'Bingo.' Sparkle said, 'Get her in the van. Quick.' They got her in the van so quick I hardly even saw it happen."

The pencil slipped from Clarissa's hand, onto the floor beneath the table. She groped for it, bumping her head as she surfaced, blinking away reflex tears.

149

"She was dead white. I'd never seen anybody so frightened in my life. She was biting her lips. She was wringing her hands. Her head was down, trying not to look at anybody. After about ten minutes they drove into the end of my street, told me to get out."

"Why are you crying, Miss Martin?"

"I could hear her screaming as the van pulled away. I was so relieved to be out myself, but I knew they'd hurt her. I still see her face. I'll never forget it."

Mr Belford was unmoved by Sally Martin's tears. "One month before Miss Lockyer's alleged kidnapping and assault, the police observed the two of you loitering and soliciting."

Sally Martin was under-awed by Mr Belford's erudition. "You know, I can see you're super educated and you use big words and all that but nobody can understand you."

"Allow me to be more direct. Was Carlotta Lockyer a working girl?"

"Yeah. She was. So what? That doesn't mean those men didn't rape her."

Clarissa and Annie were rushing down the stairs.

Annie grimaced. "Miss Martin's probably the only person we'll see in that room who will be just fine."

"Not Miss Lockyer?" Clarissa said, holding her breath for the answer. "Miss Lockyer won't be fine?"

"No," said Annie. "No hope for Miss Lockyer."

They were sitting across from each other on the train with a table between them. The heaters were blowing

150

lovely hot air. Clarissa squirmed out of her coat and put it beside her, smiling at Robert as she did.

This was normal. She was being normal. There was no Rafe. She and Robert were alone in the carriage. She was with a man she liked, being normal. She was almost happy, but she had to quell the pang of guilt that she'd put Robert on Rafe's radar. She wracked her brains for a way of warning him to be careful without telling him about Rafe.

Her first attempt wasn't too inspired, but it was all she could come up with and probably better than nothing. "Do you think we need to be more aware of things, because of the trial?" she tried.

He looked puzzled.

"I mean, just to be more alert, to look around us more," she said.

He raised an eyebrow.

"In case, well, maybe someone might follow us, or try to find out about us?" She was sounding more ridiculous by the minute.

"I'm not worried about the defendants, Clarissa. You shouldn't be either."

She bit her lip, prepared to give up already. "You're right."

"The defendants aren't going to bother you."

Great job at warning him, she thought. Well done, Clarissa, she thought. "Of course they're not," she said. "I shouldn't think like that."

"It's understandable you might be nervous. I could see you were the other night. I just want to reassure you."

"You have." She tried to tell herself that Robert was a big boy who could look after himself; if anyone had anything to fear, it wasn't Robert.

"I saw you on the train that first day. You were on your mobile. Very" — he searched for the right word — "absorbed."

She was secretly pleased that Robert had noticed her before she'd even been aware of his existence, and couldn't help but acknowledge the difference to herself; of how she felt about this man watching her when she didn't know it, and Rafe doing it.

"Tell me about a fire," she said, wishing that Rafe didn't keep creeping into her thoughts. He's not here, she told herself. Don't let him spoil things when he's not even here.

"They're boring," he said.

"You don't think that. You know they're not."

"It's your turn to tell me something. Why do you love sewing?"

She blinked at him, surprised by the question. "It's not my turn."

"Just the first hundred reasons. I want to know." He had dimples. They deepened when he smiled.

"It's a family thing and I've caught it, I suppose. Or been brainwashed. My grandmother sewed absolutely everything. My mother is — she's so incredibly good, such a passionate seamstress — she used to teach it. She knits too. Have you noticed I have a lot of knitwear?"

He laughed. "You made that dress?"

It was blackberry-coloured jersey, very fluid. The square neckline was low enough for a hint of her breasts to be visible. The bodice clung softly, a gently stretched accordion of vertical gathers, vaguely Grecian. The long sleeves were closely fitted — the marks on her wrist hadn't quite disappeared yet. She felt her face grow warm. "I did."

"It's beautiful. It —" He stopped himself. "Why else?"

"It's good for the soul, my mother says." She laughed at herself. "But I think she's right. It matters, taking time over things, making something with your own hands, creating something you can touch. My mother brought me up not to take for granted the value of materials, and what mass production does to people. Some people I know, they think it's a waste of my talent."

"Anyone in particular?"

"This is a test, isn't it?" she said, gently avoiding his question — and the subject of Henry.

The train was pulling into Bath. They were slipping on their coats, standing, stepping onto the platform, saying goodbye for the night just outside the station.

She could see Rafe, standing in the shadows across the road, wanting her to notice him watching. She refused to let him stop her. She would show him his threats and his spying didn't matter. She would have her life. She would have a boyfriend, too, if she wanted one. What did it matter that Rafe knew who Robert was? It was no secret.

153

Robert was only a few feet away when she called out, "I won't forget, Robert."

"Forget what?"

"That it will be your turn, next time, to tell me something."

He promised yes with a serious nod and she walked away smiling, defiant in the face of Rafe, realising that she'd made Robert stop and look back.

Monday, 16 February, 6.45 p.m.

The two digits are flashing slower than the beat of my heart. After so many months of near blankness since Henry left I'm startled by the red number on the display of my answering machine.

Forty. There are forty messages. Only you could leave forty messages. All the people I know put together couldn't leave forty messages in one day.

I plunge my finger onto the button for the first message. Nothingness. Silence. I make myself listen to them all, surprising myself with a faint hope that there might be one from Rowena. But of course there isn't. Of course they're all from you; the caller ID draws blank on each one, which only confirms it. However shaky I feel, however short-lived my tiny victory over you at the station, I force myself to think calmly, logically.

I try to puzzle out how you got the number. You might have found some pretext for asking Rowena, but I think this would have sent her radar into alert mode. It's more likely that my old habit of putting phone bills in the recycling box is to blame, which means you've had that bill for at least a week and a half. I was scrupulously careful three days ago, when I sorted out what went into the recycling box and what I fed to my new shredder.

I am puzzled that you waited to use that number. I know I need to understand why this is. And then it comes to me. I see the control you can exercise, when you want to. You are carefully measuring the doses of what you are doing, plotting your attacks in some careful order that only you understand, making sure they come regularly.

I'll change my landline and set it to block all calls from hidden numbers.

I've been putting all of your things in the old wooden cupboard my father refurbished for me. That's where the answering machine, with its forty blank messages, will go too.

Proof is essential. Keep all evidence in a safe place.

Just as I reach for it, the phone rings. I let out a small scream and clamp my lips shut, furious that you've got to me again. But you've been watching. You know I'm home now; you know I'm listening to that ring. Another unknown caller, I can see on the handset display. I will not answer you.

Despite the sensation of being in a nightmare where I've been paralysed, I fall onto my knees. I tear the phone plug from the connection in the wall before the answering machine can pick up. I cut you off, not giving you the satisfaction of getting through this time; not letting you into my bedroom. I will never let you into my bedroom again.

Tuesday

Tuesday, 17 February, 8.05 a.m.

Don't you have anything better to do? Don't you get bored, and frozen, standing here morning after morning?

I don't say these things when I find you outside my front door yet again. I don't look at you. I make my way steadily towards the taxi.

"Your answering machine seems to be broken, Clarissa. Did you know that, Clarissa?"

If you say my name just one more time I might punch you. You open the taxi door for me as if you are being courteous and well-mannered. Small as I am, I quell my urge to give you a shove.

"I warned you to stay away from that fireman, Clarissa."

I reach for the handle to shut the door behind me, telling the driver that you aren't someone I want to share my journey with. He tells you to step away from his car.

"Certainly," you say to him politely, man to man, as if you are reasonable, though you are still gripping the door and you don't take your eyes off me. "I was just saying goodbye to my girlfriend. Did you know that when I miss you too much, Clarissa, I look at your photographs?" With that you release

156

the door. It slams hard, all at once. But it isn't the door's slam that is ringing in my ears. It is your parting shot.

A slim, white-haired, gentlemanly looking man was sitting behind the blue screen, very straight in his chair, when they filed into Court 12. Lottie's grandfather.

"The jury will see that on Sunday, July twenty-ninth, at three thirty in the afternoon, a call went from Carlotta Lockyer's mobile telephone to Mr John Lockyer's landline," said Mr Morden. "Do you recall the conversation, Mr Lockyer?"

"Carlotta asked me for fifteen hundred pounds. She sounded scared. Upset. Extremely distressed."

More external evidence that Lottie had been kidnapped. That she did not want to be where she was and in the company she was in.

Mr Lockyer bowed his neck and looked down at his hands. The gesture made Clarissa realise how old her own parents were, and that she must protect them from seeing her in pain or grief or fear.

Tuesday, 17 February, 12.50 p.m.

I assume that I'm safe, over lunchtime, wandering through the second-hand bookshops in the dusty halls behind the court district's central street. Surely your morning glimpse of me will be enough for the day. Even so, I am twisting my head all over the place, searching for you. I must look manic, as if I have some kind of nervous tic. I actually catch myself wondering where you are. This scares me even more: it makes me see that there is a danger of my becoming as fixated on

157

you as you are on me. That is what you want, in your constant mission to keep my attention. I have to stop that from happening.

For a few minutes, I succeed. As I approach the court building I'm thinking only of the new treasure in my hand, a precious volume of Anne Sexton's *Transformations*. The goblin creature peeping out of the dust jacket is covered by the stallholder's flowered paper bag, but its face stays with me. It's that wizened face, tender and disturbing, that I'm thinking about as I walk. I'm not thinking of you at all. But then I see you, standing just outside the revolving doors, and you are all I'm thinking of.

My vision is more acute. Everything is vivid. The sounds grow louder. A white prison van glides by; its exhaust fumes make the inside of my nose burn.

As if in slow motion, I see Robert, rounding the corner from the opposite end of the road. He's sixty feet away.

Passing you will be unavoidable. I make myself approach the revolving doors.

Robert is fifty feet away.

I am praying you will do nothing to make Robert notice you, do nothing to show there is any link between us.

Forty feet away.

Keeping as much distance between us as I can, I step past you. But I say quietly, without looking at you, "If you follow me, I'm telling the security guards."

Your voice is low but easily discernible. "I've seen you as no other man has, Clarissa," you say, and then I am through the doors.

Robert is out of my view, but I am blindly calculating the relationship between his speed and your position. Twenty feet away. Ten. The screech of a faraway horn makes me jump and look behind me. You walk on, in the opposite direction from Robert, never actually crossing his path.

Robert caught up to her in the foyer, smiling as they put their things onto the X-ray machine belt and chatted together to the guards who were now like old friends and could barely bring themselves to pass the wand over them, despite the stance of polite readiness they both took up after passing through the metal detector's arch. She acted as if everything was as normal as it could be, hoping Robert wouldn't notice that her face was too flushed and her breathing too fast.

Clarissa pressed the top of her mechanical pencil several times, to extract more lead.

Mr Morden was asking an old lady with white hair about something that had happened one hour before Lottie was kidnapped.

"Four men invaded my garden. One of them was kicking my kitchen door. Another shouted at the upstairs window that they'd seen my daughter Dorcas through her bedroom curtains and he knew she was there and could hear him and she'd better come out or they'd break in and get her and that would be worse for her. He said she should have learned that lesson already. He used nasty words."

"Can you repeat for the jury what the words were?"

"I don't use those words."

Mr Morden appeared suitably chastened but also faintly amused.

"One of them saw me with the phone in my hand, calling the police, and they ran off.

"That door hasn't closed properly ever since," she said.

The snow fell softly as Clarissa and Robert went through the revolving doors at the end of the day. There was no sign of Rafe.

"I wish I could fix that old lady's door for her," Robert said.

"You want to help people even when you're off duty."

"You're right about me. I saved a snail from a thrush last weekend. The thrush was dashing it against a stone to try to break its shell."

"Poor thrush," Clarissa said. "It was so clever, a tool user, and now it's probably starved to death."

"I'd do the same thing again." He nodded to confirm it.

But they both smiled, as if each of them liked the other for their difference.

They'd only got as far as the bridge when a voice interrupted. "Fireman. Hey. Fireman."

The voice sounded nothing like Rafe's, but she still caught her breath for an instant. She stood aside as a young man set himself in front of Robert. "You talked to my sixth form in December about road safety." The reminder had the air of a challenge.

160

"I remember you. You came and chatted to me after. Sharif, isn't it? Live with your grandmother." Robert planted his feet more firmly, looked at the boy in his direct way, and waited patiently. She was amazed that he could recall all of this a couple of months later, after one meeting, in what must have been a large room full of schoolkids.

"I thought about what you said, all those slides you showed. I'm still gonna drive fast."

"I'll cut you out alive or dead," Robert said.

Clarissa felt a chill, imagining Robert's hands, indifferent, wielding huge instruments, hacking through wrecked metal so the paramedics could get to the human meat tangled inside it.

"Makes no difference to me," Robert said.

Sharif bit his lip.

"Might make a difference to your grandmother though." Robert put out his hand. Sharif shook it. "Thanks for stopping me to chat again and letting me know about your plans."

Clarissa aimed a goodbye nod at Sharif, knowing he wouldn't return it, and she and Robert walked on. "Does it really make no difference to you, if they're alive or dead?"

"None at all."

"What if it were someone you knew?"

"Depends who."

She smiled but felt another chill. "What if it were me?"

"That would make a difference."

161

Tuesday, 17 February, 6.20 p.m.

A small rectangular package is propped against the door of my building, wrapped in brown paper and tied with string. My name is written by hand in carefully controlled calligraphy. But I know your writing in any guise. My heart pumps harder as I carry it up the stairs to my flat. I drop my bag, not bothering to take off my coat, and fall onto the sofa, pushing aside the string and stripping away the wrapping with shaking hands.

It is as I guess: a miniaturised book about the height and width of a typical postcard. You cut the pages to size by hand out of thick, expensive cream paper. You bound it by hand too, with heavy thread that you stitched tightly through the holes you cut. It is a beautiful thing. I would admire such an object if you hadn't made it.

A Collection of Four Fairy Tales, Selected by Rafe Solmes, the cover says, and below the title, *Limited Edition: Number 1 of 1*. There is a dedication: *For Clarissa, who is beautiful and likes wine*. I look at the Contents page. I know every one of these stories all too well. First comes "The Castle of Murder". Second comes "Blue Beard".

I open the book to the third of your sequence, "Fitcher's Bird", and see that you have underlined a passage.

There was once a wizard who used to take the form of a poor man, and went to houses and begged, and caught pretty girls. No one knew whither he carried them, for they were never seen more.

It is the story of sex crime and murder, repeated and patterned. He has his "type", too; his victim profile. The targets are young and beautiful, of course. Why else would he be interested in them? It is the story of lovely maidens who disappear mysteriously, as so many fairy tales are, and the titillating question of what happens to them after that blink of an eye when they vanish so completely out of their everyday lives. It is his pretence of vulnerability that allows him to capture them. It is their compassion for a seemingly poor man that makes them susceptible.

All of this, wrapped up in two sentences. The fairy tales set out the template and methods long before any infamous twentieth-century serial killer snatched his first victim.

The fake sling or pretend crutches. The practised sighs of embarrassment and bravely fought pain as he struggles to load the groceries or box of books into his windowless van. Playing on the woman's kindness and pity as she walks by. Playing on her romantic hopes, too, as she approaches the handsome stranger and offers to help. Perhaps she even wonders if the next moment will become a story for future children about how their parents met. Perhaps she even thinks of those other stories; the ones that promise good deeds will always be rewarded. He doubles the dose of charm, of course, and flashes that beautiful smile again just before he shoves her in, slams the door, and slaps the chloroform-soaked rag over her face.

I turn to the fourth and last of your stories, "The Robber Bridegroom", where you have again highlighted the passage you want me to notice above all.

They dragged with them another young girl. They were drunk, and paid no heed to her screams and lamentations. They gave her wine to drink, three glasses full, one glass of white wine, one glass of red, and a glass of yellow, and with this her heart burst in twain.

163

Thereupon they tore off her delicate raiment, laid her on a table, cut her beautiful body in pieces and strewed salt thereon.

A young woman is drugged, stripped, displayed upon a flat surface, and tortured. That is how the sequence goes. Her screams and pleas only make it more exciting; they show that she cannot close her eyes to the terrible new world she has fallen into. They make clear the kind of story it actually is. Sex crime disguised as fairy tale. Sex disguised as cannibalism. Sexual sadism disguised as meat preparation. Gang rape disguised as a band of robbers. That's how the Grimms got it past their censors, who were not careful readers. The burst heart is not literal. It is not a story of necrophilia. She is not dead before these things are done to her. She is distraught and aware and in terror as they are being done. That is what the burst heart means.

I know how you read these stories, and how you want me to read them. I see how you've linked me to the horrifying things these girls suffer, their dreadful fates, in your dedication.

I remember Mr Morden saying in his opening speech that what happened to Lottie was no fairy tale. But he was wrong. What happened to her was right out of the fairy tales.

Even before I ever set foot in that courtroom I'd known how important evidence was. My impulse, still, is to be rid of anything you've touched, not to have it poisoning the air around me. I want to minimise your presence — in my mind and in my flat. But it's not an impulse I can give into.

When it comes to the police, the leaflets are impossibly contradictory.

164

Call the police immediately — Don't call the police until you have irrefutable proof.
The police are there to help — Don't expect the police to be able to do very much.

When it comes to evidence, though, the advice is unanimous: I can't have too much; I can easily have too little.

I need more evidence — so much evidence the police cannot possibly doubt me or ignore me. So much evidence that they can never make me look as they've made Lottie look.

I pull open my father's beautiful cupboard. I shove your book and its wrappings towards the back, near your other things. I am careful to bury it all behind piles of stashed fabric. I slam the doors shut so hard I make myself jump. I wash my hands, not wanting a crumb of your DNA on my skin, transferred by touching what you have touched.

I swallow two tablets and climb into bed. *Transformations* is in my hands, but I only read a few pages before the knockout drops carry me away.

When I wake the next morning, the book is open on my chest. The words have seeped beneath my skin and into my blood. I cannot stop thinking of Sexton's "Briar Rose". Nothing can heal her from the things that were done while she was trapped in the dark. She is haunted into a terror of closing her eyes even after the prince's kiss rescues her from the nightmare of that hundred-year sleeping spell.

She wandered through the outside market. She didn't want to rush into the court building to hide before the day had even begun.

With Annie's commands about iron in mind, she bought some organic stewing steak. She'd make a casserole over the weekend, using her mother's recipe. She visited the vegetable woman for leeks and carrots and sprouts and parsnips and strong onions. She bought a bottle of red wine, too. She wasn't going to stop cooking with wine, or stop drinking it, because of that story. It was pale wine that she'd drunk that November night, and that she now had an unconquerable aversion to. But she needed to tell herself that red was safe. She needed to believe that. There still had to be some safe things.

She packed it all up in a tote that she'd sewn in less than an hour with a beautiful fabric in blocks of crayon-like charcoals and blues. The groceries would be fine in the locker all day. The market would be all but gone if she waited until after court to do her shopping and she didn't want to miss the chance of a walk with Robert that evening. She wouldn't let Rafe steal that from her.

He was stealing enough already. She paused for a minute to type furiously into her phone, answering an email from Caroline, a work friend who was secretary to the Vice Chancellor. Caroline had wondered if Clarissa wanted to meet for lunch on Saturday. Though Clarissa doubted that Rafe had much to do with Caroline, she couldn't risk it. So she sent a polite excuse, her expression of disappointment more genuine than Caroline could have guessed.

She slipped her phone back into her bag and looked up. A man with a football supporter's scarf around his neck was laughing with a stallholder. He handed over money, took his coffee, then sensed Clarissa's close observation and turned. Their eyes met; she saw recognition in his, though his face was impassive. A voice made her break Mr Morden's gaze.

"Good morning, Clarissa." Robert was standing beside her. "I made you jump. I'm sorry."

"No," she said. "No you didn't." She waved her nearly empty paper cup. "Too much coffee already, that's all." She didn't say that her need for coffee was growing in proportion to her increased use of sleeping pills.

"I had a dream about you last night." He added hastily, "Nothing bad. I can't remember it. Just that you were there."

"I hope the defendants weren't," she said.

"Definitely not." He smiled. "I think it must be all the time we spend together."

She nodded agreement. "I'm probably dreaming of you too," she said, "but forgetting by the time I wake up."

"That's for the best," he said, closing the subject.

"It was funny, running into that boy with you yesterday. He didn't know your name. Just 'Fireman, hey, fireman.' It made me see what a huge part of your identity that must be. Is it strange for you not to be that, while you're here?"

He laughed. "It's great."

They paused in front of the grand, mock-Renaissance building that now housed a bank but looked like it belonged in Venice.

"I was also thinking what an other world that fire station must be. But like a kind of second home to you, too."

"You don't get much sleep there, when you're on nights."

They rounded the corner, side by side, navigating themselves around the queue spilling out of the sandwich and coffee shop.

"When you sleep at the station, are you not sure where you are, when you wake?"

"I always know where I am."

She gazed at him as if he were a magician who'd told her of an extraordinary trick, and she didn't doubt he could do it. "Do you have a favourite place in it?"

"The drying room. It's where the dummies hang. They're full of sand, different weights. God, some of those bad boys are heavy. They get splashed and we have to save them."

"Do they swing slightly? The dummies? I imagine they do."

They were waiting for the custodial services vans to turn into the underground passage that led beneath the court building.

"The dummies are still. I like to read in there. It's peaceful."

"What do you read?"

He hesitated. "Poems."

"What poems?" She was deeply interested, and a little surprised.

"Keats especially. I like Keats."

Once, she'd noticed him holding a paperback thriller — an airport-type spy book with an image of an imperilled woman clinging to the gun-pointing hero. About as far away from Keats as it was possible to be. But she wasn't being fair to him. Rafe had made her too suspicious of people. She herself read thrillers as well as poetry, and it hardly made her a serial killer. Why shouldn't Robert read lots of different kinds of things too?

She thought of Henry. Henry did not like Romanticism. He thought poems should be about contemporary economic and social and political issues. Henry wrote about negative equity and polluted landscapes and butter mountains. He played clever word games. He impressed her, but she did not love his poems. They were ceaselessly ambitious, as he was.

"I love Keats too," she said. And then, "So it's a reading room as well as a drying room."

He grinned. "And a talking room. Firemen like to talk. You get a new boy — maybe it's his first death. You need to talk him through it."

169

"That's an important thing to do. One of those rare, difference-making things."

He shrugged it off. "The drying room's the warmest room in the station. We drink tea in there in winter. Sometimes I go there to be alone. Or I take one of the young pups in there, get him to practise knots. You need to be able to tie knots without looking, quickly, without thinking about it." He moved his hands decisively, as if the rope were between his fingers.

The vans had long since disappeared underground. They walked on again, both of them flushed. They were at the revolving doors, then through security and putting things into lockers and on their way up to Court 12. The fun was over.

When Clarissa sat down in the jury box Mr Morden studied her and Robert for a few seconds, then turned to his next witness. She was delicately boned and slight, with long black hair.

Three months before Lottie's kidnapping, when Clarissa was still weeping over the failure of IVF number three, Polly Horton had been heavily pregnant. If she'd run into Polly, her face serene and complacent over her bump, Clarissa would have had to look away.

Polly had been at the farmers' market when Thomas Godfrey approached her. "When I saw it was Godfrey I was so scared. Elias — my partner — owed them money. Godfrey said, 'You're coming with me to London.'"

"Did you want to go with that man to London?"

170

"I did not. Godfrey encircled me with his arm, to stop me moving away." She stretched her arm in a curve. "Like this."

Godfrey shook his head in ominous denial; he seemed to want to threaten her telepathically through the blue screen. Mr Harker turned and frowned at him.

"I started to cry. A man asked if I was okay. Godfrey said, 'Mind your own fucking business,' but he ran off. If that man hadn't intervened" — she wiped away a tear — "I'm sure Godfrey would have forced me to go with him."

What Clarissa heard above all else was that Polly went to the police but Godfrey was never interviewed, let alone charged. What she inferred above all else was that attempted kidnapping could not be proved; even with a witness. She was unsure whether Court 12 was educating her or paralysing her. Perhaps it was doing both.

Mr Harker stood to defend Godfrey. "Explain to the court, please, why you have a conviction for the possession of heroin and crack cocaine, for which you received a one-year suspended sentence."

"They weren't my drugs," Polly whispered. "I didn't want Elias to go to prison."

"You took the rap for your boyfriend. You will go to any lengths to protect him and try to deflect attention from his drug-related crimes. Including slandering an innocent man. Mr Godfrey had no motive to kidnap you. And it's hardly credible, is it, that he would attempt to do so at a crowded farmers' market in broad daylight?"

★ ★ ★

171

Annie and Clarissa were inspecting the cloakroom, making sure it was deserted.

Annie's words practically burst from her. "I hate obsessed women." Unusually, Annie had make-up on. She was wearing a blue pencil skirt and a low-cut black blouse that she'd hidden from the defendants beneath a cardigan she'd just removed and stuffed in her bag.

"You look so pretty, Annie," Clarissa said.

Annie lifted her shoulders and made a face and shook her head in dismissal of the compliment. "I'm thirty-five, Clarissa. I'm a boring accountant and I look like one."

"Accountants aren't boring. They know everyone's secrets. And accountants look as different from one another as anyone else. You're beautiful — and there's no one accountant look."

"My husband's new girlfriend is a twenty-five-year-old fitness instructor and she definitely looks like one." Annie puffed out a little snort of something that was almost a laugh. "He's too dazzled to notice that since he left our six-year-old's index finger is on a constant loop between her nose and her mouth, she scratches her bottom every five seconds, and she's started doing this jutting thing with her head that makes her look like a turkey."

"I did all that as a child. I grew out of it. Mostly." Annie managed a smile and Clarissa went on. "You'll help her through it. I know you will. You'll do whatever you have to do. And it sounds like a temporary thing, with a clear reason for why it's started happening. Not like there's anything medically wrong."

Annie nodded and gave Clarissa a gentle push towards one of the sinks. "Wash your hands. We have to stop meeting like this."

The two of them waved their hands about after they'd finished, not even bothering to try the always-broken driers, then walked out of the jurors' waiting area and down the stairs. No Robert, Clarissa saw. She wondered where he'd rushed to.

They paused outside the revolving doors. Clarissa glanced up the road with a mixture of hope that she'd see Robert after all and fear that she'd see Rafe. She saw neither, and her disappointment at Robert's absence was greater than her relief at Rafe's.

"I must run," Annie said. "My husband — or whatever it is I should call him — is delivering Lucy. They're meeting me at that burger place around the corner. Happy families."

Clarissa picked a piece of fluff from Annie's dark hair. "He'll see what he's missing."

Annie's eyes welled up. "Thank you." She gave Clarissa's arm a squeeze. "Funny duchess," she said fondly. And then she turned and hurried away. Clarissa waited until Annie was safely out of sight before she did too.

Wednesday, 18 February, 5.45 p.m.

At least you aren't waiting for me in person when I get home. But Miss Norton has left an envelope on the white shelf, reflected in the gold-framed mirror on the wall above it.

173

Inside, on a small cream card, you've written five words. *I dream of you, still.*

I try not to let myself imagine what you do to me in your dreams. I wonder how I got myself into them. Can I get myself out, if I make sense of how it happened? Is that the key? I want a spell to unwind time, to spool it back to the moment just before it all went wrong, so I can send it forward again in a better direction. The trouble is working out which instant was the crucial one.

But hindsight only shows me that I couldn't have stopped you. Nothing I could have done would have stopped you, however clearly I can see you coming when I look back.

Thursday

Thursday, 19 February, 8.13 a.m.

You are standing between the station's dark green double doors. If I want to go in I must pass within a foot of you. That's why you chose this position. I whirl around to try the other entrances, only to find they're both sealed.

You smirk when I return after a few seconds, watching me shrink myself as far away from you as I can as I walk in. I'm so close to the door frame I bash my funny bone against it. You follow me to the queue, right behind me. I want to behave as if you're a mere shadow I can't see or hear, but it's difficult when I'm rubbing my elbow to stop the weird numbness. Because of the risk of bumping you I have to suppress the urge to flap my arm up and down like a mad chicken.

You do not speak until I get to the ticket gate. That's when you move in. As I hurriedly feed my ticket through, counting the micro seconds for the turnstile to release, you whisper, "You look so pretty in your sleep, Clarissa." This is you in nice mode as opposed to angry mode. The ticket pops up, the turnstile snaps, and I push through.

You don't see me when my knees buckle in the tunnel. But I quickly pick myself up and stumble up the stairs and get

175

myself onto the train and fall into a seat, realising that my body is becoming unglued. You are ungluing it. Ungluing me. Piece by piece.

The man beside me is staring, and asks if I'm okay, and I don't think I can speak, so I gulp and make myself nod yes. He hesitates but turns back to his newspaper.

I have torn a stocking and it's sticking to my skinned knee, but it's only a minor scrape. The tips of my fingers are tingling, as if they are thawing after frostbite, but I know it's not the fault of the cold or my funny bone.

I consider phoning my doctor's secretary during lunch to see if she can get him to post me a prescription for anti-anxiety medication. But I decide against it, remembering how Lottie had taken anti-anxiety tablets. I'm already following her too closely down the sleeping-pill path. And I know that more drugs will not make you go away. The cliché about needing to treat the problem and not the symptom is completely true. I know that to neutralise my anxiety would be very foolish. That anxiety is warning me that there is danger; something I can't allow myself to ignore.

The day was a carnival of fear. One witness after another shot nervous looks at the blue screen as if to check it hadn't suddenly become transparent. Each and every shaking quaking wreck claimed that their heads had been so messed up with drugs they didn't remember saying or doing or seeing anything. Annie swore and muttered and nodded and hissed and looked as if she wanted to kill them all.

★ ★ ★

They were walking to the train station again, side by side but not touching. It was sleeting. Robert was holding an umbrella over both of their heads. Clarissa liked this very much and was working hard to seem coherent. More and more clearly, she saw that Robert was an unfailing Rafe-repellent: he wouldn't come near her when she was with Robert. She saw also that it hadn't been an accident that Rafe had left her alone until Henry left.

A car slowed alongside them. A stab of fear clutched her stomach. But the face peering at them was not Rafe's. Waves of relief went through her. Robert nodded in greeting and Mr Tourville returned the gesture before driving away.

"He *is* preposterous, isn't he, Robert?" she said. "It's not just me?"

"It's just you."

She considered the possibility with intense mock seriousness for a few seconds. Then she shook her head to confirm her confidence in him. "Do you think we'll be kicked off for walking together? We're sharing an umbrella. Mr Tourville might report us to the judge."

"Not against any rules I've found."

"Have you looked?"

"We can't be the only ones." His phone was ringing but he made no move to answer it.

"You're popular."

"I'll ignore this one."

"If your fingers are tired I can text for you again."

177

"How helpful you are. But I think Jack's had enough excitement lately."

"I hope he greeted you warmly when you got to the pub last week."

"A great smacking kiss, Clarissa. Our relationship will never be the same again. He calls me his beloved now and I owe it all to you."

"That's very sweet. I like to help along friendships whenever I can."

"You're too kind."

The sleet had stopped. She didn't know how long the windscreen wipers on the passing cars had been off. She only knew that she was sorry when he closed the umbrella.

Thursday, 19 February, 9.00 p.m.

I'm in my sewing room, hemming a skirt. I will wear it tomorrow with boots and a clingy black cashmere sweater. It is brown and mock-suede, slightly A-line, above the knee. It fastens with silver buttons up the centre. I am secretly hoping Robert will like it — I've caught his eyes flicking over me before, when he thought I wasn't looking.

Just as I finish, the smoke detector starts to scream and I rush into the kitchen. The lentil soup I set to cook has boiled away to thick, inedible sludge. I do this kind of thing a lot. I switch off the gas and snap on the extractor fan to clear the smoke.

I climb onto a chair so I can reach the smoke detector's red button. I push it in with a satisfying plunge. Even in the new silence my eardrums continue to vibrate.

On the countertop are the letters I grabbed before coming up to the flat. I'd tossed them there, nervously, putting off examining them until I'd finished my skirt.

There is nothing remarkable about the envelope I find in the middle of the pile, but I know it's from you as soon as I see it. I have a kind of instinct for it now. I pull out the white sheet of paper, unfold it, and read.

You know the *Arabian Nights*, Clarissa. You know what King Shahryar did to his first wife, for being faithless, and to her lover. You know what he did to the ones who followed her, after he'd enjoyed the wedding night, Clarissa, to make sure they had no chance to betray him.

My chest squeezes and I wonder briefly if this is a heart attack. My legs become things that will not hold my weight. I crumple onto the charcoal blue slate. I'm not sure how long I stay there, sobbing into my own lap, trying to replay my own life. How many snapshots have you stolen from it? Watching when I know. Watching when I don't know.

And to her lover.

Even though Robert isn't my lover, you imagine that I would like him to be, and you want me to know that you are watching him too. I'm furious with myself for letting this happen to him. I can't pretend any more that Robert is too big and strong for you to hurt.

I begin to stand, curling my fingers around the top of the oven to heave myself up. My left hand presses hard against the cast-iron saucepan, still fire-hot. I cry out, staggering to the sink and plunging my skin beneath a stream of icy water. Already, inch-long, angry red strips are visible on my ring and middle fingers. I blow out little puffs of air, like a woman in labour.

I abandon the kitchen mess, leaving the letter where I dropped it. I will stuff it in the back of the living-room cupboard with your other things later.

I wrap my fingers in a dripping-wet washcloth. They are throbbing fiercely. I swallow some painkillers with sleeping medication added to them that I bought when Henry took me to New York two years ago. The pain dissolves the tight locks I normally keep on all memories of how happy he'd made me then, so that my heart is burning too.

You have done this. It is your fault. As if you'd taken an iron and pressed it into my fingers yourself.

Friday

Friday, 20 February, 8.03 a.m.

As I walk from my front door to the taxi I see that the black rubbish bag I left outside is gone and my recycling box is empty, though all the others on my street are untouched. It doesn't matter. You will find nothing of interest in any of it.

You are positioned in front of the station when the taxi drops me off. You watch me as though I'm a scientific experiment whose reaction you are awaiting.

Wordlessly, you follow me in, making me catch my breath and shake and feel my face redden as I try to act like you aren't here. Would you be pleased to know the bandages on my fingers are because of you? I do not tell you. I do not look at you.

I drop my season ticket wallet as I hold it clumsily in my bad left hand while attempting to extract the ticket with my right. I bend to pick it up, my face reddening more as the queue builds behind me. At last, I manage to feed my card through the ticket gate. All the time your eyes are on me. I can feel them. Serious and intent and only on me. This time, you feed your own ticket through and follow. You walk through the tunnel beside me.

There is a rushing in my ears. Although I can see their mouths moving, the voices of the people around me sound as if they are coming from far away. It is like being in a surrealist film.

"What happened to your hand, Clarissa?"

Or a bizarre children's cartoon. People look so large, zooming towards me and swerving out of my path just in the nick of time.

"Would you like some company on the train, Clarissa?"

The tunnel is growing darker. I blink my eyes rapidly, hard, trying to squeeze away the mist that seems to be gathering.

"Been reading any good fairy tales lately, Clarissa?"

My breathing is heavy and fast.

"Few people understand them as well as we do, Clarissa."

I can't get enough air.

"Clarissa? Clarissa. Clarissa." Your face is above mine, your tongue darting out to lick your lips, quickly, like a reptile. "I have the missing piece, Clarissa." Your hands are under my arms. I am slipping to the ground.

I open my eyes. The tunnel is very bright. I am lying on my left side. The chill of the concrete beneath the slushy tiles is seeping through my clothes and into my skin. My head is resting on a strange coat.

A railway guard and a plump, middle-aged woman are crouched beside me. The woman is tugging at my skirt. I nearly swat her hands away but that's when I see how exposed I am. The skirt's ridden up so much that the flesh above my stockings is showing. She's trying to cover me.

People slow to stare as they walk by: I am the car crash.

182

I struggle up, first sitting, then getting to my feet and leaning against one of the huge framed advertising posters, lit up on the tunnel wall. It is for the *Cinderella* I refused to meet you at. I am searching the tunnel but I don't see you anywhere. The guard and the woman are telling me I fainted and it should be investigated; they want to call an ambulance or at least put me in a taxi home.

The woman picks up her coat and I see the damp splashes of trampled, soiled snow that have stained it. I apologise, thanking her again for her kindness, offering money for dry-cleaning, but she refuses.

"A man caught you," she says. "You'd have fallen hard and hurt yourself if it hadn't been for him. He was so careful and gentle with you, before he had to run for his train."

You made yourself look like a hero, a rescuer. The thought makes me lean more heavily against the poster. My knees are weak again. I fear I'm going to slide down the tunnel wall, bump bump bump with my back along it, and land in a little heap. If ever you need witnesses, they'll testify that you're a chivalrous knight.

The guard hands me my newly made bag and I loop it over my shoulder, promising that I'm fine now, really fine, and much better for their care, but I have to get to Bristol. Greying and gentlemanly, he insists on seeing me up to the platform and onto the train.

She was sitting with Robert at one of the horrible plastic tables. She kept her bandaged hand in her lap and out of his line of vision. The burnt skin was pulling. Already her fingers were covered in blisters. At least it wasn't her writing hand and wouldn't affect her note-taking. She'd swallowed three ibuprofen on an empty stomach before leaving her flat, imagining her mother frowning at her for overdosing. That might have contributed to the fainting. At least the drugs were working and her head wasn't pounding any more.

It was small, the injury to her fingers. It was nothing compared to the things Robert must see every day. Yet everything about her felt raw, like her skin. She thought she probably looked normal, but feared she might, mortifyingly, start to cry.

Robert squinted slightly. "You look sad."

She wanted to form a smile to deny this, but only managed to bite her lip; another twinge of guilt for bringing him to Rafe's notice but not having the courage to tell him. What sane man would want to be involved with her when she was in such a mess? And to tell Robert would presume a degree of closeness, even of obligation between them, that she wasn't confident of. It was way too much to lay on him.

But she knew it wasn't fair to do nothing. She tried again to think about how she could warn him to be alert. Subtlety completely failed her; she just blurted it out: "You can defend yourself, can't you?"

"I'm six foot three. I boxed and fenced every weekend when I was a boy, and I coach kids in both. You don't need to worry about me."

"I can see that," she said.

"I once had to knock a guy out who tried to stop us going in to save his wife."

She managed to laugh, but only feebly. "Did you save her?"

184

"Yep. Not a mark on her. But he had a black eye."

She managed to smile, but only briefly. "I was thinking about how hard it must be. The not-being-able-to-save-people part of it. Having to see them suffer. Maybe being able to live with that is the bravest thing of all."

"You get used to it. No bravery involved."

"There's something," she said, "that I was wondering about."

"You're not going to ask me to introduce you to Jack, are you?"

"It's a little soon. Maybe in a week or two."

"Very wise." He was soon serious again. "What were you wondering about?"

"Is it very hard," she asked, "when a child dies?"

"It's just another body, Clarissa." He reached over the table, gently touched her arm. "I'm sorry. I can see that I've shocked you. Yes, in some ways it's worse when it's a child — I was wrong to think the lie would be easier for you than the truth. But you're fragile today, aren't you?"

"Maybe a little."

"Each death is sad in its own way. The deaths we see aren't necessary. They're premature. But I forget sometimes how it seems to others. You get hardened to all the death. You have to, to keep doing it. Most of us, we don't talk about it except to other firefighters, so I'm not practised at that. I'm not careful enough, around you, of how I talk."

She smoothed down her skirt before entering the courtroom. The skin on her fingers felt as if it would pop as she stretched them.

The blue screen was glaringly absent. They'd never had a witness who hadn't hidden behind it. The door opened. In lumbered a man with a barrel for a chest and arms the size of tree trunks. His fair blond head was bowed. Beside him was a prison guard.

"I'm not happy to be here. I'm in prison. There could be" — Charlie Barton paused to let the word sink in — "repercussions. I'm only here in the name of justice, to talk about the rape. What happened to that poor girl was terrible. I liked that girl."

Mr Morden nodded in seeming admiration of this rare example of gallantry. "You're visibly a strong, large man, and I say that with true respect. Yet Mr Azarola beat you up?"

"Yes. I was scared of him. I ran away."

"I have no further questions."

"But I'm here to help the girl. I don't see how this can help the girl. You haven't asked me anything about the girl."

It was almost twenty to five. Clarissa wanted to speed-walk out of court to try to catch the five o'clock train. Her fingers were burning horribly, so taut and hot she thought the skin would split even without moving them. She wanted to swallow more of Henry's tranquillising painkillers and get straight into bed and lose herself in sleep. His hands had been on her that morning. She couldn't let herself faint again, let herself be unguarded and helpless and in his power, even for a second. But unconsciousness at night was safe, and she needed a powerful dose of oblivion.

186

She hurried to collect her things and walked out of the jurors' area with Wendy, wondering if Robert was already ahead, running for the train. And Rafe. Would he show himself again, wanting her to see, enjoying her reactions as he had this morning? Or would he be lurking in the shadows, all along the journey home? What were the places he could hide?

She realised she was beginning to live with the daily fact of his doing these things, as if she accepted that she had to fit him into her life as discreetly as possible. So much of her concentration went on minimising his effects on everything else and above all on keeping him away from Robert. She mustn't accept it, she thought, angry with herself. She must think about how to fight him more effectively.

At the bottom of the stairs was the giant witness, surrounded by seemingly tiny prison guards, his wrists in cuffs before him. He looked respectfully at Clarissa and Wendy and she fantasised Barton beating the crap out of Rafe. In grave recognition of the two of them, Barton bowed his head slightly before disappearing through a door she hadn't noticed before, his little guards in tow.

Friday, 20 February, 5.40 p.m.

You see that there is no Robert with me. That must be why you decide to do it when you do. Just past the bridge, in the midst of the hurrying businessmen, you bump into me so hard I can't help but look at you.

"Aren't you going to thank me for catching you, Clarissa?"

187

"Your hair smelled lovely this morning, Clarissa."

"Your cheek is so soft, like the rest of you, Clarissa."

"Remember how I said you looked so pretty when you're asleep, Clarissa?" You briskly overtake me, hold a gloved hand high above your head, and let a photograph flutter onto the pavement behind you.

It lands face up. You turn to watch as I kneel to try to grab it. My hands are shaking so much I drop it twice and have to scrabble around for it on the filthy pavement with my clumsy fingers before I can get it out of sight. Satisfied, you smile and walk on.

In all of my fearful imaginings of what you might have done to me that night, I never saw this coming. I never let myself envision this.

Even hidden away in my bag the image blazes in front of my eyes as if it were blown up on a large screen. Lying on my back, asleep in my own bed, my body stretched into a straight line. I am wearing a pair of lavender bikini underwear. That is all I have on. My stockings and bra are dropped next to me. My arms are extended above my head, my fingertips grazing the bedstead. My eyes are closed.

I realise that I haven't seen the underwear since your night in my flat. There's no doubt that that's when you took the picture. And a sick fear in the pit of my stomach makes me sure you didn't stop at one.

It had been a week since she first tried and she had to attempt it again. As soon as she got home she dialled James Betterton's number.

This time a woman answered.

Clarissa attempted to sound natural, as if the call were nothing out of the ordinary. "Hello, is Laura there?"

The woman drew in her breath. She spoke as if she'd been trying to keep the words in but couldn't help herself. "Do you have news?"

"I don't. I'm sorry. I'm trying to find —"

"Don't bother us again." The woman ended the call.

Clarissa held the phone for several seconds, listening to the dead dial tone, her heart bang bang banging in her chest. Rafe's allusions to fairy tales were all mixed up with her fears for Laura Betterton. She wanted to dismiss herself as mad. That was preferable to being right. But she was growing more certain by the minute that his references to those stories were no mere threats, no teasing hints of his fantasies, but clues about what he'd already done.

She envisioned the chopped-up bodies of the young women in "The Robber Bridegroom". The sorcerer's basin of dead girls in "Fitcher's Bird". The torture devices and gore-soaked floor of Bluebeard's secret room. King Shahryar's series of punished queens; each of them knew on her wedding night that by morning she'd feel the blade of a sword on her neck in place of his lips.

Rafe's house was remote, in a village outside of Bath. Did he have his own bloody chamber filled with corpses? A burial ground in his garden? A bathtub filled with acid?

Her imagination was too lurid, she tried to tell herself. It was the drugs she'd swallowed for her

189

fingers, and the nagging pain, and irrational fear, and the ugliness of the trial. More than anything it was the mortifying image he'd given her of herself.

Two hours later she was drifting into sleep on the living-room sofa, having decided she would have to buy a new bed because she couldn't sleep where he'd stolen that image of her. Her nightdress — old fashioned and girlish and comforting and made by her mother — had ridden up. She tugged down the soft, pale blue cotton with her good hand. She tucked the blankets she'd dragged in more snugly around her shoulders. She was trying to excise the photograph from her head but it seemed to be painted on the insides of her closed eyelids. The photograph wasn't evidence against him. It was evidence against her. Evidence that she had invited him in. Evidence of intimacy — or at least an illusion of it — that he knew she wouldn't want anybody else to see.

Week 4

The Potion of Forgetfulness

Monday

Monday, 23 February, 8.00 a.m.

It is your usual routine. You are outside my house, though you stand in the centre of the grass near Miss Norton's bare apple tree instead of the path. I am walking quickly to the taxi.

"You've lost my respect, Clarissa," you say, from several feet away.

I look straight ahead.

"I warned you, Clarissa. I warned you several times. But you haven't stopped. You've brought it on yourself."

You still don't try to get close to me. You do not move from your spot. Calmly, you watch as the taxi drives away.

Will you blow the photograph into a poster and display it somewhere public, somewhere Robert will see it? You know where my parents live. Will you send it to them?

When I think of my parents my stomach does a flip and my heart hammers even harder, but I know they are safe from you, at least physically. I know you won't bother them in Brighton. Brighton is too far away from me. Brighton is where they must stay. Brighton is where, at least for now, I cannot go.

★   ★   ★

She was glad when the door to the jury assembly room snapped shut behind her. She hadn't cooked her mother's beef casserole that weekend, or touched that red wine, despite not having left her flat a single time. She hadn't even looked out her windows, in dread of seeing him there.

She knew she couldn't let herself spend all of her weekends locked in. Had Laura locked herself away somewhere? That was more likely than the Gothic film of chopped-up bodies she'd been playing in her own head.

Something Lottie had said kept haunting her. *I thought if I ignored it, tried to avoid him, it would disappear.* Clarissa understood the desire to believe that, but knew she couldn't afford to.

She had rejected him, and that could be a trigger. Evidently, Laura had too. Rejection was probably the key to it all. Nobody liked rejection, but the vast majority of people found ways to cope with it and didn't put themselves in a position where they'd have to face rejection multiple times a day. She'd only ever thought of him as sadistic, but it occurred to her that he was masochistic too. She pictured him coatless and half-frozen, and wondered if he made himself suffer in that way so he'd have another thing to blame her for.

But as she puzzled over it, she realised that she might learn something useful if she tried to view him as tormented; if she tried to see his behaviour as the product of a severe illness or wound. If he felt spurned, again and again spurned, then he must feel powerless;

he was trying to assert sadistic power over her in the face of what he saw as repeated, cruel rejection. All she ever said to him — whether through words or actions or freezing him out — was no; it was all she could say; the power of veto was her only power; and with each no, his actions became more punishing and dangerous. Not just to her: to him, too.

But it didn't work; she couldn't sustain her effort to see him as a damaged and anguished human being who ought to be understood; she was actually glad that he was beyond her comprehension; she hated giving him any more space in her head than the space he was already stealing. Her parents had brought her up not to believe in evil, but she wasn't sure they were right. They had brought her up to believe that everyone deserved forgiveness, but she wasn't capable of feeling that he did. They had brought her up to acknowledge other people's points of view, however difficult it might be; maybe there was someone on the planet who could acknowledge his, but it was impossible for her to be that person. He was her enemy, pure and simple. As if to remind her of this, the burning in her fingers deepened for a few seconds.

She'd come across so many definitions and pieces of advice she could hardly keep it straight. But she hadn't found what she was looking for; the thing that might have made her feel less alone: none of them admitted that the victim of a stalker might be reluctant to come forward because of what it revealed about her own past behaviour.

It's your fault, they'd said to Lottie in too many ways to count. Is that what they would say to Clarissa too? That she had no right to complain, because she'd had consensual sex with him, and slept beside him all night, after? That's what that photo appeared to show. And that she'd been too drunk to remember.

She felt sick at the idea of Robert ever knowing. Each time she told herself it wasn't fair to keep it from him she buried the thought.

When the usher called them to line up she was still replaying it all and trying to work out what to do. She couldn't bear for anyone to see that photograph. But if she went to the police and didn't show it, and then he produced it to defend himself, that would make her look bad; it would make her look not credible.

The blue screen was back for the next witness. Alex Wyerley kissed the Bible after taking the oath. But before Mr Morden could even begin his questions Mr Williams was standing to object and the jury was filing out the door once again.

A few minutes later, the twelve jurors were arranged in a misshapen oval, sipping coffees around three shaky tables that they'd moved close together in the jurors' waiting area. The legal argument would take half an hour, their usher had said.

Clarissa winced as she curled her left hand over her right, out of habit, around the white mug.

"Let me see."

It wasn't until Robert spoke that she realised she'd forgotten to hide her fingers. She stretched out her arm, smiling apologetically at Wendy, who was sitting between them, and rested it on the table nearer to Robert. "It's not that bad," she said. "Just a bit tight when I move them."

Wendy lightly touched Clarissa's shoulder. "Poor you."

Robert carefully lifted her hand from the table to examine it. "When did you do it?"

She pretended to consider for a few seconds. "Three or four days ago. Thursday night, I think."

"How?" He still held her hand, but was looking acutely at her face.

"Clumsy. I knocked them against a hot saucepan."

"That's gotta hurt like hell when you shower," one of the men said.

Robert gently put her hand back on the table. "You don't strike me as clumsy about anything."

"I can be." She laughed, and it sounded fake in her own ears.

"They say — what is it — if it's more than two inches you need to see a doctor. You're close to that."

"There's an NHS Walk-in Centre one street over," Wendy said. "You should go during lunch. Let them have a look."

She was in too much pain to concentrate, but she forced herself to pay attention when Mr Belford rose to defend Tomlinson. He peered in his intent way at Alex Wyerley. "How would you describe your relationship with Carlotta Lockyer?"

"Friends. We were both part of the Bath drug scene. I'm clean now, praise God."

"Have you slept with her?"

"None of your business," said Wyerley.

"I appreciate that you are a gentleman," the judge said, "but you must answer."

Wyerley slowly inhaled, then let out his breath. "I slept with her, yes," he said.

"Who's on trial here?" Annie whispered. "Miss Lockyer or those men in the dock?"

On the way to the station that night, Clarissa and Robert paused on the bridge. The skin on the back of her neck prickled but she decided not to think about it, not to look for Rafe, just to enjoy being with her fireman.

Her fireman, she thought, smiling to herself. She couldn't give him up. She wouldn't let Rafe take this from her. She had to believe that Rafe presented as little danger to Robert as a pigeon to an eagle.

Robert used to box: he would knock Rafe flat like he'd knocked out the man who'd tried to stop him from saving his wife. Robert ran every morning: he had endurance. Robert knew how to fence: he was observant and strong and tactical; his reaction time would be quick; he would stop a weapon hitting him, and he would use one with perfect aim. Robert was left-handed: Rafe wouldn't anticipate a strike coming. Robert was several inches taller than Rafe, and much leaner. Robert was level-headed and sane, two things Rafe certainly wasn't.

Robert looked approvingly at the new dressings on her fingers.

"You were right," she said, displaying her left hand. "They popped this morning. Everything you said about burns, that's what the nurse said too."

He wouldn't acknowledge his own rightness. "They hurt, don't they?" He looked seriously at her, so that she had to admit with a slight nod that they did. He caught her eye fleetingly and smiled. "Lottie has a lot of friends, doesn't she?" he said.

"She does. She really does. She's a busy girl."

They both laughed.

"I like her," Clarissa said. She could hear gulls above them.

"So does Mr Wyerley," Robert said. "And Mr Barton."

Clarissa wondered if there was an official rule that jurors shouldn't sleep with each other. "I'll be sorry." Her words were nearly lost in the wind, she spoke so softly, watching a swan glide along the water below. But she knew he'd pick them up.

"Sorry?" he repeated.

"It's been lovely getting to know you." She could feel him looking hard at her. "I'll be sad not to see you any more, when this finishes."

"It's not looking like this will be over any time soon," he said.

Monday, 23 February, 6.15 p.m.

You're sitting in your unremarkable blue car, waiting for me. I am sick to death of finding you on my street. I fumble for pound coins and drop them into the taxi driver's hands.

I consider that it's a lucky thing I don't have a car of my own. You'd probably hide a tracking device on it. It would be another place to ambush me.

I lean forward on the seat of the taxi, wondering if I should ask the driver to wait until I'm safely inside. Impatient to pick up his next fare, he is muttering into his hissing communication system, an exception to my mother's belief that all taxi drivers see themselves as bodyguards.

"All right?" he asks. Hint hint. Let's get a move on.

I unzip my anti-stalker bag — getting things ready. "Just give me a second." I don't need the taxi driver to wait and protect me. There is something better I can do to protect myself. To fight you.

I grab my new phone from the special compartment I made for it. I set it to camera. I've been practising doing it quickly, just in case. I've been reading up on things I can do, remembering that Lottie had struggled with her phone in her pocket, failing in her attempt to sneak an SOS text to her boyfriend. The instant I shut the door the taxi speeds away.

You've parked two houses up from mine. The nose of your car is pointed towards me as you watch me standing in the middle of the quiet road. You nod slowly. At least you aren't getting out and dropping more horrible photographs onto the pavement. You just want me to know you're here, sitting and observing. Because you can.

I think of Lottie coming up her own road and finding that van. Lottie was one against four. My odds are better. One against one. Me against you.

My hand is curled around the phone and I'm zooming in without even needing to look, just as I'd rehearsed. My street is well lit. The phone has an automatic flash. You aren't the only one who can take photos.

Not feeling my burnt fingers, I lift my arm and point.

Click: your car in my street. I zoom in more. Click: closer, your number plate, just readable. And then I zoom in as far as I can. Click: still closer, your face. It may not come out through the glass, but it's worth trying.

Three photos, taken so quickly it has to come as a surprise to you; so that your recognition of what I've done, and your reaction to it, cannot help but be delayed.

You open your door to come after me. This wasn't part of your original plan for tonight. I'm running already, though I cannot help but turn to check quickly that there is still enough distance between us. But you're large, not a man who can leap from a car with agility. I glimpse your thin mouth, twisted in rage, and I speed up, flying along the path to my house so fast I know you can't catch me. My keys are out and ready — another useful pocket in my bag — I'd been thinking strategically when I designed it. By the time the metal slides into the lock and the heavy wood pushes forward I know you've given up. For once, I'm in a nightmare where everything is going right.

I'm not sure how long I lean against the door, waiting for my breathing to slow down. Long enough for Miss Norton to emerge from her flat.

"I'm so happy to run into you, Clarissa," she says. "It's good to see some pink in your cheeks for a change," she says. "Will you join me for a cup of tea?" she says.

A cup of tea is just what I need. And Miss Norton's sweet, sharp company.

"I'd love that, Miss Norton." She looks so pleased I feel a stab of guilt that I don't accept her invitations more often and extend more of my own. As I follow her in, I grab my latest sewing magazine from the shelf, where she has left it for me.

Miss Norton motions for me to sit on her chintzy sofa. It is draped in lace antimacassars, once cream, now dyed tan by time. "Just relax and rest, dear," she commands. "Read your magazine. Let me look after you for a while. You deserve it for what you're doing. It must be very exhausting and upsetting." She toddles off to the kitchen.

I smile to myself as I gaze around Miss Norton's living room. All of her furniture is dark wood, and heavy, and belonged to her parents, who used to own the whole building before Miss Norton sold it into flats; Miss Norton was born in this house.

I turn my attention to my sewing magazine. I open the envelope, thinking how welcome it will be to wash away the last few minutes, to push you entirely out of my head. But you will never let that happen, will you?

I exhale as if you've punched me hard in the stomach. The blonde cover model is not wearing a new spring dress pattern.

She is wearing belts and chains and wires that circle her arms and legs and torso and hips. She is bound tightly to some kind of specially modified operating table with adjustable limb extensions. Plenty of pale skin is still exposed. Her spread legs are bent at the knees, her ankles elevated. Every part of her is immobilised. Even her hands and feet and fingers and toes are held in place by some kind of surgical tape. Her nipples are pierced with metal hoops, her breasts squeezed by a criss-cross of ropes. A leather gag wraps her mouth. A man's muscled arm, ending in a leather gloved hand, clasps a shining instrument. The owner of that arm is off camera. The woman's neck and forehead are attached to the table too, by dog collars, so she cannot turn her head, but her wide eyes are aimed pleadingly to the side, at the invisible man.

"You like your tea weak with no milk, don't you, Clarissa dear?" Miss Norton calls.

Is the pose really just modelled? I try to tell myself it must be. This cannot really be a captured woman. That table cannot really be real. But her terror looks entirely real to me.

This is what you like to see.

"Clarissa?" Miss Norton calls again. "Is that right?"

"Yes, Miss Norton," I manage to say, not knowing what I'm agreeing to.

The article titles are jumping out at me.

Shivering Slave Girl Confesses: Fear Makes Me Wet.

This is what you like to read.

"Biscuits?" asks Miss Norton.

Straightjacket Seduction: Keep Her Helpless.

This is what you like to do.

I think of my arms pinned behind my back in the park. Your hand squeezing my neck, holding me in place. The dreadful things I had to let you say, as if I yearned to hear them, and how you loved my responses — all those yeses — as your glove moved over me. Yes, yes, yes.

"I baked them this morning," Miss Norton says. "I'd so hoped to run into you. I wanted you to have a treat. And you were so kind to buy me those wonderful chocolates. You chose all my favourites."

Enema Ecstasy and Home Operations.

"Clarissa? Did you hear me?"

Realms of Torture: Inside Our Readers' Forbidden Rooms.

Do you have such a room?

"That sounds lovely, Miss Norton," I somehow say.

"I'm glad to hear it, Clarissa. You're much too thin, dear."

Bound Beauties Stretched and Plugged to the Limit.

Again I think of that November night. And the marks on my body the next morning.

That photo. Should I actually be grateful it is nothing like what this magazine must contain?

"Clarissa?" Miss Norton appears in the doorway.

In a panic, I shove the magazine back into the envelope, struggling with my stiff fingers, still swaddled in the NHS bandages, so that I tear the thick brown paper.

I've looked at it long enough. Even with the magazine out of sight the other article titles are popping in my head. The titles are absurdly bad. Annie would laugh at them in disdain. She would tell me it's all one bad fake. She would smack you, hard, across your horrible face. But I can't laugh. It isn't funny. You don't mean anything about this to be funny. The magazine's cover photo is the most frightening and ugly and grotesque thing I've ever seen.

Tied Twist: Rough Roped and Ridden Raw.

I hurry across the room to take the beautiful old china plate from Miss Norton. It is yellowing and cracked with age. The biscuits are golden. "They look delicious," I say, though nothing in the world could look delicious to me right now. I try to set the plate onto the coffee table gently, but my fingers don't seem able to grip properly and it crashes onto the wood. I'm astonished that I haven't shattered it.

Animal Positions: Restraints for the Farmyard.

"Will you help me with the tea tray?" Miss Norton calls, oblivious to my spectacular clumsiness. It is a lucky thing that Miss Norton's usually infallible ability to notice absolutely everything is entirely derailed by the all-consuming attention she gives to her role as hostess.

I lurch into the kitchen, which is a pristine 1970s time warp of brown and tan.

Painful Pleasures to Keep Her Captive: Picture Perfect Punishment.

I'll punish you for this. That was what you said in the park. Is this what you meant?

"I can't find my tea strainer, dear," Miss Norton says.

I rummage blindly in Miss Norton's overcrowded drawers.

Obedience School: Lock Me Down and Whip Me Hard.

I think of your theory about why Bluebeard murdered his first wife. *The worst form of disobedience*, you said. I remember the alarm bells going off when you used that word. *Disobedience.* Even as your wine made its way through my veins I could still see what an ugly part of your vocabulary it was; an ugly part of your outlook on what men and women could be to each other.

You need to do what I tell you. You said that in the park, too.

The terrible titles may differ, but they all come down to the same thing.

"What's wrong with you, Clarissa?" Miss Norton laughs fondly. "It's right by your hand." She takes the tea strainer and places it beside her dainty rose-covered cups and teapot. Steam curls from the spout and I nearly burn my other fingers as I take the tray, then stagger into the living room and set it on the table, china clattering.

205

Fill Every Hole: Lessons She Won't Forget.

"Sit down, Clarissa," Miss Norton says.

I sit down.

Taboo Tortures and Training Torments She Can't Possibly Resist.

"Take a biscuit, Clarissa."

I pick up a biscuit, bite off a tiny piece, and try to chew. I think I may choke. I force myself to swallow and when Miss Norton concentrates on pouring the tea I slip the remainder of the biscuit in my bag.

Workout Equipment for All Parts: Forcing Her into the Shapes and Sizes You Crave.

Miss Norton chatters happily, excited to have me in her territory, but I am hardly taking it in. "It is so lovely, having you here. You must visit me more often, Clarissa," she says, and I promise that I will.

My hands are shaking. As I pick up my cup, I spill tea over Miss Norton's antique green carpet. I rise to get a towel, apologising, but my balance is off and I knock into the coffee table hard, bruising the bony front of my shin and letting out a cry as I slosh more tea onto her rosy Axminster flowers. Miss Norton waves me down, telling me not to worry; she can see how tired I am and anybody would be reeling at the end of a gruesome day in a criminal courtroom; she'll go herself; I must rest and not even think about moving.

Shamed Slave Suspended and Flogged in Dungeon of Discipline.

While Miss Norton is out of the room I examine the envelope. There is no subscription company name or other identifying detail. There is a stamp. There is a sticky label typed with my name and address. That is all. Did you buy it

206

from the back room of a sex shop, where only their special customers are invited? Order it online from a website that can't be found through any normal search engine? Maybe you belong to a secret club of men with access to such things. The worst possibility of all is that you made it yourself. But there must be a chance that the police will be able to find out who sent it and somehow trace it to you.

Quickly, I look again at the front of the magazine itself.

No glossy airbrush has been used on the cover model; there was nobody to ask any awkward post-production questions. Her mascara is smeared by what look like real tears; they didn't hire a make-up artist who could be a witness to what they were recording. Could it be Laura Betterton? The lighting is poor, as if the whole thing was set up in somebody's sound-proofed and windowless garage; they didn't use a studio where the model could be seen entering, and could then freely exit.

I put your magazine away for the second and last time, knowing that I will never take it out of the brown envelope again. There is something about its amateurishness that makes it more sinister and real. Something that makes me ask again how clear the line is between actuality and pose. I cannot stop wondering who the woman is on the front of the March issue, and how she came to be photographed like that, and who could think up such things, and where she is now. I do not wonder if you have done such things yourself. I am certain that you have.

Tuesday

The witness was slumped in her chair, eyes half closed. Dorcas Wykes. The one whose little old lady mother didn't say bad words. Dorcas wasn't hiding behind her bedroom curtains any more; a prison guard sat close by.

Clarissa realised that she was slumped too, and made herself sit up straighter.

"I know it was almost two years ago, but I need to talk about something very upsetting that happened to you then." Mr Morden spoke gently. Dorcas glared at him.

"Do you recall travelling by car from Bath to London on Saturday, May fifth?" Mr Morden asked. "You were driven there by people you know."

Dorcas twisted to look behind her. Moved her head from side to side slowly, glaring and insistent. "No," she said. She shook her head violently. "No." She wrapped her arms tightly around herself and began to rock. She pulled her blonde hair in front of her jail-pallid face, a curtain to hide behind. She began to sob. Her breathing grew laboured.

"I need to ask the jury to retire for a short break," the judge said, "to allow Miss Wykes to collect herself."

★ ★ ★

The door between Court 12 and the intensely lit waiting room hadn't even closed before the boy with the purple-tipped hair spoke. "Crazy woman. Good looking though."

He looked like a male pixie, though in fact he was an apprentice locksmith. What marked him out for Clarissa was that he seemed always to be plugged into earphones, and they were the same shade of purple as his hair. He'd once walked into the jury box still wearing them, though Robert gave him a discreet nudge to take them out before the judge noticed.

"Shhhhh." Several of them said it at once.

Annie actually elbowed him and told him to put a lock on his mouth. But then she rolled her eyes. "She's wasting my time. I don't like people who waste my time. How dare she waste my time?"

"I'm sorry for her," Clarissa said, deflated. "This case is a contest. Who's the saddest of them all." She was rummaging in the main section of her anti-stalker bag for lip balm, digging deeper, moving things around, puzzled when her fingers came across something silky. She pulled it out to look. Immediately, she scrunched it into her fist.

Tuesday, 24 February, 11.45 a.m.

I try to smooth my face into a composed expression, but I haven't released my grip on what I found in my bag.

What I found is a piece of slashed lavender jersey. What I found is the underwear I wore the night I spent with you in

November. You must have slipped them into my bag when I fainted in the station tunnel.

You altered them after you took the photo. You slit them at both hips, at the side seams. You cut away the crotch, which is not in my bag. When did you do this? Was I still wearing them when you did? Did the scissors touch my skin when they sliced the fabric? I can see the photograph as clearly as if I held it before my eyes. Your words are playing over and over in my head. The missing piece. *I have the missing piece, Clarissa.*

Clarissa was back in her seat in the jury box. People's mouths were moving, but no words were coming out. Mr Morden appeared far away and much smaller, as if he were standing at the other end of a long tunnel and she was looking at him through a shrinking glass instead of a magnifier. After a few minutes, the noises started to return, and Mr Morden began to grow until he was the right size again, like Alice. She wasn't sure how much she'd missed, but at least she hadn't fainted, and even Annie hadn't noticed. Clarissa deliberately pricked the pad of her thumb with the lead of her pencil. Concentrate, she told herself.

"You voluntarily went to the police station on Monday, May seventh. You spent two days there, Miss Wykes, as a witness."

"Don't remember goin' there."

Annie's head was moving from side to side in disgust. That could be me, Clarissa thought, understanding the woman's terror and degradation when faced with talking in public about whatever had happened to her. Clarissa, too, could become a person who filled someone like Annie with revulsion.

Over lunch, Clarissa moved numbly from the women's cloakroom where she threw up to the café where she got a bottle of sparkling water to the quiet area where she held a book she didn't read; then she repeated the circuit.

When they returned to Court 12 she pricked herself with the pencil again, not realising what she'd done until Annie reached over and plucked it out of her hand, shaking her head no and looking appalled as she pointed to a tiny pearl of blood.

Clarissa's ears were buzzing. Mr Morden's voice wasn't making sense. She pressed her hands to her temples, looking down at her pile of notes, thinking her own handwriting looked like indecipherable hieroglyphics. All she could see were chains and belts and ropes. The woman's terrified eyes above the gag. The gloved hand and the shining instrument. The horrible titles describing the magazine's contents.

Mr Morden adjusted his wristwatch, straightened his papers, rocked back and forth on his feet, visibly struggling to form his next question. "Did you visit a London park on Sunday, May sixth, just before you journeyed home?"

Dorcas nearly jumped from the chair, but glanced at the blue screen and remained where she was, still under cover but even more agitated. "No."

As a little girl, parks had been places of delight to Clarissa. In parks, she and her parents ate the picnic feasts her mother carefully prepared and packed. In parks, her father helped her to build castles and mermaids out of damp sand. Parks were not dangerous places.

She thought of her local park, the place she once had loved. Now that park was a pair of gloved hands gripping her wrist, leather pressed between her legs, words to humiliate her, a car she had to stop herself being dragged to. Now she hated that park. She never wanted to go there again, even though she knew she'd been lucky.

There'd been no computer geek to rescue Dorcas from that London park. No Bruce with his silky black head.

Mr Morden changed tack. "Miss Wykes, your mother appeared before this jury. She —"

"The jury can fuck themselves."

The judge looked furious. "This court is suspended until tomorrow."

It was an unasked for gift, finding herself sitting with Robert in a café near the bridge, a whim of his to stop there, to drink something hot before they got a later train.

She took a small sip of the tea he'd bought her. The nausea hadn't left her since she'd touched that magazine; it had deepened since discovering the underwear; it had become a kind of poison since the aborted hints of what Dorcas had suffered, and the visual spectacle of the wrecked woman in the witness box. Though being with

Robert was such powerful happiness that the sickness eased, at least for a few minutes.

"One time," he was saying, "not on my watch, a woman was crying outside the house, 'My babies, my babies, somebody save my babies.' I told you we always go in in pairs, didn't I?"

She nodded, wondering how she could be fooling him into thinking she was normal.

"Two firefighters went in for her babies," he said. "Both men died."

"And her babies?"

"Turned out her babies were budgies."

Clarissa shook her head. "You wouldn't ever go back in, Robert, would you?"

"I don't take unnecessary risks." He took a bite of the lemon cake he'd bought himself, looking like a young boy who'd stolen a forbidden treat, chewing and swallowing with exaggerated pleasure, sighing out his appreciation. He pushed the plate towards her. "Except when it comes to dessert." There was one fork. "Share with me?"

She felt herself smiling so much it made her jaw ache. She picked up the fork and scooped up some buttercream sprinkled with citrus zest, though she barely tasted it.

"Don't think I didn't notice that you only ate the frosting."

"I always do that. Now you really have discovered my darkest secret."

"And you know mine," he said. "I never talk about the work stuff. My wife, she never wants — never wanted — to hear it. I worry that it's boring."

"Nobody could think it's boring." She knew she was flattering him with interest and attention and admiration, and that it was working, but she meant it, too, all of it.

Was her infatuation with Robert as dangerous as Rafe's was with her? Of course not, she told herself. They weren't comparable at all. She tried not to think of the eviscerated underwear in her bag.

She lifted a hand, stretched it towards him, let it hover. He squinted at her, encouraging but quizzical, until she reached the rest of the way to brush a yellow crumb from his chin, making them both freeze for a few seconds, afterwards.

She was startled by a memory of Henry, wiping a smear of chocolate from her lips with his finger, then kissing her.

She shook her head, shaking Henry away at the same time, and spoke lightly. "Are all firemen like you?"

"Yep. Simple needs. Plenty of meat and potatoes and we're happy. We're all the same."

"I don't believe that."

He laughed. "I think you haven't met many firemen . . ."

She laughed too. "You're definitely my first."

". . . or many people."

"I fear you're right. I'll have to enlarge my lists of acquaintances by asking Grant to join me for coffee tomorrow. And you must ask Sophie." Grant and Sophie were their least favourite jurors.

"There's one thing I'm certain about," he said.

"What?"

"I will not be inviting Sophie to join me here."
"Well, I'll still be asking Grant," she said.

Tuesday, 24 February, 7.00 p.m.

This time, there is only my name on the brown envelope. My full name. Typed. No note. No message. Just the photograph. Just the one.

In my own room, almost naked, limbs pulled taut so my body is like an X, my wrists and ankles bound to the bedstead, a black blindfold over my eyes and a black scarf tied over my mouth. I am still wearing the underwear, but you have cut out the crotch. The stockings and bra have not been moved, but now there's a pair of scissors next to them. You've also added a whip, coiled beside me on the bed.

All of your deluded talk of love. But the real truth is here in this photo. How you've always seen me, how you've imagined me from the beginning, what you've always wanted to do. Trapping and controlling and hurting. It's what you are doing to me every day, literalised. It's how you want me. A blow-up doll who can't speak or move, whose face is barely visible, who isn't even conscious — you can do whatever you want with her.

She can't possibly say no. As much as you love to hear the word yes, you don't need to. It makes no difference. You'll do as you please with or without yes, if you can get away with it.

I see also that you might have covered my face so you can use the photo. I think of the section of one of my sewing magazines where readers send in snapshots of what they've been making. These are accompanied by stories about the occasion the garment was made for, how they went about

215

sewing it, the specialist tools they've used or the ordinary household things they've improvised with or adapted. Your magazine must have a readers' section akin to this.

Maybe that photo was your contribution to your own special community of freaks, with a narrative of all the things you did to me. Should I actually be glad that I can't easily be recognised?

I try to tell myself that that thing on the bed is not me, that it's only my shell, but it doesn't work.

I think again of the passage you underlined in "The Robber Bridegroom". The glasses of wine and the burst heart, the display of the woman's naked body, the salt in the wounds. That is what you did to me. What you are still doing.

How long did you spend posing me and taking your pictures? I remember your overstuffed briefcase with its locked catch. Now I know exactly what props you carried with you that night. I know where the marks on my body came from.

I never doubted we had intercourse. The pain between my legs the next morning, and the bladder infection, made that clear. I know now that I must have been tied up when it happened. I only just make it to the bathroom sink to vomit.

You had the photo all this time, and I never knew, never remembered such a violation. How can I not have remembered? There is only one explanation: there is no longer even the tiniest sliver of doubt in my mind that you drugged the wine.

I splash my face with cold water and brush my teeth. I shove your disgusting trophy into the bottom of my wardrobe. Not in the cupboard with the rest of the evidence. I know better than to destroy it, but you're shrewd enough to know that I could never bear to let anyone else see it. Your other photo seems harmless by comparison.

I turn on my laptop and order a new mattress and bed. I'd been meaning to but now I must. It helps, doing something. The headboard and footboard are solid. No slats. No posts. I pay extra for them to take away the old one. I will continue to sleep on the sofa until my new bed arrives in four weeks.

Each morning I will pile up the blankets and pillows and put them in the old cedar trunk that had been one of my parents' wedding presents. Doing this will remind me that the arrangement is temporary, and for night time only. My bedroom will be my bedroom again. But I can never again sleep in my old bed, where you did those things to me, that place of nightmares you won't let me forget.

Wednesday

Wednesday, 25 February, 8.07 a.m.

You are not at my house so I know you'll be at the station. It will be too much of a treat for you, seeing my reaction to your latest gift. You won't be able to resist that. You won't be able to wait for that.

I am right. As soon as I get out of the taxi you're walking next to me. I wish I weren't right. I wish I didn't know you as well as I do.

"Do you like the mementos of our night together, Clarissa?"

I do not look at you or speak. You know I will not. We don't surprise each other any more.

"We can get more elaborate later, Clarissa. Like the magazine. So much inspiration in that, don't you think?"

I make the mistake of glancing at you, briefly. Your lips may be thin and pale but they are clearly glistening, as if you have just licked them.

You are wearing the leather gloves you wore in the park. I see now that they are like the glove on the cover of your magazine. The skin on my right wrist bristles, remembering the twist of your Indian burn, though the marks and tenderness went over a week ago.

218

You lean towards me. "You loved it, being tied up like that. I had to gag you, to stop your neighbours hearing. The gag made you even crazier. And the blindfold."

I shove my elbow into your side, hard, satisfied by your grimace of shock and pain. "Get away from me." The words escape as if I have been holding my breath for too long and cannot stop myself.

"There are other photos, Clarissa. There was a lot of foreplay. I'm considerate that way. Would you like to see them? Do you think the fireman would like them? I know where he lives."

I push through the turnstile, not looking back, expecting you to follow. You don't, but I can hear you, calling out from the other side of the barrier as I turn to walk through the tunnel. "I'm only teasing, Clarissa. I'll keep my souvenirs to myself. You know I'll never share you." You are laughing. It is a rare thing, to hear you laugh, though your laugh is bitter and full of hate and I think you are cursing me with it.

Clarissa squeezed her eyes shut, but couldn't stop seeing herself, a nightmare creature from the pages of his magazine or a gruesome S&M film. She forced herself to concentrate and tried to resist stabbing herself any more with the pencil. She wondered if the police looked at magazines like his to try to find criminals and victims, to try to solve crimes.

She wrote in her index: *Betty Lawrence, Forensic Scientist, 146*. Annie tapped the paper and shook her head in mock despair at the number of pages Clarissa's notes were running to. Robert sometimes teased her too; he'd filled a handful of pages at most.

219

Mrs Lawrence was explaining DNA profiling. Clarissa imagined crime scene investigators around her bed, taking swabs, snapping more photographs of her. He had turned her into a spectacle, into something grotesque. Somehow, she had to resist letting that overwrite the way she saw herself.

"I examined items of clothing belonging to Carlotta Lockyer," Mrs Lawrence was saying.

Clarissa tried to sit straighter and close down the image of herself. She tried not to imagine the revulsion Robert would feel towards her if he ever saw it. She imagined it displayed to a jury on a screen like the one to her right, and prayed it never would be.

"These included a pair of pink bikini underwear found behind a cupboard in the bathroom of the flat where Miss Lockyer alleges she was held. There was a significant amount of blood staining on the underwear. The blood was Miss Lockyer's."

She imagined her own shredded underwear: their shell as one numbered exhibit, found in her flat; the crotch as another exhibit, retrieved from his house — perhaps discovered in a display case. What would a forensic scientist uncover on his souvenir? She tried to quell her humiliation at the idea of somebody studying the stains on it. His semen on a slide. Her fluids under a microscope.

Wednesday, 25 February, 1.15 p.m.

I want to resist hiding. I hate that you make me hide. I am queuing in an over-lit mini market to buy a pot of yogurt.

220

I am absurd to think I can do something as ordinary as going to a nearby shop. I am stupid in my desperation to breathe fresh air, just for a few minutes, to walk there and back. I am foolish in my refusal to give up on normal acts. I am feeling very, very sorry for myself, and I know I absolutely have to stop this.

I hear you before I see you. Your voice is so low it is only for me. Your warm breath is in my ear. "I didn't actually get to use the whip on you, Clarissa. Not properly, anyway, though you did enjoy the beginnings of our experiments with it. Next time."

Escalation. That's what the checklists in the stalker leaflets all warn of. That's what they all say will happen. When I first read that word I didn't let myself properly imagine what escalation might feel like, what escalation might mean in real life, the particulars of what you might do to escalate things. I didn't let myself properly inhabit that word. Your hands on me in the park. Your vile pictures.

I shove the yogurt onto a shelf as I flee the shop. I am a terrible runner. Within seconds I am breathless and there's a stitch in my side. People stare as I weave through the crowds, running my ridiculous flapping run through the outside market to rush back to the safety of the jurors' waiting room. All the while I'm hoping like mad that Robert isn't among them and doesn't see. I check behind me as I round the corner into the street where the court building is, panting, tripping and only just catching myself, but you aren't following. You must realise how obvious it would be that you were chasing me if you came after me at speed.

* * *

It must have been the intensification of the sick terror that was with her all the time now. That must have been what made her think of the Bettertons again. She found a quiet corner of the jurors' room and dialled. The woman answered.

It was a pitch; she had an instant. "I need to know what happened to Laura," she said.

"So do we." The line went dead.

She tried again. "Please talk to me," she said. "Please."

"Leave us alone." It went dead again.

She tried a third time. There was no answer.

If they didn't want to be phoned and asked about Laura, why weren't they ex-directory? Why had it been so easy to find them? She'd left her number unblocked each time she called, in the hope that they'd be less suspicious of her then, or even that they'd call her back, though deep down she knew that they wouldn't. So why were they continuing to pick up?

Her adrenaline was still pumping at the end of the day, as they waited in the annex room for the usher to escort them downstairs. She was trying to reassure Annie, who was wondering why Clarissa looked as if she'd been bleached around both eyes.

Grant's booming voice came as a welcome diversion. "Why was there so little of Tomlinson's semen? It don't make sense. If he came in her face and then she wiped it off on the shirt and jeans like she said, there'd be more."

222

"The quantity of semen varies between men. As little as one millilitre is considered normal, and as much as five." Clarissa's voice sounded calm. It wasn't how she felt. "The fact that the forensic people only found a few small areas on the clothes doesn't mean Miss Lockyer was lying." She caught Grant's eye and felt colour rush to her face. "He may just not make a lot of it."

Clarissa and Robert had taken to lingering at the end of the court day, then walking out the door together. She did truly enjoy being with him in his own right; the fact that he made her Rafe-proof, that he made her walk to the station entirely safe, was only a bonus.

She was pretending not to be waiting for him to come out of the locker room. As if it were urgent that she commit them to memory before leaving, she was dutifully reading the stern warning signs above the jury officer's desk. No jury tampering. No taking photographs. No talking about what happens in the deliberation room because that's a criminal offence punishable by a fine or even prison — a rule that lasts for ever.

She solemnly repeated these important precepts to Robert when he appeared. He nodded in mock-stern appreciation at each one.

"Did you see Grant's face when you started talking about semen?"

"I deliberately refrained from looking." That was a big lie. They both smiled.

"They shouldn't be, but most men would be uncomfortable hearing that," he said.

She wondered if he was right.

"It was an important thing to say," he said. "How do you know about it?"

"I'm good at human biology."

"I'm sure you are. But I think there's more to it than that."

"Too many failed IVFs. What they call severe male factor infertility."

"Ouch," he said.

This time her straight gaze was aimed at him as she spoke. "I know more about semen than I ever wanted to."

He laughed, but then quickly turned serious. "It didn't work?"

"No," she said. "No baby." She tried not to look sorrowful, but feared she did anyway. "Henry made me swear never to tell anyone why we needed treatment, but I think the confidentiality clause has expired."

It wasn't a betrayal, she told herself: Robert would never meet Henry; the truth was that she didn't want Robert to think the fertility problem was hers.

"Babies weren't what drew us together, anyway. He's not the kind of man who coos over them. But he agreed to it for me, because he knew I wanted a child so badly."

"Would you have stayed with him if he hadn't?"

"I wanted to be with him very much, so yes," she said slowly. "But Henry made me a promise early on that we'd try for a baby. I'm not sure the relationship could have survived his breaking it. As it turned out, it couldn't survive his keeping it. He was terrified of how a baby would disrupt his writing."

224

"That's understandable," Robert said.

She nodded. "He was secretly relieved each time the IVF didn't work. It was an unspeakable thing between us, but I knew that's what he felt."

She remembered a note Rafe had sent, just before the trial, now with the other things that she hoped Mrs Lawrence would never inspect. *I could give you a baby, Clarissa. Let me.*

"I'm sorry for you," Robert said.

"I'm not sure I deserve it. I didn't let myself stop and properly take in how ambivalent Henry was about the whole thing. I was too scared to let myself see it; scared that it would get in the way of what I wanted. I told myself he'd love the baby once it was there, and be glad of it. I got too obsessed. I'd even bought patterns for baby clothes and nappies." She rolled her eyes in embarrassment.

"He must have cared for you a lot," he said, "to have done that for you, if he's as you say."

"He's — He was complicated. But he didn't want to try any more. All that failed baby-making was too much for him. For us both, really, though I couldn't admit it then. He felt . . . bad, and angry — as much as Henry could express such a feeling — watching me take those drugs, seeing what they did to me, when it was all because of him, and for something he didn't even want." She tried feebly to joke. "I rivalled Lottie for needle use."

He didn't laugh. "You were sad."

"I was." Her eyes were on the pavement. "I was very, very sad. I'd so wanted a baby, to be a mother. It made me lose sight of Henry. I wasn't fair to him." She was relieved to have told Robert something true about herself; she wanted to see what he did with it.

"Do you mind my asking why you two never married?"

She did mind, though only because she hated to think about it. "His wife was Catholic. She didn't want a divorce. Said they were married forever in God's eyes. Henry felt too guilty about her to push it. So did I."

"Sounds like they'll die married."

"It's five years now since they separated and he still hasn't divorced her."

"So he was ready to have a baby with you, and put you through all of that medical intervention, but not marry you."

"That's what my mother used to say."

"Glad to know I remind you of your mother."

"My mother is wonderful." They both smiled. "I always thought, always told myself, that if I got pregnant that would change things. That he'd push for a divorce if he had such a powerful reason."

"Maybe." Robert didn't sound convinced.

"I think perhaps he was too scared to marry again. He'd already failed at it once. He also felt that the important thing was our being together. All that stuff about not needing a piece of paper. There's truth in that, I think."

Robert was looking ahead of them, onto the other side of the road and frowning. She didn't doubt that Rafe was there. She slipped on blackened snow that had melted to ice, and Robert steadied her.

She couldn't squander an opportunity to make Robert look for danger. "Did you see something?" she asked. She wanted to solidify any awareness he had that something was off kilter; she wanted to make sure he was ready to protect himself.

He shook it off. "It was nothing."

She wasn't sure if she was more frightened of his denial, or of what it would mean for her if he were to admit that he'd noticed Rafe. She made herself press the point. "I thought maybe you saw something that was worrying you."

"I told you I don't worry about things."

"But you should. Everyone should, sometimes."

"You don't need to worry about me. That's not your job." She must have looked stung — he seemed to force himself to smile. "I think you're too hard on yourself about Henry," he said, changing the subject. "And about his wife. People can't always help who they fall in love with."

She was too anxious about Rafe to take in what he'd just said, though she replayed it later. At the time she could only wonder if there was something else she could do to alert him, but she soon gave up in the face of yet another failure.

"Will you tell me what happened to your wife?" She felt he'd licensed her to change the subject, too; and to something difficult and personal, given his questions about Henry.

"It was a road traffic accident. Late morning. Another car veered onto the wrong side of the road and hit her head on. She'd have died instantly. I'd come off nights and gone straight to bed. I've no idea where she was going. I wasn't aware she'd left the house."

He sounded detached. He was looking at the ground as he spoke. She'd never seen him do that before. Revealing himself, but at the same time hiding.

Thursday

It was the first time she and Robert spent lunch together. They detoured through the quiet paths of a nearby park, where the sounds of Bristol traffic seemed to disappear as soon as they entered. Without Robert there, she never would have ventured into a park. She missed parks.

Robert sat down on a wooden bench beneath a tree and she did too, curling her legs beneath her. His sudden stiffness of the previous afternoon seemed to have melted away.

"Lottie doesn't do much to help herself, does she?" he said.

She shook her head in sad agreement, hoping the same would never be said of her. "Tell me the worst thing you've ever done." She startled herself, asking this.

He considered for a few seconds. "I met my wife on a blind date. She —" He broke off. "Another time. Not a story for now." But he smiled, a brave and philosophical seeming smile to diminish the refusal, and she thought the subject pained him too much. She didn't want to press him to talk more about his dead wife, especially after seeing what the subject had done to him yesterday.

"You'd be well within your rights not to answer," he said, "but will you tell me your worst thing?"

She was watching a robin, hopping around on the grass, seeming to find nothing. She forced herself to raise her head and look at him. "Sleeping with someone I didn't care about." Her voice was very soft.

"That isn't so terrible," he said. "Or so uncommon," he added.

"It is — was — pretty terrible." And there were other terrible things she could have told him.

The phone ringing a couple of months after Henry left his marriage and moved into her flat. His wife screaming down the line about male mid-life crises and younger women and clichés. She said Clarissa was far from the first woman Henry had had an affair with. She said Henry was infertile. She said Henry didn't want children anyway, so not being able to have them suited him just fine. She said Henry would deprive Clarissa of the chance to have a baby and before Clarissa knew it, it would be too late. She said she knew all too well what that felt like.

Henry had wrested the handset from Clarissa's clenched fingers and tried to soothe the woman, but Clarissa could hear her final screamed words before she cut Henry off: Clarissa was an evil husband-stealer and would get what she deserved. It was a curse that Clarissa had begun to fear was coming true.

Afterwards, Henry had held Clarissa and comforted her and promised he would do his best to give her a baby if she wanted one, though he explained they wouldn't be able to do it naturally. But Clarissa couldn't stop thinking of the poor woman who wasn't in Henry's arms, yet wanted to be; the woman who had never had a child, despite yearning for one. His wife's behaviour was not that of someone who no longer loved her husband, though Henry had sworn that was the case.

Robert was looking at Clarissa intently, as if trying to see inside her skull, which was exactly the place she didn't want him looking. "Tell me more about fires," she said. Her teeth were chattering.

"You're too cold, out here."

"I'm not." She didn't want to leave.

He took off his scarf, reached his arms behind her, wrapped it around her neck. "Much prettier on you," he said.

She shifted along the bench, closer to him. "Tell me," she said again. "Please."

"I can see that fighting you is hopeless." He was soon looking serious again. "You've got to feel what the fire's doing," he said, "how it's going to behave. Use all of your senses, not just your mind. You can see the fire breathing," he said, "see it pulsing. Dancing angels," he said, "are deadly. It's like looking at a ceiling made of stars. You can't let yourself be lured into watching them."

"Like the Sirens," she said.

He nodded. "Just like the Sirens, yes. When you see dancing angels you need to get out before the flashover. There'll be nothing left of you if you don't get straight out."

231

★ ★ ★

Mr Belford rose unhurriedly, paused to read his notes, then leaned over and whispered something to his junior. His box of tricks for unnerving witnesses. This one nervously pushed her hair behind her ears when he finally spoke to her.

"At the time you examined Miss Lockyer you had been a police medical examiner for only two months. The truth is that you were not very experienced at this, were you?"

Dr Goddard shifted in her chair. "I've been a qualified doctor for twenty years."

He lowered his spectacles slightly to study her. "You noted that Miss Lockyer had tenderness to her chest and painful breathing. These are reported injuries: the patient's subjective account of her symptoms. You had no means of verifying whether she was telling the truth about them."

Thursday, 26 February, 8.40 p.m.

I am startled by a soft knock on the door of my flat. I feel as if I have just run a long distance and abruptly stopped. I grab my phone. I'm ready to dial 999 if it's you — if you're actually in my building then that counts as a real emergency. But it is only Miss Norton's voice that answers my anxious "Who's there?" I remember the apprentice locksmith telling me and Annie we should get peepholes for our inner doors, his purple earphones still in place as he spoke. I promise myself I'll arrange for a security specialist to do this over the weekend, after this false little fright.

Miss Norton is wearing her powder-blue dressing gown. It's made of thick felt. She smells of baby talc. A dusting of it is visible on her wrists and hands, which are holding a large, white, oblong box. I follow her into my living room as if it is her flat and I am the guest. She lowers herself onto my sofa and pats the cushion next to her. "Sit down beside me, dear," Miss Norton says. But she is not entirely her usual hostessy self: she is frowning. She keeps the box on her tiny lap. "There was no card or name, Clarissa."

I do not need a card or a name to know that the box is from you.

"That's why I opened it," she says.

I know that whatever is in this box cannot be good. If I had a pet I'd expect the box to contain its corpse.

Miss Norton lifts the lid and I make myself peer inside, refusing to hesitate, refusing to act as if I am frightened, even though I need to remind myself to breathe steadily.

But no monster jumps out. No bomb explodes. No scent of death wafts from the container. There is only the fragrance of roses.

They are black roses. I don't think I've ever seen a black rose before, and find myself wondering if they are an odd hybrid, a rarity. I imagine somebody painting them, like the flowers in *Alice in Wonderland*. I cannot help but think they are beautiful. If they weren't from you I would let myself love them. The roses are startling. They are twined with red poppies and crimson anemones.

Until Miss Norton speaks again, I think that maybe this is not so terrible a gift, though I know that my sense of terrible is now formed by the most extreme relativism.

233

"They're death blooms, Clarissa, all of them," Miss Norton says. "It's a coffin spray. Being as old as I am, I've seen quite a few. They go on a casket at a funeral. I know I'm not long in this world, but I'm quite certain it's not meant for me."

I squeeze Miss Norton's hand. The saliva seems to have dried in my mouth. I picture your scissors cutting my underwear, your scissors between my legs, your scissors cutting these flowers. There's a brief sharp stab, low and central and in my cervix or pubic bone, a kind of convulsion. I know the physical sensation is a real thing and not an imagined one; my period is due tomorrow and this sudden spearing must be to do with that.

"You think I'm just a sweet old lady, Clarissa, a kindly spinster who knows nothing and has experienced nothing" — I am shaking my head in protest — "but I can see that something is very wrong. Your parents would be extremely upset by this. Shall I phone them? They always put their number and address on Christmas cards, dear, just in case. So kind . . ."

"I need water." Miss Norton does not take her eyes from me as I lurch up from the sofa and stumble into the kitchen. I gulp two glasses, spilling a lot of it down my chest. I drag my sleeve over my eyes and mouth to wipe them. I stand against the fridge, pressing my forehead against the cold metal, as if to cool my brain.

I return to the living room and sit beside Miss Norton again and kiss her cheek. "Please don't phone my parents, Miss Norton." I touch the box. "May I?" She nods and I take the box from her and examine it. No trace of the flower shop on it. "They worry about me too much as it is." I search beneath the spray, ruffle through the tissue paper on which it sits.

Miss Norton is right. You have left no clues. "I don't want them upset." There will be other ways of finding out where you got it, though; it must have been a special order.

"It's very unpleasant. It's threatening, to send such a thing to a young woman," Miss Norton says. "I've been considering, Clarissa dear, since you became so distressed on Valentine's Day. And that man who upset you so much. I haven't seen him since, but I suspect that you have. You need to ask for some help, dear. You need to make a complaint."

I am calmer, in my relief that it isn't another photograph. That extreme relativism kicking in again. A lesson you're teaching me well. You've made it clear how much you like to give lessons.

I close the box and cross the room, pulling another stack of fabric from the cupboard to make space for it. "I do intend to complain," I say. "I promise. There are just a few more tiny details I need to sort out first, to make sure it will work. I want the complaint to stick."

Like all the best fairy godmothers, Miss Norton is bossy. She stands up to leave, waving away my offer to see her downstairs, but not without a final order. "Don't wait too long, dear."

Friday

The jurors for Court 12 had taken to playing poker. Sitting around two wobbly tables they'd pushed together, they shouted and clapped and screeched out laughter, gasping in disbelief or comic annoyance. Other jurors came and went, doing their nine-day stints but pausing as outsiders to observe and even envy the strange camaraderie and seasoned ownership of the jurors' waiting room that came from being thrown together for such a long trial.

Clarissa didn't know the game, but once in a while she'd sit companionably nearby, quietly reading or sipping coffee. Robert did sometimes play, though Clarissa secretly suspected it wasn't because he wanted to, but as a kind of goodwill effort. Firefighters must need to be skilled at working in teams, she thought; they must be hyper-aware of how groups of people function, and how to manoeuvre them. The others always embraced Robert's participation heartily, or at least the men did. She was certain they'd elect him jury foreman.

Usually the poker happened during lunch, but on Friday morning of their fourth week their usher apologised for a mysterious delay that would take at least an hour, so the Court 12 jurors gathered with their cards. Clarissa was surprised to see Robert sitting separately, at a table on the other side of the room. He was near the window so the light could fall on what was clearly a sketchbook.

He was working so intently. She watched him for a few seconds, not meaning to draw his attention away as she quietly stepped closer, not wanting him to notice her observing him, but he looked up and caught her inspecting his cartoon. It was of Mr Morden. Robert had caught him exactly, and though it was comical, he'd managed nonetheless to capture Mr Morden's seriousness and intelligence; his air of goodness.

"So you draw, too?" she said. "When you're not reading poetry and performing heroic rescues?"

He'd been saving that poker face of his for her. "I like to doodle."

"It's good."

He flashed a smile, as if he'd decided it was the right move, and she could see how shy and stiff he was in the face of what he was doing, but also secretly proud without wanting to admit it. "Amuses the guys at work, my cartoons of them."

"You have an amazing visual memory, to pull that off. Like with the lighter. You should give Mr Morden that drawing."

The smile melted into something deeper, something he seemed not to be able to control. "The judge might throw me in jail if Mr Morden shows him. Literal contempt of court." He closed the sketchbook. "There are nicer things I could draw. Out of this place."

The night before, she had at last cut out the nightdress from the Japanese pattern book, using the bruise-coloured silk. She was determined not to let Rafe and his grisly flowers and repulsive photos take over her world. She imagined wearing the nightdress for Robert. To be with Robert would obliterate any trace Rafe had left on her. It would undo those photographs like a magic spell, and what Rafe had done would have no power.

Mr Belford resumed his evisceration of the police medical examiner. "Come, Doctor. A brutal rape by two large men and no visible vaginal injury?"

"Rape victims do not necessarily demonstrate evidence of vaginal trauma. Many comply out of fear and offer no physical resistance."

She thought of Rafe's astonished rage in the park. *You were only pretending.* She would never know with certainty what her fake compliance had saved her from; but there was no doubting that the pretence had bought her time.

"This is the medically accepted view," Dr Goddard went on. "It's also worth saying that consensual sex can result in vaginal trauma. Vaginal tears, and a lack of vaginal tears, are both neutral findings."

"Why did you question Miss Lockyer about her sexual and menstrual history?"

"It can be relevant to the alleged assault. If you observe vaginal bleeding, you're asking yourself, is this menstrual bleeding? Or could it be a post-coital bleed?"

That was what she'd had after the night with Rafe: a single day of spotting. Her period had come a week later. She always knew where she was in her cycles. It was a habit she'd formed when she and Henry started trying for a baby. It was made easier by the fact that her cycles were dependably twenty-seven or twenty-eight days long; even severe stress didn't affect them. Despite her dread that Rafe had made her pregnant, she'd known it was highly unlikely.

"The blood that the forensic scientist found on Miss Lockyer's clothes could have been menstrual blood," Mr Belford said. A well-thumbed medical dictionary lay on top of his files. "They cannot distinguish menstrual blood from other vaginal blood."

"True. But the alleged rape took place on day five of her menstrual cycle. Usually a woman has finished bleeding by then — she'd have some spotting at most."

Friday, 27 February, 6.30 p.m.

All the way home I do not think of you at all. I do not think of the photographs. I do not think of your magazine.

I have forgotten my umbrella. Robert holds his over us both as we walk. He sits next to me on the train and when he lets his arm rest against mine my face goes warm. He stands with me in the taxi-queue at the station, the two of us talking and talking until I reach the front and he carefully opens and shuts the taxi door for me, smiling his slight, closed mouth smile as he watches it drive off.

As the taxi winds its way up the hill I think only of Robert, imagining what it would be like to sleep with him.

239

The instant I walk in the door and see your envelope you are back inside my head, where you want to be. I know it is another photograph before I've opened it.

It is the next step from the last one. The blindfold and gag and bindings are exactly as they were, but you've removed my underwear. You've dropped them beside me, sliced at the hips so you could get them off without untying my ankles. You've uncoiled the whip and draped the last foot of it over my stomach.

I am forcing myself to think rationally. The whip is just part of your display. You didn't actually use it on me. I'm sure you didn't. I wouldn't have missed the marks if you had. The sore spots and chafing wounds had been on my wrists and ankles. I'm actually relieved to think of them. They suggest that even unconscious I was still pulling at the restraints and straining to get free, trying to fight you. Even if you got off on my struggling, I'm glad of this evidence that I didn't want you. There'd been red compressions that turned into bruises on my inner thighs, probably from your hands, but those came after you took your pictures. There were no bloodied welts that could have come from your whip.

I put your photo in my wardrobe with the others. I look at my bed, the sheets clean and never slept in, covered in my newly sewn quilt cover. I think of Lottie curled in the corner of the sagging mattress in that London flat. I haven't eaten or showered or brushed my teeth. I haven't taken off my clothes. I am very, very cold.

I go into the living room and huddle on the sofa beneath blankets. Gradually, I've been moving my night-time things in here. I reach onto the side table for my sleeping potion and gulp down two pills, knowing my mother would say I'm getting addicted. I curl onto my side, trying to consider and plot as calmly as I can about what I will do tomorrow, not thinking I will ever sleep but astonished to feel myself floating away, carried by the force of drugs that work as well as any witch's spell. I am frightened that you wait for me in my dreams, too.

She was in a golden coffin, holding the death blooms, and Rafe was wrenching them from her grasp, dragging her from the coffin's white silk lining, throwing her onto concrete that felt like sandpaper. She was on the ground, naked, trying to hide beneath a quilt. The defendants were gathered in a circle around her, tearing the quilt away, kicking her, beating her with a broom. The broom became a whip. They were lifting her high into the air and forcing her back into the coffin, which was displayed on a table. They were holding her down so she couldn't move, cheering from the sidelines as Rafe climbed on top of her, pressing the thorns of the black roses into her bare breasts with the weight of his body, stopping her from being able to breathe. Robert was standing there, silently watching, a pair of scissors in his gloved hand. She tried to cry out his name but the words made no sound.

Saturday

The alarm woke her at 5.00 a.m. She'd taken off her clothes in the night and was shivering in tangled blankets that were drenched with the sweat of nightmares. She groped for the phone and dialled the taxi company she always used, asking them to collect her just before 6.00. She'd worked out every step she would take. She would make the first train of the morning. The timings were tight and that was deliberate; she didn't want to leave him even the smallest chance of finding her at the station.

Her life had become a Monday-to-Friday life, where there was no room for anything beyond the trial. But today would be different.

She showered, soaping away the sour coating of bad dreams, feeling the chill leave her bones as she stood beneath the stream of hot water. She blasted her hair with the blow-drier and twisted it into a careless knot, then chose clothes to keep the warmth in her skin. Boots and thick stockings and a navy wool dress, her usual coat, a scarf her mother had knitted. She threw mittens and a hat and umbrella into her bag, then remembered to toss in her London map. As an afterthought she grabbed her passport.

First, though, she'd turn his own tactics on him. When the taxi driver rang the bell she told him she'd be down in a minute. Quickly, she dialled his home number — he'd given it to her too many times to count. She was careful to punch in 141 first so he wouldn't be able to see who was phoning. He answered, startled out of sleep. Her stomach lurched at his voice — it went against all of her instincts to put herself in the position of hearing it when she didn't have to. She cut off the call without saying a word herself, secure in the knowledge that he was five miles away and couldn't track her. Then she dashed out the door.

She was taking a risk. For all she knew they might not be home. Or they might not let her in. Warning them she was coming certainly wouldn't help. But she wasn't going to let herself think beyond getting there.

By 8.30 she was in London, standing in front of their carefully tended Edwardian terraced house, gathering the courage to knock. Before she could, the door opened, though only a few inches, and a well-groomed, brisk-seeming woman in her mid-sixties peered suspiciously through the crack, demanding to know why she had been loitering there for five minutes.

There was no time for preliminaries or politeness. "Because of Rafe Solmes."

The woman's hand trembled slightly and her lips were pinched. "Are you his friend?"

"No. God no. The opposite of his friend."

"You would say that." The woman began to shut the door.

"Please." Clarissa stuck her foot in the crack. "He's making my life impossible."

"Allow me to close my door."

Clarissa could hear someone coming down the stairs, quickly, noisily — a man's tread, she thought — but she didn't move her foot. "Please," she said again. "I need to know what happened to Laura. You're her mother, aren't you?"

"Charlotte?" came the man's voice.

The woman shoved hard against the door, making Clarissa think the bones of her foot would fracture despite the heavy protection of her boot. "How dare you," the woman said.

Horrified with herself, Clarissa stepped back and the door slammed.

She didn't know what to do next. She stood there, contemplating knocking again, knocking and knocking until they let her in, but she knew she'd totally blown it. She sank onto the low wall that ran along their footpath. She bent over, her elbows on her thighs and her head in her hands. She wasn't sure how long she sat there, numbly; the rare interlude of blankness was a relief.

After a while she became aware of voices talking urgently on the other side of the door. To her astonishment, the letter slot opened. "Wait," the woman said through it, grudgingly.

It was ten minutes before the door opened again, this time widely. The man stood there, hardly taller than Clarissa. He wore dark grey trousers and a black sweater. He smelled of shower gel. He was probably in his late sixties, but he looked as if he still possessed a wiry strength.

"You're the woman who's been calling us," he said, and Clarissa nodded yes. "You don't give up, then."

"I couldn't. I can't."

He said nothing more but moved aside, motioning for her to enter. She could smell toast and coffee, which made her queasy rather than hungry. It struck her as she limped after him that nobody knew where she was. She was walking into the house of strangers and nobody knew. The rules she lived by, the rules her mother had drummed into her, were being ripped up by the day.

The walls of the corridor leading from the front door and through the house were covered in family photographs. At the centre of them all was one girl. Clarissa didn't doubt it was Laura.

A pink swaddled lump in the arms of a younger version of a smiling Mrs Betterton, looking down at her new baby. A toddler taking her first steps towards Mr Betterton — his hair dark brown, almost black, back then — crouched and holding out his arms. A teenager standing between her proud parents at her sixth-form graduation day. In her early twenties, dressed as a bridesmaid, posed with the rest of the wedding party.

She was recognisable at all ages, always fair and slight, delicate featured, strikingly pretty. But she froze at about thirty; Clarissa felt a stab with the realisation. Thirty was as old as she got — about the age Gary said she'd been during her relationship with Rafe ten years ago.

Clarissa thought of the woman on the cover of the magazine, trying to work out if it could be Laura. The colouring was similar, but with the bottom half of the woman's face obscured and the lurid lighting it would be almost impossible to tell, at least for a non-expert. The Laura in the photographs was happy and free. As far away from the magazine cover as it was possible to be.

Mrs Betterton stood in her perfect kitchen, neatly dressed in shades of olive and brown: a tweed skirt, knitted sweater, sensible shoes. She was like her daughter, and still beautiful, with her cap of silvery blonde hair cut sharply to her chin and pushed behind her ears, where it obediently stayed.

"My husband only has a few minutes," she said stiffly, not offering to take Clarissa's coat, not offering her a chair at the kitchen table. "He has a business appointment."

Right, Clarissa thought. Business meeting on a Saturday. She detected a trace of an American accent with the pointed lie.

Mr Betterton said he could arrive late, earning a darting glare from his wife. He gestured towards a chair, pouring coffee into a deeply blue earthenware mug painted with a hummingbird. He set the steaming drink on the table in front of Clarissa. She thanked him softly and took a sip, not knowing what to say or ask. How could she possibly voice her lurid questions to these people?

"How do we know you're not his friend?" Mrs Betterton asked.

"He doesn't have friends, Charlotte," Mr Betterton said. "He's not natural enough to have friends."

246

"How do we know he didn't send you? Is he paying you? He's done such things before, though not since — not for the last few years. It's not beyond him, though, to gloat, even now."

Clarissa's hand shook so much she sloshed coffee onto the scrubbed wood of the table. She attempted to mop it up with the sleeve of her coat but the wool repelled the fluid, something she would normally, automatically be aware of.

"Don't worry about that." Mr Betterton applied a towel while his wife frowned behind him. Gently, he squeezed Mrs Betterton's shoulder. "Charlotte, she's clearly not with him." He passed Clarissa a box of tissues, pretending not to notice as she wiped her eyes and blew her nose. Then he turned back to his wife. "Do you want her parents to go through this too?"

Mrs Betterton gulped. "We know nothing about her, James. She hasn't even told us her name."

Clarissa apologised and did so, eliciting Mrs Betterton's immediate demand for identification. She handed over her passport and watched the Bettertons examine it together.

"I can see why he targeted you," Mrs Betterton said, dropping the passport on the edge of the table, so Clarissa had to strain to reach for it before putting it away. "You look like Laura."

So many times Clarissa had asked herself why he'd chosen her. What she might have done to draw him. She'd wondered if it was his jealous admiration of Henry's acclaim as a poet, and Henry's charisma and power, that made him pursue her. As if taking the things Henry had — primarily her — would somehow give him Henry's qualities, and Henry's life and success.

But she saw now that that wasn't what it came down to. She was a type, just like the archetypal victim of a serial killer. Something entirely out of her control. Her colouring and features and hair and body and maybe even her voice and gestures reminded him of someone else's. Even her profession was the same as Laura's.

"There's little we can do for you," Mr Betterton said. "But we can't do even that if you don't tell us more about your relationship with that man."

"It's not a relationship," she said. But she told them all she could, as quickly and honestly as she could. She didn't mention the three photographs.

"Could he have followed you here?" Mrs Betterton said.

She explained about the early morning phone call, and that the station and train had been quiet. She was sure she hadn't been followed. She'd watched carefully, something she'd grown good at.

"He knows where we are," Mr Betterton said. "We can't move, in case —" He broke off. "It would be better for you if he didn't discover any connection between us."

"Why would we want to help you?" Mrs Betterton asked. "What good will it do our daughter now?"

It was hopeless. She was inexcusably trespassing and Mrs Betterton profoundly resented it. Clarissa stood up. "I'm sorry I bothered you. I shouldn't have come."

Mr Betterton looked sharply at his wife before turning back to Clarissa. "Sit down, Clarissa. It's good that you don't give up. Don't start now. You need to be someone who doesn't give up if you're mixed up with that man. You need to know what you're up against. You're right about that."

She saw that they hated to say his name. Just as she did.

Mrs Betterton turned her back to them and began to load the dishwasher with the breakfast things. It seemed a paradoxical gesture of consent and protest, but she didn't try to stop Mr Betterton as he began to recount Laura's early days with Rafe.

Mrs Betterton soon interrupted him with flat bitterness, still with her back to them. "What seemed like great passion — all those romantic gestures of his — was actually just obsession." Clarissa was surprised by how readily she'd spoken.

Quickly, too quickly, Mr Betterton continued, Laura moved in with him.

Almost immediately, Laura grasped the extent of his possessiveness, and the impossibility of escaping it. She couldn't have a bath or make a phone call or receive a letter that he didn't peek in on or listen in on or open.

His sexual demands began to upset her. He wanted to try bondage games and she wouldn't agree. Had Clarissa ever encountered this, with him?

Mr Betterton had begun to clear his throat between every sentence. He hadn't been doing that at first; she was certain it was the nature of what he was saying that caused it.

She answered his question with the slightest negative shake of her head, ashamed of lying.

Mr Betterton peered doubtfully at her. "That's surprising," he said.

It was pointless, hiding anything from them. They knew the worst, already. "I'm sorry. I find it very difficult to talk about," she said. "But I have encountered that, yes."

He nodded grimly and resumed, not pressing her for more details.

Rafe seemed not to understand any talk of their splitting up or Laura moving out. He seemed not to have any family or any history. Laura was frightened by the absolute lack of anybody in his life but her. There'd been dramatic fights between them, followed by promises that he'd change, that he'd be less controlling.

The lucky thing for Laura had been his getting the job outside of London. After his post-PhD phase of short-term teaching posts in London he was unstoppably ambitious to secure a permanent academic job in an established university English department. Laura knew nothing would get in the way of his moving to Bath, and that was when she decided to disappear. When he took a day trip to visit his new department she packed her things and left without even giving notice at work.

At first, she went back to her parents, but Rafe soon found her and hovered and followed and watched whenever he could. Odd nights. Every weekend. Incessantly ringing. Somehow discovering every changed phone number. Refusing to accept it was over.

Continuing to speak to Laura and to the Bettertons as if she were his girlfriend.

She moved several times but he always found her, probably led there by tracking her parents. He began to send Laura compromising photographs, taken when they'd lived together, taken when she was asleep and unaware, probably after he'd drugged her. Her parents grew more careful in their visits. Once, this drove him into breaking into their house and finding evidence of Laura's new address and phone number, though they couldn't prove it. Even if his move to Bath meant he couldn't watch Laura every day of the working week, the presents and letters and horrible images he'd stored up — so terrible they made Laura sick — never stopped arriving.

He stole her life. She had no privacy. She was shrinking, not eating, not confident, no longer herself. She'd lost her friends. She'd make new ones — she'd had such charm — but she couldn't tell the old ones where she'd gone for fear he'd find her through them.

The police wouldn't do anything. They just saw it as a broken relationship. He'd never actually assaulted her physically and he was clever. Even the photos looked merely like sex games. There was no way to prove they weren't consensual — the shops and the Internet are full of perfectly legal toys for perfectly legal S&M.

Mrs Betterton remained standing but she'd moved closer to them. She was leaning against the kitchen counter. "The police are better these days," she said. "Just in the last few years they've got better about this. But too late for our daughter."

Laura moved five times, to five different cities, in the two years after she left him. He found her each time. She'd get a few months at most of being free of him. Then she'd turn around and there he was again. They were growing fearful that he really would hurt her.

At last Clarissa voiced the question she'd wanted to ask since she walked in the door. "Where is Laura now?"

"She was hit by a car." Mr Betterton's voice was hollow. He stroked his startlingly white hair, and Clarissa had a conviction that the loss of colour had happened overnight, from absolute shock and grief. "He'd found her again. She was about to cross the road and she heard him say, 'Hello, Laura. I've missed you.' She stepped right into that car, forgetting herself, trying to flee."

Clarissa was weeping silently, still clutching the now empty, no longer warm hummingbird mug.

"She'd broken both legs and had a concussion. She woke up in hospital with him by her bed, holding her hand. He'd told the doctors and nurses he was her fiancé. She became hysterical and they asked him to leave. She got them to call us. By the time we arrived he was well away. He knew better than to let us find him. He was getting less smart and careful, as he got more desperate, and he was growing more dangerous. The more frustrated he gets, the more careful you must be. Bye-bye goes the pretence of Mr Nice Guy. He can't hide the malice.

"Charlotte was born in America. She has family there. We saw Laura couldn't stay in England and have any sort of life. After she recovered — physically, anyway — Laura emigrated. We arranged it very carefully."

"But we see now that we didn't protect her. We only made her more vulnerable." Mrs Betterton's voice came from low in her belly, a throb of pain shaking it. "We were so careful about how and when we contacted her. We were so cautious about what we kept in the house. One year after she moved — she was in California, living under my family name — she disappeared."

Clarissa recalled his UCLA sweatshirt, and her powerful instinct when she saw it that it meant something to him; that it was some kind of trophy.

"All contact stopped that summer," Mrs Betterton said. "None of her neighbours knew her, or noticed her sudden absence, she'd kept such a low profile. They hardly blinked an eye at work either — it was all clerical temping — they were used to people not turning up."

She felt how unbearably lonely Laura must have been, living like that, and how much she must have missed her parents. She knew that she herself could never be that brave.

"She was just one of the countless missing," Mr Betterton said. "The police there couldn't find any evidence of wrongdoing, in the land of the milk-carton children. They ought to put adults on those cartons too. The British police wouldn't get involved. We've sent private detectives. We've tried everything."

It was the way they said "we". Again and again it was "we". And their way of so smoothly passing the baton

253

of their terrible story back and forth, despite the very different impulses Clarissa's appearance had initially produced in them. That was what made her see how very in synch the Bettertons were, regardless of what they had suffered; what they were continuing to suffer. It could have torn them apart, but by some miracle, she thought, it had done the opposite.

"We hope, always we hope, that she did it to free herself," Mrs Betterton said. "Maybe she's safe and happy somewhere. Maybe the phone will ring one day and there will be her voice. Maybe it isn't as we fear and it wasn't him."

"But we know it was," Mr Betterton said. "Even though we tell ourselves that as long as there's no body there's hope. We've let ourselves pray that she's got some kind of amnesia but that she's otherwise all right and she'll remember who she is someday and get in touch."

Mrs Betterton nodded. "But we know Laura. She'd never put us through this. She'd always get through to us, if she could."

Now Clarissa understood why her phone calls and sudden arrival had filled them with such a strange mixture of hostility and suspicion and hope: worrying that she was somehow approaching them at his behest, yet desperate not to cut off someone who might have news, however unlikely the odds of that were.

"You need to get proper help, Clarissa," Mr Betterton said.

Mrs Betterton put her hand on top of Clarissa's. "You need evidence, better evidence than we had, iron-clad evidence and lots of it, and you need to fight hard. If you don't want to vanish out of your life you're going to need to get the police involved. You can give them our name and number if you'd like. They didn't listen to us then, but maybe they will now. You're going to need to do a better job at getting them to help you than Laura managed. He'll never stop."

By the time Mrs Betterton finished speaking Clarissa's hand was red and aching, marked by the pressure of her wedding ring; but Clarissa hadn't wanted to pull away.

Week 5

The
Guardians

Monday

She'd dragged Henry to too many films about serial killers, and they were all coming back to her. She was filled with horrifying — and she hoped, preposterous — ideas about what might have happened to Laura. Was she buried in a shallow grave on the edge of some farm in California? Undiscovered beneath leaves in woodland? Dumped in a culvert somewhere, or a disused quarry, unnoticed? On the ledge of a mountain, far off any footpath? Stored in a freezer in some derelict building? Crammed into a coffin with a stranger's corpse and buried or cremated so she would never be traced? Was it luck, or cunning, or both, that had kept her hidden?

As terrible and vivid as her thoughts were, Clarissa could not bear to picture what might have happened to Laura during her last hours or days. Envisaging her dead body was nowhere near as dreadful as imagining what might have been done to her while she was still conscious and aware. She could picture Laura's face: all of those photographs of her at different ages, overlaid. And her parents in their never-ending fear and grief. Laura was so real to her now.

She had investigated statistics about the missing. It happened more often than people realised. Hundreds of thousands of people were missing in Britain. The numbers would be even more frightening in America.

She tried to shake away her sensational conjurings and concentrate on what Annie was saying.

"You look like crap" was what Annie was saying.

They were walking up the stairs to Court 12. "Thank you," she said sweetly. "You don't."

"Seriously. Eat, woman. And sleep. And get out more. You're so white you look like the undead. You won't be able to keep up that pretty vampire look for much longer."

Clarissa glanced down at herself. Annie was right. Her arms were like bleached sticks beneath the filmy fabric she'd used to make the sleeves of her top. More and more, she was depriving herself of weak winter sun. It was probably just as well that her mother hadn't seen her for a while. She'd know just from looking that something was wrong.

"My, my, you're chatty today," Clarissa said.

"Hair's still bright," Annie conceded, as they lined up in the annex. "Bottle?"

"No, Annie!" Clarissa said truthfully.

Annie touched the clasp of enamelled flowers Clarissa had used to pull it back. "Nice," she said, as if by way of apology.

A minute later they sat down in the jury box. The witness was an expert in facial mapping. Exactly the sort of person who could determine if it was Laura on the magazine cover.

As the woman droned on without inflection, Annie sighed dramatically and squeezed her eyes shut and tipped her head back in agony. As ever, Clarissa was amazed that only she heard Annie, that none of the barristers ever turned, and none of the other jurors. She sometimes wondered if she only made up Annie's responses. Annie was like her own secret voice. Her head was pounding; Annie's must be too.

At last, Mr Morden asked, "What was your final conclusion?"

There is the most powerful level of support available for the contention that the woman on the magazine cover and Laura Betterton are one and the same person, Clarissa imagined the facial-mapping woman saying.

"There is a moderate level of support for the contention that the suspect in the CCTV images and Mr Godfrey are one and the same person," the facial-mapping woman actually said.

Monday, 2 March, 12.40 p.m.

Bearing in mind Annie's horror of my pallor, I take a walk during lunch, in icy air. The sun is lemon yellow but low in the cloudless blue sky.

More and more I am exploiting the fact that you aren't the only one capable of tracking other people. I don't want a repeat of what happened in the mini market. I know from the university timetable that you're giving a lecture. Henry once told me you bitterly resent teaching and think it's beneath you, dragging you away from your paradigm-breaking research.

On my way back I cross the street. At first I don't notice you in the crowds milling about on the green in front of the cathedral. But despite the timetable, there you are. I nearly trip over my own feet as you approach and then begin to walk beside me.

"You need some new stockings, Clarissa," you say.

What fantastic social skills you have, I think. Only you could start a conversation with that sentence as your opening gambit, I think.

But this attempt to make myself feel brave through unvoiced sarcasm is a pitiful failure. My heart is thumping more than ever as I aim myself back to court and pretend not to know you. I am searching for Robert, grateful each time I scan that he doesn't materialise.

Fine, pale brown hairs sprout from your knuckles. I imagine your hands circling Laura's throat, circling my own. I swallow hard. My neck hurts, remembering your fingers around it in the park three weeks earlier. I think I am choking and struggle to swallow again, though I know the sensation can't be physical; I know that it can only be in my head now.

"I like you in stockings," you say. "But you know that."

I keep walking. I won't let what I've learned of you make me less effective and more terrified. It must do the reverse. The Bettertons drummed this into me.

Just before I turn the corner you speak again. "I need to take some new photographs, Clarissa. It's going to be a private sitting." And you walk straight on, leaving me to turn left by myself.

But there will be no private sitting; your saying those words will not make it happen. However much you think you know about me, you have no idea about the new friends I made on Saturday. You're not the only one who can uncover secrets. I am learning yours, too.

Robert was pacing angrily back and forth in the jurors' waiting area, his phone to his ear.

A few minutes later, she stood at the back of the line with him, waiting for the usher to come and count them and return them to Court 12. Robert took his phone out, double-checked he'd turned it off, glowered a bit more as he shoved it back into his pocket. He was in his usual stance, feet apart and firmly planted; but not relaxed.

"Something wrong?" she asked. It was obviously a stupid question.

He tried to smile but it evaporated as if it had been pressed onto water. "Some kids, probably. Poured paint remover over the car last night. Slashed the front tyres."

She sat down quickly, practically falling onto the upholstered bench that was running behind the line of jurors.

"You're pale." His hand floated to her forehead, then pulled away as he realised he'd touched her in front of the others. "You're clammy."

"I'm fine, really. I just felt like sitting."

"You don't look fine. You haven't looked well all day."

"It's just — It's horrible. So mean." She looked over at the jury officer's desk, where the usher was still talking.

"It's fixable. Just inconvenient. I was angry. I don't stay angry."

"I'm sorry, though."

"Not your fault."

But there was no doubting that it was.

Monday, 2 March, 6.15 p.m.

As soon as I step onto the path and trigger the outside light I see it. You've propped it against the door. This envelope is fatter than the last one. I am numb and cold and dead. I tiptoe up the stairs as quietly as I can, not wanting to turn on the tap of Miss Norton's kind concern.

You've wrapped them in a single sheet of white paper. I'm actually thankful. They are not what I fear. You didn't take these in my bedroom. They're all from last week, a batch for each day, carefully ordered.

Standing with Robert on the bridge, my hair blowing beneath my knitted hat, mittens tucked into my coat pockets against the cold. Robert is stealing a look at me. We are almost touching but not quite.

Sitting with Robert in the café before catching the train, leaning towards each other over the table as we share his cake and I look up at him as if he is a birthday present.

Talking about my failed IVF attempts and his wife's death. In one shot, Robert looks across the road, where you must be. He frowns directly into your lens. In another, he is holding my arm.

In the park. Snap snap snap. The series of photos is like a film broken into stills: eight inches between me and Robert as I confess my worst thing; four inches as Robert wraps me in his scarf; the side of his body against mine while he speaks about fires as if he is reciting a poem.

Walking towards the train station after the medical testimony. Robert is carefully holding an umbrella over my head — I'd kept asking him to make sure he was covered too, but in the photograph I can see that he is getting wet with sleet and I am dry. In the taxi queue before we parted that night, standing so close to each other but again not quite touching.

You haven't written a word but I know what you are saying. *I can watch you all the time and I hate what I am seeing.*

Do you not know that even stolen photographs are not always ugly? You didn't mean to, but you've inadvertently given me something beautiful, in these glimpses of me and Robert together.

Laura had been alone, in California. I am not alone, despite your best efforts. You are stupid to overlook that. It gives me pleasure, calling you stupid, and makes me feel better, stronger somehow, though I know it is a childish, pointless indulgence.

Mr Belford's words are flying around my head. *Reported injury. Subjective account.* They are not words the legal system will be able to use about me. You are about to find this out, though I have known it for weeks.

I open the cupboard and stuff my collection of evidence into a huge plastic bag in readiness for tomorrow. I feel a spasm of doubt when I deliberately leave your pornographic photographs at the bottom of my wardrobe.

I take out the notebook and sit cross-legged on my living-room floor, flipping through it. I'm clutching an eraser, letting it hover over the pencilled notes about what you did to me in my bedroom. I lose track of how long I sit like this.

Rubbing it out won't make it untrue. The words are already inside my computer anyway, because I've scanned every single page, dutifully obeying the leaflets' advice to make copies of everything I can. It's supposed to be a kind of insurance against loss as well as electronic proof that I haven't tampered with anything at a later date. I let the eraser drop from my fingers. There is a dull thud and it rolls beneath the sofa. Mr and Mrs Betterton spoke so strictly to me, warning me not to hide anything from the police; they'd guessed those photographs existed, despite my inability to talk about them.

Briskly, I get up and go into my bedroom and snatch them from my wardrobe.

I think again about how the leaflets say that it takes an average of 110 stalking-related incidents before a woman actually goes to the police.

Do those three repulsive photographs amount to one incident, because you took them all that same night; or three, because you attacked me on three separate occasions with them? Is a batch of three texts calculated as one or as three? Are forty answering machine hang-ups over a lunchtime one incident or forty? Will each of your photos of me and Robert be tallied individually or as one because they arrived simultaneously, in a single envelope? Are the Valentine's chocolates with the accompanying card worth one or two?

266

Perhaps they are worth three, if they factor in your personal delivery service.

I cannot begin to imagine how the police do their sums. I only know that there have been way too many incidents for me. I only know that I have reached saturation point and cannot bear even one more incident from you. I only know that numbers do not feel like they have anything to do with any of this. Your effect cannot be measured by figures of any kind, however fine-tuned their methods of calibration may be.

I know exactly what my next step will be and I'll take it early tomorrow morning. It never crosses your mind how hard I will fight you, how meticulously I've been preparing. There's more than enough evidence against you now, whatever counting methods the police may employ.

Tuesday

Tuesday, 3 March, 6.30 a.m.

This is where I belong, where I should be, the place that's been waiting for me. I am climbing the steps of the rectangular stone building that Lottie spent so much time in. Behind me are half a dozen calmly parked cars and vans, ready for action, painted in their comforting Battenberg grids of yellow and blue blocks. Above me is a bright blue sign with the word Police on it. I take a deep breath, grab the handle of the metal-framed door, and step over the threshold.

The station is virtually deserted so early in the morning. Within a minute I understand the significance of this, staring in disbelief at the protective glass reception window with its notice that they are open for enquiries from 8.00a.m. until 10.00p.m. All at once I am deflated, on the verge of tears. I will have a fit of hysteria right here and they'll think I'm a madwoman in the grip of anti-social behaviour and slap some kind of order on me and throw me in a cell. How can I not have thought to check something as basic as the opening hours?

I turn, searching for the door I used to enter, but I'm disorientated and lost and dizzy, like a child who has spent

268

the last minute spinning in circles, which I suppose I have. They'll charge me with being drunk and disorderly too. I stumble along, trying again to find my way out, and a policeman wanders by, peering curiously at me. He must be ten years younger than I am. He says, looking concerned, "Can I help you?" and I think he means it, and that his question is not simply the polite rhetoric that millions of people reel off on autopilot zillions of times a day.

I stutter unintelligibly and hold up my huge bag of evidence as if that will explain everything. I know I need to tell him about you, at least a very quick version, so he will listen to me, so he won't make me leave. But each time I try to speak I can't get beyond the first word of my sentence. I don't know where to begin the list of the things you've done. "He . . . He . . . He . . ." I sound like a broken record or a bad mockery of laughter. I try again, opening and closing my mouth, and though nothing comes out the policeman asks if I need to make a complaint. I choke out the words "I do" and he says something about getting me into an interview room and I somehow say, "But aren't you closed? Aren't I too early?"

He says that that doesn't matter. They're only closed to routine things, like people who want lost property. He speaks to me with the gentle sorrowfulness of a surgeon talking to a patient whose condition is inoperable. He says that it's the job of the police to help those who are distressed or fearful, which isn't something that can wait. He says that he's going to get a detective constable to come and talk to me in a few minutes. Will I please follow him? He leads me through a door that is locked to the general public, a door that makes me think of the special gateway out of the jurors' waiting room and into the world of Court 12. It is a passage that people do not pass through every day, but only at rare points in their lives.

Without quite knowing how it has happened, I am sitting down and there is a glass of water in front of me and I'm being offered a cup of tea but I shake my head and mouth the words no thank you without any sound coming out. A box of tissues is sliding along the table, pushed by a hand. The hand belongs to DC Peter Hughes, a very tall, very thin, very stooping man in his late forties with a shock of soft hair the colour of steel and the thickest glasses I have ever seen. He looks tired towards the end of what must have been a long night on duty. He is drinking black coffee. I take some tissues and wipe my eyes and blow my nose and then I clear my throat but it doesn't work so I try again to clear it. I take a sip of the water. DC Hughes says, "No rush. Just sit quietly for a few minutes, until you're ready. I can see it's been a big step for you to come here."

The evidence of how wrong everything is must be etched on my face and rumbling beneath the words that are sticking in my throat. I must be visibly disintegrating; I'm about as solid as a piece of cardboard in a gutter puddle.

On the wall behind DC Hughes is a framed sign.
All victims will be treated with sensitivity, compassion and respect by professional and dedicated officers.

Already, I can see that this is true. DC Hughes. The baby-faced policeman who brought me to this room and is now sitting almost invisibly, taking notes. Both of them seem to be all the good things the sign promises. But what of the word that describes my role in all of this? *Victim*. It's a word I've resisted using about myself, a word that has unremittingly pricked at me from the leaflets and the trial. I do not want to start using it now. But that word is clearly what the young policeman and DC Hughes see when they look at me.

The chairs that the three of us sit on are made of fake plasticky wood. The matching round table between us is the only other piece of furniture. The floors are linoleum, so even DC Hughes's calm voice sounds tinny and echoey as he asks me if I want to wait for a few hours until a female police officer becomes available to interview me and I gulp out that I think I need to do it now, if that's okay, and he says yes, of course. There is a large mirror that must be an observation window, though I doubt it is being used for me. I hope it will soon be used for you.

Despite my repeated derailments of his methodical processes and my impulse to blurt everything out in distraught chaos, DC Hughes is expert at taking me through it all in logical order. I tell him that I've tried to do everything right. I tell him what you know all too well: that I haven't made it easy for you. Not at all. My urgent determination that DC Hughes should know this takes me by surprise.

I tell him that I don't belong to social networking sites; I don't advertise every intimate detail of my life or announce every journey I'm about to take. I tell him how Rowena's electronic trail led you to gate-crash my already strained friendship with her; it wasn't my own Internet presence, which is otherwise non-existent. Such public exposure is against my nature, I say. I tell him that you don't have my private email address — few people do — and that so far you've never pestered me through the university's.

I tell him that I suppose you've had no option but to track me the old-fashioned way, doggedly hanging around the places you know I have to go, even though I've reduced them almost to the point of self-imprisonment. As I say all this, I see for the first time what should have been obvious all along. My computerised existence, small as it may be, doesn't interest you at all. It is only physical contact that you want.

I tell DC Hughes about that night in November, explaining that I can't remember much. I tell him of my certainty that you will say it was consensual, and my worry that you slipped something into my wine. Despite his unflappable professional kindness, I am waiting for him to look at me in derision and tell me there is nothing he can do. That isn't what happens, though.

"The word consensual may well not apply here," he says.

I remember Lottie's eyes welling with tears when Mr Harker told her that he didn't dispute any of her evidence. I understand her stunned gratitude now in a way that I didn't then. My own eyes are prickling with tears but I blink them away, not wanting to stop DC Hughes.

"But even if we presume for the sake of argument that it does," he says, "a night of consensual sex in the past, whatever its nature, doesn't make this your fault, or give him the right to behave as he has since. We can't prove anything about the drugs now, though. You would have needed a medical exam and urine tests at the time to establish that they were used, and what they were. The tests aren't conclusive, anyway. These substances aren't all detectable, and many of them leave the body within hours."

I know that DC Hughes has probably been on too many training courses to count. He seems so natural, though, so

272

restrainedly but not overbearingly nice. So truthful. So trustworthy. I think his decency is real. I do not think it is merely the result of all those staff-development days on how to deal with the victims of sex crimes.

And now the moment has come that I can't put off any longer. I take out the obscene photographs. I packaged them separately from the rest of your grisly things, uncertain even when I walked out my front door this morning about whether or not I'd be able to bring myself to hand them over. But I place them in front of DC Hughes, babbling that I have no recollection of your taking them, telling him of my fear that you will claim it was a consensual sex game, warning him of what that envelope contains. "It's terrible enough" — my voice shakes — "being faced with you looking at them — with seeing you seeing them . . ." I trail off.

"I understand," he says. "And I think you're very brave."

I remember Mr Morden saying exactly the same thing to Lottie. The very last thing he said to her after all those days in the witness box.

I voice my fear about how many people will need to look at them.

"We're very careful of such materials," he says, but I note his avoidance of answering directly, and the vagueness of his reply.

DC Hughes's face is expressionless. I think of a doctor performing a gynaecological procedure, masking all thoughts and response to reassure the patient that there is no trace of desire; he is just doing his job. He slides out the pile of photos and glances briefly at the top one, the first one you sent me and the least terrible of them; the one before you tied me up and arranged all your props. Without looking further at

273

it, or at the others in the stack below it, he puts your souvenir images away.

I am trying to keep myself as still as I can be, blushing fiercely from head to toe in front of this uniformed man, a stranger to me. Because of you, he has seen me unconscious in my lavender underwear. Because of you, he will see worse of me than that when he looks at the rest of the photos later. He does not want to mortify me further by doing so now, before my eyes.

I take another sip of water and then he says, "It would be very difficult at this point in time to prove that you were not a willing participant, though I believe you when you say that you were not. But even if you had consented to his taking those photographs, the images are clearly not welcome to you now and you've made that clear. That is what matters about them."

He excuses himself for ten minutes, taking the quiet young policeman with him. While they are away I phone court to say I will be late. I tell them I have been detained by a family emergency. I tell them I will get in as soon as I can. I half-expect to be kicked off the jury then and there, but they are entirely kind and understanding.

DC Hughes returns with cataloguing and storage materials, again accompanied by the young policeman, who continues to operate his pencil so noiselessly I almost forget he is there. Only DC Hughes's voice and mine are allowed to bounce off the bare white walls of this interview room. I know this must be a strategy worked out between the two of them, so that I can feel as comfortable as possible in the most uncomfortable of circumstances; so that I don't feel any more overwhelmed than I already do.

Every item I've brought is carefully examined and labelled. Your letters. Your handmade book. The desiccated flowers and disused communication devices. The heart-shaped box of chocolates with its matching card. The photos of me and Robert. The ring. Your magazine and the envelope it was posted in, which I'm again grateful to DC Hughes for not looking long at. The black notebook. The photos of you on my street, snapped with my camera phone, and the one I took of my reddened wrist after the park.

Already, under the Protection from Harassment Act, I have provided evidence of much more than the minimum two instances of harassment. I have convincingly documented your persistent obsessive behaviour, and that the incidents have occurred relatively close together in terms of timescale.

More than enough grounds, DC Hughes assures me, to justify the visit he will be making to you later today. That, he says, is quite often all it takes.

I tell him about Laura's vanishing, giving him the Bettertons' contact details, mentioning that the police hadn't been able to do anything to help them, asking if he can get someone to compare the magazine cover with one of her parents' photographs of her. DC Hughes seems to sit up straighter at this, despite his stoop, and I think he actually looks worried. He plays with his heavy glasses, sliding them down his nose so I can see the red mark they've left, then up again — the first fidget I've seen from him in a very long morning. He seems to take a long time before speaking, considering his words with extra care. The police take stalking extremely seriously, he says. Though he cannot comment on another case, he says. But he will certainly retain the Bettertons' details in my file for future reference, he says.

You will be given verbal and written warnings. The clear import will be that if you persist in unsociable conduct that causes me to feel harassed, alarmed or distressed, then you will face prosecution and a restraining order. And if you breach that, you will be looking at up to five years in prison.

I tell him what you did to Robert's car, and though DC Hughes makes a note of it, he explains that unless Robert makes a complaint himself there is nothing the police can do about it. I say that I don't think Robert will be going to the police, at least for now. I don't say that this is because I am still hoping Robert will never need to know about you. For the first time, this seems possible.

By 11.00a.m. I am finished, clutching DC Hughes's card. He has written his mobile number on it, and a crime reference code. I fumble in my bag for the new notebook that is identical to the old one, all the way down to its black cover; I bought it just in case, though I hope its pages will remain blank as I slip the card between them. Then I curl my fingers around the personal attack alarm DC Hughes has given me and shown me how to use. He's also issued me a Victim Care Card with the basic information about my crime and all of the actions and paperwork that will happen next. Lottie must have had one of these too. *My* crime. The crime that belongs to me. As if you belong to me. And that word again. On the wall. On the card. In the leaflets. In the courtroom. *Victim*.

Five minutes after saying goodbye to DC Hughes I am on the station platform. I feel a pang when I realise that the young policeman vanished before I could thank him. The 11.08 train to Bristol pulls in almost immediately and I step onto it. You are nowhere in sight. You must be puzzled that you haven't found me today. All of your lookout points and routines, and nothing. I have evaded you.

Clarissa spent an unexpected afternoon break studying a vintage dress pattern, pausing occasionally to make a note to herself in her funny spidery hand. She was sitting in a small puddle of sunlight that fell through the window, sleepy in the pleasure of its warmth. She wasn't sure how long Robert had been standing there before she felt his eyes on her.

He sat down when she smiled at him. "That's an unusual-looking pattern," he said.

"It was my grandmother's. From the fifties. Patterns weren't multi-sized, then. I have to grade it down."

Carefully, lightly, he touched the yellowing sleeve piece her grandmother had cut. "It's a beautiful thing."

Their usher walked in with his usual steady stride. The other jurors, all playing poker on the other side of the room, immediately ceased their chattering and watched him. He only needed to nod and they rose from their chairs at his command. Wordlessly, they followed him. But Robert remained near the table, waiting for her as she folded away the delicate pattern.

"You have to be good, don't you, to make something like that?" he said, just before they caught up with the others. He spoke in a voice too low for anyone else to hear, for her ears alone, a lover's voice.

★ ★ ★

She walked by herself to the station that night. Robert had run for an earlier train so he could get back to Bath and deal with his vandalised car. She'd have slowed him.

She tried not to look in the shadows for Rafe. She tried to picture him getting his written and verbal warnings from DC Hughes; surely he'd have had them by now; surely he'd see that if he didn't leave her alone he'd end up with prosecutions and restraining orders and even prison. No normal person would want that.

But Rafe wasn't a normal person. She couldn't quell her apprehension that he didn't discriminate between the different types of obstacles that kept him away from her: whether he faced a police warning or a judicial command; whether he was locked out or locked in. It was all the same to him. Mere impediments that needed to be cleared away with whatever methods at his disposal, whatever the consequence; he'd say or do or promise anything.

When she was back in Bath she made herself put these thoughts out of her head. She needed to let herself trust that it would all be okay now that she'd involved the police.

She had the taxi let her out in front of the local supermarket so she could buy milk and fruit and eggs. She wasn't holding her breath when she turned down the cleaning goods aisle; she wasn't expecting him to be waiting there.

She walked those last few blocks to her house, alone in the dark. She knew he wouldn't be standing on any of the roads she crossed. She knew he wouldn't pop out at her. Not around the corner. Not on her street. Not on the path to her front door. Not by Miss Norton's lavender bush. Not in any of the usual places.

Wednesday

Wednesday, 4 March, 9.15 a.m.

I can't stop myself from writing in the new notebook. Even yesterday after I'd got home I couldn't break my habit of scribbling and then slapping the inky pages onto the shiny glass bed of my scanner. There are too many loose ends, still, before I can entirely exorcise you.

In two days' time my rubbish will be collected. Even with the police alerted and on my side I'm still not confident enough to stop my new habit of censoring what I put into the black garbage bags that I leave in front of my house on Friday mornings. I fantasise about sticking in a note. *Fuck off — I'm onto you*. But I'm not about to start speaking to you now. I'm not about to warn you or give you any useful information. And I'm certainly not about to incur my mother's wrath by letting you drive me into swearing.

As soon as I arrive in the jurors' waiting area and the key-padded door locks behind me I go to the women's cloakroom. You could never get in here. Even you never could. I take out the shopping bag I sealed before leaving this morning. Its contents are compacted into the bottom, so that my plastic-wrapped waste products resemble a misshapen balloon. I knotted the opening — airtight — before I stuffed it firmly into a second bag and knotted that too, to make the contents extra secure and keep any bad smell inside.

As I dump the bag into the cloakroom bin I'm furious that I still feel I have to do this. I'm furious that I ever needed to start doing this. But now it's all out of your reach. The sanitary towels covered in my blood from the previous five days. The empty pack of sleeping pills that I've been taking too often. The wrappings from the new body cream I just bought and the foot scrub I just opened. The wax strips I used early this morning, speckled with the fine hairs I tore from my calves and underarms. The intimate details of what comes out of my body and what goes into it, what I rub onto my skin and what I use to strip and polish it smooth, are not for you. They will never be for you.

When she left the cloakroom, she found Robert sitting at one of the shaky tables, drinking the horrible court coffee and reading the paper.

He hooked out a chair for her, smiling as she sat down with the huge latte she'd bought at a café. She needed it; she hadn't slept much. But it was over-excitement and relief, more than fear. She'd made herself skip the sleeping tablets last night; she wanted to wean herself off, and to believe that the reason she'd needed them no longer applied.

"Don't think I didn't notice the disdainful look you gave my coffee," Robert said. "Everything okay with your family?"

For a split second she was puzzled. Then she remembered the lie she'd told them all yesterday, to explain her lateness. "Yes. Thank you." She took a sip of her latte, hoping he hadn't noticed her delayed response. "And your car?"

He shrugged, as if to say it was of no importance, not worth talking about. His hand was so huge around the court's dinky white mug.

She thought about that hand. It picked up body parts. It cut car-crash victims from mangled wrecks, dead or alive. It guided frightened old ladies out of high windows and down turntable ladders. It controlled jets of water with a fine balance of expert precision and instinct and power. It dragged human beings from burning buildings or dug them out of piles of rubble.

She wondered what it would be like to be touched by a hand like that.

Robert's face had reverted to its default impassivity. But it was his job to control his face, with people dying and in pain and extremity in front of him all the time. Such physical and emotional discipline must be a skill he could transfer to everything, a skill he'd developed over many years because he had to use it every day. But could he turn off the detachment at will, too?

She tried to imagine if anything could make him lose control. She thought of the knight in Waterhouse's painting of La Belle Dame Sans Merci. The knight was off balance, bending his knees, leaning towards the fairy woman, disarmed, his sword lowered. He was still so strong, though, in his helmet and armour and tunic. Clarissa thought that that was how Robert must look when he wore the things he had to wear to go into fires.

The door swung open. Annie headed towards them. The boy with the purple-tipped hair was with her, his matching earphones in place as usual. Annie seemed to be marching him by her side with his wrists in invisible handcuffs.

"Don't marry her," Annie was saying. "You're too young to get married. When you're forty you'll just leave her for someone younger, leave her stuck on her own with three kids and a fat bum."

The boy looked scared. He looked to Robert for saving, but Robert picked up his backpack and stood. "Locker time," he said.

As he walked away, Clarissa realised that she hadn't let herself look at his startlingly blue eyes since the first time she ever spoke to him. She never dared to let her own eyes touch his beyond a moving glance. If those Romantic paintings and poems showed anything, it was how dangerous looking — really looking, directly and with intent, actually was.

Mr Morden appeared nervous and Clarissa soon saw why. "The next phase of the Crown's case concerns Mr Sparkle's police interviews," he said. But before Mr Morden could begin another sentence Sparkle's barrister was furiously declaring a need for legal argument and the jury was dismissed for the remainder of the day.

Wednesday, 4 March, 6.20 p.m.

I don't see it when I walk in. I'm too preoccupied with the important job of taking off my hat and stuffing it in my bag.

283

That's why I don't see it. That's why I step on the brown envelope, leaving mud on its corner. It is only the sensation of paper sticking to my boot that makes me look down and peel it off. Miss Norton must have been napping when it went through the door slot.

My full name is typed. I hate your using my full name, but I do not yet realise it is you, so I am not yet upset. There are a few seconds left before that happens. Nothing else is written on it. There is no address or stamp. But your hallmarks do not register because I've already made myself stop looking for all signs of you. I so wanted to do that. It was all too easy for me to do that.

As I float dreamily towards the staircase, thinking of my walk with Robert, I absently tear the envelope open and take out the contents. In the instant that I see your handwriting I slap my hand onto my head and run it over the top of my skull several times. My hair fizzles and crackles and I actually see electric blue sparks. When I move my fingers away my hair follows them as if they are magnetised.

Slouching against the wall, my bag still heavy over my shoulder, I read your letter.

You're so good on "Blue Beard". Here's another fairy tale I'd like your opinion on.

You know what the king did to his shameless wife in "The Three Snake-Leaves". She and her lover were placed in a ship "which had been pierced with holes, and sent out to sea, where they soon sank amid the waves".

Do you think he was foolish, that king, giving her those last moments alone with her lover? Do you think he should have spent them with her himself?

284

I have fallen hard and far from the great hope DC Hughes raised only yesterday. It is akin to going to sleep trying to convince myself that tomorrow's pregnancy test will be positive, only to be crushed by the clinic's call on my mobile the next afternoon or the show of blood on my underwear before the lab has even faxed through the results.

I reach into my bag for my phone and the card with DC Hughes's number. I manage to get out only a few words but it's enough and he tells me he is on his way; I needn't go to the station myself as mine is a high-priority case.

Slowly, trying to calm myself with deliberate and careful motions, I walk up the stairs to my flat and make myself a cup of tea to try to get warm and wash the horrible taste from my mouth. And the horrible phrase from my head.

High-priority case. The worst kind of honour. As if I've been given access to a perverse executive lounge or fast-tracked to hell.

I can't stop replaying those words. High-priority case. It's as if I've suddenly come down with some kind of obsessive compulsive disorder. High-priority case. High-priority case. High-priority case. The words won't leave me alone, as if a broken record is endlessly repeating itself inside my head.

Until DC Hughes said it, I hadn't known that that was what I was. I hadn't let myself think that that was what I could be. That that was what you'd made me. A high-priority case.

Last moments.

Spending them with her himself.

I see it from the outside as if for the first time. Even to the police it must all look very, very bad. Even to the police, who see terrible people every single day, you must look very dangerous. A high-priority case.

Thursday

Thursday, 5 March, 9.30 a.m.

I sit alone in the jurors' assembly area, trying to be invisible, even to Robert. I am envisaging what is happening to you. DC Hughes explained it all.

The police will knock on your door. They will arrest you. They will interview you under caution. If you don't answer "no comment" under questioning you'll probably blame me. You'll probably say we were in a relationship and I never told you your attentions were unwanted. You might even say that I was the one pestering you.

Will they show you the photographs? Will you gloat? I try to convince myself that they won't give you the satisfaction of looking at them there, of showing off your work. Or if they must, that you probably won't say much or want to peer at them for long — not with others — part of your possessiveness. Whatever they do, however you react, it won't diminish the huge weight of other evidence.

They will refer the evidence to the Crown Prosecution Service for advice.

Then, hopefully, they will charge you with the *Offence of harassment* and with *Putting people in fear of violence*, under the Protection from Harassment Act.

They will take you to appear before a court and seek the immediate imposition of a restraining order, though you'll be granted conditional bail.

You will probably be out by the weekend. DC Hughes is likely to give me this news within the next few days. But by the time you're free again it will be against the law for you to come anywhere near me or communicate with me in any way.

It will make it impossible for you to go to work. Personnel will probably take legal advice. They'll send letters, working out whether they can or should or must continue to employ you. You will be absolutely furious. If I didn't hate you so much I'd be sorry for you about this. But I can't afford pity.

More than that, I can't afford the fear that work kept you in relative check, and that that has now been taken away. There's another thing, too, that goes against me. Even if Robert's presence offers some protection, it also incites you. With Laura, there hadn't been another man to make you so obsessively jealous. At least not one her parents knew of, though you might have known more than they did, with your spying.

I try to tell myself that if anything does happen to me, the police will immediately suspect you. That's a comforting thought. You know this, too. There'd been no scrutiny of you, with Laura. They'd left you free to do as you pleased. That's not the case with me. But a tiny part of me can't help but suspect that the police are only going through all of these motions so that if you end up killing me they'll have ticked every bureaucratic box; they'll have protected themselves from blame. Tangled in all of this is the thing I've known all the time but not wanted to speak: your murdering me is a real possibility. That's why I'm a high-priority case.

She sat in Court 12 thinking about the mystery of what happened to Laura, and Mr and Mrs Betterton in their endless despair, and the woman on the cover of the terrible magazine.

She tried to concentrate on Mr Morden as he rose. "Detective Constable Mallory will read the questions he put to Mr Sparkle, while I read Mr Sparkle's responses. You will hear extracts."

DC: Okay, Isaac. Can you take me through what happened when you woke up on the Sunday morning?

IS: I found Carlotta in the bedroom. She were kinda like, curled on the bed, pressing herself into the corner, to tell the truth. Like, they call it the foetal position, innit?

I signalled her to come into the lounge with me. She were . . . a bit sceptical . . . a bit quiet like. Not like the night before when she were chattin' to me and Godfrey and Azarola. So I asks her, did something happen, and she were like, yeah, I was manhandled, they manhandled me.

289

DC: What did you understand "manhandled" to mean, Isaac?

IS: Dunno. I guess, like, you know, the rape charges and all that you lot have been talking about. So I was kinda like, who done this, and she goes, the two biggest, and I thought she meant Tomlinson and Doleman. So I says to Tomlinson later, Carlotta says you manhandled her, and he goes, it were nothing, it weren't anything. But he weren't looking at me. He didn't wanna be talkin' about it.

Instead of walking straight to the station, they stopped at a nearby bistro that had caught Robert's eye. *Just a quick dinner*, they both said, playing it down. *Too charming and hidden-in-plain-sight a place to neglect*, they both said, smiling as they slid into the red leather booth.

His mouth fell open in mock astonishment when she ordered a steak sandwich. "You're not vegetarian? For some reason I'd assumed you were."

"Definitely not. But I know how embarrassing I am, asking for it to be well done." Henry could never stop himself from cringing when she did that.

"No you're not. You should order your steak how you like it."

A zillion points for you, she thought, beaming at him. "I'm glad you see it that way."

She excused herself for a minute and headed for the cloakroom, fumbling in her bag for her phone as she walked. She wanted to check hurriedly, out of Robert's sight, for a message from DC Hughes. But there was nothing.

When she returned her breathing froze. In Robert's hand was the black notebook.

"It fell out as you walked away." His voice was calm, not guilty; not the voice of a man who'd been snooping. He held it towards her.

She took it, slowly and gently, and murmured a thank you. She held it by the wire binding, letting it dangle. She made the pages swing back and forth a few times, creaking with suitably creepy sounds as they moved.

Robert poured sparkling water into a glass for her. "Just in case you're wondering, I didn't look in it."

"I'm sorry if I made you think I thought that." She rolled her eyes at herself. "Was that a tongue-twister?"

He laughed. "Possibly." But he hadn't given up the subject. "Just so you know. I wouldn't do something like that."

She thought of Henry, rooting around the pile of papers on her bedside table, coming across the information pack from the fertility clinic before she was ready to explain to him that she wanted to start trying; his fury that she was plotting behind his back; but then his quick willingness to go with her and keep his promise that he would let her have a baby. "I know you wouldn't."

"So you trust me?"

"I do."

"Good. It's understandable if you wondered." He drank down an inch of his French beer. "Are you writing a novel?"

She shook her head no.

"You're always scribbling in it. You look like you're pretty addicted to whatever you're writing. I think it must be a work of art."

"Definitely not a work of art."

"You don't see anything else when you're doing it. This morning you were at it and I waved at you but you didn't notice. Annie did a jig to try to distract you and you still didn't look up."

"I can't believe I missed that. I'm going to have to make her perform it again."

"You didn't even hear the two of us laughing."

She gave the notebook a little glare, as if it had misbehaved by commanding too much of her attention. It was hardly bigger than the hand she held it in. "It's a bit tiny to fit a novel."

"Whatever you're writing, I bet it's good."

"It isn't good." She slipped it back into her bag, which she fastened carefully, double-checking it was safely shut.

The waitress was arranging plates in front of them.

She examined her steak sandwich. Caramelised onions leaked from the baguette and soaked the inside of it into a deep golden brown. She took a careful bite and made an appreciative noise, knowing this would make Robert look pleased, though she was secretly cursing herself for ordering something that was so impossibly messy. She wiped her mouth with her napkin as soon as she'd put the sandwich down, in case there was any steak juice around her lips. "It's truly delicious. Is my mother paying you to make sure I eat?"

Smile, quick negative shake of the head, brief pause before an amused and definite "No."

It was too difficult to fit her mouth around the huge sandwich. She cut a small piece of steak and speared some onion onto her fork along with it. She dipped it into the little pot of red wine sauce they'd put on the side of her plate. She put the fork down, the bite of steak and onion and sauce uneaten. "I wanted to say . . . about the notebook, Robert . . ."

He had a mouthful of sautéed potatoes. He swallowed before he was quite ready. "Don't worry about that."

"Are you actually choking?"

He exaggerated a croaking voice. "I can see how deeply concerned you are." He looked at her plate. "Your mother might not pay me if you don't eat your potatoes."

"I like the crispy ones best. They're the only ones worth eating."

He sorted through his own potatoes, weeded out all of the crispy ones, and piled them onto her plate.

"My mother will love you." She popped one in her mouth immediately.

His phone buzzed. "Jack's in a bad place. Otherwise I'd leave it." He slid the mobile from his pocket and squinted at a text, frowning. "I don't want to, but we're going to have to make a move soon. I need to get to him. Drag him out of the dark tunnel before he's in too far."

She nodded understanding. "Friends are important." She was thinking of Rowena, wondering whether it might still be possible to get her back, but wondering also whether she wanted to.

Friday

It was exactly how Robert would have done it, she thought, as Azarola walked sure-footedly to the witness box and gazed steadily out, straight and unflinching and looking more than ever like a Spanish pop star. He wore a grey knitted V-neck vest over a dazzlingly white scoop-neck T-shirt.

"You say you can't remember what you were doing over the weekend that a young woman was allegedly kidnapped and falsely imprisoned and raped." Mr Williams was being tough with his boy.

Azarola shook his head in helpless bewilderment. "Yeah. Because I don't know her. I've never met her. I wasn't there." He wasn't quite as tall as Robert, but he had the same narrow hips and waist and long legs.

"Then why would your own supposed friend, Mr Sparkle, tell the police you were?"

"He's lying. He's a competitor." Maybe firemen had to spend part of each day in the gym. Prisoners probably chose to, if they were smart. "He wants me put away. Out of the way."

★ ★ ★

295

Robert and Clarissa were on their usual walk to the station. "I've never been caught by a speed camera," he said. "Never even had a parking ticket."

"Were you a Boy Scout?" She pushed her hair over her ears to try to warm them. She'd left her hat in her bag. Though he'd seen her in it before, she was suddenly self-conscious, wondering if it was too little girlish a thing to wear in front of him.

"Nope."

"I was teasing you again. I'm sorry."

He didn't look as if he minded. "You're shivering. Don't you have your hat? You can wear mine."

His was shaped like a Russian Cossack's hat; the dark navy fleece definitely covered his ears. She rummaged for her own, making herself look surprised and pleased to find it.

"Nice," he said.

"My mother knitted it. She likes me to be warm."

"She sounds very wise." Apparently satisfied that she would be safe from frostbite, he resumed their subject. "Boys need structured frameworks for their aggression. Need to learn to discipline it. The Fire Service is the thing. If our friends in the dock had joined at eighteen they wouldn't be sitting there now."

"It's not for everybody, though, is it? Not anyone can join. You need special qualities."

He looked surprised by this idea.

"What percentage of applicants get in?" she asked.

"One in four. There are aptitude tests, personality tests. You can't fool the tests."

296

"I'd bet Azarola could. He'd win on charisma alone." She was reaching into her bag for her ringing mobile as she spoke. "And I think he's smarter than all the barristers put together." She could see DC Hughes's name on the screen. "I'm so sorry, Robert." She pulled her hat off again so her ear wouldn't be muffled. "I need to take this."

"I'll walk ahead. Catch up to me if you finish. Otherwise I'll see you Monday."

She spoke very little as she listened to DC Hughes. She told him she was walking on a public street, with an acquaintance nearby.

He seemed instantly to understand the position she was in. "Happy to fill you in while you listen." He hadn't wanted to leave her wondering all weekend, but he was about to go off duty.

Robert paused to glance around at her and she tried to smile at him. She rolled her eyes, as if she wished she could get the call over with and finished, and he moved forward again.

DC Hughes's information was first-hand; he'd been in court himself that afternoon. He warned Clarissa that though Mr Solmes's account of his actions was as they had predicted, she would still find it ugly and painful to hear.

Mr Solmes had bowed his head as his solicitor explained that from his client's point of view it was all a terrible and sad misunderstanding; a tragic case of poor communication which should never have been brought within the legal system. Mr Solmes had certainly never meant to intimidate Miss Bourne or burden her with unwelcome attention.

The photographs had been part of sex games that his client and Miss Bourne had enjoyed together as two consenting adults, and which Miss Bourne in particular had sought. Mr Solmes had reluctantly agreed to them because he wished to please her; he profoundly regretted that Miss Bourne had felt the need to share something so personal with the police.

Clarissa's throat tightened. She coughed, to clear it, and a choking noise came out. Robert turned once more to look at her. They were crossing a busy road at the green man's signal. He seemed to want to check she wasn't too distracted to do this safely.

Mr Solmes had been particularly shocked that she could regard the beautiful flowers as a death threat. He worried that she must be under considerable strain and exhaustion to imagine such a thing.

He'd thought that she reciprocated his feelings; they'd even chosen an engagement ring together, which Miss Bourne had accepted and retained. Until three days ago, he'd had no indication that Miss Bourne had come to feel differently since the night they shared back in November, when she agreed to marry him. He'd been completely blindsided when the police knocked on his door on Tuesday; it had taken him time to absorb this new state of affairs.

Despite what she had done to him, Miss Bourne's withdrawn and distressed behaviour was causing Mr Solmes high levels of concern about her well-being. She appeared to be quite visibly deteriorating in health and it was known that she had become addicted to sleeping pills. He had persisted in trying to contact her only to offer much-needed assistance. He'd even joined with her best friend in staging an intervention, but Miss Bourne refused that too. It was a sign of how desperate her condition was that she did not recognise the importance of accepting help.

Mr Solmes felt it to be a painful injustice that he should be dragged into court as a result of his kindness and humanity. He would now cease all attentions to Miss Bourne. However, he had instructed his solicitor to express the fact that despite his deep hurt, it was his sincere hope that Miss Bourne would seek personal and medical support elsewhere; Mr Solmes only wished her well.

The judge didn't buy any of it, DC Hughes said. He granted bail but issued a restraining order.

Mr Solmes's solicitor protested that the restraining order would make his client's job impossible, destroying his livelihood and career, as he and Miss Bourne worked on the same site.

DC Hughes hastened to reassure Clarissa that the judge did not change his mind. More than that, he made it clear to Mr Solmes's solicitor that if his client breached the restraining order the penalty would be severe and certainly involve a significant prison sentence.

DC Hughes advised Clarissa to remain watchful and careful, but to be optimistic that Mr Solmes would now leave her alone.

She had a terrible realisation, then. It occurred to her that she had actually been lucky that his behaviour had been so extreme. It wasn't such a bad thing, after all, to be a high-priority case. Had his pestering been of a more moderate nature, it might not have been taken so seriously. The police might not have helped. She might never have got that restraining order. She might have had to live with a low level of his constant presence until she died; every minute of her existence diminished by slow poison.

All she wanted now was to grab at her own life, to possess it again and bask in it being entirely hers and entirely private. That wasn't something she would ever again take for granted, as so many people did.

By the time she slipped the mobile back into her bag she was calmer. As she walked along the approach to the station Robert slowed to wait for her.

"Interesting call?" he asked, neutrally.

"No." She shook her head, too, to insist, convincing herself as she spoke. "It's a very boring thing that's all over."

He paused to consider, then spoke as if unable to stop himself. "I wondered if it was a man. Maybe someone you're seeing . . ."

"No. Goodness, no." Robert's face relaxed. She said softly, shyly, "There's no one like that, Robert." She tried to think of how she could tell him something close to the truth. "It was a colleague. There's something I'd been worried about, a work thing, but he had good news for me. The problem has gone away."

She and Robert were standing in front of the ticket gates.

"That's good," Robert said.

She nodded. "It is." She fed her ticket into the machine and walked through the turnstile. "It really, really is. I don't want to think about it any more." They paused at the top of the stairs that led down to the trains. "I'm not seeing anyone." She looked straight into his blindingly blue eyes. "There's only one person I'd want to see."

Saturday and Sunday

She tested herself over the weekend, to see if she could feel free and not look over her shoulder. On Saturday she wandered through the town centre, shopping slowly at the farmers' market, wondering fleetingly about the possibility that Polly Horton was nearly kidnapped there by Godfrey; she was struck by what a busy and safe-seeming place it was.

She ordered a latte at the coffee bar. While she was waiting for it, she texted Caroline on the off chance that she was free to come to dinner that night; though she wondered if Caroline would be annoyed with her for declining that lunch invitation two weeks ago. Almost instantly, taking her by surprise, Caroline texted back that she'd be there at eight, and that she couldn't wait to tell Clarissa about a top-secret plan to restructure the university.

The latte still wasn't ready, so she texted Rowena too. *I love you and miss you.* That was all. There was no immediate response to that one, though. She feared Rowena would take shears to the silk nightdress she'd posted earlier that morning, but pushed the thought out of her mind and let herself be excited by the prospect of Caroline's visit.

She bought bright red tulips, the first of the season, and olives and oak-roasted tomatoes and ricotta-stuffed peppers and sweet dark rye bread and handmade halloumi cheese and a bottle of her favourite Amarone. From the French chocolatier she bought pralines and truffles and cocoa-dusted almonds. She bought the ingredients for her mother's beef casserole too.

When she returned home there were no letters or presents. There was only a credit-card bill that seemed like a lovely thing.

On Sunday she walked for a long time in quiet fields where she and Henry used to watch foxes in the late summer twilight. It always seemed magical that somewhere so quiet and rural-seeming could be so close to a city.

She liked the feel of springy moss beneath her feet as she wandered through the overgrown old churchyard that bordered a small farm. She was moved by the sight of fresh flowers and a new-looking teddy bear on the grave of a young child who'd died forty years earlier. Had the mother left them? She'd probably be an old woman now, but Clarissa didn't find it surprising that she could still be mourning her lost child all these years later. Clarissa knew one child could never be replaced by another, but hoped nonetheless that there'd been at least one other for that grieving mother.

Only when the sun was so low that she had to squint did she cease from looking at the dates and names on the stone angels and ornate crosses. Only then did she pause in her impulse to make up stories for lives that were cut short, trying not to count Laura's among them.

Week 6

The
Forbidden Key

Monday

"He's intelligent," Annie said to the room.

They were in the annex, waiting for the usher to take them back into Court 12 to witness Mr Morden's final attempt at smashing the unsmashable Azarola. Mr Morden had spent the day being thwarted by Mr Williams's interventions, and the jury had spent the day popping in and out of their chairs to allow for matters of legal argument.

Annie leaned towards Clarissa and whispered, "Pretty bra strap, by the way. Do you think Azarola likes pink silk?"

Annie's whisper was not very whispery. Robert had probably heard it from his usual seat across from Clarissa, though he carefully appeared not to.

Clarissa hid the straps beneath fabric. "I'd have welcomed that information earlier, Annie," she said.

"Your cheeks are matching it now," Annie said. "Better than your usual ghost look."

Wendy was sitting on Clarissa's other side, hurriedly texting her boyfriend, but she looked up. "Any chance of Azarola using his talents in a good way, some day?"

"I'm thinking no." Annie sat back in her chair again. "And I'm thinking we're the ones who'll be turning his evil genius loose."

Mr Morden eyed Azarola with undisguised scorn. "You told Mr Williams that you gave your phone to one of your boys, Aaron, and that that's why it moved along the route to London while Miss Lockyer was being kidnapped. If you really weren't there, then tell us Aaron's real name."

Smile, quick negative shake of the head, brief pause before an amused and definite "No". Clarissa realised that Robert sometimes used this exact sequence of gestures.

"There is no Aaron." Mr Morden appeared so furious she wondered if he might actually lose control. "You know it. This jury knows it. You were in that van."

Monday, 9 March, 6.20 p.m.

There is no writing on the envelope but Miss Norton has stuck a small yellow note to it. *This came this morning, Clarissa. Probably for you? Knock on my door if I'm mistaken.* Even before I open it, I know Miss Norton is not mistaken. Miss Norton is never mistaken.

Inside is the next in your series of photographs, as if you wanted to flip through them one after the other to make a crude film. You've changed only one thing in it. You've moved one of my stockings, arranging it in a U. You've looped the centre of it around my neck. You've brought the tip of the toe and the rim of the thigh up to the bedstead and tied them to it.

I replay the examination I made of my body the next morning. There'd been no marks on my throat. I'm certain of it. I'd have noticed.

The stocking is merely decorative, if such a word can be used; entirely a reflection of your taste. It's symbolic, too, though as symbols go the message is hardly subtle: you want to strangle me, you easily can, you had a chance and didn't, and you won't be so generous next time.

I force myself to look carefully at the photo again to confirm that you didn't actually hurt me with your makeshift noose. However horrifying and threatening the image, your loop is loose.

I am working hard to be rational. It doesn't matter if you told the police and your solicitor that it was a consensual game, as you did with Laura. It doesn't matter that this image is even more disgusting and frightening than the last one. What matters is that you've hardly got beyond the weekend without breaking the restraining order. That's a criminal offence which will result in your being brought back to court within twenty-four hours and a certain prison sentence. At least eighteen months, DC Hughes said: the judge warned you that the consequences of a breach would be grave. Plus, you'll be subject to a lifetime prohibition of all contact with me.

I'll be rid of you. I'll be truly safe and free. You've actually done me a favour, sending this. I can survive the mortification of having to go to DC Hughes with it.

I call a taxi and go straight to the police station, where I spend the remainder of the evening being interviewed again; I'm growing as expert at this as Lottie must have been.

Afterwards, I'm driven home by the same young policeman I blundered into the first time I went there, and I'm glad I get a chance to thank him for being kind and helping me and not making me leave before they'd opened. He smiles sweetly as he concentrates on the road, telling me it's his job and what he's there for and he was glad to be able to help.

When he glances to the side at me, my face begins to tremble and redden and I gaze at my lap in a flash of certainty that he has seen those photos. I try to bury the thought. I try to tell myself that I have absolutely no evidence of this. I try to convince myself that if he has looked at them, it was out of pure professional necessity. I try to remind myself that I have just given the police the last and worst of your terrible pictures and it's probably being studied at this very moment by others so what difference does it make if this young man knows what I look like naked and tied up; thanks to you, he's far from alone in that.

By the time the policeman pulls into my road and parks the car and insists on walking me into the building I have got control of my face again and managed to steady my hands. He checks with me that you haven't made any new deliveries, then sees me safely up the stairs and into my flat.

I have to resort to the pills to calm myself, but I fall into my deep doped sleep knowing you will be arrested again. It will happen while I'm dreaming. And you won't be getting out any time soon.

Tuesday

Clarissa wandered through the outside market. Already he was in jail, remanded in custody. No bail this time. She'd heard early that morning from DC Hughes, who was about to go on holiday for two weeks and wanted to let her know before he left that she shouldn't worry any more; Mr Solmes would be out of range for quite some time.

Beneath her boots she wore thick socks. After she'd rummaged in her drawer for stockings that morning, out of habit, she couldn't then bring herself to put them on. Her thighs were bare, freezing under her coat and dress. This made her furious.

"I've decided you're the Lady of Shalott," said a voice.

She turned to Robert, just a few feet behind her, and her anger evaporated. "Is that a good thing?"

"Have coffee with me. There's time." He steered her towards the place on the corner. "It's not going to be pretty if Tomlinson goes into the witness box. We'll need fortification." He put a latte in front of her, and the sugar, and held out an old book.

It was a slim edition of *The Lady of Shalott*, just the one poem, illustrated with carefully placed reproductions of various scenes as depicted by different painters. "This is completely wonderful," she said. "How can I not have seen it before?"

"Something I picked up second-hand," he said.

She paused over Waterhouse's painting of the Lady sitting in her boat, floating towards Camelot and death and looking as though she had a small baby bump, a symptom of her desire for Lancelot. Clarissa wondered if it was a phantom pregnancy arising out of the Lady's wish to bear his child. She voiced this thought to Robert, then worried that he'd think she still saw babies and pregnancy everywhere.

He said, possibly with restrained amusement, "I'd never have seen that." He hesitated. "I want to draw you. Will you let me, when this is all over?"

She felt what it would be like, sitting as he wanted, as he arranged her, letting him look at her. He wouldn't just look. He would touch. She would touch back.

There would be no Rafe, spying on them, any more.

"Yes." Her voice was very soft. She held the book towards him, to return it, thinking it was a rare and expensive old edition, not quite daring to let herself wonder if he'd got hold of it since they'd met, despite his casualness. She wondered also if he'd been looking over the poems recently, too, and the paintings; as if she were a teacher he wanted to impress — the idea touched her.

"It's yours," he said.

312

"I can't." She put it on the table, gently. "It's too special a thing."

He laid his hand over the book. "It was made for you."

She'd grown habituated to refusing gifts, to seeing each one as an assault. But that wasn't what this was.

Hardly daring to do it, she rested her own hand on the book too. Very lightly, she pressed the tips of her fingers against his: there was no mistaking that one; he couldn't possibly think the contact was accidental. "Thank you," she said softly.

Antony Tomlinson lumbered towards the witness box. He wore dark jeans and a long-sleeved white shirt, untucked over his large stomach. His tie moved her: the pathos of his failed attempt to polish himself for the occasion.

He gave his account of what happened when he and Doleman got back from the nightclub. "The others were dozing. Carlotta was awake in the chair. Asked if she could pay us for drugs with sex. It was her idea. I said, 'Are you sure?' She said, 'Yeah.' She led us to the bedroom. I gave her a wrap of crack cocaine and a wrap of heroin. She smoked both."

Sally Martin had said that Lottie charged forty to eighty pounds as a working girl, depending on whether the man wanted a blow job or full sex. By Tomlinson's account, Lottie had proposed a threesome in exchange for twenty pounds' worth of drugs. It just didn't compute.

★ ★ ★

Mr Morden got to his feet, a boxer eager to throw his punches. "You say Miss Lockyer could have got out of that van at any time?"

"Yes."

"May I ask the jury to look at page eighty-two of their files?"

The white van again. And something on its side door that Clarissa couldn't believe she hadn't noticed before. She leaned forward to peer more closely, shifting her feet as she did so and stepping on her bag, which she'd placed beneath the table before sitting down.

Tuesday, 10 March, 3.20 p.m.

The noise is so piercing and sudden. Everyone is looking in my direction. Jurors are slapping hands over their ears.

I do not yet understand what is happening. I do not yet understand that it is all because of you. You have found me again.

Everything seems to be in slow motion, like an underwater pantomime. Robert is turning in his chair, managing to seem both urgent and calm at once. His lips are moving, soundlessly. They seem to be shaping the word "below". He's pointing to my desk and tapping it. Annie is bending down and when she comes up, as if for air, she drops my bag on the table in front of me.

I lift the bag and the decibel level intensifies. In a kind of bewildered nightmare, I begin to dig through it, not caring what I heap on the table in full view of them all. My coin purse, a hairbrush, lip balm, my switched-off phone, a sewing pattern, moisturiser, Robert's precious book, keys, the notebook.

The siren blares all the time, so piercingly I think it will never stop. And then I have it, silver and no bigger than a key ring, shrieking in my hand. The personal attack alarm DC Hughes gave me. I'd forgotten it was there. I must have moved my shoe onto the ripcord and activated it through my bag.

I pull at the cord, my hands shaking, but nothing happens. I search for a button to turn it off, but I can't find one, can't make it stop, can't remember what DC Hughes said to do to shut it up. My fingers have healed since burning them, but they are throbbing again, and stiff, as if I were still wearing the bandages. Robert's hands are on mine and he pulls the alarm from my grasp. He gives it one firm twist and the room is silent.

"I'm so sorry." As I speak, I have a sense of what a transgression it is, my own voice in this room. My ears are ringing. My words sound loud and echoey. I am certain my face is poppy red. I glance over at the dock. Four of the five are looking at me, Azarola with a poker player's inscrutability, Tomlinson and Sparkle with pity, Godfrey with contempt and irritation. Only Doleman stares straight ahead like a guard at Buckingham Palace.

Maybe the judge will throw me in jail for the night, for contempt of court. I am scared to look up at him, but I make myself, just a quick glance, and I see that his expression is benevolent.

Mr Morden and Mr Harker toss sympathetic and encouraging smiles in my direction. The man who sits on my left — who hardly ever reacts to anything — gives my arm an awkward pat of solidarity. Someone else passes the water jug to Annie, and she fills a plastic cup and wraps my fingers around it and watches while I drink, then looks satisfied and takes the empty cup from me. Robert turns in his seat as if to check that I'm still in one piece.

A day that began with the loveliness of Robert and his book has crumbled into this. Even in prison you are still getting at me. But the kindness all around me still seems stronger than you. Even in a room so full of ugliness and fear and meanness it is still stronger.

Mr Morden resumed at the judge's nod, putting the interruption decidedly behind them. "Please read the warning on the van's sliding door, aloud to the court."

Tomlinson read slowly. "*Warning: This door can only be opened from the outside.*"

"Which means not from inside," Mr Morden said. "And the door on the van's other side carries an identical warning. Miss Lockyer could not have simply opened a door and got out, could she?"

Tuesday, 10 March, 4.40 p.m.

I haven't taken in anything Mr Morden said, though I can feel in the air that he has been saying important things.

Eyes on the floor, I stumble out of Court 12 in a daze. For once I'm not dreaming about walking to the station with Robert. I'm not imagining what it will feel like to sit next to him on the train. I'm not wondering if I might get the courage to touch him accidentally-on-purpose. I'm not plotting about how I might be able to brush up against him as if the crush of other people is to blame and I just can't help it. I'm not full of the fantasies and plans I'm usually full of by the end of each day; they are one of my secret pleasures.

"Clarissa."

I have reached the bottom of the stairs. I blink in confusion, as if Robert has just woken me up. I hadn't even realised he was near me, which must be a true first.

Yet again you've overwhelmed everything else. You've overwhelmed me. But I let you. I won't let you again.

"I think this is yours." Carefully, Robert places the alarm in my hand.

"I think I may leave it at home tomorrow." I drop it in my bag.

"Tomorrow will be a better day."

To my surprise, I'm actually smiling. "This one did start so beautifully."

I remind myself that it was a false alarm only. I remind myself to be grateful that I don't even need that alarm any more.

And I don't need the notebook any more either. I vow that after today you will never again be second person present to me. Not ever. No more. That is no longer what you are.

Wednesday

Mr Morden gave himself a shake, as if steeling himself to confront something unpleasant. "Do you find Carlotta Lockyer attractive?"

"You don't have to find someone attractive to have sex with them. I thought I was doing her a favour."

Annie's hand fell flat onto the table, making a small slapping sound.

Tomlinson spluttered on in the face of Mr Morden's hammed speechlessness. "I had drugs. She wanted drugs. It was her idea. She said she'd give me sex for drugs. It was only for a few seconds — I didn't like the feel of it. I thought that didn't count as sex, but my barrister explained to me that any penetration of a vagina by a penis is defined as sex, no matter how brief."

Mr Morden looked as if he were going to vomit. "I'm done with this witness," he said.

Robert shook his head as soon as the door to the courtroom shut behind them. "He's a horror." The statement was delivered without inflection. The others all nodded agreement.

"Gee whiz," Annie said. "What's sex? Do you mean if I put my penis in your vagina we're actually having sex?"

"Do me a favour," Grant said.

A few minutes later, Clarissa and Annie and Robert were sitting in a wine bar around the corner. It had been Robert's idea to stop for a quick drink. Annie nearly fell off her chair when she looked up and saw Grant standing by their table, ready to join them. "We're safe with you, Clarissa," Grant said. "Anyone attacks us — we've got your alarm."

"Any special reason for carrying it?" Robert asked, as if casually.

She told a literal truth. "I forgot I had it. Someone gave it to me a while ago."

"Seriously, Clarissa." Grant sat down. "What are you? Five four? Seven stone? You've seen the size of the boys. Think how easily they could just lift you away."

She tilted the huge glass of red wine Robert had bought her, watching it swirl, feeling it hit her bloodstream.

"I don't like thinking about that," Robert said.

Robert was already on his third pint but the only sign of its effect was that every time she turned to look at him she'd find his eyes on her face, studying her too intently to avert them.

Annie played with her half-drunk pint of bitter. "That's why personal safety alarms are good."

"For someone who can manage to use them," Clarissa said. "Obviously not me."

319

Grant stretched out his legs, so he was almost lying down, and folded his arms. "Tomlinson's big. My kind of size. She's your kind of size, Clarissa. Imagine him with his knees on your shoulders like she said they were during the blow job. You'd snap."

She sat up straighter. "The mattress was on a low frame in the photo. In Tomlinson's version of events, he said she was lying on the bed on her back while he stood next to it for the blow job. That can't be right. Her head wouldn't be high enough to reach him."

"Let's try it, Clarissa. Convince me. Here and now." Grant pointed. "Plenty of room behind the table."

She glanced at Robert. His mouth had stiffened. His eyes had narrowed.

"Maybe your wife can help with your investigative work." She gathered her coat and bag.

"Or maybe you have a rubber doll?" Annie was also readying herself to leave.

"See you tomorrow," Clarissa said. She let herself sneak one last look at Robert. Please come, she thought. Please, please come with me.

Robert swallowed the last two inches of his pint, stood up, and said exactly the words she wanted to hear. "I'll come with you, Clarissa," he said.

"He can be your new personal attack alarm," said Annie.

"I'd like that," she said, addressing both of them at once.

She stepped onto the train and let herself fall into a window seat. He sat down next to her. She could smell

320

the beer on his breath. She wanted to taste it. He stared straight into her face and said her name in that simple, confirming way she'd liked when they first met over the Japanese pattern book. He swooped in to kiss her on the lips so swiftly before swooping away again she almost wondered if it had happened at all.

As the train pulled into Bath she fumbled on the floor for her bag, leaning over him to reach for it, knowing he could smell her shampoo. They stepped off the train and he walked alongside her, down the stairs, through the ticket gates, out the station doors. His hand was on her arm. He guided her into a taxi and got in next to her.

She wasn't sure how she got out of the taxi, was only vaguely aware of his dropping money into the driver's hand as she fumbled for her keys, somehow getting into the building and even introducing him to Miss Norton, who stepped out of her flat and into the hallway to intercept them. Miss Norton beamed as Robert gently shook her hand, but they quickly got away and were up the stairs to Clarissa's flat.

As soon as the door closed behind them they were tugging each other's coats off and she was wrapped around him, tasting him properly at last, his mouth, his skin, her hands in his hair. She could smell his own smell, and the clean lime note of his aftershave, which she thought he'd only recently started wearing, lovely and still there, though faint at the end of the day. He was tugging the silk jersey of her dress from behind her with one hand, watching the effect as it clung to her breasts and waist and hips while moving his other hand

321

over the fabric. He started to slip the dress off her shoulders. Before she let it fall to the floor she stepped out of her boots and socks, trying but failing to be graceful, not wanting him to see how very unglamorous they were, all the while pushing from her head the reason why she still couldn't bring herself to touch a pair of stockings and probably never would again.

He was leading her towards the bedroom, somehow knowing where it was, perhaps his fireman's instinct for house layouts, and she was sitting at the edge of the bed she hadn't slept in for two and a half weeks and he was kneeling on the floor, his head against her stomach, his hands hooked into the sides of her underwear, kissing her belly, undoing her bra.

She watched him pull his sweater over his head, quickly. Another thing he did with certainty. There was a scar on his shoulder, a branding the colour of his lips that was roughly two square inches, and another not far from it, slightly smaller and on his chest.

"Molten lead," he said, seeing her look at them. "From a roof."

She wondered if it was the accident she'd read about when she searched for him on the Internet. It scared her, that he could die, that something terrible could happen to him any ordinary day or night at work, however expertly trained he was at minimising the risk. The scars made her feel the truth of that in a way that the news stories hadn't.

"They're nothing. One of the guys who mentored me when I first joined, Al, you should have seen him. The Fire Service was a different world then. He'd push it as far as he could. He liked the burn marks. He was a work of art." He smiled. "He liked showing them to women. Lots of women. He once took his shirt off in a bar and started flexing his muscles, started . . ."

His voice trailed off as she rose onto her knees, drew him towards her, traced her fingers over each scar, then her lips, examining them; then she was kissing his stomach, so flat and beautiful, and his belly button, which made him catch his breath. "It's not fair for my clothes to be off but not yours," she said, making him laugh as she unbuttoned his trousers. He pulled them off himself, at the same time as his boxer shorts.

He was pushing her onto her back, on top of the mossy green quilt cover with red blossoms that she'd made since meeting him, that she'd bought the thread for the first day she ever saw him, that the man whose name she never wanted in her head again hadn't seen or touched or photographed, that she herself had yet to sleep beneath.

"Clarissa," he said. "Open your eyes. Look at me." She did. "Did you know" — he forced a small gasp from her — "this is sex."

"Yes."

He smoothed her hair from her face. His mouth was against hers as he whispered. "In case you weren't sure of the definition."

"I'm sure."

"Good."

Thursday

She woke as he pulled her on top of him, though he seemed to be asleep, still, and deep in a dream. "Robert," she said, softly. "Robert." She kissed him and those bright blue eyes of his fluttered open.

For a few seconds he seemed lost. She remembered his saying to her once that he always knew where he was when he awoke. She was glad that he could be wrong about himself, sometimes, at least in a small way, if only for a tiny instant. She thought he was perfect, and that wasn't fair to him. Nobody should know himself perfectly, she thought. Anybody who knew himself perfectly would be terrifying. He could never change. He could never be wrong. There could be no surprises.

He brought her face back to his, seeming still to be partly in his dreams, but he murmured her name and smiled and said good morning and moved his hand slowly along her back and pressed her hips down into his as he met her eye and there was no doubt then that he'd realised where he was.

She was replaying all of this as she looked dreamily at her own face in a cloudy metal mirror. She was in the

324

cloakroom, the single one for the jurors attached to their small private waiting area just outside Court 12. It must be what they called a body memory; she could feel it all again, his hands on her, and his mouth, the things they did to each other. What was he thinking of, sitting with the others?

There was a piercing ache below her belly, low down on her left side, that had started while she slept and been there when he woke her up. She knew what the cause was, and that it would be gone within a few hours.

She heard them getting up on the other side of the door, heard Annie loudly reporting to the usher that "Clarissa's in the loo." Hurriedly, she washed her hands and came out.

Mr Tourville's robes were wrinkled. He was breathless, as if he'd had to chase his only witness for Doleman up all those flights of stairs and into Court 12. It was probably a lucky thing for the ceaselessly wheezing Mr Tourville that Jason Leman didn't need much prompting to tell his story.

"On August eighth of last year I was hanging out with Carlotta. She said she'd have sex with me for drugs. She pulled my boxer shorts off me like she couldn't wait."

The defendants sat forward in their chairs. Even Doleman looked almost interested.

"I know you wore a condom. Who put it on you?"

"She did, but she did it wrong. I had to redo it."

Clearly a seasoned professional, Clarissa thought.

325

"I left the room to get her some vodka and when I came back she was gone and my wallet was empty. So I found her on the next street and I was like, where's my money? She said she'd spent it but she'd work as a prostitute to get it back, so we walked to a place she knew and she was talking to kerb-crawlers, but it felt like something was off, so I got closer and she was telling one of them I'd raped her. She came right up to me and in my face and slapped me twice."

"So this prostitute falsely cried rape against you. What did you do about that?"

"Nothing. I didn't want to stoop to her level. I don't hit women. I don't hurt women. I was like, fuck this shit, I'm outta here. But the next day the police are all over me and manhandling me and I'm arrested. They never brought any charges."

Mr Morden observed Leman as if he were a cross between an insect and a gift that Mr Tourville had accidentally given him. "Do you deplore violence against women?"

Leman leaned forward and gazed challengingly at Mr Morden. "Sometimes."

"You've served several prison sentences for assault. All of your victims were women."

"No evidence. Just allegations. *Allegations*. Lies."

"The guilty verdicts would suggest otherwise. Ever hear of Mary Barnes?"

"You know I have."

"Went to hospital last month. Broken eardrum. Violence against women seems to be normal operating practice for you."

"Again the police didn't bring any charges. And Mary's still my girlfriend, still living with me, so that should tell you something."

Mr Morden nodded his head slowly before speaking. "Yes. It does."

They were trailing down the stairs in their usual end-of-day formation.

Grant squinted his little maroon-coloured eyes. "About six per cent of the population commit all the crime there is," he said. "Exterminate them like vermin. Problem solved."

That night, Robert walked with Clarissa from the station. Snowdrops encircled the grave of the mother and her two babies. She made her secret ritual prayer to them with Robert by her side.

The snowdrops reminded her of how quickly winter was dissolving into spring, and that in days the trial would be over. She loved being able to see him each day; she didn't want that ever to end. The scent of wild garlic was in the air as they climbed the hill. It seemed only a few minutes before they were in her flat and she noticed for the first time that the top of his head was only inches from the low ceiling. She stood before him, surprised by her own shyness.

"Do you want coffee, Robert?"

"Ah — No." He took a long time to say "Ah", then shot out the "No" with wry decisiveness.

"Do you want tea?"

There it was again. Smile, quick negative shake of the head, brief pause before an amused and definite "No".

She stood on her toes and kissed him, feeling his arms go around her. "Is there anything you want?"

His hands were sliding down her back. He was unzipping her dress. "I just want you."

He didn't finish taking the dress off, though it had fallen from one of her shoulders, leaving it bare. She was leading him into the living room, towards the sofa, sitting him down, unzipping his trousers but not taking them off either, slipping off her underwear and moving onto his lap, so that he was inside her, his mouth against hers as she wrapped herself around him and felt him whisper her name against her lips and she whispered back his own name and that she just wanted him too.

Friday

She turned her head to the side so her chin rested on her shoulder and her nose was close to her hair. She hadn't washed it that morning. She'd wanted to keep the scent of his soap and his body in it, which she'd caught from brushing against him and sleeping with her head on his chest.

She breathed in once more, then straightened and looked forward as Mr Harker called his one witness on behalf of Godfrey.

Joanna Sinclair was short and solid with black-and-blonde-streaked hair that made Clarissa think of a zebra. She tottered awkwardly towards the witness box in high-heeled red shoes. Godfrey grudged her a cool nod and sat forward.

Mr Harker began his questions, Annie huffed, and Clarissa studied Robert's shoulders, remembering what his muscles felt like beneath her hands.

She made a supreme effort to surface from her daydream of Robert when Mr Morden rose to cross-examine. "I know your first name is Joanna. Does Mr Godfrey ever call you Jo?"

Godfrey gave his head a quick negative shake, coaching her.

"No," Miss Sinclair said. "Nobody calls me Jo."

"Mr Godfrey says the phone the police seized from him on his arrest wasn't his. That phone was used in the van that carried Miss Lockyer to London, and in the flat where she was held. Your number was saved in that phone under the name of Jo."

"So?"

"So Mr Godfrey sent two texts the day before his arrest. Both to 'Jo'. Both found in your own seized mobile. This was the first: 'I'm on my way. I want you waiting for me naked.'"

Miss Sinclair's pale face flashed red beneath her caked-on make-up. "I don't recall receiving that text," she said. "He could have been sending it to any number of girls called Jo."

"Let's try the second one. 'Talk to you in the park 'cause this phone is gonna die.' Can you think of any reasons why Mr Godfrey would want to kill that phone?"

Annie was talking in a low voice in the cloakroom again. "Those two have a little boy together." She sighed. "Hardly Romeo and Juliet, are they? Though their future's about as bright."

"I hope you're wrong, Annie."

Very lightly, Annie reached out and smoothed a stray hair from Clarissa's eyes. "You poor sweet thing," she said, shaking her head in affectionate wonder. "I hope so too."

★   ★   ★

On the way back to Bath that night, Clarissa sat alone, just as she'd walked to the station alone that morning. Robert had left her flat very early, kissing her goodbye when she was still half asleep and whispering that he needed to stop by his house before court.

As she stepped off the train, walked down the stairs, exited the station, she watched Robert, ten steps ahead of her. She nearly called out to him but stopped herself; it was her intractable reluctance to impose herself on anyone. The distance between them increased as he hurriedly crossed the road and walked on without turning back for even a second. Then he disappeared from her sight altogether.

Week 7

The
Drying Room

Monday and Wednesday

They spent Monday morning waiting around for the boy with the purple-tipped hair.

It didn't take long for the poker game to get into full swing. Clarissa hovered on the edges, hand-sewing the last touches of a bag for her mother's birthday, knocking off the classic Chanel flap style in dark blue silk that made her think of a midnight storm.

"I want one," Annie said. "Are you taking orders?"

"And me," said Wendy.

Clarissa smiled but only briefly lifted her eyes. "You're both too nice."

"The usher should take away your needle and scissors." Sophie was arranging her cards and looking cross. "The security guards should have stopped you."

"Yeah. Think of the damage she could do to Sparkle with those little things," Annie said. "Are you going to tell on her?"

"The usher can see what she's doing," Wendy said. "He isn't bothered. He already knew she had them anyway. From when she mended my skirt."

Clarissa's chair was just behind Robert's. He couldn't have failed to hear this exchange. His back remained straight as he concentrated on his hand. The men laughed loudly at his jokes, nodding in agreement with everything he said. She wondered if firemen were all automatically popular.

She tried to tell herself that she was wrong in thinking he hadn't met her eye all morning, that he hadn't looked at her or even spoken to her since he'd left her flat so early on Friday. But she hadn't caught even a flash of the blue of his eyes.

Robert was talking about an actor in a spy film he'd just seen. "He's a hunk." There was more riotous laughter at one of his jokes. Clarissa didn't laugh. She didn't think it was funny.

She pricked herself with the needle. A drop of blood fell from her finger and onto the fabric.

"I wonder where he is?" she said softly, thinking of their missing fellow juror. "It's not like him not to turn up. There must be something wrong."

"Clarissa's right," Robert said, making her heart clutch.

Grant guffawed. "Put him in the cells overnight with the boys. He'll be Sparkle's new bitch. But first the judge is gonna call him into his chambers and spank him."

The others laughed, Robert too, but Clarissa did not.

They didn't take their seats in the jury box until noon. The judge looked solemn. "I am sorry to say that Mr McElwee is unwell. It is permissible to drop down to a jury of eleven, or even to the legal minimum of nine. But my preference — as long as it does not result in too long a delay — is not to lose any jurors at this late stage. I am therefore dismissing you until Wednesday morning, when the doctor hopes Mr McElwee will be able to return. If he is not, then I will discharge him from this jury and we will resume without him."

On Wednesday morning all twelve of them filed into Court 12 as usual.

The trial was almost over, Clarissa thought. The room seemed to be spinning. She studied the soft brown hairs on the back of Robert's neck, and the faint snail trail of clean sweat behind his right ear. She wanted to smell him, to nestle her face between his shoulders. She'd have to go away from here, out of this building, back into a world where she would no longer see him every day, the world where he wasn't. Though she wasn't sure how much she liked this new version of the world she was about to lose, where he no longer seemed to want to look at her.

She fantasised a blizzard. Anything to shut the court down, to delay the end, to give herself more time with him. She'd counted on days and days of defendant testimony and counter testimony but they'd blown away without even beginning as Doleman, Sparkle and Godfrey all declined to go into the witness box.

She felt a funny quiver, low down and in the centre of her belly. Then it was gone.

Mr Morden scanned the jurors, meeting each of their eyes as he began his summing up.

Her head was so foggy and tired she couldn't pay attention. Besides, she'd listened carefully enough when he first said it all. By the time she tuned in again he was finishing. She was so confused by how many minutes had passed since he started she wondered if she was getting ill.

She was the worst juror ever. Mr Williams was sitting down before she even realised he'd ever stood up. Then Mr Belford was on his feet and once more her mind wandered. Had her brain, after seven weeks, reached true saturation point?

Mr Tourville was the only one who didn't cast a sleeping spell upon her. "Mr Doleman is no rapist. He is no kidnapper. He is no drug dealer. He is a hardworking family man who was in gainful employment until his arrest. He is the long-term partner of a beautiful young woman. He is the loving father of their young son. Mr Doleman is guilty of only one thing. He made some very bad choices in his friends. You cannot send him to jail for that. Oh, no. You cannot."

Clarissa was shivering on the platform, waiting for them to unlock the train doors so she could board. Only Sparkle's barrister and Mr Harker still had to do their closing speeches. Then there'd be the judge's instructions. She'd need to be more alert.

A hand brushed her shoulder. She wheeled around, surprised to find that the hand belonged to Robert, who was apologising for startling her.

Her own words were out before she could stop herself. "Come back with me." She tried to smile. "You're an addiction."

"So are you." His voice was low, as if he were whispering to her in bed. "But I can't tonight. You see that, don't you? We're about to go into deliberation. Last week . . . we should have waited. I'm glad we didn't, but we should have. I'm cautious. I know I haven't behaved as if I am, but I am. I should have explained. Once this is over . . ." he said. "It won't be long . . ." he said.

He was practised at breaking bad news; he did it every day at work; much worse news than this. She could feel her face growing warm. Still, she couldn't keep herself from saying what she did: "If you change your mind . . . I mean, even if it's late . . ." But she saw he was a man who never changed his mind about anything, big or small, once he'd made it up. She'd known that from the start, really. She hated begging him; she didn't want him at any cost.

There was a click of the lock release as the lights on the train doors switched from amber to green. Robert swung a door open for her and she stepped carefully over the gap.

She made herself turn to half-look at him, standing on the platform, just a few feet away. "I'll see you tomorrow, Robert." She tried again to smile, but something weak and weird took over her face instead. "I need to . . . do some things," she said feebly.

"I understand," he said. "Clarissa," he said. "I might . . ."

"Goodnight," she said, and she walked quickly through the carriage. It was her turn not to look back.

Wednesday and Thursday

She thought she'd never sleep, lying in her old bed, the bed that was no longer the bed where the awful things had happened, no longer the bed where those photos were taken. It was now the bed that Robert had been in. She was beneath the quilt cover she hadn't washed because she didn't want to wash away any part of him. But she did fall into sleep.

She was in the drying room, his favourite part of the fire station, a place she'd never actually seen, a forbidden realm not meant for her, but he was with her, kissing her, lifting her up, running his hands down her arms, holding them above her head and standing back to look at her. "Robert," she tried to say, but the word wouldn't come out and he wasn't there any more.

The drying room wasn't the drying room any more. It was Bluebeard's chamber and the dummies were no longer dummies. They were dead women with sheeted faces and blood on their mouths that seeped through their shrouds like garish kisses. They swayed from the nooses they hung from, as if blown gently by a quiet wind. She couldn't breathe, couldn't get air. She tried to raise an arm to the doorknob, to turn it, but her arm

wouldn't move. She tried to scream but her lips wouldn't move. There was a weight over the entire length of her body. Bile was rising from her stomach and it hurt her throat to try to gulp it back. Her arms were above her head. She tugged, but something cut into her wrists.

She opened her eyes to the face she least wanted to see.

It wasn't possible, she thought. He couldn't really be here. He was supposed to be in jail. DC Hughes had said he was in jail. This was only a nightmare. She told herself to wake up.

She tried to twist, to throw him off her, tried to kick at him, but he only pressed his body into hers harder, panicking her that she couldn't move at all. There was an inhuman muffled noise, and she saw that she was making those animal noises, not making words.

She squeezed her eyes shut against him, trying again to force herself back into sleep, telling herself again that it was only a nightmare, he had to be in jail. Had to be. They wouldn't let him out and not tell her.

"Open your eyes." He grabbed a handful of her hair and jerked her head back; something dug into her neck. "Open your eyes if you don't want to choke, Clarissa." She opened her eyes. He released the pressure on her neck. "You were waiting for me, weren't you? You wanted me to come. You just couldn't let yourself say it."

Her heart was pounding so fiercely she thought it would burst. She thought it was beating too much to keep going, that it would give one last squeeze and then stop. She tried again to push him away, but the skin of her wrists felt as if it were being flayed and her shoulders strained so badly she thought her arms would fall off.

He buried his face in her stomach, put his hands beneath her hips, kneading through the silk of her nightdress and pulling her up against him. "You smell so good. It's all for me, isn't it? You've been thinking about me, haven't you? And my plans for you. Can you imagine what they are?"

He scoured her cheeks with the quilt. "Are you crying because you're sorry?" She tried to nod yes, but only moved her head a little, scared that she would strangle otherwise.

He reached down the side of the bed. When he brought his hand back up there was a knife in it, the blade tapered into a spear-point, and she heard herself moan. "Shall we talk about how you've been treating me? I promised I'd punish you, didn't I?" He put the knife down, the end of its tortoiseshell handle touching her waist.

"Pretty nightdress." It was bunched up, high on her thighs. She was jerking her arms, wanting to tug it down. He smoothed a hand over the smoky purple silk. He grabbed her shoulders. "Did you make it for the fireman?" She started to move her head, no, but again felt the ring around her throat tighten. He ran a finger along it, testing it, then loosening it. "Throttling's too easy, Clarissa. You're not getting out of this that simply and quickly."

342

He picked up the knife. "This is very sharp." He lifted the hem and held it taut, then split the nightdress all the way up through the centre, sliding the blade slowly forwards. "Are you frightened?" She was trying to squash her back into the mattress and away from the knife, sobbing noiselessly. "You should be. I can see you are. I like that."

The knife was resting between her breasts, pointed towards her chin. She was holding her breath, afraid that even the smallest movement of her chest would make him draw blood.

"I'd thought you were a true princess, but you're not. You're like the others. You don't look like a princess now." He jerked the knife straight upwards, abruptly, and she screamed, but the only sound was a sickening squeak that didn't stop until she realised the knife hadn't touched her. "I could have undressed you while you were still chloroformed, but I wanted you awake for this. I've been dreaming about this." He sliced through one of the spaghetti straps, then the other.

He put the knife down near her head, parted the shorn fabric, and twisted one of her nipples, making her cry out another muffled cry. "How do you think I felt, seeing you with him? You didn't care, did you? You've been provoking me, Clarissa. Deliberately." He shook her so hard she thought he'd given her whiplash, thought her brain was smashing inside her skull.

"You're worse than my previous girlfriend. No matter how much I do for you, it's never enough. You tell me to go away and you find someone else. Another married man, no less. Not that you'd spare a thought

343

for poor Mrs Fireman." Spit was foaming in the corners of his mouth. "You fucked him when I was in jail, didn't you? But he got bored of you, once he'd fucked you."

He was pressing a hand between her legs. "He doesn't know what you need." He was creeping his fingers beneath the underwear she'd made from the same silk as the nightdress. He was pulling off his shirt, unbuckling his belt. She was squeezing her thighs together, but he was cutting her underwear at the hips with the knife and ripping them away. He was jerking her legs apart. "You don't make it easy for me to control myself."

She tried to kick him. He punched her, hard, in the stomach, leaving her floppy, making her retch so that she thought she would die by choking on her own vomit. She could taste salt and metal. He wrapped something around each of her ankles, lashing them to the bed posts. She was trying to pull her legs free, trying to say the word no, again and again, no, but she couldn't make even that one syllable sound like a word.

Then he was taking photographs. Each time the flash went off it stabbed through her eyes and he shook her until she obeyed his command to open them again and look at him. At last, he put his camera down and lay on top of her. She was squirming, thrashing, trying to roll herself away.

He raised a fist and smashed it into the side of her head. There was an explosion, and a noise like a drill in her skull. Those must be dancing angels, she thought, on the ceiling. There was that muffled crying again, coming from somewhere.

Something cold rested against the side of her face. She knew it was important to work out what it was and to keep very still until she did, to keep absolutely frozen. And then she realised it was the knife. It was in the split second before she felt the blade tilt and slice through her cheek that she realised.

She felt her body shift into limpness, vaguely saw that his face was changing, that his hands were tearing at whatever he'd put over her mouth. Then she was gasping for air, trying to swallow huge gulps of it as he cut the loop around her neck to free it, lifted her head and shoulders. He was holding a glass of water to her mouth, ordering her to take a sip, but it was running down her chin as she panted, dripping onto her breasts, mixing with something red. Why was there so much red? He was blotting her face with the gashed nightdress.

For an instant, he looked at her as if shocked to see what he was doing; his face crumpled in uncertainty and exhaustion, as if puzzled by how it was turning out. His head trembled and he blinked several times, like he'd been temporarily blinded but was now seeing clearly again.

Then he was kneading her breasts, pinching and sucking, biting so hard she cried out and he smacked a hand over her mouth and told her to shut up. He was tugging his already unbuttoned trousers off, and his boxer shorts. He climbed on top of her, grabbing her hair and pulling her face close to his. His expression

345

made her think of a painting of Apollo flaying Marsyas, looking tenderly at his victim as if he were nursing instead of killing him. His voice sounded almost loving when he whispered, "You've made me wait too long for this," and forced himself into her.

She was weeping softly, thinking that she wanted to get his DNA beneath her fingernails but couldn't because her wrists wouldn't move. When he came, his DNA would be inside of her; there would be evidence there, at least, when they found her body.

"Look at me. Say my name."

A drum pulsed in her temple. Her neck was too heavy and her eyes wouldn't open fully. She thought the wetness in her eyes must be blood, squeezing out through the pressure she felt inside her head.

"Say it."

Keeping his name from her head, from her voice, was her last talisman.

"Say it," he said. "You do what I tell you."

But she realised she couldn't remember what his name actually was.

He told her again to say it, supplying the word himself at the end of the phrase he wanted from her, and she repeated it, though the words were fuzzy.

"Kiss me," he said.

She tried to move her head away, but even a millimetre made her brain shake too much, made it ache too much, and he fastened his lips to hers, pushing his tongue into her mouth. She considered biting him but was too scared to try.

"Tell me you love me."

"I love you."

"Say, 'I love you, *Rafe*.' "

"I love you, Rafe."

"Tell me what I'm doing to you."

She didn't know what he wanted her to say. She said the only thing she could think of. The only true thing. "You're hurting me," she said.

"Good." He grabbed her hair again. "Now tell me that you're going to come, that no other lover can do for you what I can, that you belong to me, that this is how you like it."

She parroted all of this, listened as his breath grew faster, braced herself as his movements became more violent.

When it was over his body slumped over hers, tamping her into the mattress. She thought he was breaking her ribs, bruising her lungs, boring a hole into her stomach in the place where he'd punched her. It was several minutes before he pulled out.

"You loved it. I could tell you did," he said. "I could feel you coming. I know better than anyone what excites you, Clarissa."

She could feel wetness between her legs like acid, and her chest too constricted and scalding to breathe, and her shoulders as if they had been ripped from their sockets, and her ankles chafed and raw from how hard she'd tried to pull them free. Her hands and fingers were numb because the blood had drained from them.

He had the gag in his hands. She could see it was leather, like the one the woman wore on the cover of the magazine. She was weeping again, her breath

347

laboured. "I promise I'll be quiet." Her voice was a croak, squeezing out of her raw throat.

"I don't trust you. I told you I'd never trust you again after the trick you pulled in that park. You're going to learn that I mean what I say. That's going to be the last thing you learn." She tried to turn her head away, was tugging again at her wrists to escape, but she was barely able to move at all as he fastened it.

"You need to be gagged for the other things I'm going to do to you. We don't want you disturbing your neighbours with your screams." He threw himself onto the bed beside her, shoved an arm over her breasts and a bent leg over her hips, and fell deeply asleep.

The whooshes of air in and out of her nose were so loud. Her chest was heaving, up and down, lifting and dropping, pumping and deflating. She was certain she would wake him, but she couldn't slow down her breathing, however hard she tried.

Please do not let him wake, she thought. Please, please do not. Please God. Please help me. It kept going through her head, an unspoken incantation, over and over again. A charm to keep her alive and bring help. But it was soon overpowered by another chant that she couldn't stop. There was no God. There just wasn't. There couldn't be. There was no hope. Laura must have prayed and God hadn't saved her. God had let Laura suffer unimaginably.

Her breathing was getting worse. She thought the room was filling with smoke and she was choking on it. She tried to tell herself she was imagining it. She tried to tell herself there couldn't be a fire because if there was the smoke alarm would go off and she wasn't hearing its siren. But she knew there wasn't enough oxygen. There wasn't. There just wasn't. She would bite her own tongue as she died, like the wicked queen who couldn't speak or cry out as she danced to death in the red-hot iron slippers they'd forced onto her feet with tongs.

She couldn't understand why the room was spinning. She squeezed her eyes shut as tightly as she could, then opened them, but she was still in the centre of a whirlwind. Everything was in a haze. She couldn't pick out a single object to anchor herself.

When she next opened her eyes she wasn't sure where she was or why it was so hard to move or what had happened to make her hurt so much everywhere. But she was sure that there really was a fire and she was dying from inhaling smoke and almost blind because the air was so thick with it. Robert said that if she ever got caught in a fire she should get low on the floor. He said that staying low was the only way to find air. It was smoke that killed, he said. She was trying to move because she knew that that was what Robert would want her to do. She was trying to get herself onto the floor, trying to get her arms and legs free, but something had frozen her and something else had fallen on her. Maybe it was the roof. A roof had once fallen on Robert in a fire. Maybe the roof had fallen earlier, when the room had been spinning. She wondered if she was dead and in her coffin, with the lid bearing down on her.

There was a bell coming from somewhere far away. She thought it must be the church bell tolling her funeral. Something was heavy on her breasts. She opened her eyes and saw it was an arm. And then she remembered where she was and what had happened and who the arm belonged to, and realised there hadn't really been a fire. But she knew she had been in deep terror, and that he had done something very bad to her head that made her unable to think properly or stay awake, and she was certain she had had some kind of absolute and uncontrolled panic attack and lost consciousness, and she knew she had to try as hard as she could not to let that happen again because somebody had once told her that if you fell asleep with a head injury you would die.

There was a rattle, then a crash of metal. He was stirring, looking around sharply and listening, muttering and swearing under his breath. He slammed a fist into the top of her head. There was a blast of tiny dots, then only dark.

She thought that she must be dreaming. She was peering through a shimmering fog and Robert was bending over her, pulling at something on her face. She opened her mouth but nothing came out. He was at the bottom of the bed by her ankles and moving her legs, laying them alongside each other instead of so far apart. He was reaching above her and then she could see her hands, held in his, and he was rubbing them. His face, his beautiful face, was white. Why was it so white? And his cheeks were wet. Was it raining? The drops were like tears but that couldn't be right. Didn't Robert once say that he never cried? Or was it the man called Azarola who'd said that? Robert seemed to be whispering. Why did he sound as if he were choking? His voice was so odd. And he was wrapping her in the quilt, arranging her on her left side. He was holding a phone and punching numbers into it and giving her address.

There was something very important that she must remember. She was trying so hard, but couldn't make herself. And then it came to her. "You must watch," she tried to say.

He only shushed her gently. He was holding her fingers again, rubbing them. Her fingers were very white, whiter even than his face.

But then she could see a shadow in the doorway. She knew the shadow belonged to the man. Robert followed her gaze and jumped to his feet, putting as much space as he could between himself and the bed, as if to lead the man away from her.

The man was waving the knife in his right hand. With the blade pointed up and out, he advanced towards Robert. Robert took a step back and also leaned back, but the man stepped forward to maintain his face-to-face proximity to Robert and held the knife out farther.

Robert feinted a punch to the right. When the man thrust his knife out to meet it, Robert pivoted, used his left hand to hit the top of the man's right arm, used his right hand to grab the wrist with the knife in it, and jabbed his left forearm into the man's nose. All at once, there was an ear-splitting crack of bone, a burst of

351

bright blood, and the clanging of the knife onto the floorboards. As the man swayed on his feet, blinking and dazed, Robert brought his right fist to the man's left temple and his left fist to the man's jaw so his head snapped back and his body recoiled. Like the loser in a boxing ring, the man wavered for an instant, then crashed down, thumping so hard onto his side that the whole room seemed to shake.

Robert kicked the knife away as he stepped forward to inspect the man, who was entirely still but for the ragged rise and fall of his chest. He checked and double-checked for signs of consciousness, as if the man were a rabid dog he didn't want to turn his back on. He leaned over to lift the man's limp hand and then drop it, watching it fall with a resounding thud. It was his fingers Robert seemed especially concerned with, as if wanting to assure himself there wasn't the slightest twitch.

There was a fresh rush of blood from her cheek and a sharp cramp in her stomach. She didn't realise she'd groaned until Robert turned his back on the man, calling out her name as he took a step towards her. It was only a few seconds of inattention, but it was too many, and it was all her fault.

The man stretched his right arm over his head and reached beneath her bedside table. When his hand emerged it was holding a second knife. More of its mass was in the black rubber-grip handle than the blade, which was short and wide. The man sat up and drove the knife into the back of Robert's upper thigh.

Robert screamed, an animal noise that went right through her. He fell to his knees, straight down.

The man spat crimson from his mouth and blew it from his nose. He reached up, the knife shining silver above his head, held high to finish Robert off. As the knife swept down Robert twisted around, grabbed the man's right wrist with both hands, jerked him onto his back, and half-sat on him, pinning him down with a knee on his abdomen.

Robert seemed not to notice his other leg, which was splayed on the floor, the light brown corduroy of his trousers darkening with blood. His navy jersey was damp with sweat under the arms, on his chest, over his back.

The man punched Robert in the face with his left fist, splitting Robert's lip, but nothing would make Robert let go of the man's right wrist. Nothing would make him stop trying to get the man to drop the knife. Nothing would make him give up his effort to keep the knife away from his own body.

There was so much blood. Robert's dripped down his chin. It pooled from his leg onto the floorboards. The man's left a track from his nose, which had spattered his bare chest and chin as well as the sleeve of Robert's jersey.

The man slapped his left hand over Robert's two hands, fighting to control the knife. It juddered between them as each tried to drive it towards the other, as each tried to turn the blade towards the other. The man was on his back so he had to push the knife upwards against gravity. It was Robert's only advantage

353

but the advantage wasn't enough. It was a kind of awful arm-wrestling match, and Robert was slowly losing, weakening as he lost more and more blood. His face was grey. His forehead was beaded with sweat. He grunted.

Neither of them noticed her slipping off the bed. She lifted the first knife by its tortoiseshell handle, from the floor where Robert had kicked it. She stepped shakily towards them, looking like a newly made vampire rising from her grave for the first time. Blood snaked along the inside of her thighs. Blood streaked from her face and down her neck and over her breasts and belly. Blood matted her blonde hair, staining it dark red.

The kind and helpful policemen had lied to her, feeding her all of that false, deadly hope, telling her she was safe when she wasn't, when really she was as far from safe as anybody could be. The things they did didn't work. Only she herself could truly make the man disappear. Only she could make him vanish so completely he'd never ever be able to come back. It was the only way. Nothing else would make him leave her alone. Nothing else would help Robert. The next time the man's knife went into Robert it would kill him. She knew it would. She knew exactly what she had to do, and she knew she'd only have one chance.

She really was extremely good at human biology, as she'd once told Robert. Her obsession with reproduction spilled over into a fascination with the whole body, but it was an interest she'd had even as a schoolgirl. All of those details had imprinted themselves on her. She remembered the pictures of the heart, the photographs and illustrations and anatomical diagrams that she'd always thought so beautiful. She'd studied them all over again when her father had his bypass.

The man was wearing only boxer shorts. She could see those pictures as if they were drawn on top of his chest in layers: the heart and its labelled chambers beneath the thoracic cage, the thoracic cage beneath the skin. Even with her pounding head and blurry eyes she could see them. She didn't even have to try. She knew that there was a gap between his ribs, just above the right ventricle. She knew that that was the deadliest place. She made herself focus on the target, in line with his nipples and slightly off centre, trying not to let herself be distracted by the pain etched on Robert's face.

She didn't let herself take her eyes off that spot as she aimed the knife into the man's chest with all the force of her own downward rush. It was easy for her to fall to her knees on the floor just above his head; falling was what her body wanted to do. There was a split second of resistance, like the instant just before she penetrated the rind of a melon with a very sharp point; then the metal sank deeply, as if his flesh were the inside of the fruit. The knife went all the way in. It didn't stop until the hilt reached his skin.

He wheezed and sucked, but only briefly. His lips were no longer pale. They were blue. Bubbles of red were leaking from between them. The blood didn't spurt from the knife wound, as she'd thought it would; it seeped up steadily, to shape itself into a dessert plate around the handle. Her hands weren't working like they

355

usually did, and the knife was getting so wet and warm and slippery it was difficult to grasp. But she knew that she mustn't let go. No matter what happened. She knew that. She kept trying to hold it for fear of it not working. In case she'd miscalculated or missed the spot she'd aimed for. As if he would recover if she let go. As if he'd grab up the other knife again and plunge it into Robert. As if the hole she'd made would seal over and he'd pop up and come after her if she didn't make absolutely sure the knife had done its work.

His eyes rolled, then froze. They were still open but she knew that he wasn't seeing her. At last he wasn't looking at her. He really wasn't. She knew he could never look at her any more.

Robert's arms were around her and she let go of the knife. He was sitting on the floor, pulling her across his lap, scooting them as far away from the man as he could get them, smearing a trail of red over the floor as he dragged his stabbed leg. He was holding her and rocking, somehow tearing off his jersey at the same time and wrapping her in it, both of them soaked with blood. He was saying her name. Again and again he was saying it, as if he were trying to call her back from somewhere else. But she felt herself falling away, and his voice seemed to come from a great distance even though his lips were still shaping the word.

The room was full of strange people dressed like policemen and paramedics and Miss Norton was there too, weeping. She could feel them tearing her from Robert, hear them telling him that he needed urgent treatment himself. She tried to cry out his name so they wouldn't take him from her but she couldn't make any sounds come out. All at once, the pain in her head exploded and the world snapped into black.

Eighteen Weeks Later

The Maiden
Without Hands

Monday, 20 July

The clinical psychologist asked me to start a new notebook. It's handmade by my mother, covered in dusty plum fabric sprinkled with lily of the valley. The psychologist calls it a "Recovery Journal". I flash the handwritten pages at her during our appointments to demonstrate what a sensible and sane patient I am. If I actually let her read it though she'd probably give me a big fat F for what I'm writing — and to whom I'm writing it.

Tuesday, 21 July

My father is golfing with another retired teacher. My mother sits beside me in the soulless hospital waiting room. She is reading a newspaper while I try to think about anything other than the test results I'm about to be given.

What I think about is you. What I spend way too much time thinking about is you.

It is eighteen weeks since I've seen you. Eighteen weeks since you rescued me.

Eighteen weeks since that man's lawyer conned them into letting him out so he could break into my flat.

The police arrested and charged him with the harassment and violence offences on the morning of Thursday, March fifth. But the judge didn't issue the restraining order until the afternoon of Friday, March sixth. The catastrophic mistake was that they didn't get him into court and before the judge within the twenty-four-hour legal deadline. That meant the restraining order he breached a few days later wasn't legally valid, so they couldn't keep him in prison for violating it.

Would it have happened if DC Hughes hadn't been away? I think even DC Hughes couldn't have prevented his release for the legal technicality. But DC Hughes might have warned me that they'd freed him. He might have found some way to get him back in jail. He might have sent someone to watch over me; to stop him before he did the things he did. I've pieced that night together, or most of it, with the help of the sexual offences liaison officer. But I keep going over and over these contingencies; these countless what-ifs.

I am torn from these thoughts when the doctor comes out to get me. He says hello to my mother and she practically blushes in delight at the attention, despite the fact that she's as scared as I am of what I'm about to find out. I give my mother's hand a goodbye squeeze and rise to follow Dr Haynes. My back is soaking wet and I'm flashing between heat and chills.

362

Sometimes I wonder if it is because of the things that happened that I am so sick, but Dr Haynes says no. He says that extreme nausea like mine even has a name. *Hyperemesis gravidarum*. He says that some people think it's what Charlotte Brontë died of, and I like it that Dr Haynes knows such a thing. He says there's a physiological basis for it. The multiple hospital admissions to get my hydration and electrolytes back up, as well as the anti-emetics I have to take each day, certainly feel physiological. I don't think the clinical psychologist agrees with Dr Haynes on this one, though.

Dr Haynes is very Oxbridgy and very kind and also very handsome in an intelligent superhero kind of way. In different circumstances, I would almost certainly have a crush on him; the different circumstances would be my never having met you.

Dr Haynes gives me a serious look. "I have the results back, Clarissa."

I thought I'd composed myself over the past two weeks, waiting for this moment. But icicles seem to pierce my heart.

Dr Haynes reaches across his desk to touch my hand. "The genetic tests eliminated the possibility that Rafe Solmes is the father of your baby."

I can feel my lips trembling, and my hands, and my eyelids vibrating too, and I think it must be because my body is registering some kind of physical symptom of my relief. But Dr Haynes tells me that twitching and tremors can be a rare side effect of the anti-emetics, and though he hopes it's just a one-off, he wants to try

363

me on a different medication. He says I'm very pale, and he makes me sip some water and climb onto the examination table to rest for a few minutes. He sits and writes in my notes, though he breaks off a few times to recheck my pulse and blood pressure.

Even before I had proof I had faith. I knew that baby was there as soon as we made it, when you woke me up after our first night together. But I mustn't let myself think like that. For me to think of our first night together suggests we had a long series of nights together. There were only two nights. I tell myself that there will only ever be two.

At last, Dr Haynes lets me sit up, and I immediately start to babble. "I knew deep down it wasn't his. The police asked me to have the test and I was scared to refuse. I didn't want them thinking I was motivated to kill him so that he couldn't have any hold over me through the baby."

"Well, they couldn't think that now. Based on dating scans and your early pregnancy hormone levels, you are twenty-one weeks pregnant. This means the egg was fertilised nineteen weeks ago. My report concludes that you conceived a week before you were assaulted; you couldn't have known at the time of Mr Solmes's death that you were pregnant. I have consulted with other specialists. Their views concur with this, and are also part of the report."

They had plenty of his DNA to compare to the baby's. I didn't need your permission for the test. I didn't need your DNA either. Now that they have officially ruled him out, you are the only option. A process of elimination.

"And there's more good news. No genetic anomalies were detected."

I'd been so anxious about the paternity test I never thought to worry about the baby's health. What kind of mother will I be?

He pauses. "I can tell you the sex if you'd like to know."

"I think it's a girl," I say. "Is it?"

Dr Haynes is smiling so much I think he really does care. "Yes."

"I think she has dark hair and bright blue eyes like her father. I think she's very beautiful."

He laughs. "We'll have to wait until she's born to see if you're right about the hair and eyes, but there's no doubt she'll be beautiful. Shall we take a look at her? I know how concerned you were about the amniocentesis needle and the risk of miscarriage."

Dr Haynes squirts cold jelly on my belly and she pops onto the screen as soon as the probe touches my skin.

Her lips are exactly like yours, Robert. She shapes them into a rosebud and blows me a kiss. I blow one back.

Wednesday, 22 July

The sexual offences liaison officer is here. She isn't wearing a police uniform. She's wearing a navy skirt and a cream shirt that hang elegantly on her willowy frame.

Compared to her I am curvy, a new experience for me. My breasts are fuller beneath the white gauze blouse that is like the one Lottie wore her first day in court. My stomach makes a small mound above the stretchy waistband of yet another skirt my mother whipped up for me.

The officer's name is Eleanor, and that's what she likes me to call her. Not PC This or DS That. Just Eleanor.

You'd tell me I mustn't let myself forget for an instant that even if those understanding nods are all sincere, Eleanor is still watching and listening for any crumb of intelligence she can gather so that they'll have a big juicy file to send to the Crown Prosecution Service. You'd tell me that I shouldn't swallow the police line that they've given Eleanor to me because they regard me as a surviving victim who needs a single point of contact for all police communications. You'd tell me that the police keep sending Eleanor here because they regard me as a suspect.

Eleanor and I sit in my parents' living room in the two armchairs inside the bay window, my usual place for the view of the sea. Two cups of tea sit on the table between us, where my mother left them before disappearing into the garden with my father.

Eleanor pushes her black hair behind her ears and shoots a look of gentle straightness in my direction with her dark eyes. "I promised I'd never keep any information from you that I am permitted to disclose," she says.

"Is it the Crown Prosecution Service?" I am struggling to sound calm. "Are they going to charge me in connection with his death?"

"There are a few final pieces of evidence for the police to gather before they send the complete file to the CPS for a decision on whether to charge. I believe they're awaiting some reports from your obstetrician?"

"Those are on their way."

She nods. "Good. There's also the coroner's final report. It's for your protection that the police need to be thorough. It's a serious and complex case, Clarissa, involving a violent death. It's always in the public interest to ensure a proper investigation is conducted."

"I just wish it were over with."

"I know it's hard to have this hanging over you, but I want to stress again how very rare it is for the CPS to bring a prosecution in connection with the death of an intruder into somebody's home. Especially when the intruder acted violently and had a weapon. There's a strong argument that you used force to defend yourself and another person. Diminished responsibility is an important factor too, given your head injuries."

"Okay," I say slowly, though I don't feel very okay.

She takes a breath. "I already told you that the five defendants in that trial were found not guilty on all counts."

The judge let the other ten members of the jury go into deliberation without us. All five of the defendants walked free while I was still in hospital under police guard and you were having an operation on your leg.

"It's hardly a surprising result, given the way the defence barristers all tore Miss Lockyer to pieces." I look down at my lap. "She was so brave." I speak very softly, still not looking up. But then I do. I make myself. And I see that Eleanor is frowning.

She unzips her brown leather portfolio. "The police thought you'd want to be informed." She hands me a newspaper clipping.

A verdict of death by misadventure was recorded at the inquest into the death of a popular 28-year-old Bath woman. Tragic Carlotta Lockyer died of an overdose on 10 May. Coroner George Tomkins noted that significant amounts of heroin and crack cocaine were found in her body, and that their toxic effect had been enhanced by high levels of methadone in her bloodstream. Mr John Lockyer, 78, told the hearing that his granddaughter had successfully completed a detoxification programme but relapsed shortly before her death. He discovered her body on the bathroom floor when he returned from church.

I hug myself and rock back and forth in the self-comforting behaviour one of the police witnesses described Lottie engaging in. I sob wretchedly. Some bile chokes up and dribbles down my chin and I wipe it with a tissue. Eleanor waits patiently until I've calmed down. I don't know how much time passes until I do. I blow my nose loudly.

"I can see how very, very sad you are," Eleanor says. "I'm sad too. So are my colleagues. She was a courageous young woman, and she fought a terrible fight."

I glare right into Eleanor's night-sky eyes, trying but failing to unnerve her.

"I can see you're very angry, too, Clarissa," she says. "That's understandable."

"That article's a fake. It was published last week, after the supposed inquest on July thirteenth. They don't have those inquests that fast, just two months after someone dies. You said yourself that we're still waiting for the coroner's report on that man — he died four months ago — that's twice as long a time. Lottie is somewhere else, somewhere far away, and the police want those men to think she's dead so she can have a new safe life. That article's a lie, to trick them." I am snatching at hope. Maybe Laura did something like this, too.

"I don't think so, though it's a clever theory and I'd like you to be right. We all would."

"You wouldn't say. You might not even know."

"True on both counts," Eleanor says.

My father shouldn't have named me Clarissa. Pollyanna would have been more fitting. But there can be no glad game here. Laura is lost, probably for ever, and so is Lottie. I cannot save either of them, now, by making up silly stories.

It's therapy morning with Mrs Lewen, the clinical psychologist. I had to promise to see her each week. That was the only way they'd agree to release me from hospital in Bath and make all of the arrangements with the police and doctors here in Brighton.

Patient compliance is a phrase I've heard too many times.

I hate the word compliance.

Mrs Lewen is in her late fifties, with short curly brown hair. She's a few stone overweight and wears bright-coloured kaftans. Today's is yellow and orange and purple. She looks like an earth mother, but I don't really think she is.

There's a framed poster from the film of *The Wizard of Oz* on her wall. The main characters with their arms linked, about to skip off down the yellow brick road. Mrs Lewen thinks there's a *life lesson* in that film for everyone who ever watches it. I can't imagine that you would like Mrs Lewen much.

Mrs Lewen settles into a peach armchair and smiles expectantly. I'm huddled on the sofa that faces her, my legs curled beneath me. The sofa is peach too. All of the furniture is upholstered in this supposedly tranquil peach, and I detest it. The walls are peach, too. If Mrs Lewen ever tries to make me listen to *Somewhere Over the Rainbow* there will be puke on the peach carpet.

Last week's subject was my face. The plastic surgeon's gobbledegook clotted the air; Mrs Lewen made me repeat his phrases as if they were medicine.

The good news is that faces heal fast. My scar is one and a half inches long, a diagonal slash across my cheekbone. I measured it.

We're fortunate that it was a straight wound. My scar is swollen and pinched and puckered around the edges.

Scars fade and flatten considerably over the first year. My scar is vividly red and raised.

Superficial facial nerves come back, but it can take six to eight months. My face seems not to move properly around my scar, the way a person's mouth feels after a shot of novocaine.

Today, my initial silence is too long even for Mrs Lewen. Usually she likes me to be the first to speak but this time she quietly prompts me by asking what I'm thinking about.

"Robert." As soon as the word is out I stare into my weak black Earl Grey tea. I take a sip and imagine that my stomach slows in its churning.

Mrs Lewen prods me further. "You're comfortably into your second trimester now. The pregnancy's looking secure. Don't you think Robert has a right to know?"

Mrs Lewen's skin is very pink and slightly rough. Her cheeks are flushed. I wonder if she has high blood pressure.

I shake my head. "He wouldn't want the baby."

"You can't know that. And you're still pining for him, Clarissa."

Two years dead, you said. Within a minute of meeting me you said that that's how long your wife had been gone. Within a minute of meeting me you told me the most outrageous lie anyone's ever told me. Is it a tale you automatically spin to any woman you might possibly be interested in? Later, you actually said it was a road crash. You even supplied the time of day.

Mrs Fireman, that man said, putting his knife in my heart before he put it in my face.

I must have exposed you. What happened to me had to have exposed you. There was no hiding me from her in the aftermath. Your horrifying knife wound and blood loss. The police interviews and visits. The witness statement. You were torn out of your normal life, too, because of what happened to me.

Rape victims cannot be named. Even if they might also be murderers. What happened to me kept my name out of the press, but I don't think you could have kept it out of your house.

I imagine your wife. Make it go away, she must have said. Just make it go away. You are never, ever to see her again, she must have said. Perhaps you had no choice but to make me go away.

Eleanor told me your leg was healing, but you'd always have a limp. She said you'll need more operations. You're probably fighting your own battle against post-traumatic stress disorder.

Does your wife drive you to your hospital appointments? Help you with physiotherapy? Is she punishing you? Can your marriage recover from this? Do you want it to? I try not to let the questions take me over, but it isn't easy. I try not to let myself wonder what she looks like.

After Henry, I swore I'd never again let myself fall in love with a married man. That I'd never again do to another woman what I did to his wife. You took away my choice in this, with your lie. I'd never have touched you, if I'd known. Our baby wouldn't exist, if I'd known.

Despite everything, I imagine myself kissing your leg, trying to kiss it better.

"You could get in touch with Robert, you know," Mrs Lewen says. "You could find out with certainty the situation with his wife. The man who hurt you — he wasn't a reliable source."

"The sexual offences liaison officer confirmed Robert's still married. He lives with her."

Eleanor told me your wife was in London those two nights you spent with me. She was called away again, unexpectedly, the night you changed your mind and turned up and rescued me. Are you glad you did?

"You can still find out more about him, why he did what he did."

"I should think that's pretty obvious."

What must she feel, to know that her last-minute change of plans helped to save my life?

"You're not cynical, Clarissa. People do things for complex reasons. From what you've said of Robert, he's a good man, even a heroic man. I'm not denying that what he did to you was wrong, but you must have confused him badly for him to have acted so out of character."

Was it the promise of seven weeks out of your own life? With me added to make the time of the trial even more memorable and exciting? Maybe you wanted to secure my part in it all with that whopper of a lie. You said you saw me on the train that first day. Maybe you decided then and there that you'd reel me in because you knew your wife would be away in six weeks' time: an opportunity you didn't want to miss. Maybe you even saw I was reading Keats and that's why you said you liked him — you notice everything.

You must have imagined you'd go straight back to how it all was, once the holiday was over. You must have imagined I wouldn't leave the faintest trace or imprint on you.

"Everything you've told me about Robert, all of his actions, suggest his feelings for you were powerful, that you got under his skin and into his head." Mrs Lewen has an annoying ability to guess at my fantasies. "Maybe he never expected that. Whatever Robert did to you —"

"Whatever he did to me is irrelevant, given the fact that he saved my life and hurt himself for ever by doing it. The other stuff — the big lie about his wife — is actually pretty small by comparison."

Mrs Lewen looks pleased with me, despite my impatience with her. "You saved him too," she says quietly.

"He was only in danger because of me. That hardly counts as saving him."

"He may be shy of you, after what happened. Wanting to give you space to recover, not frighten you. He's your baby's father, Clarissa. You should find him and talk to him."

"Don't you think the news might come as a tiny little bit of a shock? Besides, I don't want him to be with me just because of the baby. Not to mention the fact that I don't want to try to take him from his wife . . . I feel bad enough about her. And I can't chase him. I can't . . . foist myself on someone. That's what that man did to me."

Eleanor told me that there was a shrine in that man's house, and too many photographs to count. He knew my life better than I did.

"But Robert's the great mystery to you," Mrs Lewen says. "You need to solve it to move on. You need to understand what Robert did, and why, and what he's thinking now."

"You're wrong," I say. "I think I do understand him. I think you've just helped me to. Robert's not my great mystery."

Mrs Lewen looks surprised. "Then what is?"

"Laura."

I picture Mrs Betterton sitting beside my mother, the two of them weeping in each other's arms while Mr Betterton and my father stand there looking solemn and sad and awkward.

"I thought her parents might hate me," I say. "That they might never forgive me. For being the one who survived. For not being Laura."

Mrs Lewen tells me to take a few sips of tea before continuing and I obey her.

"You don't have any regret that he's dead, do you?" Mrs Lewen asks.

The Bettertons told us that the police say it wasn't Laura on the magazine cover. This fills me with relief, but it's a very muted kind of relief because I can't stop feeling haunted by the question of who the woman was. The Bettertons also told us that the forensic people found pornographic photos of Laura in his house, hidden beneath floorboards. Is that where he'd have put the last photos he took of me, too?

He might have got away with murdering me by means of reasonable doubt, by suggesting it could have been you. You were all over my bed too. He might have said he and I had consensual sex and then he left me alive and happy, only for you to turn up after he was gone and torture and kill me. Court 12 taught me too well.

The police only just discovered he spent a summer in California seven years ago. Laura's last summer. The trail is cold now, but perhaps not entirely gone. The American police are opening an investigation into her disappearance, at last. They are liaising with the British police, who are combing carefully through all evidence.

Do I regret that he's dead?

I can't think of a dumber question than that one. There's no way I can answer truthfully. If I do, Mrs Lewen will probably tell the police that I'm an unrepentant murdering psychopath; I really don't want that in the file they send to the Crown Prosecution Service. And I really don't want her advising social services to take my baby away.

But I do cut Mrs Lewen a very large piece of the truth and hand it to her on a plate. "I'm haunted by the idea that I ruined the Bettertons' only chance of finding out what happened to Laura. He might have told them. Now he never can."

I don't want to go back to the university, though I haven't figured out exactly what I'll do once all of the broken pieces of me have been glued together and the cracks don't show so much. If there's a way of helping to search for Laura then that's what I want it to be. Maybe through writing, or publicity, or starting some kind of awareness-raising foundation in her name, with her parents.

"That seems a natural feeling to have, Clarissa," Mrs Lewen says. "That seems very human."

Perhaps she won't say I'm a psychopath after all.

"I'm not sure though that you're being entirely honest with yourself when you say that Robert isn't your great mystery."

She'll just say I'm self-deluded. Though I can't help but admit to myself that Mrs Lewen is wise in some ways.

Friday, 24 July

Newly healed tissue burns easily. Another of the plastic surgeon's warnings. Because of it, I am wearing a huge floppy straw hat to keep the sun off my face as I walk with my parents along the seafront. My empire-line dress looks like summer. Only my mother can make a dress that does the contradictory things of stretching and clinging and falling like water all at once. The pale blue jersey swishes softly. A breeze shapes the light fabric around my small bump. We hurry past the stink of the fast-food kiosks and onto the wooden planks of the pier.

My eyes skim over the amusement arcade building. Just inside the entrance, in the shadows, a tall man stands. He seems to be watching me. I can't see his face, but I imagine something of you in his stance and begin to walk towards him in a kind of trance. He turns and steps inside, quickly, moving with a limp. I start to run, barely noticing when my hat flies off, hardly hearing my parents calling me back. I forget that I am pregnant, forget that I have lost my stamina after so many months of enforced rest, forget everything but my mad conviction that this man is you.

I halt, abruptly, near a glass tank full of toy aliens with a large claw hovering over them. I turn in a circle, then another one, then another still, thinking if I can take in the full 360 degrees of the room I will spot you. The pings and pongs of the inane machines are ringing in my ears as I scan the crowds. Somebody screams as they crash their fake car. The fairground organ is deafening, as if I am at a haunted carnival. Coloured bulbs flash brightly on the games. Strobe lights make the air pulse.

My heart is pounding, my head is spinning, and I'm hiccoughing. My chest is blotchy and damp. All of this could be from the sudden exertion. Or it could be because of the anti-nausea medication. Maybe it's from both of these things together.

I will never find that man. It was crazy to think he was you. This nightmare arcade is impossibly huge and there are too many ways out that he could have slipped through. Even if I were to search the entire pier it would be all too easy to hide and disappear on either of its long sides, in any of its countless rides and buildings.

My parents are at my side, puzzled and worried, tugging at me gently, leading me off the pier, telling me my hat blew into the sea. We step carefully through the brick-paved lanes, my father guiding us through the twisting alleyways, keeping us in the shade. We wander beneath the domes and pinnacles and minarets and chimney stacks of the old palace. I trail my fingers through the broom's yellow petals.

My parents arrange me near a laburnum in a quiet part of the gardens. Rowena and Annie are coming for lunch on Sunday, and Annie's bringing Miss Norton

379

down, so my mother wants to buy a few special things. She's dragging my father along to help her carry them.

I'm glad to be on my own for a while, watching the ladybirds and butterflies. I'm deeply drowsy, probably the fault of the anti-nausea drug again, so I lie down on the grass. People do this sort of thing in this city by the sea. When I remember that I'm not supposed to be on my back I roll onto my right side, propped on my bent elbow, my hand cupping my head to support it. The pigeons are swarming above the lilacs. They make me think of the hordes of winged monkeys in *The Wizard of Oz*. Mrs Lewen is always telling me that the monkeys are supposed to be my demons and fears. I don't tell her that I think those monkeys are ridiculous.

There's a thump thump thump in the back of my skull, and I am reminded yet again of Mrs Lewen's favourite film, this time of that intense interlude when the heroine abandons the sepia tints and unearthly quiet to enter the world of Technicolor. The peonies and rock roses and sweet william and foxgloves that border the curving path appear to deepen in their already intense hues of pink and red and purple. At the other end of the path stands a man.

It is the man from the pier. He is very tall, like you. And very lean, like you, though perhaps a bit thinner. He has your broad shoulders, too. He takes a few steps towards me and I see that he walks with a limp, as you now do. Despite the limp, I think the way he carries himself is beautiful. The late-afternoon sun is behind him. I am too dazzled by it to make out his features, except for the blue eyes that jump out at me as if they've been touched by the nearby larkspurs. He is in a heat haze.

My heart is going bump in my chest. I can hear it. I'm sure I can actually hear it. I'm growing dizzy. My head is too heavy for my neck. It slips from the cradle of my hand and thwacks onto the grass. When I open my eyes I'm on my left side in the recovery position, confused by how I got into it. I blink several times, hard, trying to clear my blurry vision. I sit up and look all around me, still feeling that I am being watched. But I cannot see the man.

I tell myself he was never there. He can't have been. I am still too ready to think I'm being followed, even if it's by somebody I actually want to see. It's a kind of vertigo, and I know that you are a delusion. I remember that hallucinations are one of the extremely rare side effects of this new anti-emetic. Fuzzy eyes are on the list too. As well as dizziness and altered heartbeat. I seem to have all of it. I'm going to have to ask Dr Haynes to change me to a different medicine again. But these are small things. Temporary things. Fixable things. I am here and I am alive.

I rest my hand on my belly. The baby stomps sharply on my bladder as if to tell me she is fine, and I make a noise that is a cry and a laugh at once. I think of the fairy tale my father used to read to me about the maiden whose hands are chopped off, and how she suffers great trials. All that she loses is returned to her, and she is rewarded with more than she ever had. Her hands grow back, too.

But the story forgets to mention that each of her wrists is ringed by a scar. She wears these indelible bracelets for the rest of her life. And she refuses to cover them up, even if they do slowly fade over time.

Acknowledgements

I didn't do any of this alone. I am deeply grateful to my agent, Euan Thorneycroft, for his belief in and championing of *The Book of You*, and for all of the extraordinary things he does. Without him, *The Book of You* would not be a book at all. The team at A.M. Heath are incomparable. Euan Thorneycroft and Pippa McCarthy offered editorial advice that helped to make *The Book of You* better than it otherwise would have been. Jennifer Custer and Hélène Ferey were passionate in bringing the novel to other countries for translation rights; it is a huge privilege for a writer to be able to speak to readers in other languages. Pippa McCarthy and Vickie Dillon helped with countless things that would have otherwise defeated me.

It is a great honour to be published by HarperCollins. To work with so many exceptionally talented people is very special and rare. Sarah Hodgson in the UK, Claire Wachtel in the U.S.A. and Iris Tupholme in Canada offered inspiring and wise editorial guidance. To have any one of them as an editor would be a tremendous privilege; to have all three is an astonishing piece of good fortune. Their perceptiveness and vision is remarkable, as is their consideration, care and attention.

From HarperCollins UK, I am particularly grateful to Kate Stephenson, for all of her hard work in seeing *The Book of You* through the production process, for her unparalleled creative input, including the breathtaking shoutlines she came up with for the cover, and for her patience and kindness; to Louise Swannell, for handling my publicity with such genius and flair; to Anne O'Brien, for her incredibly careful and elegant copyediting, and responsive reading; to Ben Gardiner, for the enchanting design and typesetting of the novel's interior; to Dominic Forbes, for the stunning and compelling cover; to Adrian Hemstalk, for turning *The Book of You* into a material object and ebook that people can actually hold in their hands; to Laura Fletcher and her wonderful sales team of Sarah Collett, Lisa Hunter and Tom Dunstan; to Lucy Upton, for the brilliant marketing campaign; to Damon Greeney, for co-ordinating the sale of the novel across HarperCollins's international markets; and to Eamonn McCabe, for his photographic artistry.

From HarperCollins USA, I am especially grateful to Jonathan Burnham for his support and enthusiasm; to Hannah Wood, for co-ordinating so many things so beautifully, for helping me to navigate the journey from manuscript to book so expertly, and for her superb creative input, including the wonderful description she wrote for the American catalogue; to Richard Ljoenes, for the hauntingly beautiful cover; to Michael Correy, for the exquisite design of the novel's interior; to

Heather Drucker, my extremely talented and lovely publicist; to the brilliant publicity team; to Kathy Schneider and Katie O'Callaghan, for the fantastic marketing campaign; to Emily Walters and Cindy Achar, for seeing the novel through the production process; and to my copy editor Mary Beth Constant, for her sharp eyes, scrupulous judgement and careful intelligence.

From HarperCollins Canada, I am particularly grateful to Doug Richmond, for making sure everything came together so perfectly; to Maria Golikova, who managed the elegant Canadian catalogue copy; to Sonya Koson, my wonderful publicist; and to the team of Noelle Zitzer, Maria Golikova, Allegra Robinson and Kelly Hope, for their collaborative effort in seeing the Canadian edition of *The Book of You* through production.

Richard Kerridge's intellectual and imaginative influence has been powerfully formative; he has my heartfelt gratitude for his constantly wise judgement, painstaking support and brilliant advice. Gerard Woodward is a generous and knowledgeable friend and mentor; his advocacy of *The Book of You* meant more to me than I can say. Sheryl's very dear friendship has sustained me for as long as I can remember. Colin Edwards and Julia Green were kind and gentle and constructive when I needed them. Richard Francis and Christopher Nicholson were there for me when I sought wise guidance. Richard Kerridge, Gerard Woodward and Richard Francis also offered insightful critical responses to the novel, as did Tim Liardet,

Suzanne Woodward, Miranda Liardet, Ellen McWilliams and Ross Davis. I am hugely indebted to the firemen who helped with this book and patiently answered my many questions; they embody all that is good. Any errors and fabrications are my own.

My father is the most patient reader imaginable. My mother has the gift of unwavering wisdom and true beauty. Her love and support, and my father's, have always been my touchstone. Uncle Gary and Auntie Barbara gave me another precious book of fairy tales, and so much else. My sister Bella always tells me the truth and is always on my side — she is all that her name suggests and I would be lost without her. My brother Robert showed his usual sweetness and good humour in the face of my unavoidable need to steal his name for one of my characters. My three daughters are magical in all ways, and make everything more meaningful and beautiful.

The epigraph from "Blue Beard" by Charles Perrault is taken from *Four and Twenty Fairy Tales. Selected from those of Perrault, and Other Popular Writers.* Translated by J. R. Planché. Published by G. Routledge & Co., London and New York, 1858, page 4.

Citations from "Fitcher's Bird", "The Robber Bridegroom" and "The Three Snake-Leaves" are all from *Grimms' Household Tales.* Translated and edited by Margaret Hunt. Published by George Bell and Sons, London, 1884, Volume I (of Two Volumes), pages 178, 165 and 72.

Other titles published by Ulverscroft:

The Two Faces of January

Patricia Highsmith

Now a major Hollywood film

Two men meet in the picturesque backstreets of Athens. Chester MacFarlane is a con-man with multiple false identities, near the end of his rope and on the run with his young wife, Colette. Rydal Keener is a young drifter looking for adventure: he finds it one evening as the law catches up to Chester and Colette, and their fates become fatally entwined.

Patricia Highsmith draws us deep into a cross-European game of cat and mouse in this masterpiece of suspense from the author of *The Talented Mr Ripley*.

The Facts of Life and Death

Belinda Bauer

"Call your mother."
"What do I say?"
"Say Goodbye."

This is how it begins. Lone women are terrorized and their helpless mothers forced to watch — in a sick game where only one player knows the rules. And when those rules change, the new game is Murder.

Living with her parents in the dank beach community of Limeburn, ten-year-old Ruby Trick has her own fears. Bullies on the school bus, the forest crowding her house into the sea, the threat of divorce.

Helping her daddy to catch the killer might be the key to keeping him close. As long as the killer doesn't catch her first . . .

Respect

Mandasue Heller

Chantelle has everything going against her. She's a good student who only wants to pass her exams and find a way out of the sink estate in Manchester where she grew up. But now her feckless mother has taken off for Spain with her latest boyfriend and she's single-handedly raising her tearaway nine-year-old brother Leon. She thinks her worst problem is the debt collectors at the door. But Leon has made some new friends: teenage gang members who have given him a mobile phone, a knife — and some drugs to hide in her flat.

A part-time job seems to be the answer to Chantelle's prayers. But the violence is about to come home to her — with a vengeance. And the only person who's offering any help seems to be just as bad as the people she's trying to escape from . . .

Broke

Mandasue Heller

Amy's marriage to Mark isn't the best — he can't resist the girls, he can't hold down a job, he has a bit of a temper. But she doesn't want to know just how bad things are until his gambling habit brings Lenny Yates to her door. He makes it brutally clear how she can pay off Mark's debts . . .

And Amy's troubles are only beginning. Lenny wants more than his money back — he wants Amy to be his and his alone. And there's another woman in Mark's life, who wants Mark for herself. She is ready to steal Amy's man, her self-respect and even her children. As the stakes rise, Amy will either lose everything, or she'll have to learn how to stand up to her enemies . . .